W9-BCL-427

DEATH COMES
TO BATH

Books by Catherine Lloyd

DEATH COMES TO THE VILLAGE

DEATH COMES TO LONDON

DEATH COMES TO KURLAND HALL

DEATH COMES TO THE FAIR

DEATH COMES TO THE SCHOOL

DEATH COMES TO BATH

Published by Kensington Publishing Corporation

DEATH COMES TO BATH

CATHERINE LLOYD

KENSINGTON BOOKS
http://www.kensingtonbooks.com

KENSINGTON BOOKS are published by

Kensington Publishing Corp.
119 West 40th Street
New York, NY 10018

All Kensington titles, imprints, and distributed lines are available at special quantity discounts for bulk purchases for sales promotion, premiums, fund-raising, educational, or institutional use. Special book excerpts or customized printings can also be created to fit specific needs. For details, write or phone the office of the Kensington Special Sales Manager: Attn. Special Sales Department. Kensington Publishing Corp, 119 West 40th Street, New York, NY 10018. Phone: 1-800-221-2647.

Library of Congress Card Catalogue Number: 2018952795

Kensington and the K logo Reg. U.S. Pat. & TM Off.

ISBN-13: 978-1-4967-0212-8
ISBN-10: 1-4967-0212-3
First Kensington Hardcover Edition: January 2019

ISBN-13: 978-1-4967-0213-5 (e-book)
ISBN-10: 1-4967-0213-1 (e-book)

10 9 8 7 6 5 4 3 2 1

Printed in the United States of America

Many thanks to Sandra Marine and Ruth Long, who read this book for me and helped knock it into shape. I spent two very happy weeks in the city of Bath last summer making sure I walked the routes and visited the places Lucy and Robert would've enjoyed. If you ever have the opportunity, I highly recommend a visit to Bath.

Prologue

Kurland St. Mary
January 1822

"Robert! *Robert,* can you hear me?"

Aware that something was vaguely amiss, Sir Robert Kurland attempted to focus on his wife's face, which appeared to be underwater. Something slobbered noisily on his cheek. He was fairly certain that *wasn't* his wife, and was one of his dogs. He blinked hard and pain shot through his limbs with such appalling agony that his back arched in instinctive protest.

"Robert."

In truth, he'd much prefer to sink back into oblivion and leave all the unsettling brightness concentrated around his wife alone, but she obviously needed him, and he could never deny her anything.

Where was he? The last thing he remembered was coming down the main staircase in Kurland Hall intent on taking his two young dogs, Picton and Blucher, for a short stroll down the drive before breakfast. The surface beneath him was hard and cold, which was a damned sight better than being buried up to his neck in the mud at Waterloo, but still uncomfortable.

"Thank you, Foley." Lucy appeared to be speaking to his butler.

Robert groaned as something soft was placed beneath his head and a blanket was thrown over his torso.

"Dr. Fletcher is on his way, my lady."

"No." Robert managed to open his eyes. "*Damnation*, not him."

"Robert." Lucy leaned closer and a tear dripped from her cheek onto his. "Oh, my *darling* . . ."

He frowned at her. "My dear girl, there's no need for tears. I'm not dead yet."

She tried to smile and wiped hastily at her cheek. "I do apologize, but the sight of you on the ground has somewhat affected me." She turned her head. Robert followed the direction of her gaze and saw several pairs of muddy booted feet approaching.

"We can't leave you out here in the cold. If you can stand it, James and the other footmen are going to lift you and take you to bed," Lucy said.

Even though he was hardly in a position to argue, Robert still wanted to object. He tensed as the men gathered around him.

"On my mark." Foley took charge. "One, two, three . . ."

Even before Robert was lifted off the ground the pain swallowed him whole, and he knew no more.

The next time he opened his eyes he was lying in his own bed with the covers drawn back, and his blasted friend ex-army surgeon Patrick Fletcher was glaring down at him.

Someone had removed all of Robert's clothes except his shirt, and that was pulled up to expose his left hip and thigh.

"Why didn't you tell me about this?" Patrick demanded. His strong fingers gently probed the massive swelling on Robert's thigh.

"So much for your bedside manner, Dr. Fletcher. You

will hardly make your fortune with the aristocracy if you shout at your patients," Robert murmured.

"I'm shouting at you because you are a special case." Patrick placed his hand on Robert's forehead. "You also have a fever."

"I *am* aware of that."

"You promised at Christmas that you would allow me to examine you properly."

"You're examining me now," Robert pointed out, and received another ferocious glare in return. "Where is my wife?"

"She is right here, sir."

Patrick stepped back, and Robert located Lucy sitting in a chair next to the fire, her hands twisted together in her lap around her handkerchief. The dogs were asleep at her feet. She looked remarkably pale but met his gaze resolutely.

"I know you said you didn't wish to see Dr. Fletcher, but when one's husband is discovered unconscious on the drive, one is entitled to ignore his wishes."

"Indeed," Robert said. "Although one *might* have considered waiting awhile and consulting the patient first."

"Lady Kurland did the right thing," Patrick replied. "I know you don't want to hear this, Robert, but this swelling on your thigh is hot to the touch. I hesitate to literally reopen old wounds, but I've heard of cases like this before from fellow army surgeons, and I'd like the opportunity to drain the swelling and see what's going on."

Robert swallowed hard. The idea of a surgeon laying hands on him again made every cowardly impulse in him stir to attention. It was also why he hadn't mentioned the swelling to anyone, not even his wife.

"If I don't try something, you will probably lose the leg, and maybe your life if the inflammation spreads," Patrick continued.

Lucy came to stand beside the doctor and looked down

at Robert. "As you might imagine, I would rather you continued your existence."

He reached for her hand. "Then I must agree to put myself in the good doctor's hands. When do you want to perform your butchery?"

Patrick shared a glance with Lucy. "Now if possible."

Robert nodded. "Then give me a moment with my wife, and I am all yours."

"I need to get some equipment and persuade Foley to give me the best brandy in the house." Patrick squeezed Robert's shoulder hard. "I'll do my absolute best to save your leg."

The silence left behind by the doctor was broken by the crackling of the fire and the whimper of one of the dogs chasing rabbits in his sleep. Lucy sat on the side of the bed and wrapped an arm around Robert's shoulders. He drew her close and kissed the top of her head.

"I do apologize for worrying you."

She cupped his chin. "You have always been a worry, but one that I willingly embraced." She searched his face. "Do you wish me to assist Dr. Fletcher or would you rather I took myself off?"

"I'd rather you were here." He hesitated. "Just in case."

"Then here I shall remain." She kissed him gently on the lips. "At your side." She glanced over at the fire. "The dogs, however, will return to the kitchen." She went as if to sit up, and he held her in place.

"If the worst happens, I've made provision for you and protected the estate as best as I can from Paul, but—"

She placed a finger on his lips. "Let's not worry about that now. I have every confidence in your ability to protect me, and I do not fear the future." She smiled and he stored the memory away like a precious jewel. Her strength and calmness had never been more vital to him than at this moment.

He kissed her fingers and then her mouth, deepening the kiss until she was molded against him and they breathed as one. Eventually, she eased away from him, her eyes grave, and patted her now disordered hair.

"I must look a fright."

"You look remarkably pretty to me," Robert said.

There was a knock on the door, and Silas, his valet, peered in. "Dr. Fletcher asked me to come and assist, sir. I hope that's all right."

"Please join us." Robert pointed at the dogs. "But take these two fine fellows down to the kitchen first and make sure one of the stable boys gives them some exercise."

"Yes, Sir Robert."

Foley came in with a bottle of his best brandy and placed the decanter beside Robert's bed.

"Good luck, sir. We'll all be praying for you."

Lucy pressed her lips tightly together and averted her gaze as Dr. Fletcher used his wickedly sharp blade to cut through the angry-looking flesh on Robert's thigh. Why hadn't her husband told her how bad his leg had gotten, and why hadn't she noticed? If Robert survived the good doctor's attentions, Lucy would be asking Robert those very questions herself.

"Hold him still," Dr. Fletcher instructed Robert's valet as his patient visibly stirred even in his drunken stupor. "Lady Kurland, I'll need that bleeding bowl positioned beneath the incision."

Despite being virtually insensible, Robert flinched as a stream of foul-smelling pus gushed from the small cut and eventually slowed to a trickle. Dr. Fletcher pushed gently on the swelling until it started to bleed.

"Ah, wait." He leaned in closely and used the tip of his knife to draw something out of the hole. "Look at that! Must have stayed in there all this time."

"What exactly is it?" Lucy inquired through her teeth.

"Looks like a piece of blue fabric from Sir Robert's hussars' uniform to me." Dr. Fletcher laughed, which struck Lucy as particularly insensitive at this particular moment, and typical of a man. "I must have left it behind last time I was in here. I'll feel around and see if there is anything else. You can take the bowl away, and I'll bind up the wound."

Fighting nausea, Lucy covered the bowl and placed it on a tray outside the door. She'd already sent a note to the local healer, Grace Turner, asking her to come and see Robert at her earliest convenience. Lucy had great faith in Dr. Fletcher, but it never hurt to consult an expert in *herbal* remedies. Grace's potions had done more to improve Lucy's well-being during the previous year than any of Dr. Fletcher's concoctions.

As she returned to the bedchamber, Lucy sent up a quick prayer to the heavens. If Robert could survive the almost inevitable fever from Dr. Fletcher's attentions, she had high hopes that the sheer stubbornness of his nature would ensure his continued survival.

Chapter 1

"And what if I don't want to go to Bath?" Robert inquired, scowling at his wife as she tidied his pillows. Rain spattered the diamond windowpanes of their bedchamber, and a cold draught whistled down the chimney, making the wood fire send out sullen puffs of smoke. "What if I prefer to stay here in my own bed, and in my own house?"

"You've been skulking in that bed for weeks," Lucy said, pausing in her efforts to straighten the sheets. "Dr. Fletcher believes the hot springs at Bath will be beneficial to you, and I am in complete agreement with him. I've rented a house close to the baths and Pump Room where you can drink the waters and take additional treatments as recommended by Dr. Fletcher."

"You've gone ahead and arranged all this without consulting me?"

Lucy met his indignant gaze. "If I *had* consulted you, you would just have said no. It seemed far more efficient to simply organize everything, and present you with a fait accompli."

Robert sighed. "What about the dogs?"

"James will remain here, and he has promised me that he will look after them as if they were his own." Lucy of-

fered Robert a cup of tea. "Foley and your valet will accompany us, as will Betty."

Robert sipped the tea and studied his wife's calm features. He had a sense that whatever objections he raised
she would have answers for them. After Patrick had doc-
tored his thigh he'd fallen into a fever that had weakened
him considerably and he had no memory of the first few
days after the operation. He still didn't have the strength
to prevent Lucy from ordering one of his footmen to bundle him up in his blankets and deposit him in his traveling
coach.

"Bath isn't exactly fashionable anymore," Robert pointed
out. "All of society flocks to Brighton."

"Which is why I thought you would prefer Bath." She
patted his hand. "I doubt you wish to meet the prince regent strolling along the promenade?"

"Good Lord, no." Robert shuddered. Even though it
had been the prince regent himself who had awarded
Robert his baronetcy he had no love for the royal buffoon.
"That would not please me at all."

"Then that's settled." Lucy took his cup away from
him. "We'll be on our way by the end of the week."

Robert lay back against his pillows and accepted defeat.
If his wife had been a man and of a military bent, he reckoned she would've beaten Napoleon in a month. She stood
to brush a kiss on his forehead and picked up the tea tray.

"I'm going down to the rectory to advise my father of
our decision. Do you have any message for your aunt
Rose?"

Robert still found it difficult to believe that his beloved
aunt had married Lucy's pompous fool of a father, but
they appeared to rub along very well together.

"Just give her my love."

Lucy nodded. "Do you wish to speak to Dermot Fletcher
about the estate?"

"I'll do that later today. How long are you intending to
keep me captive in Bath?"

She paused at the door. "At least three months."

"*That long?*"

"That's what Dr. Fletcher recommends." She smiled at him, and it occurred to him that it was the first time he'd seen her look happy in days. He was not an easy man at the best of times, and being an invalid made him ten times more cantankerous.

"Thank you," Robert said gruffly.

Lucy raised an eyebrow. "For what?"

"Arranging everything."

She had the gall to laugh. "Now I know that you are still unwell. Normally, you would be standing toe to toe with me arguing the matter out." She opened the door and left the room, leaving her warm amusement surrounding him.

It was good to see her laughing again—even at him. There was a time during the previous year when he'd thought she would never smile again. But she seemed much healthier now, and far more herself. Even if that self *was* somewhat exasperating . . .

After speaking to Foley, Lucy walked down the drive of Kurland Hall and took the shortcut beside the church that brought her out opposite the rectory. It was a brisk, cold morning that required a person to keep moving. The fact that Robert hadn't ordered her to cancel the trip to Bath had surprised her immensely. Perhaps despite his objections to leaving home he was as bored as she was staying put for three months since Christmas.

She was convinced that the change of scenery and the hot springs at Bath would help aid his recovery. Dr. Fletcher and Grace Taylor, the local healer, both spoke very highly of the notion, and that was enough for Lucy. She would never forget Dr. Fletcher's skill in preserving Robert's life and leg yet again, and would be forever in his debt.

At the rectory gate, she paused and decided to use the front door. The golden stone was now covered in reddish ivy, which softened the harsh lines of the ten-year-old exterior. The new building didn't impress Robert, but secretly, after living at the Elizabethan Kurland Hall for three years, Lucy rather appreciated the rectory's warmth and symmetry. But she no longer lived there, and her father had a new wife who should be offered every courtesy. She waited as the bell clanged in the depths of the house, and was surprised when her father opened the door himself.

"Goodness me, Lucy. How very pleasant." He pinched her cold cheek. "You look very well today, my dear. I was just about to go out for a ride. Did you wish to speak to me?"

Lucy followed him into the hallway as he shut the door. "Sir Robert and I will be leaving for Bath at the end of the week as planned."

"Excellent news, my dear." The rector rubbed his hands together. "I wish Sir Robert a full and vigorous recovery."

"Thank you. I assured him that you would offer Mr. Fletcher your assistance in estate matters if required." Lucy removed her bonnet and gloves and placed them on the hall table.

"Of course, of course." The rector surreptitiously checked his pocket watch, picked up his riding crop, and put on his hat. "May I take you through to the back parlor? Rose and Anna will be delighted to see you I'm sure."

Lucy allowed herself to be escorted down the corridor as her father opened the parlor door wide enough for her to step past him.

"Ladies, here is our Lucy to see you." The rector smiled at his new wife. "She is leaving for Bath with Sir Robert at the end of the week. I have assured her that we will render Mr. Fletcher any assistance necessary."

He bowed and stepped back, but Lucy touched his sleeve.

"There is one more thing I wished to ask you, Father." She smiled up at him. "Would you permit me to bring Anna to Bath? I would value her companionship enormously."

The rector looked over at his new wife. "What do you

think of this scheme, my dear? Can you manage without Anna for a few months?"

Rose smiled at Lucy and Anna. She was an attractive woman with Robert's dark blue eyes and a lovely smile. "It's about time I stopped relying on Anna to solve every domestic crisis large and small in this house, and took on the responsibilities of my new position." She patted Anna's hand. "If you wish to accompany your sister, I will gladly give you leave."

Anna glanced uncertainly from Lucy to Rose. "I'm not sure . . ."

The rector cleared his throat. "And I must be off. If you wish to accompany your sister to Bath, Anna, I give you my blessing and hope that *this* time you'll meet some young man you will be pleased enough with to marry." He bowed and departed whistling loudly to his dogs as he went out to the stables behind the house.

Rose patted the seat beside her. "Do come and sit down, Lucy. How is Robert faring? I am very glad that he decided to go to Bath to recuperate."

Anna chuckled. "I don't think Robert had much to do with it, Rose. Lucy organized everything and sprung it upon him at the last possible moment."

"Not *quite* the last minute," Lucy defended herself. "Although I did consider dosing him with a sleeping powder and loading him into the coach while he was unconscious if he disagreed."

Rose laughed. "My nephew is not an easy man to command, but you seem to have discovered the knack of it."

"Lucy is used to managing difficult men," Anna said. "Between my father, Anthony, and the twins she usually emerged victorious."

Rose rang the bell and ordered fresh tea before settling back in her seat. Despite her very recent and surprising decision to marry the rector, she looked quite at home in the rectory. Even more remarkably, perhaps, she seemed genuinely delighted to be married again. Her adult children from her first marriage had refused to attend the quiet wedding ceremony, but seeing as she was at odds with the lot of them that hadn't bothered her at all.

Anna poured the tea and offered Lucy a slice of cake. She'd arranged her blond hair in ringlets in a casual style Lucy could never have pulled off and wore a modest blue gown that still accentuated her exceptional figure. It *was* a shame Anna was not married yet. Despite Anna's objections, Lucy was determined to give her sister another chance to meet the man of her dreams. Bath was not London, but from what Lucy had discovered there was still a smattering of polite company, which might include any number of eligible gentlemen on the lookout for a wife. . . .

"I think you should accompany your sister, Anna." Rose accepted her cup of tea. "You have done nothing but look after me for the last three months." Her smile was full of genuine affection for her newly acquired stepdaughter. "I don't know *what* I would've done without your guidance. You deserve to enjoy your freedom for a few weeks."

Anna bit her lip. "I'm quite happy here . . ."

"*Please* come." Lucy leaned forward and took her sister's hand. "With Robert taking treatments every day I will be very much on my own. We can explore the shops, and libraries, and attend the theater together."

"That does sound appealing," Anna acknowledged. She turned to Rose. "Are you *quite* certain you can manage without me?"

"No, but I'll do my best," Rose said. "I'll have to learn how to be a good wife to the local rector at some point. It's not something I anticipated happening to me so late in life, but I've always enjoyed a challenge."

"Then I will accept your invitation, Lucy," Anna said with a smile. "And now I must go and consider the state of my wardrobe. I doubt I have a thing to wear!"

"We can purchase new gowns in Bath," Lucy encouraged her sister. "I certainly intend to."

When she'd finished her tea, Anna walked with Lucy through to the kitchen where Lucy spoke to the staff, and then out into the garden.

At the back gate Lucy stopped to consider her sister.

"Are you really reluctant to come to Bath? I have sometimes wondered recently whether life at the rectory has become . . . difficult for you."

"Please don't think that Rose has been unkind to me," Anna hastened to reassure her sister. "She is as lovely as she seems and works wonders with Father's somewhat difficult temperament." She sighed. "It's just that sometimes I feel a little de trop. They are so happy together, and after running the house all by myself I find myself resenting being expected to revert to the lowly status of unmarried daughter-at-home."

"I quite understand your sentiments." Lucy nodded. "I felt the same frustration." She kissed Anna's cheek. "Perhaps spending some time away from Kurland St. Mary will offer you the opportunity to reflect on your future."

"Perhaps it will." Anna shivered and gathered her woolen shawl more closely around her. "Now I really must go and decide which garments I can bring that won't make me look like a hideous dowd."

"I doubt you could ever manage that," Lucy said as Anna retreated into the house.

Satisfied that she had accomplished everything she had set out to do that morning, Lucy walked back toward Kurland Hall with a smile on her lips, and a spring in her step. *Some* people might call her managing. She preferred to consider herself as a woman who accomplished the impossible. Robert would regain his strength, and Anna might finally meet her match. Perhaps at some point, both of them would be grateful to her.

As she turned onto the Kurland Hall drive a horse and rider came toward her and drew to a stop.

"Good morning, Lady Kurland." Dr. Fletcher doffed his

hat. "I understand that you have persuaded my most diffi-cult patient to take my advice and retire to Bath to recu-perate?"

"I believe I have, Dr. Fletcher." Lucy looked up at the doctor, who was smiling down at her.

"Excellent news. I will join you there for the first week and stay until I find a physician of worth in Bath to carry out the regime I wish Sir Robert to follow."

"You are welcome to stay with us, sir. I rented a whole house, and there is plenty of space."

"Thank you, my lady." Dr. Fletcher touched the brim of his hat. "That would certainly make life easier. My new apprentice here in Kurland St. Mary should be capable of dealing with any medical issues that arise while I am away."

"That is good to know," Lucy confessed. "I hate to de-prive the whole village of your services."

Dr. Fletcher shrugged. "If it wasn't for Sir Robert, I wouldn't even have a community to serve. Not many land-owners would willingly provide room and board for a Catholic Irishman—even one who served in the recent war."

"How is Penelope, Dr. Fletcher?" Lucy asked.

The doctor grinned. "You know my wife, Lady Kur-land. She isn't one to suffer quietly, and the 'indignities of pregnancy' haven't sat well with her." He sighed. "In truth I'd better be off home before she comes looking for me."

"Indeed."

Lucy stood back to allow him to turn his horse and head off toward the village where he and his wife lived in a modest house between the school and duck pond. She considered sending her carriage down for Penelope to bring her back to the manor house for afternoon tea, but she had rather a lot of organizing to do, and Penelope wasn't one to take a hint when it came to helping out.

Lucy entered Kurland Hall through a side door and left her muddy half boots in the scullery before heading up the stairs to the main part of the house. The pleasant smell of beeswax polish and potpourri greeted her as she traversed the ancient medieval hall. She encountered Dermot Fletcher, the physician's younger brother and the agent of the Kurland estate, going up the stairs.

"Good morning, my lady," he said, bowing. "I hear you are going to Bath."

"Yes, on Friday," Lucy said.

Dermot nodded. "I'm just going up to see Sir Robert to discuss his plans for the months he will be away." He hesitated. "Unless you wish me to return later?"

"Please, go ahead," Lucy said. She had plenty to do before she saw Robert again. "And tell him I will join him for afternoon tea."

"As you wish, my lady." Dermot bowed and continued up the stairs, leaving Lucy to walk through to her study. She sat at her desk and considered the daunting list of tasks still required to move half a household to a new location for an entire three months. Refusing to be disheartened she reminded herself that the biggest obstacles had already been vanquished.

Robert had agreed to the trip, and Anna was coming as her companion. On that thought, she took a new sheet of cut paper and readied her pen. There was one last letter she needed to write to a naval acquaintance in Bath. . . .

Chapter 2

"Well, it isn't quite up to my standards of cleanliness, but I think we can contrive to make it comfortable enough for Sir Robert, don't you agree, Foley?"

Lucy brushed down the skirt of her sadly crumpled traveling gown and looked at Foley, who had accompanied her on the tour of the rented property.

The town house, which was faced with mellow Bath stone, comprised of five floors, a basement, and attics, which meant that after climbing many staircases Lucy was breathing quite heavily, and Foley was positively wheezing. She'd left Robert on the couch in the drawing room on the first floor, which overlooked the street, and walked through the top floors of the house with the butler at her side.

Foley nodded. "I believe we will manage, my lady. I will set our staff to cleaning the place before they depart on the morrow."

"That's an excellent idea. At least we know they will do the job properly. I see nothing wrong in the *quality* of the furnishings." Lucy took off her bonnet. "Perhaps you might ask the kitchen to bring up some tea and sustenance to the drawing room?"

Foley bowed. "Of course, my lady. Cook seems an amiable person. Let's hope her cooking skills match her appearance."

Lucy made her way down the main staircase and went into the drawing room where Robert was standing. He turned when she came in, and she noted the dark circles under his eyes.

"There isn't much of a view, is there?" Robert said.

"Not much." Lucy joined him at the window and studied the grassy center of Queen's Square, and the identical houses opposite. "I decided it was better not to be directly facing any of the major attractions in the city because of the noise."

"Ah, good point." Robert shifted restlessly from one foot to the other and went to sit down. "I am delighted not to be in the carriage. I'd begun to fear the journey would never end."

Lucy sat beside him and smoothed his sleeve. "It did seem somewhat interminable. But we're here now, and I've set Betty and Silas to unpacking our boxes. Dr. Fletcher will be here tomorrow with Anna, and then we will all be settled."

She found a footstool and deftly slid it under Robert's left boot. "I've ordered some tea, and I intend to interview Cook properly before we attempt to eat dinner."

"Poor woman," Robert murmured with a smile. "I do hope she doesn't leave in a huff."

"She came highly recommended by your aunt Rose so I doubt she will be an issue." Lucy frowned. "I wonder if we should ask Jeremiah and Benjamin to stay with us instead of returning to the hall. With all the stairs in the house, you might need some assurance getting around."

"I'll manage perfectly well, my dear. From what I understand the master bedchamber is on this floor, which means if I do wish to go out I only have to navigate one flight of stairs down to the hall."

Lucy glanced doubtfully at his leg but decided not to

comment. She could only hope that he wouldn't rely on Foley to help him, and accidentally crush the old man if he fell.

A knock on the door announced Foley with the tea tray. Lucy thanked him and poured herself and Robert a cup. She also sampled the fruitcake Cook had sent up and discovered it was both moist and flavorsome, which gave her great satisfaction.

"How far from the baths are we?" Robert asked as he ate a large slab of cake and finished off his tea.

"Within a few minutes' walk I believe." Lucy poured him another cup. "I was told that there is very little point in bringing a carriage and horses to Bath when walking or hiring a sedan chair is much quicker and far less expensive."

"I won't miss having my own horses around," Robert admitted. "Although the notion of entrusting my person to two hulking lads in this town of hills does somewhat worry me." He touched his knee. "Dr. Fletcher told me I should attempt to walk as much as possible and take the air."

"That reminds me," Lucy said, putting down the teapot. "I must prepare an additional room for Dr. Fletcher." She fidgeted with her cup. "I wish I'd brought one of our housemaids with us. I can hardly expect Betty to manage three rooms."

"As you have already observed, the staff here came highly recommended by my aunt Rose so I should imagine they are perfectly capable of dusting a room for Dr. Fletcher." Robert finished his tea, found his spectacles, and opened the newspaper Foley had somehow already acquired for him.

Knowing from experience that conversation would be limited from this point onward, Lucy rose to her feet. "I'll go and speak to Cook and the rest of the household, and then make sure our bedchamber is ready for occupation."

Robert nodded but didn't take his gaze away from the Arrivals column in the local newspaper. After one last glance at his serene expression, Lucy congratulated herself on arriving in Bath with her husband not only in one piece, but also in good spirits. She had worried that the jolting of the carriage would set off his fever again, but he had survived the long, tedious journey with its many stops unscathed.

Lucy peered into the master bedroom where her maid, Betty, and Robert's valet, Silas, were busy making the bed with the Kurland linen, and then went down to the kitchen, which was below the ground level of the street. She was welcomed by Mrs. Meeks, the cook, and took a seat at the kitchen table where her fears as to the staff's competence were swiftly laid to rest.

Mrs. Meeks had dealt with many invalids and even had suggestions as to which of the many resident physicians in Bath were men of good character as opposed to charlatans. Lucy made a list she intended to give to Dr. Fletcher on his arrival.

After discussing the details of their dinner, Lucy climbed the stairs again, peeked into the drawing room where Robert had fallen asleep over his newspaper, and took herself off to bed for a nap before dinner.

Lucy jumped up to look out of the drawing room window as a carriage drew up outside their door. Dr. Fletcher got out and turned to assist Anna's descent.

"Robert! Anna and Dr. Fletcher are here!" Lucy spun around with a smile as Robert looked up from his newspaper. "I'll go down."

They had both slept well despite the slight noise generated by being in the middle of a town and enjoyed a hearty breakfast together. Lucy had already planned out her schedule for the next few days and was feeling remarkably optimistic.

"There's no need, my dear. Foley will dispose of their luggage and bring them up to us momentarily." Robert folded his newspaper and set it on the seat beside him. "In fact, I can hear them coming up the stairs right now."

He slowly got to his feet leaning heavily on his cane and faced the door as Foley opened it.

"Sir Robert?" Foley bowed. "Miss Harrington, Dr. Fletcher, and *Mrs.* Fletcher."

Lucy's mouth fell open as Penelope Fletcher elbowed her way past Anna and came over to shake Lucy's hand and press a kiss to her cheek.

"*Dear* Lucy, it is so kind of you to offer Dr. Fletcher and myself a place to stay in Bath. As you know, our situation is not as it should be, and with a baby on the way my dear husband insists that we be even more cautious with our finances."

Lucy looked past Penelope to Anna, who raised her eyebrows and shrugged.

"It is indeed good to see you, Penelope, and it was very kind of you to accompany Anna to Bath." Lucy glanced over at Dr. Fletcher, who was talking to Robert. "Although, I have to admit, I was not *quite* expecting you."

Penelope seated herself on the couch with a flourish. Despite being pregnant she still looked her beautiful self-composed self.

"I could not allow Anna to travel by *herself*." Penelope fanned herself with her gloved hand. "It would've been quite shocking."

It was on the tip of Lucy's tongue to ask Penelope whether she trusted her own husband, but for the sake of being polite, she restrained herself. If Penelope wished to spend a week in Bath at the Kurlands' expense, then Lucy would not deny her the treat. It wasn't easy being the wife of a local country doctor, especially when Penelope had once dreamed of marrying a duke.

When Penelope turned to greet her former fiancé, Robert, Anna sat beside Lucy and lowered her voice.

"I didn't *ask* her to come to protect my virtue. She was just *there* in the carriage when Dr. Fletcher came to collect me." Anna chuckled. "Although we were given the best treatment at all the inns because Penelope looked down her nose at everyone and they thought she was royalty."

"I can imagine," Lucy murmured.

"Dr. Fletcher did tell me that he was worried about her health and thought a change of air might suit her," Anna said.

Lucy sighed. "Then I suppose I will have to put up with her. It *is* only for a week, and we owe Dr. Fletcher so much."

"That's the spirit." Anna patted her hand. "I must say that I am looking forward to my visit with you. I'd forgotten how much I missed all the excitement of being in town."

"Tomorrow I intend to obtain a subscription to the Assembly Rooms and write our names in the visitors book so that any acquaintance of our family knows we are in town and can come to call," Lucy said. "And then there are shops to visit, dresses to purchase, and the theater!"

"I am glad to see you in better spirits as well, my dear sister," Anna said, smiling at Lucy. "Perhaps this trip will do us both good."

While Anna talked to Penelope, Robert came over to Lucy, touched her shoulder, and murmured, "What maggot in your brain made you invite Penelope Fletcher?"

"I didn't invite her," Lucy whispered back. "In her usual highhanded manner, she just decided to come along with her husband and take advantage of my offer of accommodation."

Robert sighed. "As that sounds just like her I forgive you."

"You won't see much of her while you are busy with Dr. Fletcher at the baths. That task will fall on Anna and myself," Lucy pointed out.

"Indeed." He winked at her. "I suppose I will manage, and I have no doubt that you will emerge the victor in any skirmish."

Foley reappeared and offered to escort the Fletchers and

Anna to their respective bedchambers, leaving Lucy and Robert alone in the drawing room again. Penelope hadn't brought a maid so Lucy directed the girl she'd asked to look after Anna to share her efforts with the doctor's wife.

Within a few minutes, Foley reappeared with a calling card on a silver platter.

"There is a gentleman in the hall who wishes to pay his respects to you, Sir Robert."

Robert picked up the card and frowned. "Do we know anyone by the name of Benson, my dear?"

"I can't think of anyone." Lucy looked up from her embroidery. "Do you wish to see this gentleman or would you prefer it if he returned at a more convenient time?"

"Send him up," Robert commanded Foley. "The day is already full of unexpected visitors so what's one more?"

Foley retreated to the door, a frown on his face. "He is an *elderly* gentleman, sir, so it might take him some time to ascend."

In truth, Lucy had begun to believe their visitor had run away before he eventually appeared at the doorway. He wore an old-fashioned wig and frock coat and was exceedingly large around the middle. A younger man in livery who was bearing most of his massive weight accompanied him.

"Let me be, Edgar," the older man bellowed as he pulled free of his servant's grip and managed a creaky bow, his round face glowing with exertion. "I'm not dead yet, lad!"

Lucy hid a smile as Robert inclined his head. "Good afternoon, Sir William. I'm Sir Robert Kurland and this is my wife, Lady Kurland."

"Pleasure to meet you both." Sir William nodded affably at Lucy. "I saw the carriage on my return from the baths and thought I'd step in and pay my respects."

"That was very kind of you, sir," Lucy said. "Would you care to sit down and take some tea with us?"

Sir William winked. "I'd much rather a glass of port than more tea to curdle my insides."

Lucy turned to Foley, who had remained by the door.

"Perhaps you might bring a variety of refreshments for our guest, Foley?"

"As you wish, my lady."

Sir William slowly lowered himself into a chair, which creaked ominously, and set his walking stick against the fireplace. "I'm renting the house next door to yours."

"Ah, and how are you enjoying Bath, sir?" Robert asked.

"I'd much rather be at home. I'm only here because my wife and my damned physician insisted upon it."

"You have my sympathy, Sir William." Robert glanced over at Lucy, one dark eyebrow raised.

"I assume your wife and family brought you here because they were concerned for your health and well-being, Sir William," Lucy said. "I should *imagine* they only wanted the best for you."

"That's true seeing as they all depend on me to make them money," Sir William chuckled. He had a strong northern accent with a rich rumbling tone. "I'm not one of those namby-pamby gentlemen who likes to sit about doing naught—present company excepted, of course."

"Are you in the business of manufacturing, Sir William?" Robert asked. "My maternal grandfather made his money that way, which gave me the opportunity to live my life in relative comfort as a landowner and farmer. Whereabouts are you situated?"

"Yorkshire, lad. I made my first fortune in coal and then dabbled in building canals, and other local industries."

"My grandfather lived in Halifax in Yorkshire. I wonder if you knew him?" Robert asked. "His name was Samuel Milthorpe."

"Milthorpe?" Sir William patted his perspiring face with his handkerchief. "Aye, I knew a man called that. He owned a pottery or two, and mayhap a mine?"

"That would probably be him. He died when I was quite young, but I remember being taken to meet him when he visited London. He was a large man and quite terrified me with his booming voice."

"Now that I look at you, I do see a likeness," Sir William acknowledged. "What happened to his business interests after his death?"

"My uncle Wilfred ran the business for some years, and now my cousin Oliver is in charge," Robert said. "I receive a percentage of the profits through his settlements on my mother, and I attend as many board meetings as I can."

"Good for you for taking an interest." Sir William favored Robert with a firm nod. "Some of my own sons are not so diligent. They enjoy the money, mind, but don't care to get their hands dirty."

Foley came in with the drinks tray followed by the parlor maid with tea. Lucy poured herself a cup, and Robert helped himself and Sir William to a glass of port. She didn't question Robert's unusual decision to join their guest in a drink this early in the day because it was such a delight to see him so interested and engaged.

She had no recollection of Robert's maternal grandparents visiting Kurland St. Mary when she was a child. She would surely have met them in church if they had. Had they stayed away not wishing to embarrass their daughter in her new aristocratic life, or had they simply not been interested enough to travel such a great distance? It was something to ask Robert when they were alone.

"And why are you here, Sir Robert?" Sir William asked. "Is your lady taking treatment?"

"No, it is for myself." Robert touched his thigh with his cane. "I injured my leg during my service in the war and have dealt with a few complications ever since which necessitated this trip."

"Which regiment were you in, Sir Robert?"

"The Prince of Wales Tenth Hussars." Robert shrugged. "A somewhat showy-looking cavalry regiment, but a damned fine one."

"Sir Robert was wounded at Waterloo and almost lost

his leg," Lucy added as Robert poured their guest another substantial glass of port. "Our physician, Dr. Fletcher, recommended he convalesce here in Bath to recuperate from his fever and regain his strength after complications in his recovery."

"My fool of a physician believes I need to rebalance my humors or some such nonsense." Sir William snorted. "Never had a day's illness in my life until I turned seventy. I fell down the steps in my house and banged my head, and you'd think the world had ended the caterwauling that ensued from my womenfolk. At least that numbskull has stopped bleeding me, and I can't complain that I haven't enjoyed floating up to my neck in that nice hot spring water in the baths."

He finished his port and set the glass on the side table with a definite thump. "Well, I should be going. I'll send my butler around with a dinner invitation in the next few days, and I'd be obliged if you'd accept it. I'm sick and tired of staring at my own family's faces, I'll tell you that."

Sir William heaved himself out of his chair with some difficulty and accepted his footman's proffered arm. "A pleasure to meet you, my lady."

"Indeed, sir. Thank you so much for coming." Lucy curtsied as Robert walked with their guest into the hallway.

He returned relatively quickly having allowed Foley to offer his help rather than risk the stairs himself and sat down by the fire.

"What an extraordinary old gentleman," Robert remarked.

"He was certainly forthright," Lucy agreed.

"I liked that." Robert stoppered the port decanter. "He reminded me of my grandfather. I didn't expect to meet anyone in Bath who might enliven the experience, but it appears that I was mistaken."

"Perhaps you should ask Dr. Fletcher to speak to his physician so that you can join Sir William at his treatments," Lucy suggested.

"I might just do that." Robert retrieved his newspaper. "Have you any plans for the remainder of the day?"

"I shall see if Anna and Penelope wish to accompany me on a walk to get our bearings in this particular location."

"In other words, you intend to go shopping." Robert smiled at her. He was looking remarkably relaxed, making Lucy glad that the unconventional Sir William had decided to call on them.

"If we come across any interesting shops, we might be tempted inside," Lucy acknowledged. "There is very little to admire or purchase in Kurland St. Mary."

"Thank goodness, or you might bankrupt me."

"I have almost a year's worth of my pin money saved, so I doubt I shall need to call on you to finance my excesses," Lucy pointed out.

Robert lowered the paper. "You are remarkably financially prudent."

"Unless I take up gambling . . ."

"And expect me to tow you out of the river tick?" He chuckled. "I'd do it just for the pleasure of watching you attempt to explain yourself."

Satisfied that her husband was in a far better humor than she had anticipated, Lucy rose to her feet.

"I must go and speak to Cook about the new arrivals for luncheon and check that Anna is settled."

"What about Mrs. Fletcher?" Robert asked.

"I shall leave *Penelope's* comfort and well-being in the capable hands of her husband," Lucy said firmly.

Chapter 3

Despite the fact that Bath was no longer a fashionable place, Lucy found it remarkably charming. There were excellent shops in Bond Street and Milsom Street that rivaled those in London and offered her opportunities to purchase all kinds of fripperies from milliners, glove makers, mantua makers, and haberdashers. Due to the excellent allowance Robert gave her she no longer had to turn her gowns or scrimp and save to buy a new one.

Still delighted by his recent marriage and acquisition of his new wife's extensive fortune, the rector had given Anna a handsome gift of money to bring with her to Bath, so the two sisters were able to enjoy the excitement of their new purchases together. Penelope's budget was somewhat limited, but she made sure to give her opinion about everything Lucy and Anna bought—oftentimes with herself in mind.

Knowing that Penelope was only staying for as long as Dr. Fletcher was made putting up with her much easier for Lucy, who did have some sympathy for Penelope's straitened circumstances.

"That blue would suit you very well, Lucy," Penelope stated.

"It's not really a good color for me." Lucy turned to

Penelope. They were in their favorite haberdashery looking at dress lengths of fabric.

Penelope shrugged. "Then if the gown didn't suit you
when it was made up, you could always give it to me."

Behind Lucy, Anna concealed a snort. It wasn't the first
time Penelope had made that suggestion.

"The blue might look well on me." Anna fingered the
fine fabric.

"With your pale complexion?" Penelope shook her head.
"I doubt it."

"I think I prefer the rose-patterned muslin." Lucy showed
it to Anna. "What do you think?"

"I like it," Anna said in support of her sister. "Buy a
length and we can take it to Madame McIntosh to make it
into a day gown for you."

Penelope raised her chin and walked away to the other
side of the shop to look at some hat trimmings. Lucy hesitated beside the ice blue satin.

"Leave it," Anna whispered to her. "You've already
bought her two things, and she can't fit into her regular
gowns anyway at the moment."

"I do have some sympathy for her," Lucy admitted.
"She was supposed to marry Robert at one point, and all
his fortune would've been hers."

"She *chose* not to marry him, and he has done much
better with you. Penelope would have made him very miserable," Anna said firmly. "Let her pout."

The bell above the door tinkled, and a new group of
people entered the shop. Lucy went to the counter to pay
for her purchases and to give them the address for delivery. She engaged the girl in conversation while the fabric
and trimming were wrapped in brown paper.

When she turned back toward the door Anna was
standing with a group of people including a tall man in the
uniform of the Royal Navy. Something about Anna's still-
ness caught Lucy's attention, and she moved swiftly toward her sister.

The naval officer saw her first and quickly stepped back with a bow, as a flustered Anna put her hand on Lucy's arm.

"Lucy, this is Captain Harry Akers and his family," Anna said. "Mrs. Akers, may I present you to my sister, Lady Kurland?"

A small, rounded woman with a pleasant face curtsied to Lucy.

"Good morning, Lady Kurland. It is a pleasure to meet you. I believe my son made the acquaintance of your sister while he was in London."

Lucy smiled. "How lovely. Do you reside in Bath or are you visiting this fine town as we are?"

"We live out in the countryside, my lady, and came to buy clothing and other necessities for my daughter Rosemary's upcoming wedding."

The third member of the family was blushing, so Lucy assumed she was the bride-to-be.

"A wedding is always a joyous occasion in any family. I wish you much happiness," Lucy said kindly.

"Thank you, my, my lady," Rosemary stuttered, and curtsied again.

Lucy glanced over at Anna, who was conversing quietly with the young captain.

"Perhaps you might consider joining us for tea one day, Mrs. Akers? I'm sure my sister would be delighted to renew her acquaintance with you all."

"That's very kind of you, my lady."

"We are staying at number twelve Queen's Square. Do you know it?" Lucy asked.

"Indeed." Mrs. Akers nodded. "It is a fine address, and very easy to find."

"Then may I hope to see you and your family very soon?" Lucy said. "We intend to invest in a subscription to the Assembly Rooms, so we might also encounter you there, or in the Pump Room."

"Indeed, my father is quite elderly, and we often accompany him to the Pump Rooms so that he can take the waters and meet with his various acquaintances," Mrs. Akers said. "My son is awaiting a new command from the navy so we are delighted to have his company as well."

As Lucy stored this interesting information away in her head, Penelope came over with Lucy's wrapped parcel and raised her eyebrows.

"Lucy, if we wish to visit Godwin's Circulating Library before it closes, we really should be on our way."

Mrs. Akers smiled at them both. "Then we will not detain you. It was a pleasure to meet you, Lady Kurland."

She moved away with her daughter, and Anna rejoined them, her color still somewhat heightened.

"I . . . was not expecting to see Captain Akers here in Bath."

"Did he not mention that his family lived near here?" Lucy allowed Penelope to precede her out of the shop door so she could speak to Anna. "His mother said he is waiting for new orders."

"Yes, that's what Harry, I mean Captain Akers, said," Anna replied. "His last command was scuttled by a storm with the loss of many lives." She pressed her gloved hand to her bosom. "He only survived by the Grace of God."

Lucy waited for a carriage to pass before she crossed the street. "I invited his mother to call on us in Queen's Square."

"That was very kind of you." Anna hesitated. "Although I'm not sure what purpose you have in doing so. I have already made my feelings very clear to Captain Akers."

"Feelings about what?" Penelope interjected. "Have you met this man *before*, Anna? Did your father's family in London *allow* such a thing?"

Lucy met Anna's gaze. "Perhaps we should talk about this matter when we have more privacy?"

Anna nodded as they entered the bookshop and were engulfed in the smell of ink, old parchment, and leather. Despite Anna's reservations, Lucy knew her sister well enough to judge that whether she admitted it or not, her feelings were still engaged with the young man. Whatever came of the matter, Lucy intended to ensure that Anna was given every opportunity to follow her emotions to a logical and natural conclusion.

When they returned to the house, Robert was absent with Dr. Fletcher, so Lucy ordered tea to be served in the drawing room and settled down to read the local newspaper. When Foley appeared in the doorway with a silver salver containing two visiting cards she told him to bring the visitors up.

"Lady Benson and Mr. Arden Hall, my lady."

Foley stepped back to allow the visitors to enter, and Lucy tried not to stare. She'd expected Sir William's wife to be quite elderly, but the woman in front of her was a fragile, ethereal beauty who looked far younger than Lucy.

"Lady Benson?" Lucy went forward to greet her guests. "It is a pleasure to meet you."

Lady Benson's lip trembled. "Sir William insisted I come." She waved a languid hand at the tall youth by her side, who was in danger of being strangled by the height of his own collar. "This is my son Arden."

"My lady." Arden Hall bowed elaborately but looked even more reluctant to be there than his mother, which was quite a feat. "A pleasure."

Lady Benson sank into a chair as if she no longer had the energy to stand upright. Her gown was composed of several layers of thin muslin that clearly displayed the lines of her body and her generous bosom. Her very expensive shawl was artfully slipping from her shoulders in a way that Lucy envied but had no intention of emulating.

"May I offer you some refreshment?" Lucy inquired.

Arden glanced at his mother. "A glass of brandy would be nice, and I suspect Mother would like some tea."

Lady Benson pressed a hand to her brow. She wasn't wearing a bonnet, but had pinned a lace cap to her silver blond hair. "I have a headache. A tisane would be better."

"I'm not sure if Lady Kurland has such a thing, Mama." Arden laughed. "Pray excuse my mother. She believes the entire world should serve her needs."

There was a note of disrespect in his voice that made Lucy sit up straight. "As I sometimes suffer from headaches myself, sir, I can only appreciate how your mother feels." She addressed Lady Benson. "Perhaps you would be better off at home in bed, ma'am?"

"I've spent most of the day in bed," Lady Benson sighed. "But William *insisted* that I get up and pay my respects to you." She shuddered. "He actually raised his voice to me!"

Lucy stood and went over to the door. "Then consider your duty done, my lady. It was a pleasure to meet you, and your son." She opened the door. "Perhaps when you are feeling more the thing you can visit me again."

Lady Benson rose from her chair, her tragic expression visibly brightening. "And you will tell Sir William that I did as he commanded?"

"Of course, ma'am." Lucy nodded. "I'm sure he wouldn't wish you to suffer."

"You might be surprised about that," she sighed. "He *lives* to humiliate me."

Arden Hall took hold of his mother's arm and guided her toward the door. "My mother is quite correct, Lady Kurland. We all live in fear of the old man." He nodded to her as he went past. "Thank you for receiving us, and good day."

"Oh!" Lady Benson pressed her fingers on Lucy's wrist. "My husband asked me to invite you to dinner on Friday. Is that convenient?"

"I believe so," Lucy said cautiously. "I will consult with Sir Robert and send you a message if we can attend."

"Thank you for your kindness." Lady Benson's smile was almost tragic.

"And please don't tell my husband that I almost forgot to invite you after all."

Lucy watched the odd couple descend into the hallway and tried to make sense of their somewhat unconventional visit. The current Lady Benson was obviously not the first wife of Sir William. She also had children from a previous marriage, which meant she wasn't as young as she looked.

Was Sir William really a tyrant who had forced his wife out of her sickbed merely to pay a call on her new neighbors, or was Lady Benson exaggerating somewhat? Lucy already knew whose side she was on but attempted to give the lady the benefit of the doubt.

She sat down in her favorite chair that overlooked the square and finished drinking her tea. Lady Benson was a very beautiful woman. Had Sir William fallen in love with her charms and then discovered she wasn't quite what he expected? Lucy would have to see them together to make any sense of the state of their marriage, but she already had her doubts.

"Good afternoon, my dear."

She turned as Robert limped into the room, and went over to him. He looked rather tired and smelled strange. She sniffed his coat.

"What have you been rolling in?"

He snorted. "You'll have to ask Patrick. He insisted I was slathered in hot mud today and wrapped up like a mummy from one of those Egyptian tombs."

Lucy pressed her mouth against his lapel to stifle her laughter.

"Oh, dear."

He put a finger under her chin so she had to look up at him. "It was quite the scene. I suspect Patrick was hoping they'd cover my mouth and stop me from expressing my opinion of such a ridiculous waste of time."

"Perhaps you should take *another* bath," Lucy suggested.

Robert walked over to the couch. "The thing is . . . I actually quite enjoyed it by the end. The heat from the mud seeped into my bones and had a remarkably invigorating effect on me."

"Really?" Lucy stared at him wide-eyed. "I'm so pleased that you derived some benefit from such an outlandish treatment and are willing to admit it."

"Indeed." Robert pointed at the teapot. "Is there any tea left? I am rather thirsty. Patrick told me to drink lots of hot spring water, but I've had enough of that foul-smelling brew for one day."

Lucy poured him a cup of tea and resigned herself to the strange aroma surrounding her husband. If it were helping him, she would willingly put up with it, and it was no worse than when he visited the pigsty at Kurland St. Mary home farm.

"I had visitors today," she remarked as she handed him the cup. "Lady Benson and her son."

"Was she as forthright as her husband?" Robert inquired as he thanked her for the tea.

"No, she wasn't what I expected at all." Lucy fought a smile. "She was extremely beautiful, much younger than Sir William, and insisted that her husband had made her get up from her sickbed merely to pay a call on me to invite us to dinner."

Robert paused, his cup halfway to his mouth. "She sounds quite odd."

"The son who accompanied her was from her first marriage, and not Sir William's."

"Was he pleasant?" Robert inquired.

"No, he was as unconventional and rude as his mother. She invited us to dine with them on Friday."

"Then we should definitely go." Robert finished his tea in one long swallow. "It sounds as if they might be quite entertaining."

Lucy had to agree. She drank her own tea and placed the cup back on the tray.

"We also met the family of a naval officer Anna was acquainted with in London. I invited them to call on us. If they *do* come, I would very much like to further our acquaintance with them."

"Are you meddling again, Lucy?" Robert raised an eyebrow.

"Hardly." Lucy met his amused gaze. "Anna mentioned this man to me last year. I got the impression that she had started to care for him before he left to carry out his duties."

"Ah, so you are meddling, but with the best of intentions."

"Or attempting to help my sister find a man who will love and cherish her for the rest of her life." Lucy held his gaze. "What is wrong with that?"

"Nothing, my dear. Just remember that Anna is old enough to make her own decisions."

"I am well aware of that." Lucy nodded. "I would never force her to do anything she disliked."

Robert leaned forward to kiss her cheek. "I know, but sometimes you can be a little managing of those you love."

"With the best of intentions," Lucy stoutly defended herself.

"Agreed, but you also told me that Anna is somewhat reluctant to be married at all." He looked into her eye. "I can't fault your desire to make sure she is happy, but I still urge caution."

"I will do my best not to interfere," she promised, even though her interventions were usually quite successful. "But I will not stop their acquaintance from progressing if they appear to be getting along."

"Fair enough. I trust your good sense." He nodded. "With all these new friends I have so much to look forward to I can barely contain my excitement."

Foley cleared his throat in the doorway. "Excuse me, Sir Robert and my lady. You have another visitor."

"Good Lord." Robert held out his hand for the calling card and read the name aloud. "Mr. *Edward* Benson."

He raised his eyebrows at Lucy. "Send him up, Foley. It appears that our interesting day is not yet over, my dear."

The man whom Foley ushered in bore a passing resemblance to Sir William and wore the sober uniform of a successful businessman.

He bowed to Robert.

"Sir Robert Kurland? It is a pleasure to make your acquaintance, sir. My father speaks very highly of you."

His accent held a hint of the north but was overlaid by years of attending a public school that had refined his vowels.

Robert stood and held out his hand for Lucy to rise. "Good afternoon, sir. May I introduce you to my wife, Lady Kurland? She just spent a delightful few minutes this morning meeting Lady Benson and her son."

Edward frowned. "So I heard, which is why I hastened over here myself to correct any unfortunate impression my stepmother might have left with you."

Robert concealed a smile. "As I did not have the pleasure of meeting Lady Benson myself, and my wife only mentioned she had called to ask us for dinner, I cannot comment on this matter."

"My stepmother can be a little . . . *eccentric* sometimes," Edward said gruffly. "But the invitation comes directly from my father and is sincerely meant."

"And we intend to honor that summons and will present ourselves at your abode at the appointed hour with great anticipation," Robert added, and gestured at the couch. "Will you stay for some refreshment?"

"I fear I must depart. My father is waiting to speak to me." Edward bowed stiffly again. "It was a pleasure to meet you, Sir Robert, and you, Lady Kurland. I look forward to furthering our acquaintance at dinner on Friday."

He turned and left, leaving Robert staring at his wife.

"Well, that was unexpected," Robert said. "Did Sir William send him to repair his fences? What on earth did Lady Benson tell him occurred here?"

"I have no idea and the whole family is giving me a headache." Lucy pressed a hand to her forehead. "I will retire for a nap, and maybe when I wake up some sort of order will have been restored in this society."

Robert frowned. He was so busy worrying about his own health that he forgot his wife had been ill herself the previous year.

"Are you all right?" he asked bluntly.

"I'm fine." She smiled at him. "I'm worn out from shepherding Penelope and Anna around the shops in Milsom Street. I'll be perfectly capable after I've had a nap."

He went over to take her hands, searching her face.

"Are you sure?"

"Yes, I would tell you if I was feeling unwell." She frowned. "In truth I have no idea why I suddenly feel tired, but a restorative nap makes everything better." She patted his cheek. "Perhaps you might consult with Dr. Fletcher and ask him if you can take a bath to get rid of all that mud? I'd rather it didn't end up on my bedsheets."

He shuddered. "I'll ask him. Now go and rest, and I will see you at dinner."

Chapter 4

Robert stood up as Lucy entered the drawing room. Despite his initial skepticism, after two weeks of treatment at the baths he was feeling much improved. He'd also enjoyed spending time with Sir William, who had somewhat similar views to his about the state of the country, and the nature of politics and politicians. Sir William had no compunction in sharing his opinions in the most forthright manner, which, much to Robert's amusement, had soon scared off other listeners.

"You look very nice this evening, my dear." Robert considered Lucy's gown in his favorite blue.

"Thank you." She smoothed down the silk. "It is new." She touched her hair. "Anna did my hair for me. Do you like it?"

He studied the profusion of ringlets. In truth he preferred it when Lucy simply braided her long hair in a coronet on top of her head, but he had been married long enough to know not to disappoint her.

"You look lovely. Is your sister ready to accompany us to the Bensons?"

"Yes, she is just coming." Lucy came over and straightened the folds of Robert's cravat. "You look very handsome this evening."

"I do not," he demurred. "I have it on the best authority that fierce-looking gentlemen such as myself only appear dashing when wearing uniform."

"Did Penelope tell you that?" Lucy asked.

Robert grimaced. "Seeing as how quickly she wished to get out of our engagement once I was wounded and retired from the hussars, you might imagine so."

"Her loss was my gain," Lucy said.

"Yes, but somehow we have also gained *her.*"

Lucy chuckled. "That has more to do with your doctor's choice of a wife than anything we did. Has Dr. Fletcher found you a new physician in Bath yet, or is he content to leave your care in the hands of Sir William's man?"

"He hasn't said. I will ask him for his opinion tomorrow." Robert picked up his cane.

"He doesn't intend to join us?" Lucy asked with a frown.

"Seeing as he has just arrived back from Kurland St. Mary, he intends to spend a quiet night at the theater with his wife."

Lucy fought a smile and Robert held up his finger. "I know those two hopes seem somewhat incompatible."

"Robert, you are impossible . . ." Lucy reached for his hand just as Anna came through the door.

She also wore blue, but her gown was patterned with flowers, and free of the fancy Honiton lace that edged the bodice and sleeves of Lucy's gown. Even Robert had to admit that it didn't matter what Anna Harrington wore when one's gaze was inevitably drawn to her beautiful face. Unlike Penelope, who had also been an acknowledged beauty, Anna's loveliness went far beyond the perfection of her person.

"Lucy, you forgot your shawl." Anna carefully draped a paisley shawl around her sister's shoulders. "I know we are only going next door, but I don't want you to catch a chill." She smiled at Robert. "And how are you feeling today, sir? You look much better."

"As I am now capable of getting down the stairs without assistance, I am obviously improving." Robert held the door open for his ladies to precede him. "Who would've thought that floating up to one's neck in a murky pool of yellowish boiling water with a group of complete strangers would make a man healthier?"

Anna's laughter floated back to him as he carefully navigated his way down the steep staircase. He was enjoying himself far more than he had anticipated in Bath and wasn't ashamed to admit it. In truth, he felt better than he had in years.

It took them all of two minutes to knock on the Bensons' door and be ushered through into the warmth. Robert hadn't yet met Lady Benson. He'd only gotten to know Sir William at the baths and was looking forward to finally meeting the rest of the Benson family. He found the climb up the stairs slightly more laborious than the one down, and was the last to arrive in the drawing room where Sir William was holding court.

Robert's gaze was immediately drawn to the willowy young woman languishing at Sir William's side. From Lucy's description he realized that the beauty must be his elderly host's wife, and not one of his children. Behind her chair were two young men barely old enough to shave, and gathered protectively around Sir William were three older men who all had his distinctive nose.

The stark division between the two sides was obvious to even the most casual observer. Sir William stood with some difficulty and held out his hand to Lucy.

"Good evening, Lady Kurland. May I present you to my wife, Miranda, my sons, Edward, Augustus, and Peregrine?"

While Lucy curtsied, and made Anna known to Sir William, Robert noted the disgruntled expressions of the two younger men who hadn't merited an introduction.

"Sir Robert." Lady Benson didn't get up and offered him her limp hand. "A pleasure indeed. May I introduce my two sons to you as my husband did not see fit to do so himself?" She waved at the boys. "Please make your bow to Sir Robert, Arden and Brandon."

"Ah, a lover of Shakespeare I see." Robert bowed in return.

"It was an affectation of my first husband's." Lady Benson shuddered. "I had no say in the matter at all."

She turned to view Anna, who was almost surrounded by the three older Benson sons. "Is this your sister, Sir Robert? She is very beautiful."

"Anna is my wife's sister," Robert replied.

Lady Benson tittered. "Yet you chose to marry the *other* one. How . . . unusual."

Robert met her gaze. "My wife's value is far more than just a pretty face, my lady. Beauty fades, but character and goodness remain."

Lady Benson touched her cheek as if checking *she* was still beautiful. "Indeed. A lesson for us all." She stood and tapped Sir William on the shoulder. "Shall we dine?"

"When I haven't even had a chance to speak to Sir Robert or offer anyone refreshment?" Sir William frowned at her. "There is no need for such haste, my dear."

Lady Benson sighed and sat down again. "As you wish."

She made no effort to speak to Anna or Lucy, and instead spoke exclusively to her sons, who looked as if they'd rather be anywhere than at a family dinner.

"Good evening, Sir Robert." The shortest of the Bensons bowed to Robert. He wore the plain black garb favored by clerics. "I am the Reverend Augustus Benson. I oversee several parishes just outside of Bath."

"It is a pleasure to meet you, sir." Robert inclined his head. "Do you reside in Bath or at one of your properties?"

"I have a curate who ministers to the souls of my parishioners. I prefer to spend my time here where I can gain valuable benefactors for my congregation and godly work." Augustus paused. "Do you support your local church, Sir Robert?"

"Seeing as I am married to the eldest daughter of our rector in Kurland St. Mary, you might say that I do."

Augustus raised his eyebrows. "Lady Kurland and Miss Harrington's father is in holy orders?"

Robert paused. "Well, sometimes I'm not so sure about the *holy*, but he does live in the rectory and take the odd service when he has no other choice."

Now Augustus was staring at him in horror, and Robert remembered that his dislike of some of the practices of the church was not universal.

"Mr. Harrington is a good man," Robert said firmly. "He was educated at Cambridge, I believe, and is the younger brother of an earl."

"Indeed!" Augustus cast a speculative glance back at Anna, who was smiling up at Edward Benson. "I must further my acquaintance with your wife's sister. Finding a partner who is familiar with the task of running a vicarage is remarkably difficult. We probably have a lot in common."

Robert went over to reintroduce himself to Edward and met the youngest Benson, who looked nothing like his brothers but had a distinct look of Sir William.

Eventually, the butler came in and loudly cleared his throat. "Dinner is served. Please proceed into the dining room."

Unlike the house the Kurlands were renting the drawing room led straight into the dining room, and the master bedrooms were on the floor above. Sir William insisted that Robert and Lucy sit on either side of him as the rest of the family, with Anna on the arm of Edward, filed into the other seats.

Sir William bowed his head and said grace, and then the footmen left the guests to serve themselves. There was no shortage of rich food, which perhaps explained why Sir William had failed to reduce his considerable weight or improve his health during his sojourn in Bath.

*   *   *

Robert looked across the table at his wife and winked, and Lucy raised her eyebrows. Her husband appeared to be enjoying himself immensely, whereas she was still attempting to navigate the somewhat peculiar family around her. Peregrine, the youngest of the Benson sons, sat beside Lucy and immediately poured them both a glass of wine.

"Drink up, my lady. You'll need it," he murmured. "My father's been consuming port all day as if it will go out of fashion. I suspect we're all going to be in for a tongue-lashing tonight. It's his favorite blood sport."

Lucy blinked at him, but he continued to smile. He was the only member of the Benson family with dark coloring, and was the most outrageously fashionable and handsome. His hair was lavishly curled and smelled strongly of pomade, giving him the look of an erstwhile poet.

Lucy took a cautious sip of her wine. "Thank you."

"You are most welcome." Peregrine continued to regard her. "Your husband has made a remarkably good impression on my father."

"I believe they have much in common," Lucy replied.

"One wouldn't think it to look at them, but I suspect you are correct. Sir Robert is something of an anomaly for his class, is he not?"

"My husband is a man with forthright opinions," Lucy agreed. "Some of which are not in step with the current political climate."

"He's just like my father then. No wonder they get along." Peregrine picked up a platter. "Would you care for some goose, my lady?"

The meal progressed without further incident, but Lucy was aware that Peregrine was correct as to the level of his father's alcohol consumption and growing anger.

"You." Sir William pointed his finger down the table at Arden, one of Lady Benson's sons. "I had a note from my tailor this morning that you haven't paid his bill in six months."

Arden shrugged. "So what? Throw it in the fire, that's what I do. Bloody tradesmen shouldn't be bothering you with it."

"That 'tradesman' has to pay his own bills and feed his family," Sir William barked. "I pay you an allowance. Why aren't you paying your bills in a timely manner?"

"Here we go," Peregrine murmured in Lucy's ear, and finished his whole glass of wine in one swallow. "This won't end well."

Arden raised his chin. "The allowance you pay me is far less than that you give Edward, Augustus, and Peregrine."

"They are sons of my blood. You are merely—"

"An inconvenience that you put up with so that you could marry my mother?" Arden didn't back down. "We understand our position in this family all too well, sir, never doubt it."

Sir William leaned forward, one hand clenched around his glass of port. "If you're that ungrateful, whelp, perhaps you'd do better with no money at all."

"Please leave the boy alone, Sir William," Lady Benson intervened. "You will make me ill."

The glare Sir William cast his wife made Lucy wish she could think of a way to politely extricate *her* family from the table. The only person who seemed to be enjoying himself was Peregrine.

"Perhaps Lady Benson has a point," murmured Augustus. "One must show Christian charity to one's family, eh sir?"

"Christian charity?" Sir William rounded on his second son, who sank into his chair like a deflated pudding. "For those lazy do-nothings who suck off the cow's teat and wouldn't know one end of a shovel from the other? Your affairs, Augustus, are in no better order than that young rapscallion's!"

The angrier Sir William got the more pronounced his northern accent became.

"And that goes for all of you." Sir William's contemptuous gaze swept the table. "I've never seen a bunch of more bacon-brained useless ne'er-do-wells in my life."

"Steady on, Father," Edward murmured. "I work for you."

"And you ignore my advice at every turn!" Sir William snapped. "With your ridiculous ideas to cut up my peace and ruin my business . . ." He took another slurp of port, which Lucy thought was perhaps unwise. "I grew up without a sixpence to scratch my arse with! None of you would survive a day down the pit. *None* of you."

Peregrine cleared his throat. "That's remarkably unfair, Father. Your hard work and determination created enough wealth to bring your sons up to be *gentlemen*. Wasn't that the whole point? Why berate us for becoming what you wanted us to be?"

Lucy held her breath as Sir William turned toward Peregrine. He was breathing heavily like an enraged bull and his complexion was purple. Peregrine didn't flinch from the contact and looked more relaxed than ever.

"Aye. More fool me," Sir William grumbled. "I thought to better myself, and what do I have to show for it? Three caper-witted sons, and two . . ." He glared down at the end of the table where Lady Benson sat flanked by her sons. "Two ungrateful fools. Mark me well I'll rewrite my will and disinherit the lot of you!"

Lady Benson rose to her feet, her voice trembling. "I think I've heard enough for one evening, Sir William. I will retire with the ladies and hope that you manage to mend your manners before you appear in my drawing room!"

Lucy and Anna hurried to leave the room behind Lady Benson, who was moving at some speed. To Lucy's mortification, Robert appeared to be enjoying the fracas immensely. When they reached the drawing room, their hostess collapsed onto the couch and covered her eyes with the back of her hand.

"Oh, the *mortification*! I am quite undone!"

Lucy went to her side. "Shall I send for your maid, my lady?"

"Yes, because I am set to swoon away at the discourtesy shown to me by my own husband." She shuddered. "My nerves are shredded! My composure *ruined*!" She laid her head back on the arm of the couch. "While you are finding my maid, ask her to find Dr. Mantel. He will soothe me, I *know* it!"

Anna went to ring the bell while Lucy patted the distraught lady's hand and murmured reassurances. It wasn't the first time she had dealt with a woman of such dramatic tendencies, and she doubted it would be the last. She did have some sympathy with Lady Benson. Sir William had behaved very badly indeed. If Robert had berated his family in such a way in front of guests, Lucy would have considered walking out herself, or something even more shocking.

The door opened, and a young woman rushed in and curtsied to Lady Benson.

"Do you want your smelling salts, Lady Miranda?"

"Why didn't you bring them *with* you, Dotty?" the lady complained, her high-pitched whining setting Lucy's teeth on edge. It crossed her mind that if Lady Benson became hysterical she would not object to being the person forced to administer a timely slap. "Why do you all *torment* me so?"

"Now, now, Lady Benson." Lucy turned as a well-dressed man came into the drawing room and knelt by the distraught hostess. "What is all this? Have I not implored you to rest and not allow such irritation to your delicate spirits?"

Lady Benson dabbed a lace handkerchief over her face and clutched at his sleeve. "My dear Dr. Mantel, how *kind* you are, how *sensible* of the horrors of my situation."

The doctor patted her hand. "You must not worry yourself, my lady. I shall ask Cook to brew you one of my special tisanes, and Dotty will bring your smelling salts to you directly."

Lady Benson gave another shudder and raised her piteous face to the doctor's. "Thank you, sir. You are the only person who thinks of my comfort."

The maid reappeared with the smelling salts grasped in her hand, and with the doctor's gentle encouragement, Lady Benson applied herself to inhaling the noxious fumes.

Dr. Mantel came over to Lucy and bowed. "I do beg your pardon for such an unusual introduction, but I must assume you are Lady Kurland?"

"Indeed I am." Lucy curtsied. "And this is my sister, Miss Anna Harrington."

"It is a pleasure to meet you both." The doctor moved closer to Lucy and lowered his voice. "I must apologize for Lady Benson's condition. She has somewhat fragile nerves."

"So I observed," Lucy replied. "Although I must say in her defense that Sir William was not being particularly pleasant to his family over the dinner table."

Dr. Mantel sighed. "He is a difficult man, but also an admirable one in many ways. I have tried to curtail his excesses. I fear to no avail."

"He was threatening to disinherit everyone," Lady Benson spoke out, her voice trembling. "He seems to think we are all parasites."

"Surely not you, my lady?" Dr. Mantel turned back to her and took the smelling salts away. "You are a devoted wife to him."

"Indeed, I do my best." Lady Benson nodded. "But sometimes it is hard, especially when he treats my beloved sons so harshly."

As if she had conjured them with her words, the two young men strode into the drawing room, identical scowls on their faces.

"We're going out," Arden snapped. "The old man is drunk, and we're sick and tired of sitting there listening to him ranting."

Lady Benson pressed her hand to her fine bosom and implored them, "Please don't leave. He will not like it. He—"

"Devil take him," Arden interrupted her. "The old fool. The sooner he dies, the better for all of us."

Dr. Mantel cleared his throat. "Now boys . . ."

Brandon swung around toward him. "No one asked for your opinion, Doctor. Why don't you go back to fawning around the man who pays your wages instead of sniffing around our mother?"

Lady Benson pointed a wavering hand at the door. "Don't speak to Dr. Mantel like that! He is the only person in this household who understands me!"

"Mother's right." Arden elbowed his younger brother. "That was uncalled for, Brandon. Apologize."

"If I must," Brandon grumbled. "I agree that the old man is the problem. If only he wasn't so tightfisted with his money." He nodded at his mother. "He told us to go to the devil, so perhaps we will oblige him. If only there was some way to cut up a lark in this boring town."

Arden bowed. "Good night, Mother. We will see you in the morning."

Before Lady Benson could issue another plea they were gone, leaving their mother weeping, and Dr. Mantel looking very embarrassed.

"I think I should escort Lady Benson to her bedchamber," the doctor murmured. "She is quite overwrought, and is in no state to deal with Sir William."

"I quite agree, sir." Lucy smiled at him, aware that he had been put in a very difficult position. "Would you like me to accompany Lady Benson?"

"That is very kind of you, my lady, but Dotty and I will manage the task between us." He attempted a smile. "I'm sure her ladyship wouldn't want to ruin your evening."

Lucy and Anna watched as Lady Benson was tenderly escorted out of the room leaning heavily on the doctor's arm, and disappeared upstairs.

"Well," Anna said. "This evening has certainly proved

far more entertaining than I anticipated it would be." She glanced around the room. "Do you think we will be served with tea, or should I ring the bell?"

Lucy sat beside the fire. "Ring the bell. I suspect we'll be here for a while before I can prize my husband away from such a spectacle."

Chapter 5

Robert shivered as the wind curled around the stone columns and attacked him from all sides. His bones were aching, and he had to pay attention to his footing on the slippery surfaces. It was also possible that he had drunk rather too much port the previous evening when they'd dined at the Benson residence. He turned to Patrick, who was accompanying him to the King's Bath.

"Why do we have to come so blasted early?"

"Because there are fewer people around for you to intimidate?"

"I hardly look intimidating when I'm up to my neck in boiling water," Robert grumbled. "At least you haven't made me wear one of those awful mop hats."

His doctor had the audacity to grin at him. "At least admit that my treatments have been helpful to you."

"Indeed they have." Robert paused at the end of the dark corridor that led toward the King's Bath. They had passed a few brave souls wrapped up in cloaks and mufflers, but the baths were remarkably quiet today. He could already smell sulfur rising in the steam like a welcome to the entrance to hell. "I will have to consider a way to import such a miraculous invention as hot spring water into Kurland Hall."

"If the Romans could manage it, I'm sure you will, too, Sir Robert," Patrick joked. "Now, who's leaving the baths in such a hurry?"

Footsteps echoed down the hallway coming toward them. Robert had to awkwardly step to the side as a large cloaked figure rushed past him without as much as an "excuse me."

With a curse, Robert righted himself, and they continued into the baths where Dr. Mantel was just emerging from one of the inner rooms clutching a parcel wrapped in brown paper and string.

"Good morning, Sir Robert, Dr. Fletcher. I am surprised to see you on such a cold day." He chuckled. "It took all my powers of persuasion to get Sir William out of his warm bed and into the baths today. Only the promise of some conversation with your good self, Sir Robert, persuaded him to rise at all."

Robert looked idly over at the bath, but it was a gloomy morning, and it was hard to see exactly who was currently in the steaming hot water.

Dr. Mantel bowed. "I must go and attend to Sir William. I will tell him that you have arrived."

He strolled closer to the baths and then spun around, his face stricken. "Dr. Fletcher! I can't see Sir William in the water, and I can't swim, and—"

Patrick was already moving toward the almost deserted bath. By the time Robert caught up his friend was stripping off his coat and boots and jumping into the steaming hot water. There was nothing bobbing on the surface except a linen cap and a small wooden tray containing a natural sponge.

Robert grasped hold of one of the pillars surrounding the bath to stop himself from slipping and looked in vain for one of the attendants. There was another splash in the water as Patrick dived down and emerged with a body in his arms that he towed toward the side of the bath.

Somewhere a lady started screaming, the sound echoing in the cavern as Patrick hauled out Sir William's body and arranged him on his side.

"Check his mouth," Patrick shouted. "Make sure he can breathe."

As Dr. Mantel appeared to be frozen in shock, Robert awkwardly got down on his knees and made certain Sir William's tongue was in the right place, and that there was nothing untoward in his mouth. Patrick thumped vigorously on the old man's back, but Sir William was no longer breathing.

"Is he dead?" Dr. Mantel asked anxiously.

"I fear he is." Patrick sat back, laid the body on its back, and gently closed Sir William's bulging eyes. "Did you see what occurred?"

"No, dammit, I left to speak to one of the vendors about purchasing a new pumice stone before he even entered the water, and when I came back—" Dr. Mantel shuddered. "I couldn't see Sir William at all. My *God* . . . I will never forgive myself."

"Having observed Sir William over the past weeks, I suspect he suffered some form of heart failure or a stroke and simply slipped beneath the surface of the water," Patrick said.

"Yes! I would agree with that possibility," Dr. Mantel said, nodding. "What a terrible tragedy. Lady Benson will never forgive me for not having taken sufficient care of her beloved husband."

"If he indeed died from failure of the heart or a stroke then there was little you could've done about it even if you'd been in the water with him," Patrick pointed out. "I'm certain you warned Sir William that eating and drinking in excess would cause him problems."

"I did warn him." Dr. Mantel sighed. "But he rarely listened to my advice."

"A common problem for physicians the world over," Patrick agreed.

Robert rose carefully to his feet. His knee was already complaining at the hardness of the stone, and the dampness of his once pristine clothing.

"Would you like me to send one of the attendants to fetch the magistrate?" Robert asked. He looked around the almost deserted space. "It appears that the rest of the patrons have decided to flee and not indulge in a dip in the baths today."

A familiar figure came rushing up to them and bowed. "Gentlemen, as the proprietor of these baths, I understand that a tragedy has befallen Sir William Benson. I offer my condolences and offer whatever help you need."

"Thank you, Mr. Abernathy." Robert bowed in return. "Perhaps you might consider closing the baths to the public until we can remove Sir William's body to his house?"

"I've already done that, Sir Robert, and ordered a carriage to transport the body back to Queen's Square." Mr. Abernathy bowed again.

"I'll travel with him, Sir Robert," Patrick said. He was shivering as he put his coat on over his wet clothes. "Mayhap you can walk back with Dr. Mantel and help him deliver the sad news to the Benson family?"

"Yes, of course," Robert said, his gaze fixing on a trickle of red that appeared to be coming from the body. He leaned in and murmured in his friend's ear, "Dr. Fletcher, why would Sir William be bleeding?"

As Dr. Mantel turned away to speak to Mr. Abernathy, Patrick gently probed the deceased's body and then looked up at Robert.

"Perhaps Sir William didn't drown or suffer heart failure." He held up his bloodstained fingers. "It's possible that someone wanted to make certain he never got out of the baths again."

Robert held Patrick's gaze. "Please do not speak of this to anyone else yet."

Patrick raised his eyebrows. "If you insist."

"I'll explain when we get back to Queen's Square." Robert straightened up. "If anyone was a likely candidate to be murdered, it was Sir William Benson."

Robert took an involuntary step back as Lady Benson started screeching like a demented banshee and then collapsed to the floor of the breakfast parlor. He supposed he should have caught her, but Edward Benson had been closer and hadn't moved an inch.

It was Edward who addressed him now, his face pale.

"My father is *dead*?"

"Yes." Robert saw no need to sweeten the news. He'd written many letters to the families of his men who had died in battle, and believed a short, heartfelt response was better received than a lot of balderdash. "My physician, Dr. Fletcher, attempted to revive Sir William when he retrieved him from under the water, but to no avail."

"Dear God." Edward sat back in his chair as if unaware that his stepmother was still lying prone on the Turkish rug while her maid and Dr. Mantel attended to her. "He's been ill for quite some time, but I never really thought he'd die. He was something of a force of nature."

"Indeed. I enjoyed his company immensely." Robert bowed. "I offer your entire family my condolences." He noted that none of the other Bensons or Lady Benson's sons were at the breakfast table at such an early hour. "If there is anything Lady Kurland or I can do to help, please do not hesitate to call upon us."

"That's very good of you, Sir Robert," Edward said. "And thank you for bringing us this sad news."

Lady Benson was carried out by one of the footmen moaning piteously, and Robert stepped out of the way.

"I should be going. Dr. Fletcher will accompany the body back to this house. He should be here very shortly."

Belatedly Edward remembered his manners. "Would you like to await him here? Can I offer you a drink or some breakfast?"

Robert hesitated. "I *would* like to wait until Sir William's body reaches this house so that I might pay my last respects, but I do not require any sustenance, thank you."

In truth, he would rather like a large brandy, but at nine o'clock in the morning that was asking rather too much of his hosts. He also wanted to speak to Patrick before any of the Benson family began to ask questions as to what exactly had befallen their father.

A commotion on the stairs drew his attention to the door as Lady Benson's two young sons came into the room. From the disordered state of their dress they had been out all night.

Edward shot to his feet, his expression darkening. "Where in God's name have you two been?"

Arden, who was propping up his younger brother, belched loudly. "Out. What is it to you?" He glanced around the breakfast room. "Where's my mother?"

"She's upstairs in her room after receiving the most devastating news," Edward said somberly. "Sir William is dead."

For a moment there was silence, and then the brothers burst into whoops and hugged each other. Robert's lip curled in distaste. If he'd had the two of them under his command in his regiment he would've taught them a few lessons about respecting the dead.

"You're pitching the gammon," Brandon said when he finally stopped laughing. "Sir William is an immortal monster."

Robert intervened. "I can confirm that Sir William is indeed deceased. May I also suggest that you show a little respect!"

Arden faced him. "Why should we? It's the best thing that's happened since Mother married that old fool. I'm glad he drowned." He grinned at his brother. "Now we'll be *rich*!"

"Get out," Edward said, and pointed at the door. "Go to your rooms and reflect upon your appalling behavior in front of our guest, and your complete disregard for your stepfather."

"We'll go," Arden sneered. "But only because we need our sleep." He half bowed to Robert. "Good riddance, Sir Robert."

Edward turned to Robert as the pair lurched back into the hall. "I do apologize."

"There's no need. Their contempt for Sir William was on display when we came to dinner," Robert said. "I'm not surprised that they are full of vicious glee at his demise."

The butler appeared in the doorway. "Dr. Fletcher is here, Mr. Benson, shall I send him up?"

"Direct him up the stairs to Sir William's bedchamber. I have already alerted his valet." Edward went toward the door. "Shall we attend them there, Sir Robert?"

Lucy jumped up from her seat by the window as Robert appeared in the drawing room accompanied by Dr. Fletcher.

"What on earth is going on next door?' Lucy asked. "There has been a veritable procession of people and vehicles arriving all morning."

Dr. Fletcher bowed to her. "Sir William is dead."

Lucy gasped and turned to Robert, who nodded. "Sir William was in the King's Bath and apparently drowned." He hesitated. "Do you suppose you could ring the bell and ask Foley to bring up the brandy?"

After Lucy had settled Robert and Dr. Fletcher in their chairs and persuaded her husband to eat a few mouthfuls of toasted muffin to accompany his rather large brandy she sat opposite them.

"I assume you went to tell the Benson family the sad news?"

"Yes, I accompanied Dr. Mantel, who was very concerned that he would be held responsible for the tragedy."

"Why would he think that?" Lucy wrinkled her nose.

"Because he left his patient in the baths and went to speak to one of the vendors, meaning he wasn't there to see Sir William sink beneath the surface," Dr. Fletcher explained.

"Why didn't anyone else help Sir William?" Lucy wondered.

"That's an excellent question," Robert said. "To be fair, there were very few people *in* the bath at that point in the morning, and most of them are either ill or elderly. It's also possible that they didn't notice what had happened through the steam and the darkness."

"Or they chose to ignore it," Lucy sniffed. "It always amazes me how blind people become when they simply do not choose to see what is happening right in front of their noses."

"Sir William was a very large man," Dr. Fletcher added. "I doubt any of them *could* have got him out of the water. It took all my strength."

"Well, thank goodness you were there." Lucy smiled at him. "Were you able to establish why he died? Considering his somewhat choleric disposition I wouldn't be surprised if he'd had a stroke or suffered heart failure."

Robert and Dr. Fletcher exchanged a long, lingering glance, and Lucy sat up straighter.

"Is there something amiss?"

"There might be," Robert replied. "Dr. Fletcher had the opportunity to examine the body properly before he returned it to the Bensons, and things might not be as simple as they appear."

"In what way?" Lucy turned to the doctor.

Dr. Fletcher grimaced. "Just below his ribs there was a wound that looked as if he had been stabbed upward toward his heart."

Lucy covered her mouth and met Robert's gaze. "Oh, *dear.* Did you mention it to the Bensons?"

"Not yet." Dr. Fletcher looked inquiringly at his employer. "Sir Robert asked me not to say anything."

"Which was very well done of you," Lucy said approvingly at her husband. "If none of the Benson family believe there is anything suspicious about the death, then we can question them without fear."

"With all due respect, my lady," Dr. Fletcher asked slowly, "question them about what?"

"About which one of them murdered Sir William?" Lucy raised her eyebrows. "It seems quite obvious to me."

After Dr. Fletcher left to inform his wife that his departure would be delayed for at least another day, Lucy remained with Robert in the drawing room while he recounted what had gone on at the Bensons on his early morning call. Lucy listened wide-eyed as he described the behavior of the younger boys and tutted in disapproval.

"I suppose they think that now Sir William is dead they can behave in whatever manner they wish."

"Indeed," Robert said. "One can only hope that Sir William had the forethought not to give them any money in his will. That should wipe the smiles off their faces. Their contempt for him was *appalling.*"

"And Lady Benson swooned at your feet?"

Robert shuddered. "Literally. I felt as if I'd been pushed onto the stage of some overdramatic melodrama."

"You do agree that Sir William's death might not be due to natural causes?" Lucy asked.

"Yes, I do." Robert paused. "I liked the man immensely, and if there has been any foul play I intend to ensure that it is brought to light."

His determination to do the right thing resonated on his face, making Lucy quite relieved that for once she wasn't going to have to cajole him into joining her in investigating a possible murder.

"I think we should start by talking to everyone who was at the baths this morning," Lucy said. "You probably knew some of the other bathers. If they are residing in Bath they might frequent the Pump Room, and you can point them out to me."

"I'm not sure I'd recognize most of them with their wigs on and below the neck, but I'll do my best," Robert agreed. "We should also speak to the attendants at the baths." He frowned. "I noticed that there didn't appear to be anyone near the actual bath when the incident occurred, and that most of the torches had either not been lit, or had blown out because of the wind."

"If someone came in after Sir William, and before you got there, it's possible they might have deliberately extinguished the torches to make it darker," Lucy said. "It would certainly have made their task easier."

"As we approached the baths some fool came rushing out and almost knocked me over in his haste to leave," Robert added. "One has to wonder if *he* had anything to do with it."

"Did you recognize the man?"

"Unfortunately not. I was too busy trying not to fall over." Robert finished his glass of brandy. "If you wish, we can walk over to the baths right now. I feel quite unsettled, and I would prefer not to sit around worrying."

Lucy cast him a doubtful glance. "Are you quite certain? Would you prefer to rent a chair?"

"I'll be fine, my dear. Don't mollycoddle me."

"As you wish."

Lucy swept him a curtsey and went to put on her pelisse and bonnet. Her husband was a remarkably stubborn man who did not always take her advice. After three years of marriage she'd learned not to insist that he did, and tried very hard not to remind him when she was proven right.

When she came down into the hall Robert was already awaiting her, his cane in one hand and his hat in the other.

He looked her up and down as if she were one of his regiment on a parade ground.

"That is a very fine bonnet, my dear."

"Thank you. It was just delivered from Milsom Street this morning." Lucy smiled at him, aware that he was attempting to make up for his earlier snappishness. "It is also remarkably warm."

"Then we should proceed." He put on his hat and offered her his arm. "Is your sister to accompany us?"

"She has already gone ahead to do some shopping and then intends to go to the Pump Room with Penelope."

"Then we can meet up with them there after we've concluded our business at the baths."

It was only a ten-minute walk from the square to the baths, and it was mainly flat, which made it much easier for Robert. Lucy made no effort to rush, pausing to admire the architecture and to study the Theatre Royal as they went by. They threaded their way through Westgate Street past Upper Borough Walls and ended up in Stall Street.

As they entered the baths, an attendant came out to greet them.

"Good morning, Sir Robert. I regret to inform you that the baths are currently closed due to an unfortunate incident early this morning."

"I am well aware of that. Sir William was a friend of mine, and I was here with him this morning," Robert responded. "I wish to speak to Mr. Abernathy if he is available."

"I shall see if I can find him for you, sir." The man bowed.

"Were you here this morning?" Lucy asked just before the servant turned away.

"Indeed I was, my lady."

"Were you positioned close to the baths?"

"We were quite shorthanded, and what with the wind blowing so hard most of us were trying to keep warm in the back." He grimaced. "I don't think anyone saw Sir William go under the surface. If we had, someone would've gone in for him."

"Has such a thing happened before?" Robert asked.

"Yes sir, with the nature of our clientele being somewhat frail or elderly, people often fall asleep in the baths, or are overcome with the heat of the water, or the fumes. Mr. Abernathy has taught us all to keep an eye out, sir."

"But obviously not today," Robert observed. "Thank you for your insight. Perhaps you might find Mr. Abernathy for me now?"

"Yes, Sir Robert, certainly, sir."

"It sounds as if this morning was particularly appropriate for a murder," Robert mused as the servant sped off. "Not enough staff, light, nor any interest in ensuring their patrons were kept alive."

Lucy shivered as the wind howled down the stone corridor. "I can hardly blame them for not wanting to stay out in this weather. How on earth do you stand it?"

Robert patted her gloved hand. "When you get into the water, you forget about the cold. It is quite blissful."

Robert walked farther into the complex, and Lucy inhaled the noxious odors emanating from the bath. She had no intention of ever disrobing in front of complete strangers and finding out if his words were true. Steam rose from the dark surface and even at this time of the day with the sun at its brightest, there wasn't much light within the cavernous space. She could quite understand how someone might not notice a body slipping beneath the surface.

She reached Robert's side and pointed at a woman sitting by the wall with a basket beside her. "Shall we speak to her while we wait for Mr. Abernathy?"

Robert walked over to the woman and tipped his hat. "Good morning, ma'am. Were you intending to bathe today?"

"Not likely." The grin Robert received revealed the woman had half her teeth missing. "I come here to sell my perfumes and soaps to the bathers, but I won't be making much money unless that skinflint Abernathy reopens the place."

"Are you here every day, Mrs. . . . ?" Lucy asked.

"Mistress Peck and aye, ma'am. I was here at the crack of dawn when the large gentleman was fished out of the bath like a stranded whale." She cackled. "What a sight. He was a kind gentleman though. Often gave me a few pennies when he passed by."

"Did you see him come in this morning?"

"He arrived with that fancy doctor of his, and another man. I only noticed *them* because they were arguing something rotten."

"Sir William and the doctor?" Robert asked.

"The other one. He was as tall as Sir William, and had a look of him."

"Did you happen to catch what they were arguing about?" Lucy asked.

Mistress Peck looked at Lucy. "You're asking a lot of questions for someone who ain't even bothered to inquire about purchasing my wares."

Lucy obligingly chose a bar of soap. Robert dug into his pocket, produced a half crown, and placed it in the woman's grimy hand. "Perhaps you might continue to humor my wife."

"Indeed I will." Mistress Peck tucked the coin in the purse hanging from her waist. "They was arguing about money, and the old man's will. Then the doctor went off to talk to someone, the old man changed to get in the baths, and the other one eventually went off in a huff."

"Did you see his face clearly?" Robert asked.

"No, he was all bundled up against the cold."

"Would you recognize him again?"

"I doubt it. There was nothing in particular about him. He just looked like a gentleman." Mistress Peck looked past them and raised her voice. "Oi! Mr. Abernathy, are you going to open up those blasted baths? Some of us have a living to make!"

Mr. Abernathy winced as he ignored the woman and came toward Robert and Lucy.

"I do apologize for keeping you waiting. As you might imagine, I have had a rather busy morning."

"I appreciate you finding the time to speak to us, Mr. Abernathy." Robert hesitated. "Sir William was a rather particular friend of mine, and I am attempting to aid his family at this difficult time."

"I am sure that they appreciate your efforts, Sir Robert. Have you come to collect his belongings? I have them in my office. Please come this way."

Lucy exchanged a startled glance with Robert and then meekly followed along behind. They could deliver the items back to the Bensons after they had taken a look at them.

Mr. Abernathy spoke to one of the men huddled around the brazier outside his office and ushered Robert and Lucy inside. When they were seated, he stood behind his desk and shook his head.

"This is a bad business, and a very sad day for the Benson family."

"Indeed." Robert inclined his head.

"I know that Sir William was not in good health, but death is always a shock, isn't it?"

"Especially when it happens on your premises, Mr. Abernathy, and under your watch," Robert stated.

"Well, my dear sir," Mr. Abernathy protested, "I cannot *possibly* be held responsible for everything that happens in the baths. The type of people who come here, the sick, the old, and the infirm, are fully cognizant of the risk they take exposing their persons to such an environment. They do it on the advice of their physicians, mind. *Not* mine. I merely supply a service."

"Then you don't believe your staff were negligent this morning?"

Mr. Abernathy's eyes widened. "Of course not, Sir Robert. My staff is beyond reproach."

"I understand that you tell them to watch out for those in the waters."

"Indeed I do." Mr. Abernathy bowed.

"Yet no one noticed Sir William was no longer visible above the water?"

"I hesitate to speak ill of the dead, but on the one occasion when Sir William *did* fall asleep in the baths, and was awakened by one of my staff, his vocal displeasure at such treatment was such that I ordered my staff not to concern themselves overmuch with him. Sir William also had his own physician accompanying him."

"But Dr. Mantel was apparently dealing with another issue away from the actual bath?"

"That is correct. At the fatal moment, Dr. Mantel was engaged in a financial transaction with one of the vendors, and arrived back when it was too late to save his employer."

"So you think it was Sir William's own fault." Robert nodded.

"It was an unfortunate accident," Mr. Abernathy said firmly. "Sir William could have dropped dead in the street just prior to his bath, or died in his carriage going home." He raised his eyes heavenward. "Who am I to judge when our Lord will take a man of great age and in ill health?"

Despite his impertinent questioning, Robert was fairly certain that Mr. Abernathy hadn't deliberately allowed someone to pay him off so that Sir William would die in the baths. But Robert wouldn't discount him as a suspect quite yet.

A knock on the door revealed a servant carrying a pile of clothing topped by a pair of boots and stockings secured by string.

"Sir William Benson's apparel, sir."

Lucy came forward to receive the pile. "Thank you. I shall deliver these garments to Lady Benson immediately." She smiled at the man. "Are you the person who helps bathers undress?"

"I can do that, ma'am, but I also keep an eye on their things while they're in the bath. There are all kinds of folks wandering in and out of here so it stops thieving hands."

Lucy nodded, her expression sympathetic. She was much better at getting answers from people than Robert would ever be. For some reason he tended to frighten people. "Did anyone ever try to steal Sir William's clothes?"

"No, ma'am, because he always paid me extra well to keep them safe. He was a kind gentleman in his way."

"Indeed." Lucy smiled at him. "Thank you."

A few minutes later they walked out of the baths into the ever-increasing wind, and Robert came to a reluctant decision.

"It is too cold for me to walk back, and you cannot carry that unwieldy mass of clothing through the streets. It will be picked off by the beggars."

Lucy looked up at him. "We won't need to walk. We are meeting Anna and Penelope at the Pump Room and can take the carriage back with them."

"Ah, I had forgotten." He frowned. "The lack of interest in Sir William's death Mr. Abernathy displayed and his inability to accept any blame have rather stuck in my craw."

"Do you think he had something to do with it?"

"Mr. Abernathy? I suppose he could have agreed to

look the other way while someone drowned Sir William, but it seems unlikely when there is a whole collection of Bensons who seem delighted that the head of the family has died, and would be eager to dispose of him themselves."

"One of the Bensons could have paid him," Lucy suggested.

"That is true." He looked down at her. "I just remembered something odd."

"What?"

"When I told Lady Benson's sons that Sir William had died I'm fairly certain that one of them mentioned he had drowned."

"And?"

"I didn't specify exactly how Sir William *had* died, so how did they know? They were out all night. They could easily have hidden in the baths, drowned the old man, and slipped out again in the confusion while nobody noticed."

"Wouldn't you have seen them?"

"I saw that one man rushing out. Perhaps they split up. Or maybe it was only one of them who did the deed." He sighed. "Now I come to think about it, we don't even know how long Sir William *was* under the water before Dr. Mantel raised the alarm. It could've been for quite some considerable time."

"Which means that the boys could've killed him, and gone before you even got there or anyone noticed." Lucy shivered. "What a disaster."

He took her arm and continued walking toward the Pump Room. He had no desire to socialize with the town's elite, but was willing to sacrifice his principles for the sake of being warm.

"I wonder if anyone at the baths would recognize Lady Benson's sons?" Lucy mused. "I could ask Anna to sketch their faces."

"It is possible that they accompanied Sir William and their mother at some point in time," Robert said. "We can always go back and ask when Mr. Abernathy isn't present."

He held open the door to the Pump Room, releasing the hum of lively conversation and the faint smell of the hot spring water available from the fountain. Robert beckoned to the footman standing to attention by the inner door.

"Will you take charge of these belongings and put them in a secure place until my carriage arrives?"

"Yes, sir." The footman bowed and took the bundle of clothes.

"Thank you." Robert offered Lucy his arm again. "Then I suppose we should go on in and face the masses."

Chapter 6

Lucy was escorted up the stairs of the house and directly into the bedchamber of Lady Benson. The curtains were closed, and the air was thick with the sickly, overpowering scents of perfume and laudanum. She and Robert had looked through Sir William's garments and found nothing of interest. He hadn't been robbed, which indicated that whoever had wanted to end his life hadn't been after his purse.

Or at least not after his actual coin . . .

"My dear Lady Benson, how are you?" Lucy asked.

Lucy sat down on the chair beside the bed and smiled sympathetically at the new widow who was lying back on a mound of pillows, her long blond hair around her shoulders, and her expression tragic.

"Oh! Lady Kurland, how kind of you to call in my hour of need." Lady Benson reached out and grabbed Lucy's hand in a surprisingly strong grip. "I cannot believe Sir William is dead."

"It is indeed a tragedy," Lucy agreed.

"It certainly is for me," Lady Benson said. "How am I going to *cope* when we are so far away from home?"

"I'm sure Mr. Edward Benson will deal with everything for you," Lucy said gently.

Lady Benson sniffed. "If I leave things up to him I can guarantee I will be tossed out in the gutter with nothing but the clothes on my back!"

"Surely you jest?" Lucy countered. "He seems to be an admirable gentleman."

"Then you do not know him at all. Even my sainted husband distrusted him at the end. He was losing money hand over fist, and Sir William was about to take back control of his companies."

"Was Mr. Edward Benson aware of this?" Lucy asked.

"Indeed. They argued about it all the time," she sighed. "And now I am at Edward's mercy, and he hates my sons as well."

Lucy resolutely kept what she thought of the young men to herself. She was far more interested in what Lady Benson was intent on confiding in her.

"I'm also certain that Augustus and Peregrine would never allow their older brother to mistreat you," Lucy stated. "Augustus *is* a man of the cloth."

"There is nothing spiritual about that man whatsoever!" Lady Benson declared. "And as for Peregrine, who fancies himself a playwright and lives off his father just like the rest of them . . ."

She fell back against her pillows and pressed her fist to her breast. "I am surrounded by those who wish *ill* on me."

Lucy pointed to the parcel she had brought with her. "Sir Robert and I collected your husband's clothes from the baths. I thought you might want them."

To her astonishment, Lady Benson sat bolt upright and reached out her hand. "Give them to me!"

Lucy put the neatly folded clothes on the bed and watched incredulously as Lady Benson took out each garment, searched every pocket, and felt along every seam.

"Nothing . . ." she murmured. "There is nothing here."

"I'm not quite sure what you are expecting to find, my lady, but—"

Lady Benson interrupted Lucy. "I should have known it. He is far too clever for that."

"Were you looking for something important?" Lucy inquired.

"No." Lady Benson suddenly looked exhausted again. "It was foolish of me."

Lucy stood and surveyed the now tangled mass of clothing. "Would you like me to fold the clothes for you?"

"Take them through to Mr. Tompkins, Sir William's valet. He will know what to do with them." Lady Benson closed her eyes and lay back down, one hand shielding her face. "Good day, Lady Kurland."

Realizing she had been dismissed, Lucy gathered up the clothing, and rather than use the connecting door into the dressing room went through to the hallway and then into the second bedroom. An elderly man who reminded her of Foley was busy emptying out a chest of drawers.

"Good afternoon, Mr. Tompkins," Lucy said. "I'm Lady Kurland. I brought Sir William's clothes back from the baths for Lady Benson. She asked me to bring them through to you."

"Thank you, my lady. You can put them on the bed." He studied her carefully. "Your husband is Sir Robert Kurland, aye? Sir William thought the world of him."

"And Sir Robert reciprocated his regard."

Mr. Tompkins gestured at the open drawers and chests. "I'll pack up his trunks, and send them back home to Yorkshire. Mr. Edward can decide what to do with everything then, and what to do with me."

He had a strong Yorkshire accent that reminded Lucy vividly of his employer.

"Have you been Sir William's valet for a long time?"

"We were boys together, my lady. Grew up in the same village and ran away to make our fortunes. Sir William did all right for himself, and offered me a job when I had nowhere else to turn. I've been his valet for fifty years now."

"That is a remarkably long career, Mr. Tompkins," Lucy said. "I can only commend such excellent service."

"Sir William was worth it," the old man said gruffly. He appeared to be the only member of the Benson household who was genuinely grieving for the old man. "He's always been a hard man, but also a fair one, and with this lot of vultures circling him recently who can blame him? I don't know why he didn't pop off even sooner."

"I *had* noticed that there was some conflict between Sir William and certain members of his family," Lucy said diplomatically.

Mr. Tompkins snorted. "He wasn't very happy with any of them. The last conversation we had before he set off for the baths was about amending his will again."

"Indeed?"

"He liked to carry it around with him and rewrite it whenever someone displeased him. I was often called to be one of the witnesses." Mr. Tompkins smiled. "It put the fear of God into the lot of them."

"I should imagine it would," Lucy agreed. "I assume Sir William has a solicitor who will deal with his affairs?"

"Yes, my lady. I believe Mr. Edward has already sent for the man. Depending on the weather he should be here within the week." Mr. Tompkins bowed. "Thank you for bringing the clothes, my lady. That was Sir William's favorite waistcoat, and I believe he would want to be buried in it."

"Then his wish can now be granted." Lucy turned toward the door. "Do the family plan to take his body back to Yorkshire or will he be buried here?"

"Definitely Yorkshire, my lady." Mr. Tompkins grinned. "He'd haunt us all if we tried to bury him in the south."

Deep in thought, Lucy made her way down the stairs to the hallway. Lady Benson believed that the Benson brothers were against her. She had also suggested that Sir William's displeasure had embraced his entire family, a fact bolstered by Mr. Tompkins's claim about the old man's will.

"Ah! Lady Kurland!"

Lucy looked down to see Mr. Peregrine Benson standing at the bottom of the stairs. He wore an immaculate black coat but was smiling up at her as if he didn't have a care in the world.

"Were you visiting the recently widowed Lady Benson?" he inquired as he offered her his hand and bent over hers. "Did she manage to conceal her glee?"

Lucy frowned at him. "She was inconsolable."

"I'll wager she was. Edward won't put up with any of her nonsense, I can tell you that."

"So she imagined." Lucy paused and looked up at his face. "Do you think he will treat her badly?"

His expression hardened. "She deserves to be left without a penny, but I doubt the old man would be that hard on her. We'll see what happens when the solicitor reads the will, won't we?"

"Why don't you like her?" Lucy asked bluntly.

"Because attempting to seduce the son of your current husband is remarkably bad form, wouldn't you say?" He raised an eyebrow. "She is amoral, and her sons are not fit to appear in polite company."

Before Lucy could even attempt to reply to his outrageous comments, the front door opened, and Edward and Augustus Benson came in speaking in hushed tones. They too wore black, but without the fashionable flair of their younger brother.

"Lady Kurland." Edward doffed his hat. "I must commend you and Sir Robert for your tireless attentions in our time of need."

Lucy curtsied. "It is our duty to help our fellow man, sir, and Sir Robert was very pleased to have made the acquaintance of an old friend of his grandfather's."

"Indeed, Lady Kurland." Augustus nodded eagerly. "You show nothing but Christian kindness."

Behind her, Lucy thought she heard Peregrine snort, but chose to ignore him. "Well, I must be on my way. Sir Robert will be wondering what has become of me." She nodded at the three brothers, noting that none of them seemed particularly troubled by grief. "Good morning, gentlemen."

Edward hastened to open the door for her and bowed low as she passed him by. Within a minute, Foley was opening her own front door, and she went up the stairs to her drawing room where she heard voices. Anna, Penelope, and Captain Akers's family were sitting there having tea. There was no sign of Robert.

Lucy untied her bonnet and went forward to greet her unexpected guests.

"I do apologize for my absence. I hope my dear sister has entertained you adequately."

"Miss Harrington has been all that is gracious." Captain Akers couldn't hide the warmth in his eyes as he gazed at Anna. "She assured us that you would return shortly, and she was correct."

Anna blushed. "Your high opinion of me is remarkably flattering." She turned to Lucy. "I merely ordered tea, and hoped."

Lucy allowed Penelope to pour her a cup of tea, aware that no one in the Benson household had thought to extend such civility toward her.

Lucy addressed Mrs. Akers. "I was visiting Lady Benson in the house next door."

"Oh yes, we heard about Sir William's death." Mrs. Akers sighed. "He was an elderly man who from all reports lived a full and productive life. May he rest in peace."

"Amen to that," Anna murmured. "Did you know the Bensons, Mrs. Akers?"

"We met the family in the Assembly Rooms. Sir William was very pleasant." Mrs. Akers paused. "I regret to say that his wife did not choose to pursue an acquaintance with us."

Penelope sniffed. "I have no idea why. She was certainly not from the higher echelons of society herself. In truth I found her remarkably dull, and not as beautiful as everyone suggested."

Mrs. Akers blinked at Penelope and then looked back at Lucy. "Regardless it is still hard to be widowed at such a young age."

Penelope rearranged her shawl over her rounded belly. "I suspect she will do very well for herself. My mother often told me to marry a much older man who would die quickly, but I chose Dr. Fletcher, who will probably outlive *me* when I die in childbirth."

"I doubt Dr. Fletcher would allow that to happen, Penelope," Lucy said robustly. "You are the most precious of his patients." She raised her eyebrows. "And don't you have to pack? I believe Dr. Fletcher said you were leaving tomorrow."

"Dr. Fletcher is *indeed* leaving for a week or so, but I will be staying." Penelope raised her chin. "You cannot possibly expect me to expose myself in my present condition to the indignities of travel *again?*"

Lucy met Anna's amused gaze. "Of course not, Penelope. You are most welcome to stay." She turned to Mrs. Akers. "Now, how are the arrangements for your daughter's wedding progressing?"

Just before the Akers family rose to leave, Robert and Dr. Fletcher arrived, meaning that their departure was delayed quite considerably. Lucy even considered inviting them to stay and dine, but was unsure whether Cook would be able to feed them. Before Lucy could put her offer to the test Mrs. Akers revealed that she had to get home anyway, and Lucy issued an invitation for a later date.

Anna walked down with the visitors while Robert helped himself to the remains of the tea. Dr. Fletcher returned to his packing with his wife accompanying him.

"Captain Akers seems like a fine upstanding fellow," Robert remarked. "And his family are very decent folk."

"Yes, they are." Lucy came to sit opposite him. "Did you notice how often he looked at Anna?"

"With all due respect, my dear, most men look at Anna. She is remarkably beautiful." He paused to drink his tea. "The thing *I* noticed was that Anna was looking back."

"Exactly." Lucy nodded. "She met Captain Akers in London, and favored his suit until he asked her to marry him, and she retreated."

"Ah, that explains it then." Robert took the last scone and spread cream and jam on it. "Mayhap she has changed her mind and intends to wed him."

"I hope she has." Lucy gripped her hands together. "Having met him, I truly believe he is the right man for her."

Robert gave her a look. "You shouldn't be meddling."

"Someone has to," Lucy replied. "Anna needs a home and a family of her own."

"In your opinion." Robert held her gaze. "From what you have told me, Anna isn't interested in any marriage that involves the prospect of children."

"I *know* that, but—"

"Then it would be cruel to push her toward something she is mortally afraid of, wouldn't it? I know you love your sister, Lucy, but this has to be her decision."

Lucy drew herself upright. "I am aware of that. I simply meant that I would make sure Anna is given every opportunity to socialize with the gentleman and his family in the hopes that she changes her mind."

"I sincerely doubt that she will, but I will hold you to your promise not to interfere." Robert finished off his tea. "I will also do my part to engage the young man in conversation, and ascertain his worth and intentions toward Anna."

"Thank you." Lucy set her cup back on the tray with something of a bang. Robert's plain speaking was sometimes hard to stomach. "I know I can always rely on your good sense in such matters. Did you go to the baths today?"

"I did, and I spoke to some of the people who usually frequent the King's Bath at that early hour. Even those who were actually in the water were quite unaware that anything was amiss until they heard about Sir William's death afterward."

"So all we know at this point is that someone ran out of the baths at some speed when you were approaching them."

"A person no one can actually identify, and who might have nothing to do with the matter at all." Robert grimaced. "Although I have considered your idea that one of the Benson family perhaps paid someone to kill Sir William. It would be a far less risky strategy."

"I agree, but if that is the case, how will we ever find out which member of the family it was?" Lucy asked.

"I thought we should start from the other end of the tangle." Robert looked at her. "The entire family will remain here until the will is read, so we have the opportunity to observe their behavior and question them."

"Sir William's valet, Mr. Tompkins, said that the family solicitor is on his way from Yorkshire to deal with his late client's affairs," Lucy said. "He also implied that his employer liked to amend his will whenever someone displeased him."

"So I gathered." Robert half smiled. "Sir William spent much of his time in the baths railing against his family, and threatening to disinherit them."

"*Lady* Benson told me that Sir William was at odds with Edward for mismanaging the business. Did he mention anything about that to you?"

"Indeed he did. I suspect there was some truth in his grievances, but I also know that it is hard to pass one's business into another's keeping without secretly thinking they will make a mull of it." Robert set down his cup and plate. "Every time I received a promotion in the hussars I believed the man who replaced me would never be as good to my men as I was."

"You should speak to Mr. Tompkins," Lucy said. "He already holds you in high regard. He has been with Sir William for fifty years so he probably knows more of his secrets than anyone."

"I'll send Foley over to speak to him first." Robert nodded. "He might be more willing to confide in a fellow servant than he would be in me."

"What an excellent idea." Lucy smiled warmly at her husband. "And I will continue to visit Lady Benson. She is remarkably indiscreet about her late husband's family, and solely concerned about her own fate."

"I can't say that surprises me. Sir William admitted that he'd married in haste and was bitterly repenting his choice at his leisure."

"Lady Benson is afraid Edward will ensure that she doesn't receive a penny from the will," Lucy said. "And Peregrine, the youngest son, suggested that Lady Benson had behaved in a most *problematic* manner with him."

"Really?" Robert raised an eyebrow. "Well then, one might assume that Peregrine is the only member of the family who was hoping his father would stay alive forever."

Lucy rose to light one of the lamps and make sure the coal fire was burning brightly. "Sir William didn't approve of Peregrine's artistic career or of Augustus. In truth, he disliked them all."

"I agree, but if one of them did kill him, why *now*? What particular thing has happened in the past week or so to bring the situation to the boiling point?" Robert stood and paced the room, his gaze focused on the floor as he walked.

"Well, there was that dinner party we attended," Lucy reminded him. "Lady Benson's sons were even heard actually *wishing* Sir William would die, and lo and behold, the next day, he *is* dead. In my opinion they are still the most likely culprits. They hated Sir William, they are unlikely to receive much from his will, and they want their mother to be in control of her own money so they can leech off her instead."

"They are certainly of the age that act irresponsibly and think later," Robert agreed. "And their disgust for Sir William was very obvious." He swung around to face Lucy. "Perhaps I *will* ask Anna to sketch their faces so I can show them around the baths, and see if anyone recognizes them."

"I think that is an excellent notion," Lucy agreed. "And let's not forget that they were also out all night, and could easily have waited at the baths for Sir William to arrive, and murdered him."

Robert walked over to the door and opened it. "It is a puzzle. I will go and speak to Foley, and see if I can engage his help in this matter. I know he will be discreet."

His wife waved him onward, and he left the room. Had he been too sharp with her about her plans for her sister's happiness? She certainly hadn't taken his intervention well, but she did have a habit of thinking she knew best for the people she loved. The fact that she was often correct in her assumptions didn't mean that she always was.

Robert was fond of Anna Harrington, and would certainly do his part to make sure that any gentleman who wanted to marry her was thoroughly investigated before being allowed to proceed. Having met the perfectly respectable and eligible Captain Akers he suspected that Anna's aversion to marriage ran far deeper than perhaps Lucy realized. She was of a much more robust nature than her retiring sister and perhaps unable to fully comprehend Anna's frailty.

Robert opened the door into the bedchamber and discovered Foley folding his shirts and cravats.

"Ah, Foley. Just the man I was looking for."

Foley turned toward his employer and bowed. "Who else would be in here at this time of day?"

"Silas? My valet?" Robert pointed at the lengths of linen. "It's usually his job to attend to such matters."

"He doesn't do it right," Foley said stubbornly. "I sent him down to the kitchen to run an iron over your best coat while I set things to rights."

Robert was fairly certain that Silas would have a different opinion on the matter. He was equally devoted to Robert and perfectly capable of performing his duties.

"Have you met Mr. Tompkins from next door?" Robert asked as he settled into a chair beside the fire. "Sir William Benson's valet."

"Indeed I have, sir. He is a very fine gentleman indeed. Devastated by Sir William's death, devastated."

"Is he the chatty type?"

"Not at all, sir. Loyal to a fault, and as closemouthed as a clam."

"Do you think you might be able to prize some information out of him anyway?"

Foley turned to look fully at Robert. "Information as to what, sir?"

"His master." Robert sat forward, his hands clasped between his knees. "I'm not convinced that Sir William died of natural causes. In truth, I suspect someone in his family decided to murder him."

Foley didn't immediately speak, and Robert looked up at him.

"Did you hear what I said?"

"I did, sir," Foley said slowly. "From my discussions with Mr. Tompkins I had gleaned that all was not well with the Benson family, and that he himself wasn't surprised that Sir William died so abruptly. Do you wish me to seek his confidence, sir? To see if he has any idea who might have done the deed?"

"That's exactly what I need, Foley," Robert said. "But you will have to be both careful and discreet, and only share what you learn with me or Lady Kurland. I don't want you putting yourself in harm's way."

Foley's eyes gleamed and he looked positively thrilled. "I'll be careful, sir, don't you worry about me. I suspect that under his dour exterior, Mr. Tompkins is dying to share his views on this matter with someone. He is from the north, and they do believe in plain speaking."

"Then can I leave the matter in your capable hands?"

Robert rose from his seat as Silas came into the room carrying the newly ironed coat. "Good evening, Silas. I see Foley has been keeping you busy."

"Yes, Sir Robert."

The exasperated look the younger man gave the butler didn't escape Robert's notice, but he didn't remark upon it. Foley was the oldest member of the Kurland household and was treated with great respect by everyone even when he turned to meddling. Silas knew that Robert valued his work regardless.

"There will only be Lady Kurland, Miss Harrington, Mrs. Fletcher, and myself for dinner this evening, Foley. Perhaps you might tell Cook."

"Yes, Sir Robert." Foley bowed and positively skipped out of the room leaving Silas and Robert alone.

Robert pointed at the coat. "You can put that away. I don't intend to go out."

Silas put the freshly ironed coat in the cupboard and turned back to the pile of folded cravats on the bed. "Now I'll have to refold all this lot again," he murmured.

Robert clapped him on the shoulder. "I really don't care how they are folded as long as they are put away before Lady Kurland asks me why they are cluttering up the bed."

"I'll have the whole lot cleared up before dinner, sir."

"Good man," Robert said. "I know I can rely on you."

Chapter 7

Lucy sipped her tea and attempted to make conversation with Augustus Benson while she waited for Lady Benson to put in an appearance. The vicar wasn't looking well, his jowly face haggard, and he kept forgetting what he was saying. Well used to the clergy, Lucy simply smiled and attempted to make him believe that every word he uttered was perfection. She'd discovered years ago that a little flattery went a long way with a cleric.

"Do you intend to hold a memorial service for Sir William before you return to Yorkshire?" Lucy asked. "I am sure that there are many people in Bath who hold him in high esteem, and might wish to offer you their condolences in person."

"I'm not sure, Lady Kurland."

Lucy raised her eyebrows. "Not sure that your father was held in high esteem, Mr. Benson, or that you will hold a service?"

The vicar swallowed hard. "I await the orders of my older brother and the family solicitor, my dear Lady Kurland. Obviously, I am more than happy to hold a service for my own *father*."

"Do you have the living on any of the churches within Bath, sir?" Lucy asked. "Or would we need to travel farther afield for such a service?"

"Unfortunately, my lady. My parishes are too far away, and too small to merit the attention of Bath society. Any ceremony would have to be held in a more fitting location."

"What he means is, that he's too busy bleeding his parishes dry to allow anyone to see the state they are in," Peregrine spoke from the doorway. "He's got one drunken curate managing five localities. Church services are nonexistent, and his parishioners are currently petitioning the bishop of Bath and Wells to have him removed."

Augustus shot to his feet, his face now flushed red with fury. "I'll ask you to refrain from commenting on something you know nothing about!"

Peregrine's smile was that of a cat that'd just trapped a mouse. "I know a lot more than you think, Brother. And so did Father."

"He knew nothing of these slanderous and totally false accusations against me unless you told him."

"I didn't need to tell him a thing," Peregrine drawled. "He wasn't stupid, Augustus. Just because he didn't speak like a gentleman didn't mean he wasn't fully aware of what was going on." Peregrine sauntered farther into the room. "In fact I heard him shouting at you the day before he died about this very matter. The whole *house* heard him, so why are you attempting to deny it now?"

Lucy stayed very still. Both men appeared to have forgotten she was there, and she was quite willing to go along with their lack of attention.

"You are wrong," Augustus insisted. "We *never* argued. It must have been someone else you overheard, like one of Miranda's young sons."

"I heard them being read the riot act many times, but this was definitely you, Brother dear. I saw you emerge from his study, and goodness me did you look angry." Peregrine paused. "In fact, the last thing you said to him was a threat, wasn't it? That you'd be damned if he ruined your reputation, and you'd see him in hell first. Fine words for a man of the cloth."

"Why you—" Augustus's hands curled into fists, and he stepped close to his younger, taller brother.

Peregrine didn't even flinch, his gaze steady as he looked down at Augustus. "You are an abysmal human being, and I wish to God that you weren't my brother."

"And you are so much better?" Augustus snapped. "What with your *sinful* London ways, and your unmitigated depths of depravity? Do you think our father approved of *that*?"

Peregrine's smile disappeared. "No, he didn't, and he told me so in no uncertain terms."

Augustus shook his head. "But it's always been easier for you, hasn't it? The youngest son, the baby of the family, until Lady Miranda's boys came along to put your nose out of joint."

Peregrine's lip curled. "My father never liked them."

"A situation which you deliberately engineered by turning him against them because you were jealous," Augustus insisted. "You couldn't *bear* not being the favored child, could you?"

Peregrine glanced briefly down at Lucy, making her jump. "I do apologize, Lady Kurland. I didn't see you there." He bowed deeply. "Perhaps we should cease this discussion immediately, Augustus."

Augustus swiveled around to stare at Lucy, his horrified expression so ludicrous that Lucy almost wanted to laugh.

"My goodness! I do apologize for my brother, Lady Kurland. He is prone to both exaggeration and fiction. I'm certain he will reassure you himself that his remarks were meant in jest, and not to be taken seriously at all."

Peregrine raised an eyebrow. "I also apologize, Lady Kurland, but I stand by every word I uttered."

Augustus gave Peregrine one last thunderous glare and left the room, slamming the door behind him. Peregrine took his brother's vacated seat and helped himself to the brandy the butler had left on the side table. Lucy considered him, noting his hands were shaking, and that he wasn't as calm as he was pretending to be. Was it possible that some of his brother's comments had hit home as well? Had a jealous Peregrine deliberately soured the relationship between his father and the two newest additions to the family?

It was an interesting thought. Lucy would have a lot to discuss with Robert when he returned from the baths later in the day.

"I *do* apologize, Lady Kurland." Peregrine met her gaze full on. "You came to visit us out of the goodness of your heart, and ended up in the middle of a ghastly family scene."

"It is of no matter." Lucy shrugged. "My father is the rector of our parish. I have seen many family squabbles after an unexpected death. People do not always behave as you might think they will in times of crisis."

Peregrine let out his breath. "I can only agree with that. Edward is proving to be most indecisive, Lady Miranda is prostrate in bed, and I'm attempting to discover where the devil Mr. Carstairs, our solicitor, has gotten to."

"I understood that he was on his way to Bath from Halifax?"

"Indeed he is, but the weather has apparently delayed him." Peregrine finished his brandy. "To be perfectly honest, Lady Kurland, I can't wait to be rid of the lot of them so that I can go back to London."

"You could depart regardless, I suppose?" Lucy offered tentatively.

"And leave my father's body in the hands of this bunch of incompetents? If it were up to Miranda, Sir William would be robbed of everything and thrown into the river with the fishes. She is one of the most mercenary women I have ever met."

"I find that difficult to believe." Lucy wrinkled her nose. "She seems rather too dependent on others."

"She certainly *appears* that way, but you must remember

that she snared herself a golden calf, and expects to receive the lion's share of his immense fortune to do with as she pleases." Peregrine finished his brandy and stood up. "Pray excuse me, Lady Kurland. I have to go to the local posting house, and see if I have received any reply to my latest letter."

He glanced down at Lucy. "Will you be all right by yourself? Are you expecting Miranda to come down?"

"I was told that she would be with me within half an hour," Lucy said.

"Good luck with that." Peregrine winked at her, his equilibrium apparently restored, and strolled out of the door.

Lucy contemplated her rapidly cooling tea. Should she go? She certainly had enough fascinating anecdotes to keep Robert enthralled until well past dinner. Just as she placed her cup back on the tray, the door opened, and Lady Benson appeared draped in black lace, supported by Dr. Mantel on one side and her maid on the other.

"Lady Kurland, I am so sorry I took so long to come down to you. I felt a little faint when I first attempted to rise, and Dotty took fright, and insisted I waited for Dr. Mantel to assure me that I was well enough to risk my health on the stairs."

Lucy curtsied. "If you truly feel that bad, ma'am, perhaps you should return to bed? I would hate to be the cause of any lapse in your well-being."

She thought Dr. Mantel's lips twitched at her honeyed words, but she might have been mistaken.

"No, my good doctor says it is important for me to rise from my bed, or at least make the attempt." Lady Benson sank gratefully down onto the couch. Her maid took up position behind the chair, smelling salts in hand. "But it is so hard to be positive, Lady Kurland, when all around me are threats to my livelihood, and that of my sons."

"Threats, my lady?" Lucy asked. "Who would do such a thing to such a recent widow?"

Lady Benson glanced fearfully around the room as if she

suspected there were untold enemies hidden behind the curtains. "They all wish me ill."

"*They?*"

"I believe Lady Benson is referring to her stepsons," Dr. Mantel intervened.

"I'm certain that as her physician you are not *encouraging* her to doubt Sir William's family?" Lucy countered.

"Of course not, my lady." To his credit, Dr. Mantel looked appalled at the very idea. "My only job is to make certain that Lady Benson is well enough to represent herself when the family solicitor arrives."

"I have asked Dr. Mantel to accompany me to any meeting regarding Sir William's estate, but he insists that it is not his place," Lady Benson said.

"I will be close by, my lady. I can assure you of that." The doctor patted Lady Benson's black lace–mittened hand. "You are stronger than you think, and are a devoted mother and have your boys to fight for."

"That is true. I cannot allow Edward to deprive my beloved sons of their rightful inheritance."

Lucy forbore mentioning that the disbursal of the assets would be at the late Sir William's behest, and that Edward would merely be the executor of his father's wishes. From her own observations Lucy had a shrewd suspicion that Sir William might not have left the boys a penny.

"Mr. Peregrine Benson told me that he is attempting to find out what has befallen Sir William's solicitor, and why he hasn't arrived yet," Lucy said.

"Peregrine hates me," Lady Benson wailed. "He probably wishes to get to Mr. Carstairs and bribe him to destroy my husband's real wishes."

Dr. Mantel cleared his throat. "I doubt Mr. Peregrine would do that, my lady, or that Mr. Carstairs would take a bribe. He is a fine, upstanding gentleman."

"I'm certain that everything will soon be resolved, Lady Benson," Lucy murmured reassuringly. "Sir William did

not strike me as the kind of man who would leave his affairs in disorder."

"Exactly, Lady Kurland." Dr. Mantel bowed.

The butler entered the drawing room and bowed to
Lady Benson.

"Would you like some fresh tea, my lady?"

"That would be lovely, thank you."

Lady Benson sighed and eased her head back against the
couch. "It has been a very tiring day. I sorted out my
wardrobe and put away all my beautiful gowns. I will
have to call on my dressmaker. I only own this one gown
in black because it does not suit me. I fear I will have to
wear this color for *months* if not for years."

Lucy couldn't think of an appropriate reply and said
nothing. She would drink yet another cup of tea and then
escape back to her own house next door. Lady Benson's
self-absorption was remarkably wearing.

Arden Hall came into the drawing room and bowed to
Lucy and his mother.

"Good afternoon, Mother. I'm impressed that you managed to get out of your bed today."

Lady Benson pouted. "I am not well."

Arden sat down and crossed one leg over the other. "You
should be feeling a lot better seeing as you don't have to
put up with the attentions of the old man anymore."

Dr. Mantel opened his mouth as if to chastise the young
man and then apparently thought better of it.

"He's dead, Mother dear," Arden sneered. "You hated him
while he was alive, so why pretend to mourn him now?"

"How can you say that?" Lady Benson gasped, and sat
up, her hand pressed to her bosom. "I loved him *exces-
sively!*"

"You loved his money," Arden continued. "And you
certainly loved being Lady Benson, but come on, Mater,
you can be honest now. You couldn't stand him!"

Again Lucy wondered if she had perhaps become invisible or whether the Bensons had no ability to keep their dirty family secrets firmly in the closet where they belonged. It certainly made her task of ascertaining the truth easier than she had anticipated.

"I think you are being unfair to your mother and to your stepfather," Dr. Mantel said. "Their marriage is their business, and they are the only people who know what truly went on in it."

"Good Lord, Doctor. My mother loves to spread her woes around. She told Brandon and me how things were," Arden protested. "In truth, there were times when I had to forcibly restrain my younger brother from confronting Sir William and doing him bodily harm!"

"Brandon is rather hotheaded," Lady Benson acknowledged. "And there was that unfortunate incident at school when they sent him down for fighting."

"Fighting?" Arden's crack of laughter made Lucy wince. "That was the least of his crimes. The final straw was when he attempted to beat one of the schoolmasters with his own chair. But don't worry, ma'am. I have him well in hand now."

Dr. Mantel cleared his throat and glanced over at Lucy. "And how is Sir Robert enjoying the baths these days?"

"He is recovering nicely." Lucy smiled. "Although I believe he misses Sir William's company. He insists that everyone else there is either a fool or an invalid."

"Yet he is an invalid himself?" Lady Benson nodded. "He does seem quite young to be so afflicted."

"He is hardly *afflicted*, Lady Benson. Sir Robert held the rank of major, fought with the Tenth Hussars against the French, and was wounded at the battle of Waterloo." Lucy raised an eyebrow. "He was knighted by the prince regent for his gallantry on that day."

"Really?" Arden turned to Lucy, his face for once free of malice. "How absolutely splendid. I've always wanted to go into the military."

"Do not speak of such things." Lady Benson clutched her throat. "Do you wish to kill your own *mother?*"

Arden's expression clouded over again. "I'll leave that sort of thing to Brandon." He shot to his feet. "I'm going out."

After Arden left banging the door behind him Dr. Mantel spoke. "Actually, I think a military career might be the making of him."

Lucy nodded. "Sir Robert would agree with you."

"Maybe if Arden does receive a bequest from Sir William, he could use it to purchase a commission in a good regiment."

Lady Benson glared at her physician. "It is hardly your place to suggest such a thing—especially when I am so recently widowed, and fearful of being abandoned by everyone I know and love."

Dr. Mantel bowed. "I do apologize, my lady. You are quite right."

"I have a few errands to run before dinner so I must depart." Lucy rose from her seat and curtsied to her hostess. "Thank you so much for the tea. I do hope you feel better soon, Lady Benson."

"Good day, Lady Kurland."

Her hostess waved a vague good-bye and leaned back against the couch as if unable to support the weight of her head any longer.

Dr. Mantel walked Lucy down the stairs to the front door.

"Thank you for coming, my lady." He hesitated. "You might not realize it, but Lady Benson really does appreciate your visits. She knows almost no one in Bath, and is feeling rather isolated and unsure."

"I can imagine." Lucy smiled at him, aware that his status put him in a very delicate position with the family who employed his services.

"If Sir Robert gets a chance to speak to Arden about obtaining a commission—without his mother noticing—it might help him form a better plan for his future than raising hell," Dr. Mantel suggested.

"I'll certainly mention it to my husband, but I must warn you that Sir Robert hasn't been impressed by Arden's or Brandon's demeanor, and might be reluctant to involve himself further."

"I understand." Dr. Mantel sighed. "The boys have, perhaps, been overindulged by their mother."

Lucy decided not to comment on that. "Do you intend to stay with the family now that your principal patient is deceased, Dr. Mantel? Or will you remain in Bath and set up practice here?" Lucy asked.

"I intend to return to Yorkshire with Lady Benson, and make sure she is comfortably settled. After that I am not sure." He smiled and bowed. "It is most kind of you to be concerned for my welfare, my lady. I truly appreciate it."

On that note, Lucy took her leave and went out into the street. She chose the path that led back into town as she had a book to return to the lending library on Milsom Street. It was sunny outside, but not warm, and she walked quickly, her thoughts on the afternoon's encounter. There was certainly a lot of information to consider. She couldn't imagine living in a household that laid bare every emotion to the world, but it certainly helped her attempts to decide which one of the Bensons had the most reason to murder Sir William.

Robert stared at Lucy as she recounted her earlier visit to the Bensons over dinner. Penelope had retired to bed and Anna was out visiting Captain Akers's family.

"Good Lord." Robert only realized his dinner had gone cold when he attempted to eat some more lamb. "What an *extraordinary* tale."

"I know." Lucy picked up her fork. "At times I felt as if I had been relegated to a seat in the audience of a play, but

I didn't complain too loudly. It was quite educational to hear them all at one another's throats."

"What are your conclusions so far?"

"Well, my suspicions of Miranda's sons still stand, but I would speculate that Brandon was the perpetrator, and that Arden is covering up for him. This also might explain why only one man appeared to be running away from the baths that morning,"

Robert nodded. "Agreed. Anything else?"

"Augustus is obviously in some trouble," Lucy mused. "I thought I might pay a visit to the bishop's residence, and see if I can ascertain exactly what is going on."

"Do you think they will talk to you?"

"Of course they will." Lucy raised her eyebrows. "I am the daughter of a rector who also happens to be a well-known scholar, and is the son of an earl. If anyone knows how to charm their way into a clerical household, it is I."

Robert couldn't argue with her reasoning. "What do you think Augustus meant about Peregrine's 'sinful' ways?"

Lucy wrinkled her nose. "I thought I'd leave that part up to you. I was also interested in his claim that Peregrine deliberately set his father against Miranda's sons because he was jealous of them."

"Why did that concern you?" Robert asked.

"Because maybe Peregrine *knew* they had been included in Sir William's will, and he was so incensed that he decided to murder his father."

"Leaving the boys still in the will," Robert pointed out.

"Maybe Peregrine thought he could change the will somehow," Lucy suggested. "All I know is that he wasn't as calm and unconcerned about everything Augustus said as he claimed to be." She cut into a potato speckled with parsley. "Did you find out anything more at the baths today?"

"Only that both Arden and Brandon have been seen there before, but that no one could definitely say that they were there on the morning in question." Robert grimaced. "To be honest, I am more interested in finding out what is going on with Sir William's business, and whether his claims that Edward was destroying it are true."

"And how do you intend to proceed with that?" Lucy asked.

"I've written to my cousin Oliver. He knows the Benson family and their business, and will probably have an opinion about them both."

"Then we are progressing—albeit slowly." Lucy sighed. "Sometimes I wonder why we get mixed up in these matters at all."

"Because this time Sir William deserves justice." Robert held her gaze through the candlelight. "I am more convinced than ever that he died before his time. I intend to bring his murder or murderers before a judge to pay for their crime."

"Our most likely candidates are still the two boys," Lucy said. "I can't quite see Augustus murdering his father in broad daylight, can you?"

"We know from experience that murderers often do the unexpected, and spring from the most unlikely of places," Robert reminded her.

"That is true, although I still doubt that a cleric, who tend to be well-known figures, would risk jumping into the baths to drown his father." Lucy drank some of her wine and grimaced. "This tastes remarkably metallic."

"It tastes fine to me." Robert finished his glass. "And if Augustus did jump into the baths he wouldn't have been wearing his clerical attire at the time, would he? He would've been wearing the same ridiculous outfit as the rest of us."

"Which lends the wearers a certain anonymity, especially if they cover up their hair," Lucy murmured. "I hadn't thought of that."

"Augustus could've drowned his father, and then joined the other bathers on the far side of the baths, and exited with them being none the wiser there was a murderer in their midst," Robert pointed out.

"As could any of our suspects." Lucy sighed. "Do you still wish to accompany me to the theater this evening, or would you rather stay in?"

"I'd prefer to go out. If I stay here worrying about the Bensons, I will be pacing the carpet all evening, and you will probably wish me to the devil."

"Probably." She smiled at him. "But I do understand your concerns."

He reached across the table, took her hand, and kissed her fingers. "I really must thank you again for insisting I came to Bath. I am feeling so much better."

"So I can see. Apparently, you needed nothing more than taking the waters and solving an unexplained death to set you to rights."

Robert chuckled. "And a wife who understands me and allows me to follow my passions."

She blushed very prettily and looked down at her plate. "I should go and change."

"If you must." He studied her muslin dress. "You look perfectly nice just as you are."

"Flatterer." Lucy rose to her feet and Robert followed suit. "I'll be as quick as I can."

Chapter 8

"It is such a pleasure to meet the daughter of the Honorable Mr. Ambrose Harrington—a man whose theological work I have long admired."

Lucy smiled at the retired archbishop's wife and her two daughters as they offered her tea. Her note to the bishop's Bath residence had resulted in an invitation to call and she had immediately acted on it. She had no real interest in seeing the bishop himself, who was fortunately in Wells, having learned long ago that the female members of clerical families and their staff generally held any secrets.

"My father is a very well-educated man, Mrs. Lemmings, with interests that span a variety of topics including those dear to the Church of England."

In truth her father was far more invested in hunting and horse racing than anything spiritual. The theology of the church did appeal to him in an intellectual manner, which meant he was quite prepared to pontificate and argue about it with the best scholars in the land, and often wrote articles for scholastic journals.

"How wonderful," the oldest Miss Lemmings breathed. "I cannot imagine how it must have felt to hear him speak in person every day."

Lucy made a mental note to remind her father to visit Bath at the earliest opportunity.

"I often helped him with his sermons and translated passages from the original Greek and Latin," Lucy said.

"He allowed you to learn those heathen languages?" Mrs. Lemmings raised her eyebrows. "My dearly deceased husband did not consider them suitable for our daughters."

"I was lucky that my father never barred me from learning anything I wished to know." Lucy smiled. "He often said that I was far too intelligent to be trapped in a woman's body."

Mrs. Lemmings nodded as if this made perfect sense to her. "Does Mr. Harrington not have sons?"

"My brother Anthony is currently abroad with the prince regent's Tenth Hussars, and my younger twin brothers are away at school." She didn't mention her older brother, Tom, who had died during the war, because it was still not a matter she was prepared to subject to public scrutiny.

"Lucky man," Mrs. Lemmings commented. "Sadly, I only had daughters."

Lucy noticed Cora, the youngest Miss Lemmings, rolling her eyes at her sister as if she'd heard that particular lament rather too often.

"Daughters are a blessing," Lucy said firmly. "They are always so supportive."

"Do you have children of your own, Lady Kurland?"

"Not yet," Lucy said. "But I have only been married for three years. It is something I would dearly love."

"You married quite late, then?" Miss Lemmings asked, and then blushed a fiery red. "Not that is it any of my business, but—"

"Yes. After my mother's early death I was convinced that it was my destiny to stay and keep house for my father, and younger brothers and sisters. As it turned out, Sir

Robert, who is the major landowner in Kurland St. Mary, asked me to marry him. I was very happy to accept his proposal."

"What a wonderful story," whispered Miss Cora. "You give us all such hope."

Lucy smiled at the sisters. "Perhaps while I am staying in Bath you and Miss Lemmings might care to join us for tea, or even accompany us to the Assembly Rooms? My sister Anna would love to meet you."

"That would be most acceptable. We have secure lodgings here at the bishop's residence, but are somewhat cut off from the outside world." Mrs. Lemmings inclined her head making the bows on her lace cap tremble. "Since my husband's demise I simply cannot abide society. I fear that the girl's chances of making a good match are fading away along with their looks."

"One should never give up hope," Lucy answered. "I'm certain your daughters behave themselves impeccably in society, and that any man would be lucky to have them."

Her retort earned her beaming smiles from the two girls, and a doubtful look from her hostess.

"Have you ever been to the King's Bath?" Lucy asked Mrs. Lemmings. "My husband has been taking treatments there."

"My late husband enjoyed the hot springs very much, Lady Kurland, but I never cared for them."

"I wonder did he ever meet a Sir William Benson at the baths?" Lucy scrutinized all three faces. "He was recently taken ill at the baths and unfortunately died."

"I heard of this." Mrs. Lemmings pressed a hand to her heart. "The poor, dear man. I do remember the name. Was he involved with the church?"

"I believe his son Augustus is the vicar of several parishes in the local area," Lucy offered. "Perhaps you know of him?"

"Augustus Benson?" Miss Lemmings shuddered. "We

all know about *him*. He has been on the lookout for a wife for years."

"I understand that his parishes are not wealthy so perhaps he feels he needs a helpmate to manage his finances, and tend to his flock," Lucy suggested.

Mrs. Lemmings rose to her feet. "Will you excuse me for one moment, Lady Kurland? I want to ask Cook to bring up some of her fruitcake. I am quite certain you will enjoy it."

The moment the door closed behind their mother, Miss Lemmings turned to Lucy. "Augustus Benson is a horrible man. No woman would ever marry him because even within clerical circles it is known that he uses all his income to gamble on the horses."

"As in horse racing?" Lucy asked. "Dear me."

"Rumor has it that he is in great debt," Miss Cora Lemmings whispered. "And desperately seeking a means to repay his creditors before he loses *everything*."

"Then I will make certain that any advances he makes toward my sister are nipped swiftly in the bud." Lucy put down her cup. "Having met Sir William, I assumed that his son would be an excellent man of character."

"Sir William has two other sons," Miss Cora piped up.

Lucy noticed that for a couple that did not go out much in Bath society the sisters were extremely well informed.

Cora continued. "The oldest is rather staid, but the younger one—Mr. *Peregrine* Benson—is as handsome as Byron."

Miss Lemmings nodded in agreement. "We saw him once in Milsom Street with Sir William's wife, and he was most courteous toward us."

"I have met Mr. Peregrine Benson, and he is indeed a very charming gentleman, although his current lack of employment in a respectable occupation does make me doubt his prospects as a suitable husband for my sister." Lucy looked at Miss Lemmings. "He is an artist, I believe?"

"And a poet and a playwright."

"Indeed." Lucy looked up as Mrs. Lemmings returned with a plateful of cake. "How delightful, ma'am. I love a good piece of cake."

Lucy placed a hand over her stomach and smiled at Robert. They were sitting in the drawing room of their house enjoying a late cup of tea before they dressed for dinner. "I'm not sure what was *in* that fruit cake Mrs. Lemmings asked me to sample, but it feels like it was full of lead."

"Are you suggesting that you deserve credit for forcing down cake?"

"Indeed I am, but it was worth it because it seems widely known that Augustus Benson is in debt, and not the kind of debt that he can wiggle out of, but gambling debts of honor. No wonder he wanted money from Sir William."

"So you think Peregrine was right about Augustus arguing with his father just before he died?" Robert asked.

"It would certainly make sense if he desperately needed money, and was denied," Lucy said. "I still find it difficult to believe that a man of the cloth would do such a thing."

"That is because you were brought up to venerate such men," Robert stated. "I don't blame you for being deceived."

"Well, thank you for that. How did *you* get on today?" Lucy inquired. "Did you hear back from your cousin?"

"Not yet, but I did find out there are rumors that Peregrine Benson's private life is not as it should be."

"As in how?"

Robert smiled at her. "Unnatural vices, my dear."

"Whatever does that mean?" Lucy asked with a frown.

"That he preferred the 'company' of men."

"Oh. I expect Sir William wouldn't have liked that at *all*."

"If he didn't, he certainly didn't mention it to me, which in retrospect seems odd considering how honest he was about every other problem within his family."

"He didn't tell you that Augustus was gambling away the church roof fund, either."

"True." Robert sighed, and stretched out his legs. "Did you really ask all those females to join us for dinner every night?"

"Not every night." She hesitated. "I felt sorry for the girls because their mother was so immersed in her mourning that she had little time for them."

He reached out a hand to her. "And you of all people know how hard it is for a proper clergyman's daughter to meet a good man."

"I was luckier than most," she reminded him, returning the clasp on her fingers. "Miss Lemmings said I gave her hope."

"If Miss Lemmings is half the woman you are, my dear, she will have no difficulty attracting a husband. I am more than willing to vouch to any gentleman as to the value of a wife brought up in a clerical household."

She blushed very prettily as she withdrew her hand and rose to her feet.

"Cat got your tongue?" Robert inquired as he stood as well and looked down at her.

She cupped his jaw. "It is nice to see you in such good humor."

He bent his head and kissed her on the lips. "I am feeling much better." He kissed her again. "Much, *much* better." He took her hand. "Now, come along."

She didn't move. "It is still too early to dress for dinner."

"I know." He winked at her. "But I suspect we can find something far more pleasurable to do together while we wait."

"Robert . . ."

"And think of the benefits, my love. We'll already be undressed when Betty and Silas come and find us."

"Sir Robert, might I have a word with you?" Foley inquired.

"Of course, come in."

Robert nodded at Silas, who had just finished helping him undress after the visit to the theater. "Thank you, Silas. That will be all."

"Good night, sir."

Silas left, and Foley came in, and stood beside the fireplace, his hands joined behind his back.

"What is it, Foley?"

"As instructed, I have been speaking to Mr. Tompkins on a regular basis, and he has confided in me a great deal."

"Excellent." Robert gestured at the chair behind Foley. "Sit down."

"Oh, I couldn't do that, Sir Robert. It wouldn't be seemly," Foley protested.

"Sit *down*, you old fool." Robert took the other chair. "I promise I won't tell anyone."

"As you wish, sir." Foley sat gingerly on the edge of the chair. "Mr. Tompkins wanted me to give you something."

"And what would that be?"

"His master's correspondence."

"Ah. But won't the Bensons notice it is missing?"

"Mr. Tompkins says that his master always kept everything in his bedchamber so that no one else could see it or read it." Foley sniffed. "Sir William was remarkably suspicious of his own family, and very private in his business dealings."

"Possibly with some justification seeing as he is dead," Robert pointed out.

"That's exactly what Mr. Tompkins said, sir. He believes that *someone* was coming into Sir William's bedchamber when neither of them were present, and going through his papers."

"Did he have any idea *which* Benson?" Robert asked. "There are rather a lot of them."

"Mr. Tompkins didn't say, but he *did* want you to read the letters and decide for yourself what's been going on, sir."

"How much of his business did Sir William discuss with Mr. Tompkins?" Sir Robert asked.

"Almost everything, sir. They have been friends since childhood. I think Sir William trusted him more than anyone else in his life."

"Including his own sons?" Robert asked.

"From what Mr. Tompkins said, Sir William wasn't very happy with any of them. If you are agreeable to reading the letters, sir, he says it will all become clear."

"Then I suppose the best thing is to take a look at them, and hope that the Bensons don't notice their absence," Robert said. "If Lady Kurland and I share the task, we can probably get through them quickly enough that no one will even be aware that they went missing."

Foley stood and bowed. "Then I'll ask Mr. Tompkins to hand them over."

"Thank you, and good work, Foley. I appreciate it."

"Thank you, sir." Foley hesitated. "The more I've listened to Mr. Tompkins talk, the more I've come to agree with you that Sir William did not die in peace. I'd be delighted to think that I'd played some small part in bringing his murderer to justice."

"Splendid, Foley." Robert nodded. "After I read the letters I might need to speak to Mr. Tompkins in person. Do you think he would be agreeable to that?"

"Indeed he would, sir. Remember, he already holds you in high esteem. I'd like to think that if someone murdered *you*, sir, I'd make sure justice prevailed on your account, too." Foley turned toward the door. "I hear Lady Kurland coming up the stairs so I shall leave you in peace. Good night, Sir Robert. Sleep well."

"Lucy, I need to speak to you." Penelope came and sat opposite Lucy at the breakfast table. "Goodness me, no wonder you are looking so pale and wan, you hardly have anything on your plate!"

"I'm just not very hungry this morning," Lucy admitted. "For some reason everything in Bath tastes odd to me. It's quite disconcerting." She munched determinedly on her dry toast. "What do you wish to speak to me about?"

Penelope glanced around the deserted room and lowered her voice. "Anna."

"What about her?"

"She is spending a lot of time with Captain Akers and his family."

"And?" Lucy glanced up inquiringly. "They are very pleasant. I have no objection to her being in their company."

"But he is hardly a peer of the realm now, is he?" Penelope pointed out. "And Anna is the granddaughter of an *earl*."

"As am I. Do you think I should have aimed higher than Sir Robert?"

"With your average looks, and a great deal of luck, you did very well for yourself, Lucy, we all know that. But you cannot compare yourself with Anna. She is a diamond of the first water!"

"And she had a London Season, and decided that none of the titled gentlemen who courted her would do," Lucy said firmly. "If she wants to spend time in Captain Akers's company that is perfectly acceptable to me, and to Sir Robert."

Penelope placed her hands over her growing stomach. "As you wish. I really do not have the energy to argue with you when I've been kept awake all night by this baby kicking me in the ribs."

Lucy studied the mound of Penelope's belly as the pattern on her muslin gown shivered like a blancmange. It was really quite extraordinary.

"When does Dr. Fletcher think the baby will be born?" Lucy asked, hoping to redirect her guest's concerns away from Anna and back to herself where they usually resided. "It can't be much longer, surely?"

"Another three months I believe." Penelope grimaced. "I can't reach my toes or even see them anymore."

"Well, hopefully, by the time you are due you will be safely home in Kurland St. Mary with your sister, and your husband to support you," Lucy said. "Do you hope for a daughter or a son?"

"A son, *obviously*." Penelope raised her eyebrows. "We both know that the males in any family retain *all* the advantages. And you in particular, Lucy, must know that you have a duty to provide Sir Robert with a male heir to inherit his title."

"I'm doing my best," Lucy replied. "When Sir Robert is fully recovered and we return home I'm sure things will develop naturally between us."

"One can only hope that you are right, my dear Lucy," Penelope agreed. "From everything I have heard, Mr. Paul Kurland is quite beyond the pale."

"Good morning, my dear. Good morning, Mrs. Fletcher."

Robert came into the dining room with an unfamiliar leather box tucked under his arm. Lucy was pleased to see that he wasn't even carrying his cane let alone using it.

"When you have finished your breakfast, Lucy, perhaps you might spare me a moment of your time in the library?" Robert addressed her directly.

"Of course. I'm just about finished."

He bowed. "Then I will see you in a minute."

"Sir Robert?" With some difficulty Penelope turned in her chair to look at her host. "What do you know about Captain Akers and his family? Are they respectable?"

Robert exchanged an inquiring glance with Lucy over the top of Penelope's head. "I have inquired about the family extensively, and they are well-liked, financially solvent property owners."

"But not of the peerage."

"I doubt it, why?"

"Because Anna could do much better for herself," Penelope said firmly.

"Anna is an intelligent young woman who is perfectly capable of making a decision about the man she wishes to marry by herself. I will support her in that," Robert said.

"Oh well." Penelope started eating her second plate of food. "Don't say I didn't warn you."

Lucy rose to her feet. "Perhaps I *will* come with you now, Robert." She smiled at Penelope as she went past her. "Anna intends to take her books back to the circulating library this morning if you wish to accompany her."

"Then I will have to go, too." Penelope nodded. "We can't leave her unchaperoned."

"Betty will accompany her."

"Betty is hardly a *chaperone*," Penelope responded. "I will go. I've nothing else to do."

Lucy escaped into the hall and followed Robert into the library where he held out a chair for her at the desk.

"When is that woman leaving?" Robert inquired as he unlocked the leather box.

"That *woman* is waiting for her husband to return to Bath. I can hardly order her to leave in her current condition, can I?"

"Why not? I'll even pay for the damned carriage. She has a terrible habit of sticking her nose in where it's not wanted, and I do not appreciate being lectured in my own house!"

"This isn't your house," Lucy reminded him.

"Don't be pedantic." He glared at her. "She is a nuisance. The only reason I put up with her is because my best friend happens to have been besotted enough to marry the woman."

"She is quite beautiful." Lucy glanced over at him as he started emptying the box. "You obviously thought so at some point seeing as you asked her to marry you."

"As you well know, that was her mother's doing," Robert grumbled. "The pair of them tied me up, and made it impossible to escape without losing my reputation, and damaging hers."

"Yet you managed it eventually."

"Thank God." He handed her a bundle of letters. "These belong to Sir William. Perhaps we should both stop talking, and start reading."

A while later, Lucy raised her head and stared at her husband, who was reading intently, his brow furrowed in concentration.

"Sir William certainly has a way with words."

"He is blunt and uncomplimentary about everything. At least he had the forethought to copy most of his replies. It saves us a lot of time puzzling out what he must have said." Robert let out his breath. "There is so much to consider in these letters that I don't know where to start!"

Lucy found a clean piece of paper. "Let's make a list. What have you read about so far?"

Robert put on his spectacles again. "Edward Benson's complete lack of understanding of how to run a business, and a refusal by Sir William to pay Augustus Benson's gambling debts. How about you?"

"Something far worse." Lucy handed Robert a letter. "This is from an 'anonymous well-wisher' in London."

He read through the letter and winced. "Well-wisher? Let's call this what it is, my dear girl, an attempt to extort money from Sir William to protect Peregrine's reputation. One does have to wonder what the man gets up to in London and why he is apparently so indiscreet." He looked at Lucy over the top of the letter. "Is there a reply to this?"

"From Sir William?" She leafed through her pile of letters. "There is a copy of his reply, which consists of one line telling the blackmailer to go to the devil, publish, and be damned." She looked at Robert. "This letter is dated just before Sir William died."

"Then one can assume that Sir William had discussed the matter with Peregrine." Robert grimaced. "I thought he at least was not a suspect, but this paints things in a very different light, doesn't it? If Peregrine thought he was about to be exposed as a sodomite he might have been willing to murder his parent to get enough money to pay *off* the blackmailer."

Lucy showed Robert Peregrine's last letter to his father. "Did you notice there is some kind of word and numbers game at the bottom of the page?"

"Yes, I've noticed that on all their letters to each other." He sighed. "I wish I could ask Peregrine what it meant, but that would mean admitting I'd been reading his private correspondence with his father, and he'd probably call me out."

"Peregrine does seem to be somewhat hotheaded." Lucy considered the letter. "But it also indicates that despite everything he and his father had a good relationship."

"Because they shared puzzles between them?"

"Yes," Lucy said definitely. "Even when Sir William is absolutely furious with Peregrine, and you can see it often in their correspondence, he never fails to continue their game."

Lucy wrote Peregrine on her list and put the pen down. "Is that everything so far? Shall we continue? I'll ask Foley to bring us some tea."

"Good Lord."

Lucy stared at Robert, who was looking down at one of the letters as if it were about to bite him.

"What is it?"

"Sir William believed that Lady Miranda was having an *affair*!"

"With whom?" Lucy asked.

"Someone close to the family, apparently. Peregrine, maybe?" Robert squinted at the closely written script. "This is a reply from his solicitor, Mr. Carstairs, who advises his client to think *very carefully* before altering his will so dramatically." Robert shook his head. "I wonder what Sir William was going to do?"

"I have no idea," Lucy said. "But I cannot wait to hear what Mr. Carstairs has to say when he finally arrives and reveals the secrets of Sir William's will."

Chapter 9

"Lady Kurland! How nice to see you out and about."

Lucy turned to find Peregrine Benson smiling down at her. She'd gone to Milsom Street to purchase a new ribbon to trim an old bonnet and was now considering whether to join her sister at the Pump Room for tea. She was feeling rather more tired than she had anticipated and longing for a nap.

"Good afternoon, Mr. Benson." She curtsied. "I was just about to return home."

"Then it would be my pleasure to accompany you." He bowed and offered her his arm. "I am finished with my business in town myself."

Lucy placed her gloved hand on his sleeve and they set off. "Did you ever locate your father's solicitor, Mr. Benson?"

"Indeed, that is what I have been attending to this morning. The poor man thought he would never get here." He chuckled. "He is safely ensconced in one of the bedrooms at the White Hart Inn and will visit the family tomorrow."

"I am glad to hear that he arrived safely," Lucy replied. "Your stepmother was very worried about him."

"She's worried about the will, my lady, not about the man," Peregrine observed as they crossed the cobbled street, and went back toward the center of town. "Although, in my humble opinion, she should be worried about the contents of the will. My father was not the kind of man who appreciated being lied to."

"Did Lady Benson lie to him?"

"When she encountered my father in London, she pretended to be acquainted with an old friend of his, and he took her at her word. Unfortunately, my father happened to *meet* this old friend just before he left for Bath and the man had no knowledge of Miranda at all."

"Oh dear," Lucy murmured. "I wonder why she did that?"

"Because she knew an old fool when she saw one?" Peregrine's smile wasn't pleasant. "She flattered him, and he fell for her tricks."

"With all due respect to Sir William, Mr. Benson, your father is hardly the first older man to fall in love with a beautiful young woman."

"Ain't that the truth, Lady Kurland." He hesitated. "I think my father was regretting his decision well before he left for Bath. Miranda spent his money like water and lavished it on her spoiled brats, which led to a lot of disagreements."

"I can imagine." Lucy stepped off the high curb, lifting her skirts out of the way of the muddy water gushing down the hill. "Lady Benson does seem to be devoted to her sons." She paused, wondering how much he knew. "If your stepmother didn't have a previous acquaintance with a friend of Sir William's, I wonder why she pretended that she did?"

"Probably because she didn't want him to know where she really came from."

Lucy looked inquiringly up at her companion and gratifyingly he continued talking.

"She was on the stage."

"Oh."

"And not even in a decent reputable London theater, but in a small touring company that made little money. I found that out from some of my acquaintances in London." Peregrine snorted. "No wonder she wanted to marry my father."

"One can see that such a marriage would definitely be advantageous for her," Lucy said.

"And her sons," Peregrine added. "The last conversation I had with my father was on the subject of Arden and Brandon. He was considering cutting them from his will entirely."

"One can see why. They are remarkably disrespectful to his memory, and to their mother," Lucy said. "Sir William told my husband that he was unhappy with *all* the members of his family. Did that include you? Your brother seemed to suggest there was some 'friction' between you and your father."

Peregrine glanced down at her. "You're a very observant woman, Lady Kurland."

"Thank you." Lucy chose to accept his rather pointed comment as a compliment. "Sometimes, one can't help but notice the conflicts in other people's families."

"Especially when they enact them right in front of you." Peregrine sighed. "I'd forgotten that you had to sit through Augustus and me arguing." He continued walking for a while and then started speaking again. "My father didn't approve of my life in London."

"I suspect most fathers feel the same when their sons come of age." Lucy nodded. "My own father gave my older brother many a lecture about how to behave in society while conveniently forgetting that his own behavior had been equally suspect."

Peregrine laughed. "My father grew up in poverty. His expectations of us were rather complicated. He wanted us to be gentlemen, but he abhorred the excesses and laziness of the very class he aspired to. I choose to associate with artists and playwrights, occupations he didn't consider worthwhile."

His smile turned wry. "Which is slightly amusing when

you realize he was bamboozled into marrying an actress himself."

"Indeed," Lucy agreed. "Were you the person who first alerted your father to this fact?"

"I suppose I might have been. Once my father realized Miranda hadn't known his friend at all, he started asking questions." He shrugged. "It was something of a fortuitous chance that I found out who she really was, and was able to confirm his suspicions."

Lucy doubted there had been much evidence of chance involved but didn't dispute the point. His frankness about his father and stepmother was in direct contrast to his reluctance to speak about the breach between his father and himself. But who could blame him? Being a sodomite was still a criminal offense with harsh punishments and hardly something to be discussed with a stranger.

They turned the corner into Queen's Square, and Lucy was soon outside her front door.

"Thank you so much for accompanying me home, Mr. Benson." She smiled up at Peregrine. "It was very kind of you."

"You're most welcome, Lady Kurland." He swept off his hat and gave her a magnificent bow before climbing the steps and knocking on the door next to hers.

Lucy went inside, spoke briefly to Foley, and went upstairs to her bedchamber where Betty was folding newly laundered clothes and putting them away.

"My lady!" Betty turned to Lucy. "I wasn't expecting you back." She took Lucy's bonnet and gloves and helped her unbutton her pelisse. "Are you feeling well?"

"I thought I might take a nap." Lucy smiled at her longtime maid, who had accompanied her from the rectory to Kurland Hall and stood by her during the last disastrous year. "I'm not sure why I am feeling so tired all the time."

"Well, these hills do wear one out." Betty hesitated. "I wasn't sure if I should mention it, my lady, but perhaps it is due to the arrival of your monthly courses?"

Lucy stared at her maid. "That's true, I haven't . . ." She stopped, her heart thumping. "I haven't bled since before Christmas."

Betty held her gaze. "That's correct, my lady."

"Oh, my goodness!" Lucy sat down on the nearest chair. "That's four *months*. I've been so busy caring for Robert and arranging this trip to Bath that I hadn't even noticed." She pressed her hands to her mouth, and took a long calming breath. "Please don't say anything to Silas or my husband."

"I wouldn't do that, my lady." Betty patted her shoulder. "I'll always keep your secrets. There's no point worrying the menfolk when there's nothing they can do to help, is there? And you know how they fret."

"Exactly." Lucy nodded, her mind still running in circles. "At some point, my condition will become obvious or it will—" She couldn't finish that sentence. After two miscarriages she was too afraid to even hope.

"Yes, my lady. But you are already further along this time." Betty smiled at her. "Now, why don't you take that nap, and I'll make sure that you aren't disturbed."

Robert glanced over at his wife, who was staring into space neglecting the book she was supposed to be reading.

"Are you thinking about our investigation?" He smiled. "You seem quite preoccupied."

She jumped and turned her attention to him. "I'm sorry, I was woolgathering. I spent some time with Peregrine Benson this morning. He suggested that *he* was the one who alerted his father to the fact that his new wife was actually an actress in a traveling theater company."

"That explains why her sons have Shakespearean names."

Lucy nodded. "I suppose they do. Peregrine allegedly frequents the company of artists and playwrights so he *might* have heard the gossip about Miranda there."

"That's quite possible," Robert agreed.

"I was also wondering whether Peregrine was black-mailing his father."

"With what?"

"The knowledge that his father's new wife was an actress." Lucy held his gaze. "What if he told Sir William that he would keep quiet about the matter if Sir William would deal with his blackmailer?"

"That might be true, I suppose," Robert agreed. "But would Sir William care? He never saw himself as a member of the ruling classes and could marry whomever he wanted without incurring the wrath of some titled family." Robert paused. "The thing I *could* see sticking in his craw was that she lied to him. That he would not like."

"And we aren't even sure if Peregrine was the first person to break the news to Sir William," Lucy said. "The letter we read indicated that Sir William knew about it, but he doesn't reveal his source."

"Which might explain why Sir William refused to pay off Peregrine's blackmailer, giving Peregrine a very good reason to end his father's life."

"The thing is . . ." Lucy twisted her hands together in her lap. "Despite everything, I *like* Peregrine, and I cannot imagine him killing Sir William."

"Being likeable doesn't necessarily mean you aren't a murderer," Robert reminded her. "We've met some delightful people over the years who have turned out to be absolute villains."

"I know," she sighed. "I'd still prefer it to be Miranda's sons."

"Well, what about Miranda herself?" Robert asked. "If Sir William really was planning on cutting her out of his will then she would definitely have a reason to kill him before he attended to the matter."

"No one saw her at the baths that morning, and she is quite memorable," Lucy said. "Although, I suppose she *could* have instructed her sons to take care of the matter for her."

"Yes, mayhap they are working together."

"So we are discounting Edward and Augustus as likely suspects?" Lucy asked.

"Not so fast." Robert took a letter out of his pocket and handed it over to Lucy. "I had a reply from my cousin Oliver. In his usual brusque manner he informed me that Edward Benson is a failure in business, owes more money than his father probably knew, and has a terrible reputation in his town."

"But none of that makes him a murderer," Lucy objected.

"It might if his father found out and had decided to disinherit *him*."

Lucy threw up her hands. "By the end of his life it appears that Sir William might have disinherited everyone!"

"Agreed. They are rather a bad lot, aren't they? To be fair, I doubt Augustus either had the nerve or the desire to kill his father. The church will cover up his misdeeds, and he will be allowed to go on his merry way."

"I wish that wasn't true, but I fear you are right." Lucy sighed. "There are quite a number of contemptible individuals within the clergy who neither believe in God nor have a single care for their parishioners."

"I can't argue with that," Robert said, and prudently kept his thoughts as to Lucy's father fitting that description to himself.

"Peregrine did say that the solicitor had arrived, and was coming to the house tomorrow to discuss the will." Lucy read the letter and then handed it back to Robert. "I wish I could be a fly on the wall."

"There's no need." Robert smiled at her. "I had an invitation to attend."

"*You* have? Why?" Lucy demanded.

"I have no idea, but the solicitor requested my presence. I will tell you all about it when I get back."

"Get back?" Lucy raised her eyebrows and looked quite like her old self. "I'm coming with you."

"This way, Sir Robert, Lady Kurland."

Robert followed the Bensons' butler through into the drawing room where a row of chairs had been set before a table. A man Robert had never seen before was fussing about the placement of a candle while Edward Benson tried to talk to him.

"I assume that is Mr. Carstairs," Robert murmured in Lucy's ear.

"One would hope so. He looks competent."

"Apart from getting lost on the way to Bath?" Robert replied as he ushered Lucy into a seat in the back row and sat beside her. "That does not fill me with confidence."

Peregrine and Augustus came in, shook hands with the solicitor, and took up residence in the front row next to Edward. They both looked remarkably nervous, which considering the mercurial nature of their late father was not entirely unwarranted.

The clock on the mantelpiece chimed the hour as the staff that had accompanied the Bensons down from Yorkshire filed into the back of the room. Edward stood up and checked his pocket watch.

"Where is Lady Benson?"

Dotty the maid curtsied. "She is just coming, sir. Dr. Mantel is accompanying her."

"And Brandon and Arden?"

"We're here." The two young men came in and sat directly in front of Lucy and Robert. Brandon seemed agitated, and Arden was talking to him constantly in a low murmur.

Just as Edward was about to walk out into the hall, Lady Benson appeared on Dr. Mantel's arm and was tenderly led to the front seat directly opposite the solicitor. The doctor retreated to the back of the room and stood against the wall, his patient's smelling salts in his hand.

Mr. Carstairs cleared his throat. "Perhaps we might begin."

Arden raised his hand. "Why is Sir Robert Kurland here?" He turned to Robert. "No offense, sir, but you are hardly a member of the family."

"Neither are you," Peregrine murmured.

"Now, look here—" Brandon growled and Arden grabbed hold of his brother, who had started out of his seat.

"Don't let him bother you, Brother. He's like an annoying wasp full of venom, but ultimately not worth killing."

Peregrine rolled his eyes. "Good Lord, a threat. I'm terrified."

Mr. Carstairs waited until everyone had composed themselves again, and held up a letter. "I received this from Sir William just before he died. He instructed me that he had amended his will again, and that Sir Robert was now included as one of his executors."

Robert blinked as all the Bensons now turned to stare at him. None of them looked particularly happy.

Ignoring them, Robert looked at the solicitor. "I am more than happy to assist you and the Benson family in any way."

"Didn't my father tell you he was doing this?" Edward asked.

"I had no idea," Robert said. "But I consider it an honor."

Mr. Carstairs put down the letter. "Thank you, Sir Robert. Now, if we might get on to the important matter of the will itself?" He looked around expectantly and the silence lengthened until Edward gestured to him.

"Well, get on with it, man. We're all ears."

"There must be some mistake." Mr. Carstairs frowned. "I am merely the legal presence required to read the will and explain anything to the beneficiaries that is not easily understandable."

The Bensons exchanged puzzled glances and Edward again spoke up. "We understand, but what is stopping you going ahead and reading the blasted thing?"

"I don't have it, sir," Mr. Carstairs said. "Sir William preferred to retain the document in his own keeping. He brought it to Bath."

"Then why in damnation didn't you say that yesterday?" Edward growled, and Lady Benson began to weep.

Beside Robert Lucy sat up straight. "Of course he did!" she whispered while the Bensons continued to argue with one another. "You said he was constantly amending things."

Mr. Carstairs banged on the table to restore order. "Where is the will?"

Edward stood and looked toward the back of the room. "Mr. Tompkins?"

"Yes, sir?" The old valet stepped forward.

"Were you aware of Sir William's will amongst his possessions?"

"I know he had it, Mr. Edward, but I don't know what he did with it."

"What do you mean you don't *know*?" Augustus joined in. "Was it in his possession or not?"

Mr. Tompkins didn't look impressed by the shouted question and took on a more truculent tone. "I saw it when he took it out to change something, but where he kept it, I have no idea. I'm just his valet. It's not my place to inquire what he chooses to do with his important documents now, is it?"

Edward turned back to Mr. Carstairs. "This is ridiculous! Why didn't you say immediately that you didn't have the will? We all assumed my father had sent it back to you before his death."

"Because nobody asked me, sir," Mr. Carstairs snapped. "One would assume you would know how your own father preferred to deal with such matters. He *always* insisted on keeping the will on his person."

Lucy nudged Robert. "Peregrine is enjoying this. Look at his face."

Peregrine Benson looked as if he was desperately trying not to laugh, Lady Benson was moaning and sniffing the smelling salts the doctor had offered her, and her two sons were furiously muttering to each other.

"Then I suppose we must adjourn this discussion until we have thoroughly searched the house and found the will," Edward announced. He bowed to Mr. Carstairs. "We will continue to pay for your room and board until this matter is successfully concluded."

"Thank you." Mr. Carstairs looked thoroughly put out as he stood and pushed in his chair. "I will return to my hotel. Please let me know when I can be of service."

Within seconds of his exit, the whole Benson clan erupted into a flurry of accusations, insults, and panicked questions. Poor Mr. Tompkins was bombarded with questions and grew increasingly red-faced as his character was called into question.

"We should go," Robert murmured to Lucy.

"Not yet. This is all remarkably interesting," she replied. "Edward and Augustus are furious, Peregrine seems to think it's all a big joke, and Lady Miranda and her sons are huddled together possibly plotting their next move."

"None of which is our business," Robert reminded her.

"Well, it *is* if you think one of them is a murderer," Lucy reminded him. "Poor Mr. Tompkins is being most unfairly blamed for this whole debacle."

"Perhaps not unfairly seeing as we both agree that he is the most trusted member of the Benson household, and had known Sir William since he was a child. If anyone knows where that will is, I'll wager it will be him."

"Then perhaps when this fuss dies down we can send Foley over to sympathize with him, and find out if that really is the case."

"That's an excellent suggestion." Robert smiled at her. "Shall we go?"

No one noticed them leaving, and Robert chose not to draw attention to it. He was just knocking on their front door when Lucy looked up at him.

"I just remembered something."

"What?"

"When I took the clothes back to Lady Benson she was prostrate in bed. As soon as I mentioned what I'd brought she sat up and went through every pocket as if she was searching for something."

"Perhaps her late husband's will?" Robert asked, and then frowned. "Maybe she was worried that someone had stolen it at the baths."

"But the man we spoke to there said he guarded Sir William's clothes very carefully."

"We should speak to him again. I wonder if someone was *supposed* to steal the will at the baths, kill Sir William, and amend the will as necessary?" Robert nodded as Foley opened the door, and he stepped over the threshold and into the hall. "Maybe she was just making sure it had gone."

Lucy started up the stairs untying the ribbons of her bonnet. "I hadn't thought of that. I suppose one of her sons could've have stolen it while the other murdered Sir William in the bath."

Robert followed her into their bedchamber. "Which might explain why Lady Benson wasn't enacting her usual gothic drama when the will was discovered to be missing this morning. She might be quite glad about it, especially if she arranged for it to disappear."

"She was rather quiet." Lucy sighed as she took off her bonnet and placed it on her dressing table. "This is all so confusing. What happens if they can't find the will?"

"Nothing. It leaves everything in a complete and utter muddle."

"But there must be some legal resources to deal with such a problem?"

"Indeed there are, but they aren't quick or timely. The legal arguments could go on for years."

"Which I suspect is not what Sir William would've

wanted at all." She took off her pelisse. "It is a terrible tangle."

He walked over, took her hand, and kissed her fingers. "One we will endeavor to solve."

"You haven't given up then?" She looked up at him.

"Not at all. In truth, I suspect the fun is just beginning."

Chapter 10

"I forgot to mention that Foley is going to visit Mr. Tompkins this evening while we are out dining with the Akers."

Robert pinned his cravat in place with a modest silver pin, and put on his best coat while Silas fussed around him brushing the fabric.

"Good," Lucy said as she clasped her pearls around her neck. "It will be interesting to hear what he finds out."

She was wearing one of her new gowns, and hoped its bright pattern would eclipse the paleness of her face. She'd been feeling quite nauseous all day and wasn't enjoying the prospect of having to eat her dinner under the scrutiny of others. Admitting she *might* be with child seemed to have encouraged all the unpleasant symptoms she had so far ignored to appear.

"Are you ready?" Robert asked her as Silas handed him his hat and cane. "I ordered the carriage for six, and it is at the door."

"I'm quite ready." Lucy rose from her seat. "I will go and see if Anna and Penelope have finished dressing."

"Penelope's coming?" Robert made a face. "Well, do your best to make sure she doesn't express her opinions too loudly. I don't want to scare Captain Akers off."

"You approve of him, then?"

"How could I not? He is intelligent, kind to his mother, and a naval hero."

"But do you think Anna will take him?"

"I don't know." He kissed her brow. "We shall do everything in our power to show that we approve of the match if she wishes to move forward, and then it is up to Anna."

Lucy sighed. "I know, but it is *very* hard not to meddle."

"I'm sure it is, and you have been most restrained, my love."

"I've tried." She looked up into his amused dark blue eyes. "It is not in my nature to keep my opinions to myself, and I have practically bitten through my tongue doing so."

He laughed, caressed her cheek, and went to open the door. "Come on, my lady of restraint. I am rather looking forward to my dinner."

It was the first time that Lucy had accepted an invitation to dine at the Akerses' house in the countryside as opposed to at their rented town house in Bath. She was pleasantly surprised by the size of the stone-built house and the expansive gardens around it. Robert had assured her the family was financially solvent, but seeing it with her own eyes made her worry less. Captain Akers was the oldest son, and at some point in the future, everything would belong to him.

Anna had been quiet on the drive over, her beautiful face turned to the window, her replies distracted. Despite their close bond, Lucy had no idea how her sister was now feeling about Captain Akers. Caught up in investigating Sir William's murder, and her own recent preoccupation with the possibility of reproducing, she had neglected her sister. Perhaps seeing her with the family would answer some of Lucy's questions.

They were warmly welcomed by Mr. and Mrs. Akers, several exuberant dogs, and smaller children, and were soon chatting away with the entire family. Robert was at his most gracious, which was a blessing. Even Penelope was on her best behavior, her speculative gaze calculating the family's wealth and standing, and no doubt coming up with her own notion as to their suitability. Lucy could only hope that she wouldn't voice her opinions out loud.

Dr. Fletcher was due back in Bath in a few days. Lucy knew that Robert had every intention of asking his friend to take his wife back to Kurland St. Mary when he left. Penelope could hardly complain after a month of living at the Kurlands' expense. Although Lucy did allow that she had done an excellent job of chaperoning Anna when Lucy was otherwise engaged.

Mrs. Akers drew her and Penelope into conversation leaving Captain Akers to introduce Anna to his younger siblings, who all seemed delighted to meet her. Robert was happily discussing the military with Mr. Akers without even the hint of an argument. It was all so very different from the turmoil of the Bensons that Lucy could hardly believe such civility and kindness existed anymore.

She allowed Mr. Akers to take her into dinner, and sat down at his right hand. To her relief, the food was plentiful and not too rich. With Robert safely away at the other end of the table with his hostess, she dined without fear that he would notice how little she was eating.

By the time they reached the treacle tart, apple pie, and jellies she had established an excellent rapport with Mr. Akers, and gathered that he was not averse at all to the marriage of his eldest son to Anna. In truth, he was refreshingly direct about the qualities he saw in Anna beneath her beauty, which endeared him to Lucy even more.

The ladies left the gentlemen to drink their port and made their way to the drawing room where a roaring fire and the tea tray awaited them. The Benson children were soon dispatched to bed, and the older women settled into a comfortable circle around the fire. Mrs. Akers paid particular attention to Anna, who seemed quite at ease in her company.

After drinking two cups of tea, Lucy had to ask her hostess for directions to use the facilities and was sent up to the dressing room between the two master bedrooms. As she ascended the stairs, the gentlemen left the dining room and a waft of smoke and brandy billowed out from the open doors. They headed toward the drawing room talking amongst themselves.

Lucy completed her business and returned down the stairs, pausing in the hall to get her bearings. The sound of scratching drew her attention toward one of the closed doors, and she went toward it. A piercing whine greeted her approach, and she opened the door to discover that one of the dogs had gotten locked inside the room.

She accepted his lick of gratitude and let him go past her into the hall. She paused to admire the rather large library, her gaze focusing on a stained-glass window at the far end that depicted a family crest. The motto was in Latin, and she walked over and peered as closely as she could at the etched glass in an attempt to decipher it.

"Ah! *My home is my strength and my purpose.* How lovely."

She was just about to turn around when she heard Anna's voice followed by that of Captain Akers coming toward the library. There didn't appear to be another door, so Lucy stepped behind the bookcase closest to the wall and held her breath.

"Thank you for being willing to speak to me, Miss Harrington," Captain Akers said. "I must confess that seeing you here, in my home, has done nothing to dissuade me from my conviction that you are the woman I wish to marry."

"Oh, Harry. Your home is lovely, and so are your family," Anna replied.

"Then will you consent to be my wife?"

There was such a long silence that Lucy had to remember to breathe.

"I've already explained why I think that would be a mistake," Anna finally answered him. "And seeing you here, with your loving family all around you, just makes my inadequacies more obvious."

"Your *inadequacies?*"

"As I have already told you, I do not wish to be a mother," Anna replied. "Although that is not quite true, either, I would *love* to be a mother but I am mortally afraid of childbirth, you *know* this."

"Anna . . . as you have probably noticed, I have plenty of brothers and sisters. If you don't want children one of them can happily inherit this place."

"How can you say that when I see your rightful pride in your family, and in your position in society? If I was selfish enough to deny you heirs what would you think of me then?"

"I've spent most of my life onboard a ship. This place is my home, but it isn't who I *am*." He sighed. "I want to marry you, Anna. I can't tell my heart whom to love."

Lucy put her hand to her mouth.

"Can you really tell me you don't love me?" Anna still didn't speak, and Captain Akers continued, the conviction in his voice strengthening. "Because I believe you do love me."

"Maybe love isn't enough," Anna whispered.

"Beside my duty and obligation to my family?"

"*Yes.*"

"Those things are important to me but they aren't the sum of who I *am*. If I married you I'd want all of you. I can't promise that I won't get you with child. I won't lie to you about that."

"Thank you," Anna murmured.

"But I would do everything in my power to prevent it from

happening." He paused. "I've traveled all over the world. There are more ways than you might imagine to prevent conception."

"But you cannot guarantee it," Anna stated. "And what if I did become pregnant, and lost my mind in terror? How quickly would you regret your choice *then*?"

"You are not your mother, Anna. Science has greatly improved since she died and I would make sure that you had the best available care in the world." There was an implacable note in his voice that surprised Lucy. "You cannot live your life in fear of something that might not happen."

"And what if it did?" Anna retorted. "What if I died?"

"Then I would be devastated, and I would forever blame myself."

"But you'd still be alive."

Then was another long silence before he answered her. "Yes. I would." He sighed. "What do you want me to say, Anna?"

"I don't know."

"Do you love me?"

"Yes." Anna said it with such reverence that Lucy bit her lip to stop herself from crying. "Of course I do. Too much to bring such harm on you."

"So you'd rather not take a chance on happiness? You'd rather allow your fears to rule you?"

"That's not fair, Harry."

"Life's not fair. I've almost lost my life at sea, and I've come to understand that one has to *grab* happiness when it appears, and hold on to it because tomorrow you might be dead anyway. Will you think about that? About denying us even a *chance* to be happy when we love each other, and cannot predict what the future will hold? We might not even be blessed with children. Wouldn't a year of happiness be worth *anything*?"

The next thing Lucy heard was the door slamming and Captain Akers uttering a curse.

"You can come out now, Lady Kurland. Anna has gone."

Lucy startled, and then stepped out from behind the bookcase. "I do beg your pardon, Captain. I had no intention of eavesdropping." Curiosity overcame her. "How did you know I was there?"

"I didn't until the last second when I stepped close enough to the mirror over the fireplace to see your reflection in it." He shoved a hand through his hair. "You must think me a rogue."

"Not at all," Lucy was quick to reassure him. "I thought you presented your case very well."

"You *did*?"

"Yes, you gave Anna something to think about." Lucy hesitated. "I cannot say whether she will allow herself to *listen*, but one can only hope."

"Thank you for that, my lady."

"If Anna chooses to confide in me, I will not divulge that I was present during your discussion."

He bowed. "You have my word that I will not mention it, either."

"Thank you." Lucy gathered her skirts. "Then I will return to the drawing room."

Both Anna and Lucy were very quiet on the drive home, and, as Robert had nothing in particular he wished to say to Penelope, the journey passed in relative silence. Robert had the sense that the Akers family had perhaps expected some announcement from their son as to his engagement. Whatever had happened between the couple, neither of them had looked particularly happy by the end of the evening.

Lucy yawned and leaned against his shoulder. "What a delightful family."

"Indeed." Ignoring Penelope's pointed look he drew Lucy even closer and wrapped an arm around her shoulders. "Mr. Akers was very knowledgeable, and agreeable, and, his children and dogs were well behaved."

He looked out of the window as the carriage drew to a stop outside their Bath residence and waited for the coachman to let down the steps.

"Thank you."

He assisted his three companions out and followed them up the steps. Lucy turned to him in the hall.

"I'm going straight to bed."

"Good night, my dear." He blew her a kiss as he handed Foley his hat and gloves. "I won't be long."

Anna went upstairs and into the drawing room. Penelope followed her.

"Well, Anna? What do you have to say for yourself?"

Anna looked up as if she were in a daze. "I beg your pardon?"

Robert came into the room just as Penelope started to speak again. He closed the door so that Lucy wouldn't hear anything that might send her back into the fray.

"The entire family was obviously expecting you to accept Captain Akers's proposal!"

"I . . . wasn't aware—"

"Good Lord, Anna! The man wants to marry you, his family are agreeable, and you refused him, didn't you?" Penelope threw up her hands. "You will end up an old maid!"

Anna turned around. "So what if I do? It is none of your concern! Go away and leave me in peace!"

Penelope recoiled in shock as Anna raised her voice.

"Well, there is no need for such rudeness. I am just trying—"

"To interfere." Anna obviously wasn't done. "You are worse than Lucy! At least I know she has my best interests at heart whereas you . . . All you care about is maneuvering for money and position!"

Penelope drew herself up like an offended golden goddess. "That is a *ridiculous* thing to say when I chose to marry Dr. Fletcher! Do you think I *wanted* to marry a nonentity? I married him because he loves me, and I love *him*!" She pointed her finger at Anna. "With your looks you could marry a duke, but Captain Akers *loves* you and that, my dear Anna, is the most important thing in the world!"

With a toss of her head, Penelope burst into tears and stormed out, leaving Robert and Anna staring helplessly at each other. To his horror, Robert realized that it fell to him to attempt to aid Lucy's sister.

With a soft sound, Anna sank into a chair. "Oh, my goodness. Now I have offended Penelope."

"That's a remarkably easy thing to do."

"But I made her *cry*."

Robert hesitated, aware that tact and diplomacy weren't his strengths. "For once I have to agree with her."

"That love is more important than anything?" Anna scowled at him. "You almost married *Penelope*! What do you know?"

He sat down and took her shaking hand in his. "But I didn't. I married your sister because I love her."

"Captain Akers thinks I should marry him because I love *him*, and accept what happens."

"Isn't that what we all do?" Robert asked her. "Since marrying your sister I've had to face almost losing her, and it was awful, and terrible. She had to sit through Dr. Fletcher cutting into my thigh. Should I not have married her? Not enjoyed my life so much more with her at my side? I suspect both of us would prefer to spend our time together regardless of how short it might be."

"I'm not like Lucy. She is resilient."

"I think you underestimate yourself."

"I am tired of everyone saying that." Anna's face settled into a stubborn frown that reminded Robert all too forcibly of his wife.

"Then would you prefer me to be more direct?" He held her gaze. "You are allowing your fears to rule you."

"So I'm a coward?"

"Maybe you are. Good night, Anna." Robert stood up. "Whatever you choose to do know that Lucy and I will support you regardless."

He left her sitting there and went toward the stairs only to be waylaid by Foley.

"Do you have a moment, Sir Robert?"

Robert took out his pocket watch and checked the time. He reckoned Lucy would already be in bed.

"Yes, of course."

He followed Foley back down the stairs and into the small study that fronted the ground floor of the house.

"I spoke to Mr. Tompkins, sir."

"And what did he have to say for himself?"

"He said that Sir William had a hiding place for his will."

"Where?"

"That he said he didn't know, Sir Robert," Foley said.

"I find that difficult to believe, don't you?"

"Yes, sir, but he wouldn't budge on his story. He insisted that Sir William would send him out of the room every time he hid the will."

"And he never once peeked or caught him in the act?" Robert shook his head. "I wonder why Mr. Tompkins doesn't want the Benson family to know where the will is?"

"He did say, sir, that he was often the one to witness the changes to the will."

"So perhaps he is aware that several members of the Benson family might blame him for what he witnessed." Robert nodded. "I can see why he might not want to reveal what he knows until he is safely away from Bath, and the wrath of the Bensons."

"So can I, sir. He told me that he plans to pack up and leave fairly soon to alert the household back in Yorkshire as to Sir William's death, and prepare for his burial."

"I'm sure that Edward Benson already has these matters in hand."

"To be fair, sir, Mr. Tompkins doesn't have much faith in Mr. Edward," Foley said tactfully. "And seeing as the whole family is stuck here waiting on that will, he thinks someone needs to go back there in person and take charge."

"Well, see if you can press him further, and offer to help him finish packing Sir William's belongings. Maybe *you'll* find the damned will." Robert walked to the door. "Now I must go to bed. Thank you for your efforts, Foley. They are much appreciated."

"I must confess that I've enjoyed it." Foley bowed. "Good night, Sir Robert."

Robert went back up the stairs thinking about everything that had happened that night. He'd have to face Lucy in the morning, who would definitely wish to discuss the situation with Anna, and he'd have to tell her what Foley had discovered about Mr. Tompkins.

He had a suspicion that neither of his pieces of information would cheer her up and that she would have no compunction in sharing her displeasure with him.

Chapter 11

Lucy contemplated the dried toast on her plate and added a miniscule scrape of butter. Anna hadn't come down to breakfast yet, and, as Lucy was for once unsure of what to say to her, she welcomed the reprieve. She wanted to tell Anna to listen to Captain Akers, but despite her sweet exterior her sister had a stubborn streak that rivaled Lucy's own.

Hearing Robert's voice in the hallway, she quickly rearranged Penelope's discarded plate in front of her to make it look like she had enjoyed a hearty repast. Her husband might not be the most observant man in the world, but he wasn't a fool. His concern for her would make him ask questions that she wasn't yet ready to answer, and she would not lie to him.

"Good morning, my dear."

Robert smiled at her as he entered the dining room and helped himself to the covered dishes on the sideboard. The smell of warm ham and coddled eggs made Lucy clamp her lips together and try not to breathe too deeply. He took a seat beside her, which made it easier for her to avert her face and concentrate on putting marmalade on her toast.

"Good morning, Robert." She managed to eat a piece

of toast and swallowed it down with the help of some tea. "Are you planning on going to the baths today?"

"No, I thought I'd wait until Dr. Fletcher comes tomorrow. Did Foley tell you about his discussion with Mr. Tompkins about the missing will?"

"He did." Lucy shook her head. "I cannot believe that Mr. Tompkins never saw where the will was hidden, can you?"

"No. I suspect he doesn't want it found for some reason." Robert cut into the ham. "I wonder if Sir William made him promise something to that effect?"

"As in, if he died under suspicious circumstances Mr. Tompkins was to hide the will, and tell no one where it was?" Lucy asked, her nausea disappearing as she considered the puzzle.

"Exactly." Robert chewed the ham thoroughly before starting on his eggs. "But he'd have to release it at *some* point."

"Would he? If he suspected one of them of murdering him wouldn't Sir William have preferred none of his children to inherit his fortune?"

"That's also a possibility. He didn't strike me as a forgiving man. What a tangle. I have a great deal of sympathy for Mr. Carstairs."

"I intend to visit Lady Benson this morning. Would you like to come with me?" Lucy asked.

"Yes, I would. I might be able to get a moment alone with Mr. Tompkins, and see if I can convince him to let me take the will into my safekeeping." Robert frowned. "I am concerned that the Bensons might turn to the law and accuse Mr. Tompkins of stealing from them in order to threaten him to disclose his knowledge."

"I could certainly see Augustus or Edward doing exactly that," Lucy agreed. "Perhaps you could use that as a good reason for Mr. Tompkins to hand over the will to a gentleman who would not be so easily cowed."

"As in me?" Robert nodded. "I will certainly make the

suggestion." He glanced around the table. "Have Anna and Penelope been down yet?"

"I haven't seen Anna. Penelope was here." Lucy sighed. "She insisted that Anna had insulted her last night, but refused to explain exactly why."

"Anna did insult her." Robert poured himself a second cup of coffee and topped up Lucy's tea. "Penelope was remonstrating with your sister about not accepting Captain Akers's proposal. Anna said that Penelope was fixated on her acquiring money and wealth."

"*Anna* said that?" Lucy put down her cup.

"In truth, Anna shouted it right in Penelope's face." Robert winced. "And Penelope retorted by saying that *she* had married for love, and that she didn't regret it. Then she burst into tears and rushed out."

"*Penelope* did?" Lucy rubbed her forehead. "I feel as if I am entering some magical universe where everything is upside down."

"It was rather alarming to witness, and to find myself in complete agreement with *Penelope* of all people," Robert admitted. "I actually think Penelope was trying to help."

"Did Anna apologize to her?"

"No, because Penelope stormed out in high dudgeon. I attempted to calm your sister down, but I'm not sure if I succeeded."

Lucy stared at Robert. "You . . . *did?*"

"Anna asked my opinion." He shrugged. "I can assure you that I tried to be tactful, but I'm not sure if she listened to me."

Lucy inwardly shuddered at the thought of her husband attempting to offer advice to her sensitive sister, and was no longer surprised that Anna had declined to descend for breakfast.

"I hope Anna does think about this matter very carefully." Lucy was reluctant to share the details of the conversation she'd overheard because she suspected Robert wouldn't approve of her staying to listen to it. "I liked

Captain Akers and his family very much, and I believe Anna cares for him very deeply."

"Then she needs to be brave and reach out for her happiness." Robert wiped his mouth with his napkin. "That's what I told her."

Lucy rose and brushed the toast crumbs from her skirts. "I will go and see if she is awake before we leave for the Bensons."

"Take your time." Robert reached for the newspaper Foley had set beside his plate. "I need to read what our government has been up to since we left home. I suspect it will not be pleasant."

After failing to rouse Anna, Lucy put on her bonnet and pelisse and went back down to the drawing room where Robert was seated by the fire still reading his newspaper. Betty had suggested Lucy carry some dry bread in her reticule in case she felt nauseous when she was out. She'd never felt quite this sick during a pregnancy before and wondered what that meant. If she felt much worse, she would have to tell Robert what was going on.

He looked up at her over the top of his newspaper and folded it up.

"As I suspected the country is in a terrible state."

"Then perhaps now that you are feeling better you might consider standing for Parliament as you originally intended?" Lucy reminded him.

"I might do that." Robert put his spectacles in his pocket. "I can hardly be less competent than those buffoons running the country now."

Foley came in and handed Robert his hat and cane.

"Thank you, Foley." Robert gestured at the door. "Shall we, my dear?"

Lucy went outside, immediately climbed the steps up to the Benson house, and knocked on the door, which was opened by the butler.

"Good morning, Lady Kurland, Sir Robert."

"Good morning. I am here to see Lady Benson."

"Then please come in, my lady, and I will ascertain as to whether her ladyship has come down yet."

"Thank you." Lucy followed him up the stairs and into the drawing room where the fire had already been lit to warm the space. Robert brought up the rear. "I did send her a note yesterday to say that I would be here at eleven."

"Would you like some refreshment, my lady, sir?"

"Some tea would be most welcome." Lucy took a seat by the fire and removed her gloves. "Thank you."

Robert prowled the space, pausing to look out of the window at every turn and make a disparaging comment about the lack of view until Lucy wished he would sit down. She was just about to voice her request in a rather firmer manner when the door opened to reveal Edward and Peregrine Benson.

Edward went straight over to Robert. "It is a pleasure to see you, sir, even in such sad circumstances."

Robert shook his hand as Peregrine bowed and winked at Lucy. "I must apologize for not staying longer at the reading of the will. My wife and I felt it inappropriate for us to linger."

Edward sighed. "It is something of a muddle, Sir Robert. As it stands, the will cannot be found, and Mr. Carstairs insists that he cannot act without that legal document in front of him."

"With all due respect," Lucy ventured. "Surely as Sir William's solicitor he would have enough knowledge from drawing up the will to know what it would contain?"

"That is a very good point, Lady Kurland, but my father did have a tendency to change his will," Edward said. "Mr. Carstairs quite rightly refuses to speculate as to how the validity of the bequests he dealt with agree with the document his client amended."

"Then one has to assume that Sir William brought the will with him to Bath," Robert commented. "Is it possible that it has just been overlooked?"

"I doubt it," Peregrine said. "My brothers and step-mother have turned this place upside down looking for the damned thing. If it is here, they haven't found it yet."

"You didn't search yourself, Mr. Benson?" Lucy asked Peregrine.

"Seeing as the last time I spoke to the old man he was threatening to disinherit me, I hope the blasted thing *never* turns up."

"Peregrine is jesting." Edward frowned at his brother. "We cannot allow matters to stand like this. It will affect confidence in our business enterprises and encourage our debtors and creditors to question our continued existence."

"Indeed." Robert inclined his head. "If you cannot find the will how do you intend to proceed?"

"Mr. Carstairs says there are ways to deal with such is-sues. They would be costly and involve employing the ser-vices of a barrister, but if that is what I must do to resolve this impasse, then I will do it."

"With what?" Peregrine demanded. "You don't have a feather to fly with of your own."

"If we have to we will borrow money against our expec-tations," Edward said stiffly. "And I must insist, Brother, that you cease embarrassing our guests by discussing our fi-nancial matters."

"I don't think they are the ones who are embarrassed, Brother, *dear*." Peregrine's smile wasn't pleasant. "You seem to forget that Sir Robert's fortune comes from the in-dustrialized north, and he is well aware of the financial as-pects of our companies and not offended by my bluntness at all."

Edward looked appalled at the very thought of dis-cussing trade. He opened and closed his mouth quite a few times before he managed to get a sentence out.

"As I said, this is neither the time nor the place for this discussion."

Peregrine bowed elaborately. "As you wish, Edward. I am on my way out to see Mr. Carstairs at the White

Hart. Do you have anything in particular you wish me to tell him?"

"Why are you visiting Mr. Carstairs?" Edward demanded.

"I wish to make sure he remains in good health and doesn't bolt back to Yorkshire." Peregrine smiled. "He isn't very happy about this whole situation."

"One can see why," Robert murmured, and both Benson brothers turned toward him. "I've noticed that men who practice the law are generally rather finicky when due process isn't carried out to their satisfaction."

Peregrine strolled over to kiss Lucy's hand. "A pleasure to see you as always, Lady Kurland."

"Indeed." Lucy withdrew her fingers from his rather determined clasp.

The door opened, and Lady Benson came in flanked by her older son, Arden, and Dr. Mantel. She stiffened, pressed her hand to her breast, and stopped moving.

"Why are you both *here*? What has happened now?"

For a startled moment Lucy wondered if Lady Benson was talking to her and Robert, but she realized her hostess's fearful gaze was fixed on the brothers.

Peregrine walked over and stared down at his stepmother, the naked insolence in his eyes plain to see. "Good morning, Miranda." He leaned in closer. "Still no tears for the man who gave you everything?"

"Go away," Miranda snapped. "You horrible little man."

Peregrine blew her a kiss and pushed past her, deliberately knocking Dr. Mantel to one side.

"Oh, I say," the doctor murmured as he straightened his cravat. "There really is no need for such bad behavior."

Edward bowed to his stepmother and then to Lucy and Robert. "I fear I must be going as well. I have some letters to write."

He slipped out of the room leaving Lady Benson glaring at his back. It was the most animated Lucy had ever seen her, but within seconds the anger was gone, replaced by

the wide-eyed helpless look of a doe Lucy was more familiar with.

"I am so sorry, Lady Kurland," Miranda breathed. "As
you can see, my stepsons treat me *abominably*."

She sat on the couch and Arden took the seat behind
her. "It is so kind of you to call to inquire as to my well-
being. No one else in this house apart from Dr. Mantel
gives a fig for my health or grief. My stepsons do not care
about me at all and wish me to the devil."

Lucy smiled sympathetically. "It must be a very trying
time for you, what with the missing will and a funeral to
arrange."

"My dear Lady Kurland," Lady Benson whined, "you
have no *idea* . . ."

Robert admired his wife's fortitude as she nodded along
with Lady Benson's litany of complaints, slights, and concerns. Eventually, he glanced up as the tea tray was delivered along with some decanters for the men and excused
himself. He doubted Lady Benson even noticed he had
gone. He followed the butler out into the hall and called
out to him.

"Is Mr. Tompkins here today?"

"I believe so, sir. I haven't seen him myself this morning,
as he is busy packing up Sir William's belongings. Would
you like me to send for him?"

"I'm more than happy to go up to Sir William's room
and speak to Mr. Tompkins myself." Robert tapped his leg
with his cane. "I need as much exercise as I can, and I
don't wish to cause any trouble."

He headed for the staircase toward the center of the
house. "I won't be a minute."

"As you wish, sir." The butler continued through the
door and into the servants' area of the house.

Robert went up the stairs, pausing every so often to
gauge who was up and about on the floor above. In their

rented house the master bedroom was on the same floor as the drawing room, but in the Bensons', two separate bedrooms and a dressing room took up most of the second floor. He already knew Augustus had returned to his parish, Peregrine had gone out, and Edward and Arden were downstairs with the ladies. Foley had told him that Sir William's room was on the left, there was a dressing room in the center, and Lady Benson occupied the room on the right. He knocked cautiously on the left door, but there was no answer.

He eased down on the latch and peered inside, noticing the room was in complete disorder with clothes, trunks, wigs, and nether garments strewn everywhere. He frowned. Knowing Foley's love of neatness he reckoned that if Mr. Tompkins had left everything in such a state Foley would have mentioned it. Foley had also indicated that Mr. Tompkins was almost ready to leave.

Stepping more fully into the room Robert closed the door behind him and stood still. Not a single surface was clear and clothing was tossed all over the floor. Drawers and cupboards hung open as if a blizzard had passed through. Robert paused to pick up two books that hindered his path and placed them on the bed.

He stiffened as a curse came from the dressing room to his right. Robert carefully stepped through the debris, his cane at the ready, and opened that door to discover Brandon tipping the contents of a small leather case out onto the floor.

"What in God's name are you doing?" Robert demanded just as Brandon launched the case at his head. He managed to dodge the missile, but by then Brandon had clattered down the servants' stairs. Robert found the bellpull and rang it hard as he surveyed the damage around him. Brandon had obviously decided to instigate his own search for the will. . . .

But where was Mr. Tompkins? Had he already left, taking the vital will with him?

Robert turned a slow circle, his instincts and memories at war with the domestic scene around him. Something wasn't right; he could almost taste it.

The butler came into the room, his eyes widening in shock as he saw the chaos. "Sir Robert! What happened?"

Robert held up his hand. "Is Mr. Tompkins in the kitchen?"

"No, sir. No one has seen him since breakfast."

Robert's gaze was drawn to the wall of oak cupboards against the wall between the two connecting doors. He moved closer, his nose wrinkling even as his eyes saw nothing wrong. A trickle of brown matter on the carpet drew his attention. He swallowed hard, braced himself, and opened the largest of the cupboards, which ran the whole height of the wall.

"Oh, my God . . ." Behind him the butler recoiled in horror. "That's Mr. Tompkins! He's hanged himself."

Robert spoke without turning around. "Please go and fetch Mr. Edward Benson, and don't mention what you have just seen to anyone. Do you understand me?"

"Yes, sir. Of course, sir."

After a deep breath, Robert forced himself to get closer to the old man whose body hung like a sack of corn from the loop of the cravat tied around his neck and strung over the rail. The bulging eyes and purplish tone of his flesh were horrifying. He did not look as if he had gone willingly to his death. . . .

Robert wished Patrick Fletcher were with him, because he was certain his friend would be able to decipher the clues in a scientific way that aligned with Robert's instinct that Mr. Tompkins had not killed himself, but had most definitely been murdered.

Chapter 12

Edward Benson came back into the study where he'd left Robert drinking a restorative brandy.

"It appears that Brandon has disappeared. I've sent our servants out to look for him and insisted that Arden stays here."

"Good thinking."

Robert finished his brandy. It was barely midday. Since the Bensons had entered his life his drinking had increased substantially. When Lady Benson had swooned, Lucy and the maid had assisted Dr. Mantel in taking her back to her bedchamber—with the door into the dressing room securely locked so she couldn't accidentally venture in there and have another screaming fit.

Edward helped himself to a large glass of brandy. He looked rather pale, which wasn't surprising considering what was going on in his household as he sat opposite Robert.

"I hate to ask you this, Sir Robert, but what was Brandon actually doing when you surprised him in the dressing room?"

"He was emptying out a box of his stepfather's possessions. When he saw me he threw the box at my head."

"Dear God," Edward exhaled. "I was in Father's bedchamber yesterday speaking to Mr. Tompkins. The room was spotless, and everything was stored away."

"That's what my butler, Foley, told me when he came to help Mr. Tompkins finish the packing," Robert replied. "I have to suspect that Brandon decided to go through everything he could get his hands on and didn't care about the mess he was making."

"That boy has been no end of trouble," Edward groaned. "He's been expelled twice from school and has the most violent temper imaginable."

"Do you think he took his temper out on Mr. Tompkins?" Robert asked.

"God knows. It's possible." Edward shoved a hand through his thinning hair. "Mr. Tompkins was an old man, but he would've defended my father's possessions from anyone."

"Do you think Mr. Tompkins was the kind of man to kill himself?"

"No. He was devastated by my father's death but was determined to do the right thing and bring him home to be buried in Yorkshire soil." Edward grimaced. "And now we will be burying both of them."

"Then if you think Brandon might have had a hand in Mr. Tompkins's death what do you intend to do about it?" Robert inquired.

"I think it is too late to try to pretend that Brandon isn't dangerous. If we can't locate him ourselves I intend to contact the authorities to see if they can find him. It's probably pointless to attempt to keep this within the family. There is nothing missing from Brandon's room, and he ran off without his hat and coat. At some point unless he has a considerable amount of money in his pocket, which I doubt—he will have to come back here and face us."

"I agree." Robert placed his glass on the silver tray. "Would you object if I spoke to Arden before I leave?"

Edward frowned. "May I ask why?"

"I was a cavalry officer during the war and often dealt

with junior officers and enlisted men with very little sense and a lot of overconfidence. I suspect that the key to finding Brandon is his brother."

"Then have at it. Arden will never speak to me."

Robert stood up. "I think Arden might be redeemable. A stint in a decent regiment would knock him into shape fairly quickly and give him a defined purpose in his life."

"If we ever *find* the blasted will then I will certainly consider your suggestion, although my feelings toward him and his brother are currently not very complimentary." Edward rose and bowed as Robert went toward the door.

"There is one more thing." Robert paused. "Would you object to my physician, Dr. Fletcher, seeing Mr. Tompkins's body?"

"Dr. Mantel is supervising the laying out of the body in Mr. Tompkins's bedroom on the top floor. We will need another coffin to transport him back to Yorkshire along with Sir William. Perhaps you might ask the good doctor?"

"Thank you, I will." Robert opened the door. "Now, where will I find young Arden?"

Robert followed the directions up the stairs to the next floor and discovered one of the footmen sitting outside a locked door.

"Mr. Benson said I might speak to Arden. You can lock the door behind me, and I'll knock when I'm ready to leave."

"Yes, sir." The footman unlocked the door and Robert stepped inside the room where Arden was sitting on the side of his bed. He leapt to his feet when he saw Robert and scowled.

"What's going on? Where's Brandon?"

Robert took a seat beside the fireplace. "Don't you know?"

"I heard some cock and bull story about him wrecking the old man's room and running off, but why I've been locked in here when I should be the one going after him is beyond me."

Robert remained silent until Arden stopped pacing and glared at him.

"What?"

"I went to find Mr. Tompkins but instead discovered your brother rifling through your stepfather's possessions. When he saw me he ran away. Why do you think he might have done that?"

"Run away?" Arden shrugged. "Because that's just how he is. Whenever he's caught kicking up a lark he attempts to escape the consequences."

"*Kicking up a lark?*" Robert asked. "Destroying someone's property is not amusing."

"It is if you're Brandon and you hated your stepfather." Arden kicked the corner of the bed. "If you let me out, I'll find him. I know all his favorite haunts."

"I believe Mr. Benson is planning on setting the authorities on him."

"Why would he do that?" Arden demanded. "Did Brandon *steal* anything, or just give you a bloody good fright?"

"Did you know that Brandon intended to search for the will?"

Arden blinked at him. "What?"

"The missing will," Robert repeated patiently. "What else would he have been looking for?"

"I have no idea." Arden tried to look unconcerned. "Probably money or something to pawn to pay his debts."

"He didn't tell you anything? That seems unlikely when you are so close." Robert eased back in his chair. "In fact, I don't believe you."

Arden's expression clouded over. "I don't care what you think of me, Sir Robert. You have no say in this family, and your opinion counts for nothing."

"It might if you aspired to get into a particular regiment. I have some influence in that sphere that might benefit you."

"If I tell tales on my brother," Arden objected. "What kind of honorable man would do that?"

"A man who feared that his brother had perhaps crossed a line?" Robert suggested.

Arden came to stand right over Robert. "What exactly are you trying to say? Did Brandon . . . *hurt* someone?"

"Why would you think that?"

"Because—what has happened—tell me!" Arden shouted.

"Mr. Tompkins is dead," Robert said. "I found his body in the dressing room just after your brother tried to brain me with a leather box."

Arden sank into the chair, his head bowed, his hands twisted together in front of him. Robert didn't say anything and waited for the young man to look up at him again.

"You think Brandon killed Mr. Tompkins," Arden croaked.

"It's possible," Robert agreed. "The fact that he ran away isn't helping his case." He paused. "If you can tell me where to find him then at least he can be brought here to explain himself rather than being incarcerated in the town gaol and formally charged."

Robert tensed as Arden shot to his feet, went over to his desk, and furiously started writing. He rose to as Arden approached him with a piece of paper.

"Take this."

Robert raised an eyebrow.

"It's a list of all his favorite places to go."

"Thank you." Robert took the paper. "I will endeavor to find him and bring him home to you."

"If I came with you we would find him much more quickly."

"Alas, you will have to remain here. The thought of finding your brother and then the two of you conspiring against me and running off together doesn't sit well with me." Robert folded the note and put it in his pocket. "I will make sure that you are told when Brandon returns."

He'd reached the door before Arden spoke again.

"Sir Robert?"

"Yes?"

"Is Mr. Tompkins truly dead?"

"Unfortunately, yes. He was hanging in the closet."

Arden paled and swallowed hard. "He was always nice to me."

"He was a nice man, and a loyal employee of Sir William." Robert inclined his head. "Good-bye, Arden."

He knocked on the door and was allowed out. After thanking the footman he made his way down to the drawing room and found Lucy awaiting him. She looked rather tired, but he suspected that anyone who had to deal with Lady Benson's hysterics would look the same way.

"Are you all right?" Robert asked as she turned around and spotted him.

"Dr. Mantel finally persuaded Lady Benson to take a sleeping draught, and I was able to leave." She sighed as he took her hand in his. "She really is the most exhausting woman I have ever met."

"I wouldn't argue with that." Robert lowered his voice even though they were alone. "Let's go home where we can talk freely."

Lucy realized she hadn't eaten anything all day and hastened to send an order down to the kitchens to bring up something for her and Robert to sustain themselves with before dinner. She took a few moments to take off her bonnet, smooth her hair, and wash her face before returning to the dining room. Robert hadn't yet come back from breaking the bad news to Foley, so she was alone with her thoughts.

Robert had given her a few details about what had occurred between him and Arden. She only knew that Mr. Tompkins was dead, and was eager to hear the whole story. Unfortunately, the notion that Brandon had killed the valet in a rage was not only possible but all too likely. And if Brandon had murdered Mr. Tompkins, was it also likely that he'd murdered his stepfather as well?

Anna came in and stood by the fire warming her hands. She wore a plain high-necked gown, and her hair was pinned up in a severe fashion unlike her normal soft ringlets. She turned to Lucy and frowned.

"Where have you *been* all day, Lucy? Despite my attempts to apologize, Penelope won't speak to me and has refused to leave her room. Foley didn't know when you would be back, and I wanted to speak to you most *urgently.*"

"I was detained at the Bensons'." Lucy didn't sit down. "There was a—"

"I don't know why you bother with Lady Benson. She is an incredibly selfish woman." Anna talked over Lucy, which was most unlike her. "Her *problems* are mainly of her own making."

"And yours are not?" Lucy fought off her weariness. "What do you wish to speak to me about, Anna?"

"Captain Akers, of course. Last night he asked me to marry him again, and I turned him down."

"Oh."

"Is that all you have to say?" Anna demanded.

"What would you like me to say?" Lucy met her sister's gaze. "We have discussed this at length. The only thing that can change is you, Anna. If Captain Akers cannot persuade you to change your mind, then maybe he is not the right person for you after all."

"But I care for him very deeply," Anna whispered.

"So you said before."

Anna drew herself up. "I can see that you are not interested in discussing this properly with me, Lucy. I hoped you would *listen* to me, and—"

"I *have* listened to you, and I fully intend to support whatever decision you wish to make," Lucy said wearily. "What more do you *want*?"

"Some compassion? Some *understanding*?" Anna tossed her head. "But perhaps I should've realized you are incapable of those things."

Lucy briefly closed her eyes and held on to the back of the chair as a wave of dizziness overcame her. "Forgive me. I am rather tired. I—"

"Lucy!"

She blinked hard and managed to fumble her way around and sit before she fell down. Anna knelt in front of her and took her hands, her blue eyes filling with tears.

"I'm so sorry, I didn't mean to upset you and I should never had said such *awful* things." Anna dabbed at the tears now coursing down her cheeks. "I am turning into a *horrible* person."

Lucy offered Anna her handkerchief. "It's all right. It's just been a rather trying morning."

"Shall I fetch Robert for you?"

"No!" Lucy squeezed Anna's fingers hard. "Please don't bother him. I haven't eaten since breakfast and I'm simply hungry. As soon as I eat something I'll feel much better." She took a deep breath and managed a wobbly smile. "Can we talk later? I fear I will not be much help at the moment."

"Of course." Anna helped her up and held on to her elbow until she seemed satisfied that Lucy wasn't going to crumple into a heap. "Foley said there is food in the dining room so perhaps I'll walk you there, and you can tell me what on earth has been going on at the Bensons'."

"I fear I was rather short with Anna earlier," Lucy confessed as she sat with Robert in the dining room after her sister had gone.

"You were?" Robert raised an eyebrow. "What did she do?"

"She accused me of not supporting her." Lucy sighed. "I told her that we would accept any decision she made regarding Captain Akers. That still wasn't good enough to satisfy her."

"Your sister is rather out of sorts," Robert said tentatively.

"Yes, and I *know* I can be quite opinionated, but—"

He reached for her hand across the table. "In this instance I believe she is in the wrong, and you have been all that is reasonable. We can't force her to marry the man, and that's the end of it."

"I have to agree with you."

"Well, that is good to know." He smiled at her. "After hours of Lady Benson wailing at you I'm surprised you had any patience left for your sister at all."

Lucy made a face. "Lady Benson *is* rather trying. I don't know how Dr. Mantel puts up with her."

"She probably pays him well, or at least Sir William did." Robert hesitated. "I asked Edward Benson if Dr. Fletcher could look at Mr. Tompkins's body, and he said to ask Dr. Mantel. Do you think he would object?"

"Dr. Mantel has a very high opinion of Dr. Fletcher, so I don't see him demurring," Lucy said. "Why do you want our doctor to look at the body?"

"As an ex-military surgeon, Patrick is very good at determining the causes of violent deaths."

"How exactly *did* Mr. Tompkins die?"

Robert grimaced. "He was hanging from the railing in one of the closets."

Lucy shuddered. "Is it possible that he killed himself?"

"It's possible, but according to Edward Benson the old man was intent on bringing his master's body back to Yorkshire and taking care of his effects until there was nothing else he could do for him. He didn't look like the type of man to fall into a pit of despair to me."

"I'd agree. He seemed to be very strong-willed and stubborn."

"As are most men from Yorkshire," Robert added. "My cousin Oliver amongst them."

Lucy fiddled with her teaspoon. "Does Edward think *Brandon* killed Mr. Tompkins?"

"I assume he does, seeing as he told me that if he couldn't find Brandon by tonight he would be notifying the town authorities and asking them to apprehend the lad and take him to gaol."

"Do *you* think Brandon killed Mr. Tompkins?"

"Well, he certainly was in the right place at the right time." Robert frowned. "But as I didn't catch him in the act I can't say for certain."

"Brandon is known to be violent. He has a terrible temper and has been expelled from school," Lucy pointed out. "He might even have killed Sir William as well."

"What makes you think that?"

"Well, it stands to reason, doesn't it?" Lucy asked. "Mr. Tompkins probably knew more than he was letting on, and maybe he tried to confront Brandon and Brandon turned on him?"

"I suppose that is possible," Robert said slowly. "The sooner we can locate the young fool, the quicker the truth will out."

Chapter 13

"He suffocated." Dr. Fletcher drew the cover down to Mr. Tompkins's waist and pointed at his neck. "The cravat tightened around his neck leaving those vivid bruises until he couldn't draw breath into his lungs. It probably took a while because it wasn't done on a professional scaffold or by a skilled hangman."

Robert nodded. As military men both he and Patrick had attended their fair share of hangings, him in his capacity as an officer, and the doctor to lay out the corpse and make sure the man was really dead.

"Could Mr. Tompkins have done this to himself?"

"Yes, but look at his arms and torso." Patrick directed Robert's attention to the valet's sturdy body. "There is a considerable amount of bruising around his wrists, and his hands are badly scraped up, which indicates that whatever was happening to him he wasn't cooperating. I think he was attempting to fight someone off."

"Someone who eventually overcame him," Robert murmured. He'd never been comfortable around the dead. They brought back too many memories of battles fought long ago and the injuries that had almost ended his life at Waterloo.

"There's one more thing." Patrick cupped the back of

Mr. Tompkins's skull. "There's some damage or swelling here as well, which suggests he got a thump on the back of his head to keep him quiet while his murderer strung him up."

"Thank you for the vivid details." Robert shuddered. "I don't suppose you can hazard a guess as to how long ago he died, can you?"

"Not with any great accuracy. Was he stiff when you cut him down?"

"No, he wasn't." Robert paused. "Does it matter?"

"Well, you said Brandon was in the room minutes before you found the body. If he'd been the one doing the killing, the body wouldn't have been stiff because rigor mortis takes a while to set in."

Patrick's extensive knowledge about the processes of death had been acquired on the battlefields of the war with Napoleon and was unparalleled in Robert's experience. His casual acceptance of the many horrors of death never ceased to simultaneously impress and appall Robert.

"Have they found him yet?" Patrick asked as he drew the sheet over the dead man's head.

"Brandon? No. I went out to look for him yesterday afternoon myself, but I couldn't find him." Robert hesitated. "If you can spare me some time this evening, I thought I might go out and search for him again."

"Bath is a large town, Sir Robert."

"I know, but I have the advantage of a list of his favorite haunts supplied to me by his brother."

"How did you get that?" Patrick asked. "Both of them seemed equally obnoxious to me, so I'm surprised the older one offered his help."

"I believe Arden has aspirations to join the military."

"Ah. And you have the connections." Patrick nodded. "It makes sense. Of course I'll come out with you."

"If your wife is agreeable, of course," Robert added hastily.

Patrick made a face. "My wife is not very happy with me as she can no longer touch her toes, sleep comfortably in her bed, or fit into any of her favorite dresses. I suspect she would be quite delighted to see the back of me for a few hours."

"Do you think you might take her home with you when you leave this time?" Robert asked nonchalantly.

He was rewarded by a knowing grin. "Is she driving you mad?"

"I would never say that, but—"

"It's all right." Patrick washed his hands. "I know she can be a little trying sometimes." He turned back to Robert. "The thing is . . . I'm concerned about how close she is to giving birth."

"I thought she had another month or two to go."

"So did I, but I think we might have miscalculated." He grimaced. "I would hate to get halfway home and then have to stop in some godforsaken inn where she'd have to give birth in a bed of straw."

Robert tried to imagine Penelope's fury if that happened, but attempted to reply diplomatically. "No woman would want that."

He was already wondering how he would break the news to Lucy that not only was Penelope staying, but that she might give birth at any moment. . . .

"Ah, good morning, gentlemen."

Robert turned as Dr. Mantel came into the room and bowed to them. The doctor wore his usual modest brown coat, breeches, and scuffed boots that in Robert's opinion needed a good polishing.

"Thank you for allowing me to view the body, Dr. Mantel." Patrick shook the doctor's hand. "It was quite instructional."

"You are most welcome." Dr. Mantel nodded. "It is always a sad day when a man takes his own life, and somewhat horrifying to view the damage he has wrought upon himself."

Robert and Patrick exchanged a quick surprised glance.

"You believe he killed himself?" Patrick asked slowly.

"He hung himself using his own cravat in a cupboard."
Dr. Mantel frowned. "He was distraught because of the
loss of his master and worried about his future employment. One cannot condone such actions, but one can certainly sympathize with the poor soul."

"Did no one mention to you that Brandon was discovered in the dressing room and that he fled when I discovered him?" Robert asked.

"Well yes, I heard he was *there,* but the poor boy could
hardly have known . . ." It was Dr. Mantel's turn to stare
at the two men. "Are you suggesting that *Brandon* had
something to do with this?"

The shock on the doctor's face was evident. Robert nodded to Patrick, who took up the conversation.

"From my examination it seems that as well as the
bruising around the neck there are other injuries to the
body." Patrick pulled back the sheet again and Dr. Mantel
flinched. "There is enough evidence of a struggle to suggest that someone manhandled Mr. Tompkins into that
cupboard, knocked him half-unconscious, and then strung
him up with his own cravat."

Dr. Mantel's mouth hung open. "Oh, dear God," he
said faintly. "What the devil am I going to tell Lady Miranda?"

"There's no need to say anything to her at this point,"
Robert intervened quickly.

"But if her son is implicated in a murder . . ." Dr. Mantel sank into the nearest chair and looked up at Robert.
"She will be *inconsolable.*"

"Your concern for her well-being is admirable, Doctor,"
Robert said. "I would suggest that knowing the strain she
is under right now, *not* telling her anything would be the
right thing to do."

Dr. Mantel nodded fervently. "Perhaps you are right."

"Does Lady Benson know anything about Brandon's
presence in the dressing room?" Robert asked.

"I don't believe so, otherwise she would be in a state of

panic that would concern me deeply. She is a *delicate* soul, Sir Robert, and has suffered greatly from the unpleasantness of the Benson sons."

"Do you think she has noticed Brandon has not returned home yet?"

"He isn't the most dutiful of boys and wouldn't necessarily seek her out on a daily basis," Dr. Mantel said. "She did ask me whether Arden was home, and to my shame I told her a slight fib that he was indisposed and not able to come to her side."

"I think you did the right thing, Doctor." Robert nodded. "If Brandon comes back tonight and explains himself, then she will be able to remain in blissful ignorance."

Dr. Mantel stood. "Then let's hope that the boy returns. I suspect he ran away because he encountered you, Sir Robert, and you scared him silly."

"I do have that effect on people sometimes," Robert admitted. "Perhaps his attempt to knock me out was merely a playful gesture on his part."

"One cannot doubt it." Dr. Mantel's smile returned, and he turned to the door. "The undertaker is coming this afternoon to measure for the coffin. I must ask one of the maids to make sure that Mr. Tompkins is dressed in his finest garb before he is sent back to Yorkshire and his final resting place."

The doctor left, and Robert and Patrick regarded each other.

"Do you want me to report my findings to Mr. Edward Benson or not?" Patrick asked bluntly.

"Perhaps we should find young Brandon first, and see what he has to say for himself."

Patrick frowned. "I would prefer Mr. Benson to see the physical evidence on the body for himself."

"Mr. Benson is already predisposed to believe that Brandon is a murderer. If you write out a statement, and I witness it, I think that will be enough to convince him."

Robert glanced over at the body. "And this poor man deserves to be shut away from the madness."

Patrick nodded. "I forget that you don't like dead bodies."

"I've seen far too many of them," Robert murmured. "And they continue to haunt and follow me to this day."

"Yes, you and Lady Kurland do seem to uncover more than your fair share of fatalities." Patrick put on his coat. "Now I must go and write that letter for you and speak to my wife."

"Of course you must go and search for Brandon." Lucy looked up from her darning at Robert. "I will enjoy a quiet evening with Anna and Penelope while you and Dr. Fletcher are out."

"Thank you." Robert took the seat beside her. "There is one more thing."

"Yes?"

"It's about Penelope."

Lucy put down her work and gave him her full attention. "What about her?"

Robert met her inquiring gaze full on, thinking he might as well get it over with.

"Dr. Fletcher says she is further along in the pregnancy than he realized, and he cannot risk transporting her back to Kurland St. Mary at this point."

She stared at him for a very long time. "Oh, no."

"He is worried that she might not make it home without going into labor."

She let out her breath. "Then she will have to stay here."

Robert took her hand. "I'm sorry."

"It's hardly your fault if our doctor can't work out when his own *child* will be born, is it? Penelope might be something of a burden, but I would not wish her to suffer on my account."

Robert kissed her fingers. "You are remarkably tolerant, my love."

"That's because I have no choice. Does Dr. Fletcher intend to stay here until the baby is born, then?"

"I believe so."

"Then he can take good care of Penelope." Lucy nodded. "He can eat with her, walk with her, and accompany her on *all* her excursions."

"I'll tell him," Robert agreed. "I will make sure that he remains constantly at her side." He stood and bowed. "Well, I must be off. Wish me luck."

"Do be careful, won't you?" Lucy looked up at him, her gaze worried.

"I'll do my best, and I'll have Patrick with me at all times."

"I'll try and wait up for you."

He paused at the door. "How about we agree that I'll wake you up if something interesting has happened?"

"As you wish." She stifled a yawn behind her hand. "I must confess that all this walking around Bath does wear me out somewhat."

Robert went down into the hall where he found Patrick putting on his hat and glancing nervously up the stairs. He had the look of a man who had just faced down an enemy and was now in full retreat.

Glimpsing Penelope appearing on the landing, Robert headed for the front door where Foley awaited him. "Come on, my friend." He accepted his hat and gloves, tucked his cane under his arm, and went down the steps.

It wasn't quite dark out in the square but the lamplighters were already at work. Patrick came down the stone steps behind him and let out his breath.

"Thank goodness she can't move very fast at the moment."

Robert concealed a smile.

"She's developed this distressing habit of bursting into tears every time I say a word. I'm not sure what to do about it," Patrick confided.

"Stay mum?" Robert suggested.

"I've tried that and then she accuses me of not caring enough for her to bother to speak." Patrick sighed. "I almost wish the old Penelope was back—the one who criticized me and stood up to me at the slightest provocation."

"Don't we all," Robert said dryly. "You're supposed to be a doctor. Aren't you *used* to dealing with women with child?"

"Yes, but none of them are my wife." Patrick pulled on his gloves. "Now, where are we going to start looking for this young fool?"

"Not in the well-lit parts of town, I can assure you." Robert had already checked all the locations Arden had given him on the previous outing and had a fair idea of the route to take. "We're visiting the dilapidated inns, the whorehouses, and the gaming parlors."

Patrick patted his coat pocket. "Then it's a good thing I brought my pistol and my favorite knife."

As the evening wore on, Robert began to hate the stench of unwashed bodies, drunkenness, and despair emanating from those who frequented the lower levels of society. He'd almost had his pocket picked twice and had fended off more than one over-perfumed woman offering him her services.

They extricated themselves from yet another bawdy house and moved on down the narrow unpaved street with a clogged gutter running down the center of the cobblestones.

"Where next?" Patrick asked. He looked far less perturbed than Robert, being more used to working amongst the extremes of humanity.

"The inn on the corner." Robert pointed out the old stone building with its thatched roof and sagging doorways. "If you can call it that." Lights flickered through the shutters and a waft of ale and sweat curled around them at the entrance.

Patrick went first, and Robert followed him, ducking his head to avoid the low-hanging beams. No one looked up as they entered, which gave Robert precious seconds to look around the room. All eyes were turned to a dice game taking place at one of the crowded tables.

A roar was followed by a groan as one of the barmaids distributed tankards of ale to her customers and coins were thrown toward the dealer and dice thrower.

"There," Robert mouthed in Patrick's ear. "At the table to the right of the dealer."

"I see him."

Brandon was intent on the game and seemed unaware that he was being observed. His fumbling motions as he attempted to drink his ale made Robert suspect he was a trifle disguised.

"Let's get as close as we can on either side of him without him noticing," Robert continued. "And the second he moves, we'll take him."

"Agreed."

As Brandon was unlikely to recognize Patrick he took the longer route around the room, crossing directly in front of Brandon's gaze, but the boy gave no sign that he noticed anything. Robert went more slowly and found a position against the wall directly behind Brandon as if he was observing the game.

When the barmaid went past, he bought a pint of ale and sipped it as he watched the progression of the game. If Brandon kept drinking he'd need to piss soon, and that would offer them another opportunity to catch him.

Eventually, Brandon lurched unsteadily to his feet and attempted to climb over the bench he was sitting on. It took him a while to untangle his legs, and then he staggered off toward the rear of the inn, Robert and Patrick in pursuit. Before Robert could call out to him, two large men pushed past him and went straight toward Brandon, who was now pissing against the wall of the stables.

"Oi!"

Brandon didn't look up, and the men closed in around him. "You owe us money."

"I don't have any," Brandon snarled as he fastened his trousers.

The larger of the two men grabbed him by the throat. "Then why was you gambling, toff?"

"Take your hands off me!"

The man laughed. "Give me my money, and I'll do whatever you want, your lordship. That's half a crown you owe me, and two shillings to my friend here."

Brandon attempted to get out of the man's grasp and ended up being slapped around the face.

"Quieten down, little man. If you ain't got the coin, maybe you've got a nice pocket watch or tiepin that will do instead?"

"I don't have anything, you bacon-brained idiots!"

Another slap. Robert winced and cleared his throat.

"Gentlemen, may I make a suggestion?"

All three men turned to stare at him. Brandon's nose was now bleeding. Patrick stepped up beside Robert, his pistol already cocked.

"How about I pay this young man's debt to you, and in exchange you let me take him into my custody?"

"You the law?"

"Unfortunately not, but I am a connection of this man's stepfather. I feel it is my duty to restore him to the bosom of his family."

"I don't want to go home," Brandon slurred. "Everyone hates me there."

"We can discuss that on the way back," Robert said firmly. He took two half sovereigns out of his pocket. "Gentlemen? Do we have a deal?"

Within a few moments, both men grabbed the tossed coins and disappeared back into the inn. Patrick seized hold of Brandon just before he toppled over, and jerked his head in the direction of the stables.

"Let's leave through the courtyard so our new friends don't get any ideas about robbing us as we pass through the inn."

"Agreed." Robert took Brandon's other arm and nodded. "Let's go."

As they walked back toward the more civilized parts of the town, Robert considered what to do next. In truth, he was obliged to deliver Brandon back to the Bensons, but for some reason his instincts were telling him not to.

"Do you think we could get him into our town house without the Bensons noticing?" Robert asked Patrick.

"If we came up through the mews at the back of the garden, I don't see why not." Patrick paused. "Why do you want to do that?"

"I'd like to ask him a few questions before the Bensons get to him."

"While he's drunk and loquacious?"

"Exactly."

Patrick heaved a sagging Brandon back onto his feet. "Then let's see if we can get him back there before he either pukes on my boots or passes out."

Foley opened the back door and frowned at Robert.

"What on earth are you doing, Sir Robert? The servants' entrance is not a fitting way for a baronet to enter his own house."

"Needs must, Foley." Robert nodded at his disapproving butler as he and Patrick came inside with Brandon slung between them. "I'll need to borrow the butler's pantry for an hour or so."

"As you wish, sir." Foley wrinkled his nose as he held open a door off the main corridor that eventually led to the kitchen. "I assume you don't wish me to alert Lady Kurland as to your presence?"

"You assume correctly," Robert spoke over his shoulder. "I would, however, appreciate some coffee and brandy for myself and Dr. Fletcher."

"As you wish, sir." Foley closed the door and went off muttering so loudly Robert could hear him through the wooden panels.

Patrick lowered Brandon into one of the chairs, pulled up another for himself, and placed it right beside the drunken boy. He gently shook him.

"Brandon? Wake up. Sir Robert wishes to speak to you." Patrick glanced up at Robert. "You might ask Foley for a bucket in case this young fool decides to cast up his accounts."

"Good idea."

Robert waited until Foley came in with the requested beverages and had provided them with a bucket before settling himself opposite Brandon.

"Your family is very worried about you."

"Bloody hell, not you again." Brandon opened one eye. "Why do you keep turning up when you're not wanted?"

"It's a talent of mine." Robert paused. "Why were you in Sir William's bedchamber?"

"I don't have to answer your questions," Brandon growled. "You have no authority over me."

"That's true, but I was very fond of your stepfather, and I consider it my duty to preserve his memory."

"What the devil does that mean?"

Robert set a cup of coffee at Brandon's elbow. "Why were you going through his possessions?"

"None of your flaming business!" Brandon suddenly sat forward, his fists clenched and his gaze fiery. Beside him Patrick tensed.

Robert regarded Brandon until the boy began to squirm in his seat. "Hurling insults at me will hardly result in us accomplishing anything, will it? You might not believe it, but I am trying to help you." When Brandon said nothing, Robert continued speaking. "I assume you were attempting to steal money to pay your gambling debts?"

"Why would you think that?"

Robert raised an eyebrow. "Because I had the opportunity to view your attempts to gamble, and you have neither the ability nor the finances for it."

"That's got nothing to do with you."

"Then you weren't looking for money." Robert contemplated the sullen boy. "Were you looking for something in particular?"

Brandon's eyes flickered and Robert pressed on.

"Was I the only person you encountered in that dressing room trying to stop you stealing your stepfather's possessions?"

"I wasn't *stealing*—I was—*looking* for something!" Brandon shouted, and shot to his feet. Patrick joined him, one hand on the boy's shoulder preventing him from leaping at Robert.

"For the will?"

"No! Dammit! You don't understand!" Brandon said. "Sir William kept a lot of things from me and Arden— things that rightfully belonged to us from our father! I was trying to get what belonged to us!"

"Such as?" Robert asked.

"None of your bloody business."

"Strange that Arden didn't mention any of this when I spoke to him last," Robert mused.

"Arden?" Brandon sat back in his chair. "What are you lying about now?"

"It's no lie." Robert held the boy's indignant gaze. "How do you think I knew where to find you?" He took out the list and showed it to Brandon. "This is your brother's handwriting, isn't it?"

"Give that to me!" Brandon attempted to snatch the list out of Robert's hand, but Patrick slammed him back in the chair and held him there by his shoulders.

"Your brother is very worried about you," Robert said. "That's why he offered to help me find you."

"Why didn't he come himself?" Brandon asked. "Is he locked up as well?"

"You are hardly locked up." Robert glanced around the room. "When we have finished our conversation, you are free to leave and take your chances with the local magistrate."

"Edward would never allow me to be taken up like a common criminal," Brandon scoffed. "He's too much of a coward and is terrified of damaging the family name."

"You're wrong there." Robert paused. "If you don't return by midnight tonight, Mr. Benson intends to allow the authorities to put you in gaol."

"For what?" Brandon had the gall to laugh. "Throwing a box at your head? They'd let me out in a second!"

"One has to assume that you haven't spoken to anyone from your family since you ran away from me?" Robert asked.

"Of course I haven't." Brandon frowned. "Why?"

Robert looked at Patrick, who nodded at him.

"Because there has been a death in the house."

"Good Lord, did Edward have heart failure because of me?" Brandon's smile was full of vindictive spite. "What an excellent lark."

"No, it wasn't Edward." Robert watched Brandon's face very closely. "It was Mr. Tompkins."

"Old Tompkins?" Brandon blinked. "That's why the old man wasn't there when I went into Sir William's bedroom."

"Oh, he was there," Robert said, suddenly tired of the unpleasant individual he was dealing with. "I'm surprised you didn't come across him in your very thorough search."

Brandon smiled. "Where was the old chap, then? Hiding under the bed?"

"I think you know damn well where he was." It was Robert's turn to raise his voice and use a tone he'd perfected as an officer in the cavalry. Brandon shrank back into his chair. "Seeing as you probably murdered him and put him there."

Brandon opened his mouth and then closed it again, the color draining from his face.

"I'll give you a choice," Robert said. "Run away and wait for the authorities to catch you and face murder charges, or be an honorable man, go home, and face up to the consequences of your actions."

Robert lifted his gaze to Patrick. "Perhaps you might wait with Brandon until he makes his decision. If he chooses to run, let him. If he decides to go home, make sure he gets there."

"Yes, Sir Robert." Patrick nodded. "I'll let you know what he decides."

Robert left the room very carefully, not slamming the door behind him. He was no longer a man who sought out conflict, but the sick joy on Brandon's face as he'd talked about who he hoped was dead made Robert want to throttle the boy with his bare hands.

He continued up to the drawing room where Foley had left the candles alight and paced the floor. As far as he could tell, Brandon hadn't been telling the truth about anything. He'd claimed he'd merely been taking back his own property. But what on earth could that have been? Robert paused to consider Brandon's statement. There was no one amongst the Bensons who could answer that question except Lady Miranda and Arden, and he suspected they wouldn't be very forthcoming.

What could Sir William have held on to that belonged to the boys? The only other person who would probably have known the answer was Mr. Tompkins and he was dead. Which led Robert back to his suspicion that Brandon had been found going through Sir William's things by Mr. Tompkins and that the poor valet had ended up being murdered by the young man in a fit of rage.

A light tap on the door was followed by the appearance of Patrick, who came in and bowed to Robert.

"He decided to run."

"The little fool," Robert said. "Although I can't say I'm surprised. What a thoroughly contemptible individual." He turned away from the window and sat beside the fire. "Then we need do nothing further. Let Edward Benson make the decision to ask for help from the magistrate's court in the morning, and justice will take its own path."

Patrick sat opposite him. "Do you think Brandon killed Mr. Tompkins?"

"He's big enough and has the right temperament. If he was at the baths somewhere that morning, he could easily have murdered Sir William as well. He and Arden knew Sir William had drowned before anyone else," Robert said. "I had a young officer like him in France. He enjoyed killing far too much—took pleasure in the pain and suffering of others. I eventually had to send him home after he tortured some poor prisoner to death."

Patrick shuddered. "I've seen those kinds of men as well. You can't fix them. I wonder how long it will take Brandon to fall foul of the law?"

"If he receives no help from his brother I doubt he'll last long." Robert snorted. "He couldn't even avoid amateurs like us."

"What did you think about his story of merely claiming back his own property?" Patrick asked.

"I wasn't expecting him to say that," Robert admitted. "And it does concern me, but my first thought is that he killed Mr. Tompkins in a blind rage when the old man stopped him searching."

"I could see that happening." Patrick nodded. "And Brandon was quite bruised and battered himself, wasn't he? Almost as if he'd been in a fight."

"Maybe with Mr. Tompkins." Robert scowled. "Who knows? But if Brandon *did* murder the valet, perhaps he killed the master as well."

"Did anyone see Brandon at the baths that morning?"

"No, but no one saw anything," Robert said gloomily as he shoved a hand through his hair. His leg was hurting, and he yearned to get out of his mud-splattered clothing and wash away the filth of the slums. "This business is making my head ache."

"Then perhaps you should go to bed." Patrick stood up. "Sometimes a good night's sleep will clear your thoughts."

"Indeed." Robert rose, too. "Thank you for assisting me so ably this evening."

Patrick grinned at him. "It was a pleasure. It felt just like the old times when we fought our way through the mountains of France."

Robert made sure the fire was burning down and picked up one of the candles. "Now I will take your excellent advice and make my way to bed."

Chapter 14

"You said you would wake me up if anything exciting happened."

Lucy regarded Robert balefully over the rim of her cup. It was early the next morning, and they were alone in the dining room where Robert had just finished telling her about his extraordinary encounter with Brandon.

"I tried." Robert folded his newspaper and placed it on the table. "You were snoring and refused to stir."

"And now I find out that you caught Brandon and let him go again!"

"As I explained, I didn't feel as if I had a choice. He isn't a child and he made his own decision to flee rather than face up to his accusers like a gentleman. I *hoped* he would do the right thing."

"I'll wager you are correct that Mr. Tompkins caught him going through Sir William's things and Brandon killed him."

"That's a distinct possibility."

"But what?" Lucy asked. "You don't look quite convinced to me."

He flicked a smile at her. "You know me too well." He hesitated. "This might sound odd, but we both know Brandon has a terrible temper."

"Agreed." Lucy nodded encouragingly.

"So if he'd killed Mr. Tompkins in a fight, don't you think he would've simply left the body on the floor and continued his search?"

"Rather than hanging Mr. Tompkins out of sight in the cupboard?" Lucy considered her husband's words. "I hadn't thought of that."

Robert sighed. "Maybe I'm thinking about it too much, but Brandon did look genuinely startled when I mentioned that it was Mr. Tompkins who had died."

"Arden did say that Brandon is something of a liar," Lucy reminded him. "The most likely explanation is still the most obvious one, that Brandon lost his temper, killed Mr. Tompkins, and hid his body in the cupboard."

She refilled her teacup and added plenty of milk. On Betty's recommendation, she'd attempted to eat porridge rather than toast this morning, and it had settled well in her stomach. Robert was busy eating his way through a plate of ham, eggs, and sausages with the occasional bite of toast and sip of coffee as he talked. The return of his appetite and the relaxation of the lines of pain on his face made her quietly happy.

"Then there is this other matter," Robert said. "Brandon said he was searching for something that belonged to him that Sir William had withheld. What do you think he meant by that?"

"He could have been talking about the will."

"He denied being there to search for the will." Robert paused. "Knowing Sir William it is quite possible that he kept information about the boys to himself. He was notoriously secretive."

"But what information could he have that merited Brandon killing Mr. Tompkins over it?" Lucy set down her cup.

"That's the question." Robert sat back.

"If one believes Brandon was speaking the truth," Lucy reminded him.

He frowned at her. "Good Lord, Lucy, you are being remarkably close-minded this morning."

"I am merely pointing out the obvious, which is what *you* usually do when I go on my own flights of fancy. The most likely explanation is that Brandon murdered both Mr. Tompkins and Sir William. *Why* he murdered them might indeed have more to do with the information he was trying to retrieve than his desire to stop the publication of the will, but until the will turns up we cannot be certain."

"I don't think it will take the authorities long to find Brandon and lock him up in the town gaol. He has no money, no acquaintance in town, and very little ability to blend into the background," Robert observed.

"Then perhaps we should wait to see what Edward decides to charge him with." Lucy folded her napkin and placed it on the table.

She looked up to find Robert staring into space, an arrested expression on his face.

"What is it?"

"The will."

"What about it?"

"It must still be here somewhere."

"I think we can all agree about that," Lucy replied. "So what?"

"Mr. Tompkins was planning on taking the body and Sir William back to Yorkshire at the end of the week."

Lucy blinked at him. "Yes, I know."

"So maybe someone didn't *want* him taking Sir William's possessions away before they got another chance to search for the will. Killing Mr. Tompkins adds to the delay and keeps everything right here."

"But killing Mr. Tompkins also got rid of the person most likely to know where the will *is*." It was Lucy's turn to pause. "Perhaps someone hopes that the document will never be found, and the estate will be fought over in a court of law." She stared at Robert. "Now who on earth would benefit most from that?"

*   *   *

Robert knocked on the door of the Bensons' house, where he was admitted by the butler and led through into Edward Benson's study.

"Sir Robert Kurland, Mr. Benson."

Edward came around his desk to shake hands with Robert and offered him a seat.

"Thank you." Robert sat down. "I hope I am not disturbing your work."

"I am not able to do much at the moment." Edward grimaced. "As you might imagine, Sir Robert, the longer the will is missing, the harder it becomes to make plans for the future."

"If it is not located, do you plan to go to court?"

"I won't have any choice. The businesses cannot run without a new injection of capital to modernize our operations. My father, bless his soul, strenuously resisted change, which means we now lag behind many of our competitors."

After his correspondence with Oliver, Robert knew that Edward was speaking at least some of the truth. His lack of management skills was obviously not mentioned as a factor in his company's ills.

"It is certainly expensive when one has to turn to the courts," Robert agreed. "I have had to alter some of the inheritance requirements for my own estates since being given the baronetcy, and it cost me a pretty penny."

But he'd been willing to pay whatever it cost to safeguard his wife and potential offspring in the event his despicable cousin Paul inherited the title.

"Has Brandon returned home yet?" Robert turned the conversation in the direction he desired.

"Unfortunately not."

Robert took out the letter Patrick had written for him. "You might wish to read this account from my doctor about the state of Mr. Tompkins's body."

He handed over the letter and waited in silence as Edward read it through.

"Dear God," Edward said faintly. "Is it possible that Brandon deliberately *killed* Mr. Tompkins in a fit of rage? I wondered perhaps if it had been an accident, that he'd said something to upset the man and caused him to give up hope, or—"

"I cannot say, Mr. Benson. I can only vouch for the honest nature and intelligence of my physician."

"Why didn't Dr. Mantel mention this?"

"With all due respect, sir, I doubt the good doctor has ever encountered a body that has been violated in such a way. Dr. Fletcher served as an army surgeon. His experience with wounded and dying soldiers is extensive."

Edward's hands were trembling as he put down the letter and met Robert's gaze. "Is this why you asked if your man could view the body?"

"I must confess that after finding Brandon in the dressing room and watching him flee, I did wonder if anything untoward had taken place." Robert cleared his throat. "I do hope you forgive me for interfering in such a private matter."

"*Forgive* you? Sir Robert, your interest and help have been invaluable." Edward selected a clean sheet of paper. "I will write to the local magistrate and ask him to apprehend Brandon on the suspicion of murdering Mr. Tompkins."

Edward's enthusiasm to lay the blame at Brandon's door didn't surprise Robert in the least. It would be most convenient for the three Benson brothers if one of their father's stepsons were blamed for everything. . . .

"He can be held at the gaol while we attempt to resolve the matter of the will."

"Still no sign of it?" Robert asked.

"No. I am thinking of having the floorboards and wainscoting removed in the bedchamber to see if the damn thing was secreted there." Edward sighed. "Mr. Carstairs is not willing to stay in Bath for much longer and is asking for instructions on how to proceed. I'm wondering whether we would be better off returning to Yorkshire and settling matters there."

"With Brandon retained in Bath Gaol?" Robert asked. "Would Lady Benson be agreeable to that?"

"Oh, Good Lord, Lady Miranda." Edward groaned. "She will not take this news well at all."

"She is certainly a very devoted mother," Robert said diplomatically. "I can't imagine her believing one of her sons is guilty of murder."

"Neither can I."

Robert stood up. "Well, I must be going. Please let me know how things turn out. Lady Kurland and I are most concerned for the continuing well-being of your family."

He bowed and went out of the door. In the hallway, he spotted Arden loitering on the stairs, obviously waiting for him.

"Good morning."

Arden came over and lowered his voice. "Did you find Brandon?"

"I did, but he refused to come home."

"Couldn't you have *made* him?" Arden asked.

"I offered him a choice as a gentleman, and he chose not to face the consequences of his actions."

"Because he's a stupid fool," Arden groaned. "Now Edward will set the watch on him, I *know* it."

"Then perhaps, seeing as you have been liberated from your room, you should find Brandon yourself and encourage him to return before he is clapped up in gaol."

Aden looked up at him. "What did he say when you found him?"

"About what exactly?"

"Did he tell you why he was in there?" Arden persisted.

"He suggested he was looking for something that affected you both."

"What an idiot! I *told* him—" Arden abruptly stopped speaking.

"Told him what?" Robert asked. "Not to destroy anything while he searched? Not to lose his temper and *kill* anyone?"

"Is that what you think he did?"

"You know I do." Robert met Arden's angry stare. "And you know your own brother, which is why you constantly stay at his side and try to prevent him from exposing his rage to the world."

Arden gulped hard.

"If you did send him into that bedchamber and he murdered Mr. Tompkins, his blood is on your hands as well as Brandon's," Robert said. "So I suggest if you find your brother, you impress upon him that he needs to turn himself in and accept the consequences."

Robert stepped back and inclined his head a frosty inch. "Good day, Arden."

Arden ran back up the stairs, and Robert turned to the front door where his hat and gloves sat on the hallstand. He picked them up, and as the butler had discreetly disappeared at the first sign of trouble, let himself out.

He didn't normally lose his temper with young men, but the brothers made his blood boil. Had Arden sent Brandon to search for something? For a moment, Robert wished that he had been a little bit more sympathetic and perhaps gleaned the answer to that important question. But it was not in his nature to accept incompetence and dishonesty easily. He left the subtler questioning to Lucy.

"It is very kind of you to call, Mr. Benson." Lucy smiled at Peregrine, who had unexpectedly appeared in her drawing room. "Sir Robert will be back shortly if you wish to speak to him."

Peregrine sat opposite Lucy and smiled back. "I'm quite content to speak to you, my lady."

"Then shall I order you some coffee? Or do you drink spirits at this time in the morning?"

"I always like a drink, Lady Kurland, and seeing as my

family are currently driving me to Bedlam, a glass of brandy would be much appreciated."

Lucy gave Foley his instructions and returned to sit opposite her visitor. Anna and Penelope had repaired their relationship sufficiently to agree to go to the Pump Room together, and then on to Sidney Gardens accompanied by Dr. Fletcher for a breakfast event. The thought of attempting to eat more food under the observant eye of Dr. Fletcher had persuaded Lucy to plead tiredness and stay home.

"Has Brandon returned?" Lucy asked after Foley brought their refreshments.

"He has not, my lady. I believe Edward intends to enlist the help of the local watch in finding him."

"On what grounds?"

"I suspect Edward thinks Brandon had something to do with Mr. Tompkins's demise."

Lucy tried not to look shocked, but suspected from the smug smile on her visitor's lips that she hadn't quite managed it.

"Oh, my goodness."

"I *did* wonder why Edward allowed your Dr. Fletcher to see the body," Peregrine murmured. "It was almost as if he expected to find something was wrong."

Lucy sat up straight. "Dr. Fletcher is a very experienced physician. He was also a surgeon in the military."

"So a man who would recognize the difference between a violent death and a suicide." Peregrine nodded. "What an interesting choice for your family doctor, Lady Kurland."

Lucy sipped her tea and said nothing.

Peregrine shifted restlessly in his seat. "I suppose you've also heard that the will cannot be found."

"I was there when Mr. Carstairs asked to see the will and nobody knew where it was," Lucy reminded him.

"That's right. The solicitor asked Sir Robert to attend." Peregrine's smile wasn't kind. "I almost wish the will had been read. It would have amused me greatly if my father had left the entire company to your husband."

"I suspect such an outlandish amendment would not stand up in court," Lucy said. "Are you really disappointed that the will hasn't been found, or would you rather it was lost forever?"

"What an interesting question, Lady Kurland," Peregrine said slowly. "Why would you think I wish the will never saw the light of day?"

"I believe you mentioned that you and your father were fighting just before he died. Were you not worried that he might have disinherited *you*?"

"I didn't mention it. Augustus did, but I concede your point." Peregrine paused and let out his breath. "I don't care what's in the will, Lady Kurland."

"Even if you get nothing?" Lucy ventured.

"Even that. I *care* that my father is dead. We fought about everything, but I greatly admired and respected him." He met her skeptical gaze head-on. "Why do you think I keep talking to you about these personal family matters?"

Lucy stayed mute and Peregrine continued.

"Because I'm not stupid, Lady Kurland. I've noticed that you and Sir Robert seem to have a vested interest in proving that my *father* was murdered." He sat back, one arm draped along the top of the couch. "Will you deny it?"

"Sir Robert was very fond of your father."

"And?"

"And I cannot say anything else until I have spoken to my husband," Lucy added.

Peregrine kept talking. "If my father was murdered, and so was Mr. Tompkins, one must assume that the killer has an interest in my family."

"One might say so." Lucy decided to proceed with caution.

"In truth, one *must* say so. I can't imagine there are two separate murderers currently roaming Bath who independently decided to attack *my* family."

"It would be a remarkable coincidence."

"Then this has to be about money," Peregrine stated.

"It generally is." Lucy nodded. "And the disappearance of the will makes it all the more likely."

She half turned as the drawing room door opened and Robert appeared. He paused on the threshold, his dark blue gaze assessing Peregrine before he bowed his head.

"Mr. Benson."

"Sir Robert." Peregrine remained standing. "I was just inquiring of your lovely wife as to your interest in my father's murder."

Robert noticed that Lucy was looking rather guilty as he advanced into the room and took the seat beside hers.

"What makes you think your father was murdered?"

"I think you're the person who should be telling me that." Peregrine finally sat down. "Lady Kurland asks the most penetrating questions, and I can only assume that you both share my suspicions."

"My wife and I have some . . . experience in bringing murderers to justice. I was fond of your father," Robert said. "He reminded me of my own grandfather. Sir William's death seemed somewhat *convenient* to me."

"In what way?"

Robert shrugged. "He was far away from home, he was unwell, and was getting older, and he took a devilish delight in upsetting his family and tinkering with his will. At some point such behavior does tend to catch up with you."

Peregrine slowly nodded. "Thank you."

"For what?"

"For being honest with me. I was beginning to think that I was the only person who believed my father's death wasn't an act of God or a tragic accident."

"It still might have been," Robert reminded Peregrine. "Such things do happen randomly."

"Yes, but the fact that the will hasn't turned up tips the balance toward a deliberate act."

"Your father did not approve of the life you chose to live in London," Robert remarked and Peregrine's skin flushed.

"I know. We fought about it endlessly," Peregrine said.

"But it never occurred to you to kill him?"

"Frequently, but I would never have put those thoughts into action. Just because we didn't agree about something didn't mean we couldn't coexist amicably enough." Peregrine sat forward. "I liked him, Sir Robert. When we weren't arguing we enjoyed many similar pastimes, such as word puzzles and theatrical comedies. I was the fool who took him to the theater where he met Miranda!"

"So if Sir William hadn't died, you would not have been in any financial trouble?"

"Why do you say that?"

Robert held his gaze. "Your father mentioned some . . . unhealthy gossip about you."

"Did he." Peregrine's smile disappeared leaving his face curiously blank. "I wonder whom he received that information from? One might speculate that Miranda kept at least some of her connections amongst the scum of the theatrical world. It would be just like her to spread gossip to spite me."

"One might also guess that if you introduced her to your father she would've been more grateful," Robert suggested.

"Exactly."

"If you expect us to believe that you played no part in your father's demise, is there anything you might wish to add to help us along?"

"Not that I can think of, but I am more than willing to answer any questions you might have in the future." Peregrine looked from Robert to Lucy. "Although your wife is already quite an expert at getting information out of me in the most *charming* manner."

"Lady Kurland is an exceptional woman," Robert agreed. "And quite invaluable to me."

His pronouncement caused his wife to blush and cast her gaze modestly to the floor, which amused him greatly.

Peregrine stood up. "Well, at least we understand each other now." He bowed. "I will do everything I can to help you catch this murderer—even though it is probably a member of my own family."

"If you had to take a guess at which person it was, whom would you pick?" Lucy asked.

"Brandon?" Peregrine suggested. "He seems the most likely choice, and he is already under suspicion of murdering Mr. Tompkins. And seeing as we have already agreed that it is unlikely that there are *two* murderers at large then he definitely would fit the bill."

Robert stood and escorted Peregrine down the stairs, and into Foley's hands, and then returned to the drawing room.

"What did you make of that?" he asked Lucy as he shut the door. "Do we believe him?"

Lucy bit her lip. "I'm not sure."

"I thought you'd be convinced he was speaking the truth after all those fine compliments he bestowed upon you." Robert sat next to her.

"I'd like to *think* he was telling the truth. But there are several issues that still concern me."

"Such as?"

"We know that Peregrine was fighting with Sir William, and that he was being blackmailed from the correspondence Mr. Tompkins showed us."

"Agreed." Robert nodded.

"So despite what he said, Peregrine still had a reason to want money, and Sir William's death would provide it for him."

"He said he didn't care about the money and insinuated that any rumors that had reached Sir William had come from a biased source—that is—Lady Miranda, a woman he despises."

"But we *saw* the correspondence," Lucy said. "Peregrine knew about the accusations and was arguing the matter out with his father. That hardly sounds like the actions of an innocent man." Lucy wrinkled her nose. "I wish we'd kept copies of the letters. I'd love to read them again."

"We still have the letters," Robert said. "Foley didn't manage to get them back to Mr. Tompkins before he died."

"Then I shall *reread* them." Lucy paused. "Despite their differences their letters to each other were far warmer and full of affection than any of Sir William's other correspondence. And Peregrine did sound *quite* sincere when he stated that he missed his father more than his money."

"I have to agree with you," Robert said reluctantly. "It was the only time I have ever heard Peregrine *sound* sincere about anything."

Lucy offered Robert the brandy decanter and coffeepot, and he declined both.

"He was rather quick to pin the blame on Brandon though, wasn't he?" Robert said.

"Because Brandon is the most likely culprit," Lucy reminded him. "Had Mr. Edward Benson heard anything from the fugitive?"

"No, and after he read Dr. Fletcher's letter he wrote to the magistrate's court accusing Brandon of murdering Mr. Tompkins and asking for his imprisonment. I was quite surprised at his enthusiasm for the task." Robert sighed. "I saw Arden when I was leaving the house, and he's gone out looking for his brother. I was rather short with him."

"He probably deserved it." Lucy patted his sleeve. "One has to think that both of those boys are implicated in this murder."

"That's what I tried to suggest to Arden. As he is the older brother, and the one with a modicum of sense, if Brandon *were* searching for something then it was probably at his older brother's bidding."

"So Arden confirmed Brandon's excuse that he was looking for something more personal than the will," Lucy said. "I wonder what that could be?"

"I have no idea, and I can't think of anyone in the Benson family who would offer up that information without becoming immediately suspicious."

"There are so many things that we still don't know," Lucy complained. "The will is still missing, two men are dead, and we are no closer to discovering *why.*"

"I wouldn't say that. The fact that Mr. Tompkins was killed means that someone was determined to stop him speaking out, which indicates that our first assumption that Sir William was murdered was correct."

Lucy raised her eyebrows. "And how many more members of the Benson household will have to die before we are able to identify the murderer?"

"That's a very good question." Robert grimaced.

"Maybe Brandon will confess to both murders and justice will prevail," Lucy said hopefully. "With his temper I doubt he has the ability to stay silent for long."

Chapter 15

Lucy sat at her desk and read through the letter she had just written to Grace back in Kurland St. Mary. Unwilling to draw Robert's attention to the possibility that she might be with child she had decided to share the news with Grace and ask for her advice. As she read, her hand came to rest on the slight roundness of her belly as if seeking her own confirmation that she wasn't entirely imagining the whole thing.

She'd received a packet of letters from the rectory from both her father and Rose and intended to distribute them to the others at dinner. She'd set her own letters aside to read later with everyone else's, and would reply to them tomorrow. Unlocking her desk, she sealed the letter to Grace, added the address, and resolved to walk into town later to send it on its way.

Robert had left Sir William's correspondence on the top of her desk and she opened it again, this time carefully separating the letters into piles according to who had sent them. The first pile she read were between Sir William and Mr. Carstairs, which included much complaining about the cost of everything from the client, and a lot of explaining from the poor solicitor.

What was interesting was the advice Mr. Carstairs gave Sir William about making sure that any amendments he made to his will were legally witnessed and signed. Lucy gained the sense that Mr. Carstairs was trying to say that the volume of such changes and corrections made the will harder to interpret and might cause problems in the future.

"If we ever find it," Lucy murmured to herself. "Where on earth could it be? Could it possibly have been stolen at the baths when Sir William was murdered and already destroyed?"

Lucy made a note to herself to go back and speak to the servant who had looked after Sir William's possessions.

She returned to the letters and read through the correspondence between Peregrine and his father. Peregrine's letters were covered with excellent sketches, riddles, and Shakespearean word puzzles, and were full of lively conversation. Even when the subject matter turned hostile the letters were still crammed full of both men's personalities and respect for each other.

Lucy compared the letters to those written by Augustus and Edward, which were equally contentious, but lacked the underlying affection and exasperation bursting from the others.

Had Sir William liked the fact that Peregrine stood up to him? From what she remembered of the old man, Lucy suspected that he had. His annoyance with Peregrine sprang not from his exasperation about the lack of purpose in his life and his morals, but from the fact that he'd allowed himself to be blackmailed.

Lucy picked up the last letter Peregrine had written to his father and read it aloud.

"I don't want your money, you blathering old fool. These accusations are ridiculous and untrue! I just want you to use your influence to shut the rumors down at the source!"

In light of what Peregrine had told them yesterday Lucy

considered his words afresh. Was he suggesting that if his
father confronted Miranda, whom Peregrine suspected was
spreading the lies, then nothing further would need to be
done? Lucy read through everything once again and could
find no hint of Peregrine actually asking for money. It appeared that it was Sir William who had first mentioned the
matter to Peregrine. Unfortunately, even if he had written
another reply to Peregrine's outraged reply, Sir William
hadn't made a copy of it.

"Why *didn't* Peregrine ask for money?" Lucy wondered
aloud. "Such accusations could destroy a man's reputation."

But if he'd believed the rumors came from his father's
own wife then perhaps he'd felt justified in assuming they
might amount to nothing. Or had he already decided that
he was going to end his father's existence and solve all his
problems in one desperate throw of the dice? Despite his
lazy exterior, Lucy sensed that Peregrine was no coward,
and that beneath his devil-may-care attitude lurked a man
who hated and loved very strongly. He'd be ruthless as
well—a quality that Edward and Augustus also lacked.

Lucy shivered as she turned to consider Edward Benson.
He seemed far too mild and accommodating to be actively
involved in a murder, but the speed at which he'd offered
up Brandon to the magistrates hinted otherwise. Despite
her confident prediction to Robert that Brandon was the
guilty party, she was beginning to have her doubts. . . .

Augustus would not have the nerve to carry out a murder, and Lady Benson was too physically weak . . . Lucy
paused and searched through the letters to find the one
where Sir William was concerned that his wife might be
having an affair and read it through again. Letters in hand,
she went through into the drawing room where she'd left
Robert reading the paper.

"I wish to ask your opinion about something."

He looked up and immediately set his newspaper to one
side. "What is it?"

"In the letters to his father Peregrine insisted that he hadn't done anything that merited him being blackmailed."

"Yes, I remember that."

"He also told *me* that Lady Miranda had attempted to lure him into entering a relationship with her," Lucy said. "So which is it?"

"Ah. You're saying that he can hardly be both a lady's man, and a man's man."

"Exactly." Lucy kept going. "What if Miranda spread rumors about him *because* he refused her advances?"

"His visceral dislike of her could certainly stem from that," Robert agreed. "But it still doesn't mean he prefers women."

"But what if he does? He is *very* passionate in his dislike of her. He also contradicted himself yesterday when he said *he* had introduced Miranda to his father when previously he suggested that she'd claimed friendship with an old friend of Sir William's to get to know him." Lucy paused to breathe.

"Peregrine said he took Sir William to a play Miranda was in. He didn't say he introduced them to each other," Robert demurred.

"That's what he implied," Lucy returned. "And it's more than likely that Sir William *did* take an interest in Miranda at that point. She *is* very beautiful."

"Maybe he did it behind Peregrine's back?" Robert suggested.

"I suppose that's possible. Peregrine might not have appreciated that, either." Lucy frowned. "Maybe he was in love with her and was furious that she chose his father over him."

Robert stared at her as if she had gone mad.

"Or what if she loved him back?" Lucy persisted. "And Peregrine conspired with Miranda to kill his own father, and this whole business between them of hating each other is just an act?"

Robert recoiled. "That's *absurd*."

Lucy flung up her hands. "Think, Robert! Miranda and Peregrine knew each other in London. Peregrine *introduced* Miranda to Sir William. Maybe he wasn't expecting her to go off with his father, or maybe that's exactly what they planned all along!"

"All right." A frown appeared on her husband's brow. "I am beginning to see your point. But if he truly is a murderer why would he offer to help us discover *himself*?"

"Because he is arrogant enough to believe he is too clever to avoid detection. By befriending us he has already discovered that we believe his father was murdered," Lucy said. "Now he can keep an eye on what we do next to see if we uncover *more* evidence, and prevent us from exposing him as a murderer. What better place to hide than in plain sight?"

Robert held out his hand. "Give me the letters."

He read them through and then looked up at her. "You are making quite a lot out of some very tenuous connections, my dear, but I can't discount your opinion. You have proven to be right too many times in the past."

"Thank you for that at least." Lucy sat down opposite him. "I am aware that I might be grasping at straws, but I think we should at least be aware that Peregrine might not be behaving honorably toward us."

"Noted," Robert said. "And Sir William *was* suspicious that Miranda was having an affair. Maybe he wasn't prepared to pay off the blackmailers because he knew Peregrine was involved with his wife."

"Or Sir William thought that when he saw Peregrine in person, he would remind his son that he held the purse strings, and that Miranda was now his wife and that would be the end of it."

"And order Peregrine to leave well alone?" Robert nodded. "Which might have given Peregrine another reason for murdering his own father. You're right to be wary of him, my dear."

Lucy smiled at him approvingly, and he raised an eyebrow.

"What?"

"You are being remarkably open to my flights of fancy."

"Mainly because we have nothing else to go on," Robert admitted wryly. "I have a horrible feeling that the Benson family are going to return to Yorkshire, settle the matter of the will with the courts, and all go away much richer without anyone being held to account."

"Then we shall continue to do our best to avoid that happening," Lucy said firmly. "Now I have to go out. Do you wish to accompany me?"

"I'm waiting for Dr. Fletcher to return from his shopping expedition with his wife, so we can go to the baths together." Robert's smile was wry. "I can't believe I'm saying this, but I miss the hot springs."

"It is a shame that we don't have one in Kurland St. Mary," Lucy agreed. "Although the thought of the entire village floating around in their underthings is not very appealing."

Lucy left the room to the sound of Robert's appreciative chuckle. If there was a way to replicate the benefits of the baths in her own home then she would do everything in her power to find it for her husband.

Betty helped her into her pelisse and Lucy tied the ribbons on her bonnet before they descended the stairs and went out into the square. Lucy would miss the shops and entertainment available in Bath but was starting to long for the peace and quiet of her own home. They had less than four weeks left on their lease, and she had no intention of extending it. If she were with child, she would much prefer to be close to Grace and in her own village.

After paying to have her letter sent to Grace in Kurland St. Mary, Lucy turned toward the baths and made her way toward the room set aside for changing. Luckily, she had a good memory for faces and was able to recognize the man she and Robert had spoken to on the day of Sir William's death.

He came over to speak to her, a smile on his face.

"Good afternoon, Lady Kurland. Have you decided to sample the amazing healthful benefits of the baths today?"

"I have not," Lucy replied. "I wanted to ask you about Sir William Benson."

"The poor gentleman who died." His smile disappeared, and he looked down at his boots. "Why's that, my lady?"

"I was wondering if anyone asked you to . . . look away from Sir William's belongings that last morning he was in the bath?"

"No, my lady. No one *asked* me to do that."

Aware that her time was limited, Lucy decided to be more direct.

"Did someone pay you to do so?"

He hesitated and again avoided her gaze. "I can't say."

"Can't or won't?" Lucy asked. "I do not wish to get you in trouble, but I would like to know if anyone asked you or paid you to search Sir William's clothing and retrieve something for them?"

She took out two gold sovereigns and held them out to him. If he had been paid at some point, maybe she could offer him more of the same.

His gaze fastened on the money, which was probably equivalent to a quarter of his yearly wage, and he licked his lips.

"I left Sir William's clothes unattended for a couple of minutes."

"Who asked you to do that?"

"I wasn't asked directly." He shrugged. "One of the other servants here handed me a note wrapped around some coins."

"Do you still have the note?"

"No, my lady. I threw it away." He finally looked up at her. "You probably think badly of me after me saying how much I prided myself on guarding Sir William's clothes, but my wife's expecting our third child, and we're barely able to afford our rent and food as it is."

"Did you see the person who approached Sir William's clothing?"

"No, because I walked right away and hid around the corner." He grimaced. "I was ashamed of myself."

"So you don't know if anything was taken?" Lucy asked.

"I noticed that Sir William's coat felt lighter when I picked it up afterward, but his purse and watch were still there, so I didn't think too much of it."

"Indeed." Lucy sighed. If the will had been taken out of Sir William's pocket, she still had no idea who had done it or where the will currently was. "Well, thank you for your help." She held out the coins.

He stepped back. "I can't take your money, my lady."

Lucy met his gaze. "Why not, if you took a bribe from someone else?"

"Because I regret what I did." His mouth twisted. "I liked Sir William, and the thought that my actions might have caused him harm doesn't sit well with my conscience."

Lucy didn't press him further and let him go back to his work. She discovered Betty sitting patiently on a bench near the door of the baths, chatting to another woman, and went toward her.

"Afternoon, my lady! Back again?"

She recognized the woman she and Robert had met trying to sell her wares at the baths the morning Sir William had died.

"Good afternoon, Mistress Peck." Lucy smiled at the woman who was sitting next to Betty. "The soap you sold me was very fragrant."

"Thank you. I pride myself on the quality of my offerings." She patted the bench beside her. "I've been talking to your maid. She says you're *Lady* Kurland."

"That's correct. My husband was honored with a baronetcy from the prince regent for his conduct at Waterloo."

"My late husband was a soldier. I did wonder if your husband was a military man, he had that ramrod spine and domineering presence."

"He can be quite formidable," Lucy acknowledged as Betty moved from the bench to stand behind her.

"He was a friend of that Sir William's."

"Yes, indeed." Lucy sighed. "The poor gentleman. He is going to be transported back to Yorkshire for burial later this week."

"I saw that man again."

"Which man?" Lucy inquired.

"The one who came in that morning with the doctor and was arguing with Sir William. He came to speak to Mr. Abernathy the other day, and this time he wasn't quite so wrapped up in his cloak and scarf." Mistress Peck chuckled. "Same beak of a nose of him as his da, but blacker hair. Handsome, too."

"That was probably Mr. Peregrine Benson, his youngest son." Lucy nodded.

"He brought the widow with him as well."

"Lady Benson?"

"Aye, the beautiful blond lady who was draped in black and clinging to his arm like climbing ivy."

"They probably came to pay their respects to Mr. Abernathy," Lucy said. "Lady Benson might have wanted to see exactly where Sir William died. Did they speak to any of the bathhouse employees?"

"Can't say I noticed them traipsing about much." Mistress Peck sniffed. "When I approached her with my basket, she flapped her hand at me like I was an annoying gnat."

Lucy studied the array of soaps and lotions and picked up several before handing the woman one of the gold sovereigns and standing up.

"Please keep the change."

Mistress Peck grinned up at her. "Thank you kindly, my lady!"

Lucy handed the soap to Betty to place in her basket, and they left the baths. She had a lot to tell Robert when she got home. . . .

Robert was just knocking on the front door when a carriage drew up in the cobbled street and Edward Benson stepped out of it. He paused when he saw Robert and doffed his hat to him.

"Sir Robert, just the man I was hoping to see."

Robert walked back down the steps to the flagstone pavement and waited as Edward paid off the driver.

"Good afternoon, Mr. Benson."

"Brandon has been apprehended and is now in Bath Gaol."

"That is excellent news," Robert replied. "Is he unhurt?"

"Apart from a few bumps and bruises when he tried to escape the watch, he is quite well. I've paid for him to have his own room so he will at least be comfortable while he awaits the magistrate's decision as to whether to proceed to trial or not."

Robert raised an eyebrow. "You are now convinced that he murdered Mr. Tompkins? For what purpose?"

"I doubt Brandon had a purpose," Edward replied. "I suspect Mr. Tompkins told him to get out of the dressing room, and Brandon simply lost his temper and killed him in a rage."

"Why do you think Brandon was in there in the first place?" Robert asked.

"Who knows? Does it even matter?" Edward asked. "A man is dead, Sir Robert. That is what we need to concentrate on now."

"How is Arden taking it?"

Edward made a face. "Very hard, as you might imagine."

"And Lady Benson?" Robert persisted.

"We haven't told her yet." Edward sighed. "I'm actually

hoping I can persuade her to go back to Yorkshire with Sir William's body while I remain here and sort out this mess as best I can."

"Without her knowing her son is being held in gaol on charges of murder?" Robert murmured. "Good luck with that. When do you hope she will leave?"

"At the end of the week. I've already booked a traveling carriage to accompany the funeral vehicle. She will be quite comfortable with her maid and Dr. Mantel in attendance."

"What about Arden?"

"He'll stay here with me. I'll impress upon him that I need him to support his brother and not upset his mother."

Edward didn't sound too convinced of his own success, but Robert didn't remark on it.

"If there is anything either Lady Kurland or myself can do to help, don't hesitate to call upon us." Robert touched his hat and turned back to his own front door. He was becoming heartily sick of the Benson family in its entirety. If it were up to him none of them would ever benefit from the hard work and industry of the murdered Sir William. They were all too full of self-interest and willing to sacrifice Brandon Hall without a qualm of conscience.

Robert threw his hat at Foley and stomped up the stairs to the drawing room where he found Anna reading a book, and no sign of his wife.

"Good afternoon, Robert." Anna looked up at him inquiringly. "Can I order you some tea?"

"No, thank you." Robert bowed. "Is Lucy home?"

"Not that I know of." Anna put down her book. "Would you like me to go and see if she is in the kitchens?"

"Please don't disturb yourself on my account. Is Dr. Fletcher about?"

"He is out walking in the square with Penelope." Anna hesitated. "Is everything all right?"

Robert let out his breath. "I am just contemplating the

vast selfishness of the majority of the population, and the fact that a good man does not necessarily have good offspring."

"Are you thinking of anyone in particular?" Anna asked tentatively.

"Just the Bensons at the moment, but my theory holds true about everyone else. Look at my cousin Paul. He is a disgraceful human being, but his parents weren't. Look at your father!"

"You do have a point," Anna agreed. "Which makes one wonder why anyone wishes to procreate at all. What if you had a child who was more like Paul than like you?"

"I suppose it is possible," Robert grudgingly agreed. "But if we all held to that rule then the humankind would cease to exist. I suspect one rolls the dice and takes one's chances."

Anna's expression grew thoughtful. "I suppose you are right."

Just as Robert was about to reply Lucy came in unbuttoning her pelisse. "Ah. Robert! Just the person I wished to speak to. I've been at the baths."

He followed her down the hall to their bedchamber, and waited until Betty helped her change her dress and left.

She sat at her dressing table, looked in the mirror, and smoothed down her hair. "I have some interesting news to share with you."

"About the Bensons?"

"Yes, of course!" She swiveled around on her seat to stare at him. "What else?"

"Quite frankly, I am sick of the whole lot of them," Robert grumbled.

"Then you won't want to hear that someone *did* get to Sir William's clothing at the baths?"

"Who?" Robert demanded.

"Unfortunately, the servant was sent money and a note, and didn't see who it was."

"How convenient."

"He did say that Sir William's coat felt lighter when he picked it up, but his purse and watch were still there." Lucy held Robert's gaze. "It's extremely likely that someone took the will out of his pocket and that it has already been destroyed."

"Good." Robert sat back in his chair and crossed his arms over his chest. "If that's the case then the whole lot of them will have to go to court and fight it out. In my considered opinion they all deserve one another, and the pittance that will undoubtedly be left when the cannon smoke clears."

Lucy angled her head to one side and studied him. "Are you feeling quite well?"

"I just encountered Edward Benson, who informed me that Brandon has been apprehended and that he plans on getting rid of Lady Benson before she notices."

"I doubt that will work. She might be a little overdramatic, but she does care for her sons." Lucy pinned up a stray lock of hair. "How does Edward think he's going to stop Arden from telling her everything?"

"By appealing to Arden's good sense." Lucy raised her eyebrows. "Exactly. If he wants Miranda out of that house he's going to have to drug her, tie her up, and send that coach off at a gallop before she wakes up."

"Miranda was at the baths yesterday with Peregrine," Lucy said.

"What? I thought they couldn't stand the sight of each other."

Lucy's smile was a little smug for Robert's liking. "And Peregrine was the man who accompanied Sir William and Dr. Mantel to the baths on the morning he died."

"Good Lord." Robert sat back and studied his wife. "You have been busy today."

She shrugged. "I just thought it might be worth revisiting the baths and talking to the servant again. I didn't expect to meet the soap seller and be freely gifted all that extra information."

"Freely?"

"Well, it cost me a sovereign, but it was well worth it." She smiled at him. "So what do you think? Did Peregrine get the attendant to turn away while he went through Sir William's pockets, secured the will, and then ran off, almost knocking you down in his haste to leave?"

"You're forgetting the part when he kills his father," Robert objected.

"Ah, yes." She frowned. "I suppose he could still have done that, but wouldn't his clothes have been wet if he'd gotten in the bath?"

"Maybe Lady Miranda did the killing while Peregrine ran for it," Robert suggested.

"Perhaps she did."

"Don't be ridiculous, Lucy, I was jesting. She's a weak and rather feeble woman."

"She's also an actress who managed to snare a very wealthy baronet for a husband." Lucy didn't lower her gaze. "It's not the first time we have encountered a female murderer."

"You think she dressed up as an old crone, got into the baths, and stabbed Sir William when no one was looking?" Robert demanded.

"Why *not*?"

"Because your ideas are becoming more and more preposterous!"

"Well, *you* tell *me* what the answer is!" Lucy was no longer smiling. "I am merely trying to help, and you"— she swung around and presented him with her back—"are being very difficult and have given me a headache."

Robert took a deep breath as his wife fussed around with her earrings and resolutely ignored him. After a few minutes of strained silence, he got up and put a tentative hand on her shoulder.

"Forgive me? I allowed my frustration over this whole business to boil over, and I was unfair to you."

She shrugged off his hand. "I'm feeling rather tired. I don't think I'll bother to come down to dinner tonight after all. Could you ask Betty to bring me up a tray?"

With some difficulty, Robert persuaded her to look at him. "I'm *sorry*."

To his horror, she looked as if she was about to burst into tears.

"I really do have a headache, and you are right, sometimes I do guess wrongly why someone might be a murderer." She swallowed hard. "Would you prefer it if I kept quiet?"

"*No*." He cupped her chin. "I would be devastated if you did that. I was merely frustrated with my own lack of ideas and took it out on you. Please forgive me."

His wife was normally far more forceful when she stood up to him, and he always enjoyed their sparring. This evening he had obviously gone too far.

"Are you sure that you don't want to come down to dinner and share the joy of Penelope's complaining, and Anna's wistful sighs?" he coaxed.

She finally managed a smile, which relieved him greatly. "I'd rather stay up here until my headache disappears."

He kissed her fingers. "Then I will leave you in peace." He hesitated. "If I am truly forgiven."

She patted his cheek. "Yes, of course you are."

He left after one last uncertain glance back over his shoulder, and a resolution not to upset her anymore. He always thought of his wife as the kind of woman who could put up with anything, but perhaps he needed to remember that even she had her limits.

Chapter 16

"There's a Mr. Arden Hall wishing to speak to you most urgently, Sir Robert," Foley announced from the door of the study where Robert had retired to spend the rest of the evening after enduring dinner without the company of his wife.

"Then send him in."

Robert rose to his feet and waited for his unexpected guest to be shown through to the study.

"You've got to help me." Arden started speaking the moment Foley closed the door.

"With what?" Robert asked, and offered the young man a seat he didn't take.

"With Brandon. Edward thinks he *murdered* Mr. Tompkins?"

"Yes, I was aware of that."

"Then how can I stop it?" Arden asked. "I spoke to Brandon yesterday. He swears he didn't do it."

"And you believe your brother."

"He wouldn't lie to me." Arden met Robert's gaze. "Why *would* he? He knows that even if he *had* killed Mr. Tompkins I would still stand by him."

"So what did Brandon tell you that makes you so certain of his innocence?" Robert sat back down, sipped his brandy, and offered Arden a glass. "He was in the dressing room around the time Mr. Tompkins was killed. I saw him there myself."

"And Brandon told you that he was looking for something."

Mindful of his earlier disastrous attempt to throw scorn on his wife's suggestions, Robert attempted to be diplomatic.

"Brandon threw a box at my head and ran away. If he was looking for something, did he find it?"

"No, because the old man was really good at keeping things hidden." Arden frowned. "They can't even find his will. My mother is beside herself."

"What exactly do you want me to do, Arden?" Robert asked slowly.

"I want you to tell me how to get Brandon out of gaol!"

"Does he currently have a member of the legal profession representing him?"

"I believe so. Edward said he'd done everything he could to help Brandon." Arden hesitated. "If you would be willing to drop the charges—"

"Wait." Robert held up his hand. "*What?*"

"The charges against Brandon." It was Arden's turn to look at him as if he were daft.

"I didn't accuse him of anything, Edward Benson did."

Arden's mouth slowly opened and then closed without him emitting a sound. His hands fisted, and he swung around toward the door.

"The *bastard*!"

"Don't run off just yet," Robert called out in his best commanding officer voice. "If you lay a finger on Edward, I can guarantee he'll find a way to put you right in that cell beside your brother. Sit down and talk to me."

Arden's shoulders slowly lowered, and he turned around, his expression now icy cold. He took the seat Robert pointed at and accepted the glass of brandy.

"Now drink up." Robert waited until some color came

back into the young man's face. "I assume you still want my help?"

"If this is on Edward, then I don't need you to do anything, thank you, sir," Arden said stiffly. "I should've known all that fake sympathy and concern was a lie."

"I think Edward truly believes that your brother killed Mr. Tompkins in a fit of rage." Robert paused. "You can't deny that Brandon has a temper."

"I know he does, but he *liked* Mr. Tompkins, we both did."

"But what if Mr. Tompkins got in the way of his search? Would that not have angered your brother?"

"Brandon said that when he got into Sir William's bedchamber there was no sign of Mr. Tompkins, so he was able to search in peace until you arrived and disturbed him. If Mr. Tompkins *had* been there, do you think Brandon would've been allowed to make such a mess without the valet raising the alarm earlier?"

Robert didn't reply, but he conceded that Arden had a point.

"So Brandon said he didn't see Mr. Tompkins at all."

Arden nodded. "Exactly. So he couldn't have killed him, could he?"

"What exactly was Brandon searching for?" Robert decided to change tack for a moment. "You insisted it wasn't the will."

Arden's lips thinned, and Robert held up a finger.

"If you want my help, then you'll have to be honest with me."

"Apparently, Sir William had some damaging information about our father," Arden said reluctantly as he shifted in his seat.

"Lady Miranda's first husband?"

"Our father, yes."

"And how did you come to know about this?"

"Because my mother was upset, and she told us that someone had been spreading lies about her."

"To Sir William?" Robert asked.

"Yes, and that he had started to doubt her and was considering ending their marriage."

"That must have indeed been upsetting for her, and for you boys." Robert paused, trying to think how to phrase his next question. "Did Sir William tell her exactly what his concerns were?"

"Only that he had been deceived and was not happy about it." Arden frowned. "Mother said that Sir William had been collecting evidence against our father. Sir William was considering launching a legal case to declare his marriage to my mother invalid."

Robert considered Arden for a long moment. "Forgive me if this sounds harsh, but your mother didn't seem very happy in her marriage. If it was dissolved, would she not perhaps have welcomed such an outcome?"

"She didn't believe it would be possible for Sir William to simply dissolve the marriage as if it had never even taken place, and that he would have to take it through the courts. She told us that a divorce is very expensive and requires an act of Parliament or something to pass, and that the shame of being a divorced woman would kill her," Arden said. "And she said she would be poor again."

"Ah, I see her point. Did she ask you and Brandon to find the information for her after Sir William died?"

"No, of course not. She would never ask such a thing of us. Brandon and I decided that the documents should not be seen by Edward, Peregrine, and Augustus, and used against our mother to prevent her gaining her fair share of Sir William's fortune."

"But if Sir William hadn't actually achieved his aim of divorcing your mother, such information as he had gathered would no longer be useful, would it?" Robert pointed out.

"We don't know that." Arden sat forward. "What if Edward decided it was useful?"

Robert nodded. "One has to assume that if Sir William

did have the documents with him he would have kept them alongside his will."

"Which cannot be found." Arden sighed. "I know you won't believe me, but when Brandon went to Sir William's bedchamber, he hoped to speak to Mr. Tompkins and beg him to let us have the information about our father."

"Which leads us back to the unpalatable fact that if Mr. Tompkins had *refused* such a request your brother's temper might have gotten the better of him, and he might have accidentally killed him."

"Brandon swore to me that he *didn't* do it," Arden repeated.

"Is it possible that he lied to you because he knew you would be disappointed in him?"

Arden met Robert's gaze. "No. We stand together. We've had no choice."

Robert sat back. "I am not sure what I can do to help you, Arden, but I will make certain that Brandon is well treated at the gaol, and that he is supplied with a competent man at law to defend him if the magistrate decides the charges are valid, and he must stand trial."

"He won't stand it for long in there," Arden said gloomily. "He's already desperate to get out. I tried to tell him to be patient, but he's not the kind of person to take advice well."

"I noticed that," Robert said dryly.

"I'm worried that he'll end up dead," Arden confessed. "That he'll try to escape or decide it is easier for him to die and get it over with, and then I'll be left here all alone."

"Do you think it would help if I went to speak to him?" Robert asked.

"Probably not. He isn't very fond of you for turning him in to Edward."

"I didn't have a choice in the matter seeing as I discovered a dead man in the cupboard." Robert paused to look Arden in the eye. "You do understand that the fact that

Brandon was in the room at roughly the same time as Mr. Tompkins died might make a jury consider he was guilty?"

"I know that." Arden rubbed his forehead and suddenly looked older than his years.

"And do you also understand that if there is a trial I will probably be called in as a witness against your brother?"

"I'm not stupid, Sir Robert, and I'm not asking you to stand up there and lie for Brandon."

"That is good to know. I can, however, stress that I didn't actually see your brother *with* Mr. Tompkins at any point."

"Then you don't believe Brandon was the one who killed him?"

Robert sipped the last of his brandy before replying. "If Brandon didn't kill Mr. Tompkins, and we discount the notion that he committed suicide, who do you think *was* the murderer?"

Arden was silent for quite a while before he spoke. "I'd think it was either Edward or Peregrine."

"Why?"

"Edward isn't running the businesses very well and needs more money, and Peregrine . . ." Arden wrinkled his nose. "He likes to stir things up and make everyone unhappy just like the old man. He would consider it a big lark to upset the family like this."

"But surely Edward would *want* the will to appear rather than killing Mr. Tompkins, the only person who might know where it is?"

"Edward's the oldest son. If the will isn't found he thinks the courts will give him control of everything."

"He might well be right." Robert sighed, and then refocused his attention on the young man sitting opposite him. "Promise me that you won't provoke Edward into a fight when you return to the house tonight."

"I'd like to plant him a facer, but I won't. I don't want to end up in gaol," Arden stated. "I *will* keep an eye on him and make certain that he doesn't try to do anything to harm Brandon's chances."

"That's an excellent idea." Robert rose and put his brandy glass back on the tray. "Now you should go home or else your poor mother will wonder what has happened to her *other* son." He went to open the door. "Has she noticed Brandon is not at home yet?"

"Dr. Mantel and I agreed not to tell her the truth. She thinks he's off at a racecourse with some friends." Arden scowled. "I don't like deceiving her, but I believe it is for the best."

"I agree. That was very wise of you." Robert waited until Arden went past him into the hallway before closing the door behind them. "Good night, Arden. I promise I will keep your confidences to myself."

Arden nodded and went toward the front door, his head down, leaving Robert staring at nothing. A moment later, he headed up the stairs and went into his bedchamber where Lucy was sitting up in bed reading a book.

"Oh good, you're still awake." Robert pulled up a chair and set it beside the bed. "I was just speaking to Arden Hall."

"About what?" Lucy removed her spectacles and set them on her bedside table. She did look tired, but not as upset as she had earlier, which relieved him greatly.

"What Brandon was searching for in Sir William's bedchamber."

"He *told* you?"

"He came to me thinking I was the one who had laid charges against his brother—a notion inspired and not corrected by Edward Benson, apparently."

"Good Lord."

"Arden said that Sir William had documents and information relating to their father, and was considering applying for a divorce from Lady Miranda. He says that Brandon was trying to get the documents back before Edward got hold of them and used them against his mother."

"I suppose his explanation has some merit," Lucy mused.

"Did he say *why* Sir William was so intent on this course of action?"

"In what sense?"

"Obtaining a divorce *is* very difficult and costly. Surely one has to wonder exactly what evidence Sir William had acquired to make him think the effort was worthwhile?"

"I see what you mean. Sir William was not the kind of man to waste his money." Robert frowned. "I didn't think to ask Arden whether he knew exactly what was in the papers. I should have done so. I was more interested in why he and Brandon were so determined to suppress the information even after Sir William had died."

"And what did Arden have to say about that?"

"He was convinced that Edward would use the information to disinherit Lady Miranda."

Lucy set her book aside. "But if the evidence was gathered simply so that Sir William could obtain a divorce, then how could it be relevant to Edward now?"

"Arden said it was related to his father."

"Miranda's first husband? The one who died in mysterious circumstances?"

"Yes, and I see your point. If the papers weren't still a threat then Arden and Brandon wouldn't still be after them, would they?"

"One would assume not, especially seeing as it seems that they were willing to kill to obtain them." Lucy paused. "I wonder what Mr. Hall did? Perhaps he was a convicted felon or died in prison."

"Which might indicate that Arden wasn't quite as forthcoming with me about what was in those papers as I first imagined." Robert shoved a hand through his hair. "I knew he wasn't telling me everything, but I was so desperate to get *something* out of him that I was afraid to push too hard."

"Do we know *anything* about Miranda's first husband?"

"We don't, but Peregrine might."

"Perhaps we should ask him about that." Lucy nodded. "I'll ask him tomorrow. He is more likely to offer an answer to me than to you."

Robert sat back. "The thing is . . . I don't think Brandon did kill Mr. Tompkins."

Lucy regarded him unwaveringly but didn't speak.

"It's all tied up together, isn't it?" Robert groaned. "The will, the information about the deceased Mr. Hall, and both deaths."

"A will that might already have been stolen and destroyed," Lucy reminded him.

"And a boy in gaol soon to face charges of murder." Robert reached out and clasped his wife's hand. "We have to do something, Lucy. There is too much at stake for us to fail now."

Chapter 17

"What a delightful surprise, Lady Kurland." Peregrine bowed and offered Lucy a seat in the drawing room close to the fire. "Did you come to see Lady Benson? I understand that she is out collecting her new black gowns from her mantua maker and no doubt complaining that the color doesn't complement her beauty."

"I didn't come to see Lady Benson, I came to see you."

Peregrine took the seat opposite her, his expression amused. "Then how can I help you?"

Lucy folded her hands together on her lap. "In the spirit of cooperation you suggested regarding the recent deaths in your family, I wanted to ask you a few questions."

"Please, go ahead." He waved an airy hand at her. "Always delighted to oblige a lady."

"It concerns your relationship with Lady Benson." Lucy had decided that at this point she had nothing to lose by being frank. "I am slightly confused about how she met your father."

A wary gleam entered his eyes. "Ah, that."

"You originally suggested that Lady Benson met your father when she claimed to be an acquaintance of one of his old friends. You later told me that you took your father to a play and introduced Lady Benson to him there."

"*Did* I?" He sighed. "My lamentable memory."

"So which is it?" Lucy inquired.

"It is a combination of both those things. I did take my father to see a play, Miranda happened to be in it, and she did claim to know a friend of my father's."

"When you introduced her to him?"

"I think I might have done that." He shrugged. "Does it really matter? And to be frank, Lady Kurland, I do not see what this has to do with someone murdering my father unless you are trying to build a case against my step-mother, which I am very happy to encourage."

"Do you really think she murdered him?"

He made a face. "I wish I did, but she wasn't at the baths that fateful morning."

"How would you know?" Lucy asked.

"Because I was there." He raised his eyebrows. "Didn't you know?"

It was Lucy's turn to stare. "I heard that your father and Dr. Mantel were accompanied to the baths by another man. Was that you?"

"Yes, my father was proving very obstinate over a partic- ular matter. We were arguing over the breakfast table and continued our disagreement until the moment he stripped down in the baths. At which point, I walked out in a rage and left him and Dr. Mantel to it." He raised an eyebrow. "Anything else?"

"What exactly were you arguing about?"

"Miranda, of course. My father had something on his mind about her, and he was refusing to tell me what it was."

"You weren't arguing about your being blackmailed?"

His smile widened. "My, my, you are good at discover- ing the worst about people, aren't you, Lady Kurland? And yet you look so damned upright and respectable."

Lucy maintained her silence and offered him her bland- est inquiring smile.

"All roads lead back to Miranda, don't they?" Peregrine

sighed. "She didn't like the way I treated her sons, and invented some fantasy that I preferred to bed men to discredit me with my father. She persuaded one of her theater friends to send my father a demand for money. It was all done out of spite. I believe my father was beginning to realize that."

"Do you think he had begun to tire of Lady Benson?" Lucy asked.

"Who would not? She is a vapid and unpleasant leech." He shrugged. "There was definitely some maggot stirring in his head. He loved his secrets, and he was full of rage about something. Unfortunately, he died before I was able to get the whole story out of him."

"That was a terrible shame," Lucy agreed. "Can you tell me anything about Mr. Hall?"

Peregrine blinked at her sudden change of subject. "Dennis Hall? The boys' father?" His irritating smile returned. "My goodness, Lady Kurland, you really are out to get Miranda!"

"Sometimes, understanding what happened in the past helps one solve a problem in the present," Lucy replied. "Was he an actor?"

"I assume so. I can't say I met the man. I believe he died in prison when the boys were small, leaving her penniless. Miranda stayed on with the same band of traveling players and brought her boys up with that community until she captured my father."

"You sound as if you knew Miranda quite well before she met your father," Lucy commented.

"Amongst other things I'm a playwright. Miranda's theater company were the first to perform one of my plays. I had to work quite closely with them to make sure they presented the words I'd written in the way I wanted."

"And that was when Miranda told you about her first husband?"

"Miranda told me nothing, Lady Kurland. I met the boys first and learned their story from the other cast members who had helped Miranda raise them."

"Yet you don't seem to care for the boys or Miranda now."

"Because she went out of her way to use me to ensnare my father," Peregrine said. "I *hate* being used."

"I suspect none of us enjoy that." Lucy hesitated. "Did you ever find out exactly what happened to Mr. Hall?"

"You'd have to ask Miranda, and I doubt you'd get an answer. She's far too sensitive about the subject."

"Did the boys remember him at all?"

"I doubt it seeing as Brandon was a babe in arms, and Arden not much older." Peregrine turned to the window. "I hear a carriage. Miranda has returned. If you don't wish to speak to her, you should probably leave now."

"I have no objection to speaking to her," Lucy replied. "In truth, she probably deserves some sympathy. Her husband is dead, her stepsons seem united against her, and one of her sons is likely to be charged with murder."

"I loathe her, but don't assume Edward and Augustus feel the same way. They are both far too concerned about the family name, and despite maybe wanting to get rid of Miranda, they would never have the balls to actually do it." Peregrine rang the bell and ordered tea.

"Seeing as Augustus is a clergyman one would hope not," Lucy said. "And Edward is the oldest, and should protect his father's widow and follow through on his wishes."

"Which he will do if he can ever find that will. He and Miranda are agreed that they will take the matter to the courts if it isn't recovered." Peregrine turned to the door. "Good morning, Dr. Mantel. How is your patient?"

Dr. Mantel looked exhausted, and Lucy felt a momentary twinge of pity for him having to deal with Lady Miranda every single day.

"Lady Benson is still quite emotional but rapidly improving. She managed a whole two hours at the dressmaker's without feeling faint." Dr. Mantel bowed to Lucy. "Good morning, Lady Kurland."

"Good morning, Dr. Mantel. I am so glad to hear that Lady Benson is feeling more the thing."

"She'd feel a lot better if this will turned up, wouldn't she?" Peregrine spoke up. "But then, wouldn't we all?"

Dr. Mantel ignored Peregrine and focused his attention on Lucy. "I will accompany her back to Yorkshire at the end of the week. I feel it is only fitting."

"Is she paying your wages now, or are you doing this out of the goodness of your heart?" Peregrine asked.

Dr. Mantel finally turned toward Peregrine. "I could hardly leave Lady Benson in distress, Mr. Benson."

"So you're working for nothing?" Peregrine laughed. "Good luck ever getting your money back. Edward is as tightfisted as my father. If the will isn't found, he'll control the purse strings, and my stepmother had better remember that."

Lady Benson entered the room and glared at Peregrine. "Why haven't you gone back to London?"

He didn't bother to rise, but regarded her from the couch. "Why would I leave when I am enjoying myself so much?"

"Your father has *died*! How is that amusing?" Lady Benson said, her voice trembling.

"Because it's left you and my brothers in something of a quandary."

"I did nothing to deserve your derision." Lady Benson sat on the couch. "Yet you continue to insult me." She found her black lace–trimmed handkerchief and dabbed at her cheeks.

"Good Lord, woman, after all those years on the stage you are still a terrible actress," Peregrine drawled. "But then you never relied on that particular talent when you had so many others."

Lady Benson swallowed hard, and a tear trickled down her cheek. "You are a *horrible* man."

"I can't argue with that," Peregrine agreed. "If Edward keeps all the money to save his company, will you return to acting? If so you might want to take a few lessons."

Lady Benson sat up straight. "Edward has recently reassured me that he will do everything in his power to make sure that I receive my widow's portion."

"Has he now?" Peregrine's expression grew thoughtful. "I wonder why he did that?"

"Because he is a better man than you will ever be," Lady Benson said fiercely. "And he intends to respect his father's wishes!"

Peregrine glanced over at Lucy, and then back at Miranda. "My father told me that he had certain . . . damaging information about your first husband. I wonder how long you would have *remained* Lady Benson if what he'd heard turned out to be true?"

Lucy focused her attention on Lady Benson, who looked visibly shocked by Peregrine's provocative comments.

"I have absolutely *no* idea what you are talking about, Peregrine." She rose from her seat and stared him down. "If such 'rumors' did reach Sir William, we all know who provided them, don't we?"

He leaned back and looked up at her. "Let's just call it tit for tat, shall we?"

She turned and marched out of the room without her usual delicacy, and was quickly followed by Dr. Mantel and her maid.

Lucy raised her eyebrows at Peregrine, who grinned at her. "Why on earth did you do that?"

"What?"

"Inform Lady Benson that Sir William was suspicious of her first husband?"

"Why shouldn't I tell her what she probably already knows?" He shrugged. "She's not stupid. She must have been aware that my father's affection for her had dwindled to nothing." His gaze narrowed. "Why would it bother *you*?"

Mindful that Peregrine had no knowledge that Miranda's

sons were already searching for any evidence concerning their father, Lucy considered her reply carefully.

"Sir William didn't tell you he had damaging information about Mr. Hall, *I* told you that."

"And I considered what you said and connected the fact that my father was furious with Miranda with the interesting new information about Mr. Hall." He smiled. "The fact that she reacted to the suggestion so badly proves that we are on the right track."

"*We* are not, Mr. Benson. Your methods are highly irregular, and one might even say audacious."

"Says the lady who has discovered all my secrets," Peregrine retorted. "You are hardly in a position to be sanctimonious, Lady Kurland."

Lucy rose from her seat and curtsied. "I must be going."

Peregrine stood, too, and came over to take her hand and kiss her fingers. "Always a pleasure, my dear lady. Do come again."

Lucy suspected that the glare she gave him only provided him with even more amusement and ammunition, but she couldn't help herself.

"Give my regards to Sir Robert, won't you?"

"Indeed." Lucy headed for the door, aware that she'd been bested, but determined that Peregrine would not see it. She was beginning to wonder if Peregrine would eventually blurt out the truth—that he had been the one to kill his father after all. . . .

Lucy yawned discreetly behind her fan as the opera singer giving the concert in the Upper Assembly Rooms continued her rather long and mournful aria. Beside Lucy, Robert shifted in his seat as if either his leg was paining him, or he was as bored as she was.

When the singer finally drew to a close to rapturous applause the audience was invited to attend a light supper during the interval. Robert stood, offered Lucy his arm, and they strolled from the blue painted walls and five crystal chandeliers of the ballroom into the cozier but more packed Octagon Room, with its four fireplaces that were providing far too much heat in the crowded rooms.

Lucy fanned herself and then turned to Robert. "It is far too hot in here. Shall we venture into the card room or the vestibule?"

"Yes, please." He headed for the nearest exit, politely excusing himself as they progressed. "It's like trying to herd cattle in here."

Lucy chuckled. "I have to agree with you. Perhaps we should follow the Fletchers' example and retreat to the refreshment room. Anna is with them as well."

"As if I haven't seen enough of them during the past few months." Robert patted her gloved hand. "It is quite pleasant to spend a moment alone with you and forget about the damned Bensons."

Lucy squeezed his fingers. "Then you are about to be disappointed because here comes Peregrine, Edward, and Lady Benson."

She fixed a smile on her face as the Bensons approached. "Good evening, Lady Benson. Are you enjoying the concert so far?"

"It is passable," Lady Benson said. "Despite my protestations, Dr. Mantel and Edward *insisted* that I leave the house and attempt to forget my sorrows."

"What an excellent notion," Robert agreed. "I often find that a brisk walk outside with my dogs or a change of scenery clears my head wonderfully."

Lady Benson gently shuddered presumably at the idea of that much exertion and raised her beautiful gaze to Robert. "You do not suffer as I do, Sir Robert."

"You're probably right about that." Robert bowed. "Now, I must take my wife out of this crush and make sure she has something to eat. If you will excuse us?"

He smiled and very firmly led Lucy in the opposite direction.

"Peregrine was very quiet, wasn't he?" Lucy said as they moved out of earshot.

"Perhaps he's regretting sharing all his secrets with you."

"That might be it," Lucy said, frowning. "Lady Benson and Edward seem much in charity with each other, don't they?"

"I didn't notice. I was too busy hoping the widow wasn't going to perform one of her swoons and expect me to catch her." He shuddered. "I cannot bear weak women like that."

"You wouldn't catch me if I swooned?" Lucy asked.

He stopped in the doorway to smile down at her, his blue eyes glinting. "*You* are not a weak woman, and I seem to remember that in the past I have most definitely caught you when you've swooned."

She touched the lapel of his coat. "My very own hero."

"Hardly that. But I would protect you with my life." He brought her fingers to his lips and kissed them. "Shall we go and find Anna, and get her opinion of the opera singer?"

The second half of the concert proved to be much more entertaining than the first, and Lucy enjoyed it immensely. Even Robert was tapping his foot to the music at one point, and Anna was in heaven. Lucy did feel rather sorry for poor Penelope because every time she settled on her chair, the babe would start moving, making her feel most uncomfortable.

Lucy only knew this because Penelope made sure that everyone seated near them shared in her discomfort. Poor Dr. Fletcher looked rather beaten down by the end of the performance and eager to leave. As Robert had ordered a carriage to take them down the steep hill of Gay Street back to Queen's Square she suspected Dr. Fletcher's desire to flee would take far longer to achieve than he wished.

Even though they waited until most of the audience had left the ballroom, the lobby was still crowded. It had begun to rain and many of the patrons remained inside the building discussing the likelihood of the shower continuing, or whether they should risk walking home.

"Good evening, Miss Harrington." Lucy turned as Captain Akers approached Anna. "Lady Kurland, Sir Robert."

"Captain Akers." Anna curtsied, her cheeks reddening. "How are you? I haven't seen you for several days."

His smile to her was perfectly polite, but held none of its previous warmth. "I do apologize, Miss Harrington. I've been in London." He raised his gaze and scanned the crowd. "And now I must apologize again and leave you as I attempt to find my sister and her fiancé's family. I saw that it was going to rain and brought the carriage out to bring them home."

"How . . . kind and thoughtful of you," Anna said, her gaze lingering on the Captain's face. "How *very* like you."

He looked down at her for an instant and then away, as if the sight of her beautiful face was somehow too much for him to bear.

"Good-bye, Miss Harrington."

And he was gone, swallowed up in the crowd in an instant. Lucy reached out to touch Anna's arm.

"Are you all right?"

"Why wouldn't I be?" Anna's attempt at a smile was rather wobbly. "Are we going to attempt to get our cloaks?"

"Dr. Fletcher is attending to that," Robert spoke up, and then pointed at the wall nearest the exit. "Mrs. Fletcher is sitting over there. I suggest we join her."

After almost half an hour of waiting for the carriage, Robert put his pocket watch away and surveyed his party. Penelope was complaining about something, Anna still looked stricken from the encounter with her suitor, and Lucy was attempting to keep everyone's spirits up. He strolled over to the front door and looked up at the sky. The rain had stopped, and the cobbled streets weren't flooded. He knew from experience that it was only a fifteen-minute walk all downhill to their rented house.

He returned to Lucy and murmured, "I think we should give up on the carriage and walk."

"I am more than happy to do so." She fastened the clasp of her cloak in a businesslike manner. "Is it still raining?"

"No." Robert caught Patrick's eye. "We've decided to forget about the carriage and walk back. Do you wish to accompany us, or will it be too much for Mrs. Fletcher?"

Penelope stood up. "I am quite capable of walking. In fact, I am feeling quite restless and would like to go as soon as possible."

Dr. Fletcher shrugged. "As you wish, my dear—although I can order you a chair if you prefer?"

"And leave me in the hands of unknown ruffians who would take advantage of my delicate condition?" Penelope asked.

"I would, of course, walk alongside you," Dr. Fletcher reassured his wife, who didn't look impressed.

Anna rose as well. "I am also ready to walk."

"Then we will leave immediately." Robert paused at the front door to inform one of the footmen that if a carriage *did* finally turn up for Sir Robert Kurland to send them away with a flea in their ear.

He offered Lucy and Anna an arm, and then led the way past the architectural wonder of the Circus, and down onto Gay Street, which would lead them almost directly into Queen's Square.

The streets were reasonably well lit and patrolled by the watch, so Robert wasn't too concerned about getting his ladies home safely. About halfway down Gay Street Lucy poked him in the ribs.

"Oh, dear. It's the Bensons again."

Robert immediately slowed his step and looked farther down the road where there was a huddle of people. "It looks as if Edward and Lady Benson are about to hire two chairs." He snorted. "They are almost home!"

He waited until Dr. Fletcher and his wife caught up with him before moving on. Now that they were relieved of Lady Benson, the two remaining men were moving far more quickly and seemed oblivious to their surroundings, or to the fact that Robert and his party would be obliged to follow them all the way home.

As the ground leveled out, Robert reached an intersection and paused to allow a succession of barrel-laden carts to pass by. Anna dropped back to walk with the Fletchers. By the time Robert picked his way through the puddles and filth of the cobblestones there was no sign of Peregrine or Dr. Mantel.

"Nearly home now," he murmured to Lucy. "Although I cannot wait to be really home in Kurland St. Mary. How many more weeks are we supposed to stay here?"

"Less than four," Lucy said as she smiled up at him. "And if you really hate it that much I'm sure we could leave earlier as long as you are willing to forgo the rent money."

"I'll consider it." Robert lowered his voice so that only Lucy could hear him. "I'd still like to sort out this business with the Bensons before we leave."

"I agree. It would be a shame to walk away when we are so close to solving the murders."

"Close?" He glanced down at her. "I feel as if we are as far away from finding out the truth as we were when Sir William died."

"I don't think Brandon killed anyone," Lucy stated. "I think it was Peregrine all along. He was there at the baths that morning, he hates Lady Benson and her sons, and he doesn't care about what happens to the rest of his family. He seems to think that everything is a big joke, but under that amusement lurks a far greater sense of purpose."

"Why do you think he killed Mr. Tompkins then?"

"Because Mr. Tompkins knew where Sir William had hidden the will. If Peregrine had already killed his father and had the will stolen at the baths, he wouldn't want the valet telling Mr. Carstairs where it was supposed to be, and then everyone realizing it wasn't there. That would cause a whole other scandal."

"So you think Peregrine has the will?"

"I think he had it, and that he read it." Lucy hesitated.

"Didn't you ever get the sense that he knew too much? That he was secretly laughing at everyone all the time while we floundered around in the dark?"

"Yes, now that you put it like that, I can definitely see it." Robert walked a bit farther before he replied, "And if it is Peregrine, what do you think we should do about it?"

"Confront him?"

"For what purpose?"

"To confirm our suspicions?"

"We can't prove anything though, can we?" Robert argued.

"But we might be able to convince Edward to withdraw the charges against Brandon," Lucy contended,

"That's a good point." Robert considered her arguments as they walked onward to their destination. "If Edward wants to attempt to deal with Peregrine then that's up to him. Do you think Peregrine destroyed the will?"

"I should imagine so." Lucy sighed. "I suppose for him the idea that everyone will have to stand by and watch Edward sink all their money into his failing companies is somehow amusing."

"I thought you said you liked Peregrine," Robert reminded her.

"If he wasn't a murderer, his outrageous arrogance would be something to admire, but he is, and my opinion of him is not high," Lucy stated.

"So do you think he wanted Lady Benson for himself, or that the rumors about him preferring men are true?"

"I'm not sure," Lucy sighed. "Mayhap we can ask when we confront him."

A shout echoed down the street and Robert's head went up. He peered into the darkness ahead and saw some kind of struggle at the corner of Queen's Square.

"Stay here," he commanded Lucy, and headed for the melee, Patrick at his heels.

Three men surrounded Peregrine and Dr. Mantel, who were attempting to fight them off. The doctor went down with a crash onto the flagstone pavement, swiftly followed by Peregrine. Robert reached the men just in time to pull one of them off the doctor before all three ran away.

Neither Dr. Mantel nor Peregrine immediately rose to his feet, and Robert and Dr. Fletcher crouched beside the two men.

"Go to the house, Penelope, ask them to bring some light," Dr. Fletcher said in a tone that indicated he had no time for his wife's nonsense. "*Quickly!*"

Anna took Penelope's hand, and the two women hurried toward the house.

Dr. Mantel struggled to sit up. His face was scratched, and one of his hands was bleeding as if he'd used it to ward off a blade.

"What in God's name *happened?*" he croaked.

"You were attacked." Robert handed the man his handkerchief. "Did they take anything from you?"

Dr. Mantel searched his pockets. "My money's gone, and my watch." He used Robert's handkerchief to wrap around his hand. "Nothing that isn't replaceable, thank God." His gaze fell on Peregrine, who was still sprawled out on the ground. "Is he all right?"

Patrick turned to give Dr. Mantel a cursory glance as his hands moved over Peregrine with practiced speed. "He's unconscious. Come over to his other side and help me locate the source of this bleeding."

Dr. Mantel crawled around Peregrine's recumbent form and stared down before gingerly placing his hand on the body. He attempted to clear his throat, and then shook his head before scrambling to his feet and backing away.

"I don't know how to *do* that. I don't know bloody *anything!*"

"Sir Robert!"

Robert looked up to see Foley approaching with two lanterns, closely followed by one of the kitchen maids and an assortment of footmen. As Dr. Mantel staggered away, his hand to his mouth as he dry heaved, Lucy took his place at Peregrine's side.

"What do you want me to do, Dr. Fletcher?"

Patrick glanced over at her. "From the look of him, he's been stabbed, but in this light, and with his dark clothing, I can't see where. You'll have to feel over him to see if you encounter blood-soaked cloth."

Lucy stripped off her gloves and set to work, not appearing to notice that her new ball gown was now covered in mud and filth from the road.

"Here." She looked up at Patrick. "Just under his shoulder. The blood is pouring out."

"Then press down as hard as you can," Patrick ordered. "And don't move."

Lucy did as she was told, aware of the wetness seeping through her silk gown and petticoats and the rancid smell of the gutters around her. Dr. Mantel had fled, and Robert had followed him to make sure he went into the Benson house.

Anna had returned and was ripping up a sheet to make bandages while Dr. Fletcher and one of the footmen attempted to cut Peregrine out of his extremely tightly fitting coat and waistcoat. She continued to press down on the wound, her fingers growing colder and number with every second.

"Well done, Lady Kurland. This is definitely the only wound we need to worry about." Patrick was now crouched beside her. "You can let me take over now."

"Is he still alive?" Lucy asked.

"He is at the moment, but he's lost a lot of blood. Hold the lantern still, Foley." Dr. Fletcher cut off Peregrine's shirt to expose the area around the ugly wound. "When I ask you to remove your fingers do so as quickly as possible and then get out of my way."

"Yes, Dr. Fletcher."

He fashioned a wad of cloth and laid two strips of bandage under Peregrine's torso.

"Now, Lady Kurland."

Lucy let go, and blood briefly seeped out again before Patrick placed the cloth over the wound and tied the two bandages tightly over it.

"This should do until I can get him into the house and have a proper look."

Robert helped Lucy to her feet and wrapped an arm around her shoulders. Her knees were aching, and she was shivering with cold.

"Bring him into our house, please, Foley," Robert ordered.

"Not the Bensons'?" Patrick asked.

"No. I'd rather he survived the night."

Foley organized the footmen, and under Dr. Fletcher's direction they carefully picked Peregrine up and brought him into the bedchamber next to the doctor's. When everyone was back inside the house, Robert turned to Foley.

"Lock all the doors. Don't let anyone in unless I say so."

"Even the Benson family, sir?" Foley asked.

"Especially them." Robert patted Foley's shoulder. "Thank you for your quick response, and please thank the rest of the staff."

"I will, sir." Foley bowed. "I'll send up some brandy and tea to your room as soon as we get ourselves organized, sir."

Robert turned to Lucy, who had remained standing in the hall. Even as he watched her, she started to sway, her gaze fastened on her bloodstained hands.

He caught her elbow in a firm grip and held on to her. "Stand firm, my love. Let's get you upstairs."

"Yes . . ."

He was relieved that she hadn't actually swooned because he suspected his leg would have buckled if he'd tried to carry her up a flight of stairs. Betty was already in their bedchamber. She swooped on Lucy and took her through into the dressing area exclaiming about the state of her clothes and her hands. Robert let out a long breath as his heartbeat steadied and finally returned to normal.

"Shall I help you change, sir?" Silas spoke from behind him, and Robert looked down at his disheveled muddy clothing.

"Yes, please."

"You weren't hurt in the skirmish, sir, were you?" Silas asked, his expression worried, as he poured hot water into a basin and placed soap and a towel beside it.

"No, I simply did my best to help." Robert shook off his memories and the smell of blood, and unbuttoned his coat. "I don't know what you think, Silas, but I suspect my best coat will never be quite the same again."

Lucy lay in the bath until the water cooled around her. She'd used almost a whole bar of the lavender soap she'd bought at the baths trying to scrub the blood from her skin, and yet she still didn't feel clean. Feeling a man's warm blood pumping out under her fingers was an experience she hoped never to repeat.

The fact that Peregrine was still alive was a miracle. . . .

Betty helped her out of the bath and into her nightgown and dressing robe.

"Is Sir Robert still in the bedroom?" Lucy asked Betty as she braided her hair.

"He said to tell you that he's just gone to speak to Dr. Fletcher, and then he will be back to have supper with you. Foley is just bringing that up." Betty smiled at Lucy. "How are you feeling now, my lady?"

"Much better," Lucy said, smiling in return. "It was not quite the way I expected my evening to end."

"I'm not sure that your gown can be properly cleaned, my lady." Betty laid it over her arm along with Lucy's other clothes. "But I will do my best."

"Please, don't bother." Lucy shuddered. "I don't think I could wear that dress again anyway."

"As you wish, my lady." Betty curtsied and went out of the servants' door. "Please ring for me when you wish to retire to bed."

Lucy took a seat beside the fire and thanked Foley when he brought a covered tray of food and a pot of chocolate for her. She left the food alone, poured herself a drink, and sat staring into the fire until she heard Robert come back in the room.

"Well, Peregrine isn't dead yet, but Patrick says his life is still in danger." Robert paused to kiss the top of her head before he sat down opposite her. He had a large glass of brandy in one hand and wore his favorite silk banyan.

Lucy shuddered. "Considering how much he was bleeding I'm not surprised."

"Patrick also commended your calm good sense and had a few choice words to describe Dr. Mantel."

"He panicked quite badly, didn't he?"

"Indeed," Robert said dryly. "I made sure he went into the Benson house, and left him to it. I'll wager he'll hide in his room like the coward he proved to be and not tell anyone what happened."

"Not all physicians are used to seeing bloody wounds, Robert."

"I know, but one has to question his professional competence if he can't even act on a direct order from a fellow physician."

Lucy sipped her hot chocolate and allowed the sweet warmth to settle in her stomach.

"Does it seem odd to you that three pickpockets would venture as far as Queen's Square, which is well lit and patrolled by the watch?" Robert asked. "Because it does to me."

Lucy sighed. "I was hoping you weren't going to mention that."

"Here's the thing, Lucy. Does it strengthen the case against Peregrine—that Edward now wants to get rid of him?" Robert asked. "Or does it mean that Peregrine is innocent, and Edward is far more conniving than we thought and is attempting to get rid of all his competition?"

"I don't know," Lucy said. "Does Dr. Fletcher need someone to share the nursing of Peregrine tonight?"

Lucy's words ended on a yawn, and Robert leaned over and took the cup out of her hands.

"If he does, it will not be you. Now eat some of these buttered crumpets and let's go to bed."

Chapter 18

Lucy woke up to the sound of the scullery maid making up the fire in their bedchamber. It was still dark so she kept her eyes closed, and waited for the noise to stop and the maid to leave. She rolled onto her back, placed a protective hand over her slightly rounded stomach, and breathed out slowly. Beneath her fingers she felt a slight fluttering, as if she'd swallowed a butterfly, and went still.

After the horrible end to her night, she'd worried that she might have overexerted herself, and had feared the worst. But there had been no blood spotting and she still felt perpetually nauseous. She smiled into the darkness. Perhaps this time with God's grace she might be lucky. . . .

Determined not to dwell on her hopes and unable to go back to sleep, she considered the problem of Peregrine and the Benson murders anew. What were they missing? If Robert was correct, and Edward wanted to make sure he took complete control of the family fortune the attack on Peregrine made sense. But even if Edward got rid of Peregrine and paid off Augustus's debts to keep him quiet there still remained the problem of Lady Benson.

Unless . . .

"Robert!" Lucy rolled onto her side and shook her husband's shoulder. "Wake up!"

He opened his eyes and scowled at her. "What is it?"

"Lady Benson!"

"*What?*"

She'd forgotten that he was never at his most amiable first thing in the morning.

"What if Dennis Hall isn't dead?"

Robert came up on one elbow and looked down at her. "Her first husband?"

"Yes. It's so obvious!" Lucy said. "Why didn't we think about it sooner? If Sir William found out that Dennis Hall was still alive, then that would make Miranda a *bigamist,* and would give him grounds to have the marriage annulled."

"I suppose it would."

It was Lucy's turn to sit up. "If it *is* Edward who wants to control the entire Benson fortune, having that information would help him get rid of Miranda *and* her sons, wouldn't it?"

"Arden was afraid Edward would use his father against him," Robert said. "I wonder if that's what he wasn't telling me? That he knew his mother was a bigamist, and that finding those documents and destroying them would protect her." He paused. "But how would Edward know about them?"

"If Sir William boasted to Peregrine that he had evidence to end his marriage, do you not think he did the same to Edward? Or Peregrine might have told him, or *somebody.*"

Robert exhaled and sat back against his pillows while Lucy watched him anxiously.

"So you now think Edward is the murderer, even though we don't have any evidence that he was at the baths that morning," Robert stated.

"Maybe he paid someone to do it," Lucy said stubbornly.

"And what about the will?"

"What about it?"

"Did Edward steal it from the baths, or is it still missing?"

"I . . . hadn't thought of that." Lucy bit her lip. "But wouldn't it be in his best interests if the will never turned up anyway? If it's lost, he'll go to court and will probably be given control of the money. If he found it, and the documents about Dennis Hall, then he can keep the will hidden and use the other information to discredit Miranda."

"He *could* have killed Mr. Tompkins," Robert said slowly. "He was definitely in the house that morning, and he was very eager to place the blame on Brandon."

Lucy nodded, her hands clasped together in her lap, her long braid hanging over her shoulder.

"The thing is, my dear, we still can't *prove* anything," Robert said. "We have no witnesses who saw Edward at the baths that morning."

"Perhaps we simply haven't asked the right questions," Lucy said stoutly. "I am quite prepared to go back there and try again."

"What a mess." Robert sighed, drew Lucy against his side, and wrapped his arm around her. "And now I am wide awake and will never get back to sleep."

Lucy rubbed her cheek against his chest. "I do apologize for waking you."

"Don't be." His arm tightened around her. "If I'd had the same thought I would've woken you up, too."

An hour later, Robert was sitting with Lucy at the breakfast table eating his way through a hastily assembled meal that had apparently, according to Foley, put Cook in a right fluster seeing as they were up two hours earlier than normal. He was quite content eating what was left over from the previous evening's dinner, and as Lucy ate like a bird in the morning she was happily eating toast.

Patrick appeared in the doorway and paused when he saw them. He'd removed his coat and his shirtsleeves were rolled up to the elbow. He hadn't shaved and the white of his linen was spotted with brown flecks of dried blood. Robert beckoned him in and pulled out a chair.

"You look as if you have been up all night. Sit down and eat something before you collapse."

"Thank you." Patrick nodded at Lucy and accepted the cup of coffee she poured him. "Mr. Benson is still alive. He stopped bleeding quite quickly, which was a mercy, because sometimes a man will be drained dry and there's nothing I can do about it." He took a slurp of coffee. "I've bound up the wound, and now we just have to wait for him to regain consciousness, and hope to contain the fever that will certainly occur."

"That's good to hear." Robert handed Patrick a plate of food. "Eat."

Patrick obliged and between mouthfuls thanked Lucy for her assistance again, railed against Dr. Mantel's incompetence, and praised Betty for sitting up with Peregrine for half the night while he took some rest.

"May I visit Mr. Benson this morning?" Lucy asked.

"Of course, my lady." Patrick nodded. "Not that you'll get much sense out of him at the moment."

"Thank you." She looked at Robert. "Should I write a note to the Bensons explaining where Peregrine is, and the current state of his health?"

"No, I think I'll pay a call on Mr. Edward Benson myself," Robert said. "I'd rather the whole lot of them stayed out of my house."

Patrick set down his knife and wiped his mouth with his napkin. "I'm surprised Mr. Benson wasn't round here last night after seeing Dr. Mantel run in there in such a panic."

"Perhaps the good doctor didn't mention what happened to anyone," Robert suggested. "It certainly wouldn't reflect well on him now, would it?"

"But surely the Bensons noticed that Peregrine didn't arrive home from the Assembly Rooms?" Patrick frowned at Robert. "Unless there is yet another thing going on I am not aware of?"

"All I can tell you at this point is that if any of the Benson family do manage to convince me that they can see

Peregrine, they are not to be left alone with him even for a second," Robert stated.

"Understood, Major." Patrick stood and offered Robert an impeccable salute. "Now, thank you for breakfast. I will change my clothes, speak to my wife, and meet you in the sickroom whenever you are ready, Lady Kurland."

Even before the door shut behind Patrick, Lucy started speaking. "Do you really intend to confront Edward?"

"I don't think I have a choice, do I?" Robert replied. "The last thing we want is him setting the law on us for kidnapping his brother."

"But what if he turns violent?" Lucy asked.

"I'm not going to accuse him of murder, my dear. I'll just inform him that Peregrine is in my house and cannot be moved until he sufficiently recovers."

"Please be careful."

He reached across the table and took her hand. "I will. I promise."

Lucy leaned over the bed and studied Peregrine's flushed face. Dr. Fletcher had given him some laudanum to ease the pain, but she could already see that he was fighting a fever.

"I cleaned the wound out and used some of Grace Turner's herbs to make a poultice to put over it," Dr. Fletcher murmured as he removed his hand from his patient's brow. "I've noticed that whatever she puts in that mixture works much better than what I have used in the past."

"Then let's hope for the best." Lucy straightened up. "Has he said anything this morning?"

"Not much and nothing that made sense." Dr. Fletcher hid a yawn.

"I am more than happy to sit with him for a few hours, Doctor," Lucy offered. "I intend to have a quiet morning after the excitement of last night."

"Then I will go and sit with my wife. She isn't feeling

well herself today and is insisting that I shouted at her and treated her as if she were a servant."

"You shouted at me, too, but I understood why," Lucy reminded him.

"You are much more . . ." He hesitated as if trying to think of an appropriate word. "*Robust* than my wife."

"Indeed." Lucy walked over to the door and opened it. "If you could ask Foley to come and speak to me when he has a moment, I would be very grateful."

After Dr. Fletcher's departure, Lucy reorganized the space around Peregrine's bed to her liking. When Foley appeared, she asked him to fetch her workbasket and bring another branch of candles. She was still finishing up some baby clothes for Penelope, and as the birth was likely to be earlier than anticipated she didn't want to have things half done.

She sewed quietly for a while, occasionally glancing over at the bed to see that Peregrine remained unconscious. Anna came in to offer up her services for the afternoon, and Lucy told her to speak to Dr. Fletcher. She knew that Robert had gone out to speak to Edward Benson, and she was rather worried that he hadn't yet returned.

A groan made her set her sewing aside and walk quickly over to Peregrine. His eyes were open and he was staring directly at her.

"What the *devil*?" he whispered.

She held a glass of water to his lips and he managed to take a sip.

"You were attacked by pickpockets and injured. Dr. Fletcher is taking care of you."

He winced and grabbed hold of her wrist. "I don't remember what happened."

"You were lucky that my husband and Dr. Fletcher arrived just after you were attacked. They managed to fight the men off, and they ran away."

He blinked at her. "Is Dr. Mantel all right?"

"Yes, he received some minor injuries. You were stabbed."

Peregrine wet his lips, and Lucy helped him take more water.

"What did they take?"

"Your purse and watch are missing," Lucy said.

"Not much then," he murmured. "Hardly worth stabbing me for."

"I agree." She set the glass back on the tray. "As you once mentioned, it is quite *extraordinary* how often your family are targeted in these attacks, isn't it?"

He stared at her for one second and then closed his eyes, his mouth settling into a stubborn line that reminded Lucy forcibly of his father.

She waited for another minute, but he turned his head away and was soon snoring again. With a sigh, Lucy returned to her sewing. She had a sense that he would be feeling far worse than he was right now and braced herself to deal with his fever.

"As I said, Mr. Benson. Your brother Peregrine is in the very capable hands of my physician. Dr. Fletcher said it would be unwise to move him at this point in case the bleeding started up again," Robert repeated himself patiently.

He'd been admitted directly into Edward Benson's study, and there was no sign of any of the other occupants of the house. For once his normally calm host looked remarkably out of sorts.

"But he would be better off here with his family, and with Dr. Mantel to care for him," Edward blustered.

"I'm sure that as soon as Dr. Fletcher thinks it is safe, he will bring your brother back here to the bosom of his family. I'm quite sure that Dr. Mantel would agree. Do you wish to consult with him before I leave?"

"Dr. Mantel was also injured in the attack and has taken to his bed. I would prefer not to disturb him at this point," Edward said.

"Then if he is indisposed, he cannot possibly care for Mr. Peregrine Benson, can he?" Robert said smoothly, and rose to his feet. "I would certainly not expect him to endanger his own health."

Edward stood as well. "I will come over and see Peregrine this afternoon."

"I doubt he will be able to speak to you, but please do call at the house and Foley will let you know whether a visit would be advisable." Robert bowed. "I'd better be getting back."

"Thank you." Edward bowed stiffly in return. "Our debt to your family is substantial."

"Hardly that," Robert countered. "I'm sure that if the situation was reversed you would have done exactly the same. I'll keep you informed as to Peregrine's progress, and if he takes a turn for the worse, I will send for you immediately."

Edward frowned. "I thought you said he was on the mend?"

"He is certainly no longer bleeding, but Dr. Fletcher anticipates he will suffer a fever, and that is never something to take lightly."

He nodded again and headed for the door all too aware that Edward Benson was staring at his back. In the hallway he met Augustus Benson, who had just arrived at the house. He still wore his muddy boots and rain-soaked cloak.

"Sir Robert! I hear that my brother Peregrine has been grievously injured."

"Did Mr. Edward Benson inform you of that?" Robert asked.

"Yes, of course he did." Augustus shook his head, making his many chins wobble. "What is the world coming to when a man can be attacked by ruffians right outside his door? There is a lack of godliness in this modern world, Sir Robert, that I find quite appalling."

Robert had no answer to that. "Your brother is currently residing in my house under the care of my physician, Dr. Fletcher, who was the person who tended to his wounds."

"Not Dr. Mantel?"

"Dr. Mantel was also attacked and found himself unable to offer his professional services at the time."

"Ah, I see." Augustus untied his cloak and draped it over a chair. "Perhaps I should accompany you home and say a prayer over my brother Peregrine."

"I don't think he is ready for visitors quite yet," Robert countered.

Augustus stiffened. "I am hardly a *visitor*. Peregrine and I might not see eye to eye on everything but he is still my flesh and blood."

"And I'm sure he will be delighted to see you when he regains consciousness, but until then he is not receiving anyone."

"If you insist," Augustus sighed. "I suppose the best thing for me to do is to stay here and comfort the other members of my family."

"I'm not sure if anyone other than Dr. Mantel and Mr. Edward Benson know what happened yet."

Augustus frowned. "What about Lady Benson? She has never liked Peregrine but I'm sure that she would not wish ill on him." He hesitated. "With all due respect, Sir Robert, is it possible that my brother might die?"

"It is always possible, sir, and eventually inevitable."

"Then you will inform me if he needs my prayers, or any other services I might render him such as writing out his last will and testament."

Robert frowned. "One would assume with all this furor over Sir William's will that all of you would have written a will already—although I suppose in your brother's case he might not have a feather to fly with worth mentioning in a will."

"You mistake the matter, Sir Robert." Augustus's chuckle

was somewhat forced. "Peregrine was the only one of us who had his *own* wealth. His godmother was our father's sister. She married a wealthy industrialist and had no children. She left her entire fortune to Peregrine."

Even though he was startled, Robert kept his thoughts about that interesting information to himself. "Well, I must be going. It was a pleasure to speak to you, Reverend Benson."

Robert left Augustus standing in the hall and made his way back to his own house. He paused as he went to raise the knocker. Should he have warned Augustus to be careful? Surely Edward wouldn't be stupid enough to attempt to murder another of his brothers? Augustus was hardly worth killing and would likely accept money to pay his debts in return for his silence.

Foley let him in and Robert repeated his orders about not allowing any of the Bensons beyond the front door without Robert's or Dr. Fletcher's express permission. He went upstairs to the drawing room and found it empty. Lucy was probably still in with Peregrine, and Dr. Fletcher might be having a well-earned rest—if his wife allowed him to.

His gaze turned to the local newspaper and he sat down to read it. If Augustus was correct about Peregrine having his own fortune his behavior toward his father and the rest of his family made a twisted kind of sense. But did having that wealth make him a murderer or a victim? Who would inherit Peregrine's fortune if he died? One had to assume it would be his brothers.

Robert checked the clock on the mantelpiece and settled into his chair. Whatever the answer, he'd stay home and guard Peregrine Benson until the man was capable of defending himself.

Armed with the very interesting information that Peregrine was a wealthy man in his own right, Lucy returned to the sickroom after dining with Robert and sent Anna down to enjoy her own repast. Dr. Fletcher was frowning down at his patient as she came in the door.

"He's burning up with fever."

"Then I assume you'll want me to keep him cool, try and get him to drink water, and summon you if he takes a turn for the worse."

"Exactly." Dr. Fletcher nodded. "You would make an excellent physician, Lady Kurland."

"I'd rather not." Lucy shuddered. "I've nursed Robert and my younger brothers through many such fevers, and I've simply learned how to read the signs."

He smiled at her as he turned down the sheets to Peregrine's waist. "I have complete confidence in you, my lady. If you need me, do not hesitate to call. I have to go to the apothecary to get some more supplies, but I will be as quick as I can."

"I will be absolutely fine, Dr. Fletcher." Lucy smoothed down her skirts and tied an apron around her waist. She'd already destroyed one gown and was reluctant to ruin another. "Please make sure that you take time to eat before you even think of returning."

"I will, my lady." Dr. Fletcher paused at the door. "Did Sir Robert mention if any of the Bensons attempted to get in the house?"

"Apparently, they all did. Even Lady Benson, who was quite hysterical." Lucy sighed. "Foley managed to fend them off, but I doubt they will allow themselves to be deterred for much longer."

"By the morning, Mr. Benson's fever will either have broken, or he will start to show signs of the wound being infected and grow worse." Dr. Fletcher grimaced. "He is a man in his prime, and one can only hope and pray he will fight this off."

"We will do our best to ensure he survives," Lucy said firmly. "I will call you if his condition worsens."

She lit the extra branch of candles Foley had brought up

for her and made sure the light didn't fall on Peregrine. His breathing was ragged now, his skin flushed, and he moved restlessly on the sheets.

Lucy bathed him in cold water with a sponge and laid a cloth on his forehead, which he immediately snatched off. She'd asked Foley to purchase some ice earlier and had used it to keep the bucket of well water as chilly as possible. Peregrine didn't appreciate her efforts in the slightest. She regularly had to avoid his flailing arms and prevent his attempts to pluck at the bandages around his chest.

After half an hour of wrestling with him Lucy was exhausted and was contemplating asking for Dr. Fletcher's help. To her relief, Peregrine suddenly went still and started snoring. Lucy sat down in her chair by the fire and wiped her brow. If he grew more agitated she would struggle to control him and might have to ask Silas to aid her.

She sipped her tea, which had cooled down considerably, but decided not to bother ringing for another pot. If she started asking for things, Foley would inform Robert, and then poor Dr. Fletcher would insist on coming to Peregrine's bedside when he clearly needed to rest.

An hour passed in relative quiet. Lucy finished sewing a baby bonnet and started embroidering the brim with yellow silk. The clock on the mantelpiece ticked away as the small coal fire cracked and popped. Eventually she stuck her needle into the fabric and walked over to the bed.

Peregrine's eyes were open, but he didn't look himself. Lucy took his hand in hers and smiled down at him.

"Do not worry. You have a fever, but you will soon feel much better."

"Dying," he croaked.

"Not if Dr. Fletcher and I have anything to do with it," Lucy corrected him. "You must concentrate on your recovery."

She offered him some water, and he managed a few sips before she lowered his head back down onto the pillows.

"Have to tell you something," he whispered.

"What is it?" Lucy asked, leaning closer to hear the faint rasp of his voice.

"Letters."

Lucy frowned at him. "I don't understand."

"Letters and numbers." He blinked hard, his throat working. "*Listen.*"

She took his hand again, and he grasped her wrist, the heat of his fingers scorching her skin. "What can I help you with?"

"Key to it all. Thought it was amusing, but can't let it die with me."

"Let what die?" Lucy asked. "Does this have something to do with your father's will?"

A commotion in the corridor outside permeated through the closed door, and Peregrine's gaze intensified.

"Shakespeare was a better playwright than me."

"I would imagine so." Lucy held his gaze. "Could you perhaps be a little more *specific*? I fear we are about to be interrupted."

Just as the door opened, Peregrine's eyes closed as if he was exhausted by his efforts. "As you like . . ."

Lucy turned to glare at Edward Benson, who stood in the doorway, Robert and Dr. Fletcher behind him.

"Please have some *decency*! Your brother is very ill, Mr. Benson."

Dr. Fletcher came in and took over Lucy's position by Peregrine's head. "His fever still hasn't broken?"

"Not yet." Lucy walked away from the bed and went to stand next to Robert.

Her husband regarded Edward, his blue gaze frosty. "As you can see for yourself, Mr. Benson. No one is trying to deceive you. Your brother is gravely ill."

Edward looked from Robert to Lucy and a now oblivious Dr. Fletcher, who was busy concentrating on his patient.

"I do beg your pardon." He loudly exhaled. "My concern for my brother overlaid my good manners and common sense."

"There is very little you can do for him at this moment," Robert said quietly. "If you wish to stay here and keep vigil with Dr. Fletcher and my wife's maid tonight, you are more than welcome."

"No, I'll call in the morning." Edward touched the brim of his hat. "I do apologize. I don't know what came over me."

Robert and Lucy followed him out into the corridor and escorted him down the stairs. Edward paused in the hallway.

"Has he asked for anyone? Has he spoken about what happened?"

"He has barely been conscious, Mr. Benson," Lucy replied. "And when he does speak, his words are somewhat garbled and nonsensical."

"Would you object if Dr. Mantel came to sit with him tomorrow in my stead?"

"Not at all." Robert bowed.

"I have to meet with the magistrate about Brandon and speak to Mr. Carstairs about returning to Yorkshire." Mr. Benson bowed. "Again, I do apologize for my impatience. After the recent death of my father I am very reluctant to lose a brother as well."

"Of course, Mr. Benson." Robert held the door open and bowed their visitor out. "Good evening."

Robert shut the door with something of a bang and turned to Lucy.

"What the devil was that about? Edward pushed his way past Foley, almost knocked him down, and demanded to be taken up to see Peregrine!"

"Maybe he thought we'd spirited him away somewhere," Lucy said.

"Or he's worried about what his brother might be saying about him and thought to finish him off." Robert blinked as his wife marched off in the direction of his study. "Where are you going *now*?"

He followed her into the book-lined room to find her studying the shelves, a candle in her hand.

"What exactly are you doing?"

"There must be a volume of Shakespeare here *somewhere*. Every library in the land has the Bard's plays," Lucy murmured.

"Why this sudden interest in Shakespeare?"

"Because of what Peregrine told me—or tried to tell me. I do hope I understood what he was saying because it did indeed sound *quite* nonsensical."

Robert caught hold of her elbow and firmly turned her to face him. "Start at the beginning, and then I'll help you search."

She sighed as if he was being a particularly dense pupil. "Peregrine said he had to tell me something in case he died. That it had all been a bit of a joke, but perhaps it wasn't funny anymore."

"And what does that have to do with Shakespeare?" Robert demanded.

She wrinkled her nose. "I'm trying to remember the exact words he used. He said it had *something* to do with numbers and letters, and that was key. Then he mentioned his plays weren't as good as Shakespeare's."

"Well, that at least makes sense," Robert muttered. "*And*?"

"I asked him if he was talking about his father's will, and he didn't disagree with me." She frowned. "And then all that noise started in the corridor, and he started to lose consciousness again."

"It sounds like a lot of fustian to me."

"But remember, Peregrine and Sir William loved riddles. Perhaps he was trying to give us some clues as to how to find the will."

Robert considered her hopeful face. "All right, then let's

go over what he said again." He found a piece of paper and started writing.

"Letters, numbers, and Shakespeare." He looked up. "That's rather a daunting task. Where on earth are we supposed to start?"

"I don't know." Lucy bit her lip. "What relevance would that have to Peregrine and Sir William?"

"Lots of hawks in Shakespeare," Robert offered. "Not sure there were any peregrines, though."

"What an excellent thought!" His wife smiled approvingly at him. "Who else has a name that might have appeared in Shakespeare?"

"Practically all of them," Robert groused. "There's definitely a few Edwards and probably an Augustus in *Julius Caesar*, and then Miranda appears in—"

Lucy held up a finger. "Arden!"

"Also from Shakespeare." Robert nodded. "As is Brandon."

"But that makes sense of the last thing Peregrine said before he lost consciousness!" Lucy said.

"The thing you didn't mention, and that isn't on my list?" Robert asked.

"Only because it didn't mean anything until I thought of *Arden*. I asked Peregrine to be more specific, and he said, 'as you like . . .' At first, I thought he was merely *agreeing* with me." She gazed at Robert expectantly.

"*As You Like It*," Robert said slowly. "And the Forest of Arden. I had to study that one at school." They smiled at each other in complete accord. "Now let's see if we can find that play on these shelves."

"Don't you remember it?" Lucy asked.

"Good Lord, no." Robert shuddered at the very thought. "I hated every minute of the damned thing."

"If we can't locate it I'm fairly sure they have it at one of the circulating libraries in Milsom Street," Lucy said. "We can go and search tomorrow morning."

They both took a candle and started at either end of the wall of books, but there was no sign of the play.

Lucy sat down with a thump, her face dejected. "Well, that is disappointing."

Robert perched on the corner of the desk. "I doubt we would've done much with the information tonight, anyway. Are you *sure* Peregrine didn't utter anything else that might indicate where we're supposed to be *looking* for the will?"

"One has to assume that the will is somewhere in Sir William's room or secreted in his belongings." Lucy looked up at him.

"Agreed. But *where*? By all accounts the rooms and baggage have been thoroughly searched on numerous occasions and nothing has turned up."

"But knowing Sir William's love of puzzles maybe the will is hidden *inside* something obvious that needs a key or a code to let you in?"

"That sounds very likely."

"Then the only thing we can do is search for ourselves. Knowing that we are looking for something that needs *opening* might help us see things in a different way to everyone else."

The hall clock struck eleven times, and Robert helped Lucy to her feet. "Let's check on Peregrine and go to bed."

He held the door open for his wife to go ahead of him and they ascended the stairs together.

"I do hope Peregrine survives this," Lucy commented as they walked through the silent house. She knocked on the door of the sickroom and peered inside. Patrick came out to join them in the corridor.

"He's still fighting the fever," Patrick said, and nodded to Robert. "With your permission, Sir Robert, I'm going to ask Silas to stay with me tonight to keep Mr. Benson safe."

"Of course. I don't need him." Robert nodded. "I'm perfectly capable of undressing myself. Do you think Peregrine is going to get better?"

"I'm hopeful." Patrick met Robert's gaze without hesitation. "If his condition worsens I'll send Silas to let you know, and you can fetch the Bensons."

"Thank you." Robert patted Patrick's shoulder. "I appreciate your skills more every day."

His friend went back into the room, closing the door behind him. Robert looked at Lucy.

"Let's go to bed and do our best to get some sleep. I suspect tomorrow might be a very interesting day."

Chapter 19

Lucy deposited the library book on Robert's desk and went to find her spectacles, which she realized she'd left with her sewing basket in the sickroom. She tapped on the door and was admitted by Anna, who was smiling.

"Mr. Benson's fever has broken. Dr. Fletcher is very pleased."

"That's wonderful." Lucy crossed over to the bed where Peregrine was now sleeping soundly, his expression so devoid of mischief and malice that he looked quite unlike himself. "Is the wound healing nicely?"

"Dr. Fletcher cleaned and dressed it this morning, and detected no sign of new swelling or the odor of decay."

"Then let's hope he makes a full recovery." Lucy smiled at her sister. "Have you eaten breakfast yet?"

"I will as soon as Betty comes to relieve me. I promised Penelope I would spend some time with her today as she is feeling somewhat neglected."

Lucy rolled her eyes. "Penelope is *terribly* selfish."

"I do have *some* sympathy for her, Lucy." Anna hesitated. "She is expecting her first child and her husband is rather busy dealing with another emergency while she quietly worries about giving birth."

"*Quietly?*" Lucy snorted. "Penelope doesn't know the meaning of that word. She just hates it when she isn't the center of attention."

Anna bit her lip. "I honestly believe that beneath her rather shrill exterior she is quite afraid, and I'm hardly the right person to alleviate those fears, am I?"

"You can only do your best," Lucy reminded her sister. "I promise that as soon as Mr. Peregrine Benson and his entire family leave Bath I will give you and Penelope *all* of my attention."

She turned to leave. "If you need me, I will be in Sir Robert's study, and then we might be visiting the Bensons."

Lucy pondered Anna's remarkably forgiving nature as she descended the stairs. She had to concede that her sister might have a point about Penelope being somewhat alone. Neither of them had a mother to guide them through the process of childbirth, but Lucy at least had helped out at many births and knew what happened. She had to suspect that even though Penelope was the wife of a doctor her sheltered upbringing had not offered her the opportunity to observe a birth.

On an impulse, Lucy changed direction, and went back up to the rooms Penelope shared with Dr. Fletcher and knocked on the door.

"Come in?"

Lucy went in to find Penelope sitting by the window, her hands folded over the large mound of her stomach. Penelope held her fingers to her lips and struggled to her feet. Her belly appeared to have dropped even lower.

"Dr. Fletcher is sleeping next door. I was just about to come down to the drawing room."

"Then I will walk with you." Lucy held open the door and stepped back to allow Penelope's bulk to pass through ahead of her. "How are you feeling today?"

"I'm exhausted," Penelope said without any of her usual snippiness.

"Do you need to go back to bed?" Lucy asked.

"I can't sleep." Penelope sighed. "The baby kicks me all night long."

"How horrible for you." Lucy gently rubbed Penelope's back as they walked. "Have you tried raising your feet up?"

"I have tried everything my husband has suggested, and nothing works." She smoothed a hand over her belly. "I cannot wait until this baby is born."

"From the look of you, it won't be long now." Lucy settled Penelope by the fire and placed a footstool under her feet.

"Why are you being so nice to me?" Penelope asked.

"Because you are stuck here, without your sister, and away from your home when you are going to give birth," Lucy replied. "I want you to know that I will do everything in my power to make sure you are supported through this."

Penelope's lip trembled. "I think that is the nicest thing you have ever said to me, Lucy, and I probably don't deserve it."

Lucy sank down onto the footstool and took Penelope's hands. "We have had our differences in the past, but when it comes to this—bringing a new life into the world—we are all women together. I want the best for you and Dr. Fletcher."

"Thank you," Penelope whispered. "It *is* rather upsetting not to be home, and I am aware that my temper has perhaps been a little *uncertain*."

Lucy squeezed Penelope's fingers. "We will get you through this, I swear it."

Penelope nodded and found a smile. "Dr. Fletcher says the same thing. He insists that his professional reputation demands that I will not only survive the experience, but positively *enjoy* it."

"Easy for him to say," Lucy murmured. "When he isn't the one doing the actual birthing."

This time Penelope's laughter was more genuine, and Lucy was still smiling when she continued down the stairs

to Robert's study where he was awaiting her. As soon as
this matter with the Bensons was concluded she promised
herself she would dedicate her time to Penelope and Anna.

Robert was already engrossed in the book and barely
looked up as she joined him.

"Did you find anything yet?" she inquired.

"Yes, and I didn't have to go far. This is the first mention of Arden Wood and it's right at the beginning of the
play in Act One."

Lucy read out the lines.

*"They say he is already in the Forest of Arden, and a
many merry men with him; and there they live like the old
Robin Hood of England. They say many young men flock
to him every day, and fleet the time carelessly, as they did
in the golden world."*

She wrinkled her nose. "What docs that tell us?"

"I have no idea," Robert said. "I've copied it out and I
thought we might take it with us when we search Sir
William's baggage tonight."

"Tonight?"

"Yes, I thought we'd sneak in up the servants' stairs.
Foley still has a key to the back door."

"Peregrine said it had to do with letters and numbers,"
Lucy reminded him, so perhaps it is a puzzle or a code or
a play on words?"

"It could be any of those things." Robert took out another sheet of paper and handed her a newly cut pen. "Perhaps we should just work out as many possibilities as we
can and hope we find the right combination."

"We should look at the letters Peregrine and his father
exchanged," Lucy said. "There might be a clue in there."

"That's an excellent idea." He grimaced. "Do you think
there's any chance Peregrine might wake up and tell us the
whole truth?"

"Dr. Fletcher is reluctant to awaken him at this point.
He says he needs healing sleep." Lucy opened the inkwell
and dipped the nib of her pen in the ink. "And now that

Peregrine is going to live I somehow doubt he will be willing to reveal his secrets anymore."

An hour later, Foley knocked on the door to let them know that Augustus, Lady Benson, and Dr. Mantel were seeking admittance to the sickroom. Robert stood up and stretched.

"I'll have to let them see him, but I'm not letting them go up there alone. Will you excuse me for a moment?"

Lucy put down her pen. "Seeing as I am getting nowhere, I'd like to at least *see* the Bensons. Perhaps I could offer them some tea after their visit and find out if they are willing to talk about anything in particular."

"As you wish." Robert nodded. "You're much better at getting information out of people than I am. Perhaps you could also ascertain where everyone will be tonight."

"I'll certainly do my best." Lucy rose and smoothed down her skirts. "The Bensons do love to share all their secrets with us, so goodness knows what they might reveal now?"

Lucy had already settled herself in the drawing room with Anna and Penelope, and ordered refreshments when Robert ushered in Lady Benson, Augustus, and Dr. Mantel. She went to take Lady Benson's hand and led her toward the couch.

"Please sit down, my lady. I cannot imagine how you must be feeling at this moment."

Lady Benson uttered a mournful sigh. "You cannot imagine, Lady Kurland. You truly *cannot*! My beloved husband is dead, my youngest son had deserted me, and now *this*! Peregrine has never liked me, and one has to suspect that he is positively *enjoying* causing me such anxiety and grief."

Lucy frowned. "I hardly think he deliberately allowed himself to be stabbed purely to annoy you, ma'am."

"Oh, you'd be surprised." Lady Benson made a dramatic gesture. "He probably hoped my dear Dr. Mantel would be killed, and *he* would be the one who 'escaped' with minor injuries."

Lucy looked at Anna, whose stunned face reflected Lucy's own reaction.

"I don't think that's what happened at all, Lady Benson. You are naturally distraught and don't mean what you say." Dr. Mantel hurried into the conversation. "Mr. Peregrine Benson was as startled as I was when those men set on us."

"He was always a passable actor," Lady Benson sniffed. "And his hatred of me knows no bounds."

Lucy glanced over at the tea tray. "Would you like some tea, Lady Benson? Hopefully, Mr. Peregrine Benson will be recovered enough soon for you to take him back to your house where Dr. Mantel can care for him."

She smiled at the doctor, noting the scars on his hands and face. "How are you feeling after such a horrible event yourself, Doctor?"

He made a face. "Remarkably embarrassed by my own behavior, to tell you the truth, my lady. I panicked rather badly."

"Not all physicians are as used to dealing with bloody wounds as Dr. Fletcher, sir," Lucy reminded him.

"That is very gracious of you." Dr. Mantel took his cup of tea and sat down.

Even as Lucy smiled at him she decided she would insist that Dr. Fletcher not release Peregrine into Dr. Mantel's hands until he was capable of defending himself and he wouldn't relapse. She suspected the Benson doctor would fail his patient again.

The rest of the visit passed without any more revelations although Lucy discovered that all the Bensons were planning on being home that night. She reassured herself that the only room close to Sir William's was Miranda's, and that the widow was remarkably fond of laudanum to help her sleep.

Whatever happened, she was determined that she and Robert would succeed in finding the will and finally working out which one of the Bensons was a murderer.

* * *

"Are you ready, Lucy?"

"Yes, I'm just coming."

Lucy gathered her notes into a pile and folded them carefully so that they would fit inside the pocket of her darkest dress. She wore soft kid skippers and had decided not to bring a shawl or reticule that she might accidentally leave behind. She went down the stairs and found her husband waiting for her in the hall. The candles and lamps had been lit, and the house was quiet as everyone else had retired to bed.

Robert wore his black coat and waistcoat, which made the whiteness of his shirt and cravat stand out even more. He had a large key in his hand and was talking to Foley, who was describing which door they could use to enter the Benson residence and exactly where the backstairs were located.

Foley turned to Lucy as she came down the stairs. "Are you quite certain that you wouldn't prefer me to go with Sir Robert, my lady?"

"I'd rather go myself," Lucy reassured him. "We wouldn't wish to get you into trouble."

"As you wish, my lady." Foley sighed and opened the door that led into the back of the house. "There is a path from the mews that leads directly to the door you need, Sir Robert. Please be careful."

Lucy followed Robert out of the house and was surprised at how bright the moon was. If anyone were looking out of the Bensons' house they would spot them in an instant. But there were no lights burning in any windows, and no sign of any people.

Robert followed the path and located the door at the back of the house without much trouble. With most of the houses in Queen's Square being rented out rather than owned, there were not many dogs to advertise an intruder's presence.

The door clicked open, and Robert stepped inside, pausing to listen before he beckoned for Lucy to follow him in.

The servants' stairs were close to the back door, which meant that they didn't have to go into the kitchen.

Luckily, Robert had an excellent sense of direction whereas Lucy found the darkness rather disorientating. When they reached Sir William's dressing room, Robert cautiously opened the door, wincing when it squeaked.

"Stay there," he whispered. "In case we have to flee. I'll make sure the other doors are locked."

He disappeared into the gloom, leaving Lucy holding her breath and clinging to the doorframe. Even as her nerves tightened, her eyes adjusted to the darkness, and she made out the shape of the furniture and proportions of the room, which weren't the same as in their rented house being on the floor above.

The strike of a flint and a flicker of light focused her gaze on the far side of the room where Robert was lighting a candle. He carried it over to her, his hand shielding the flame.

"Let's start in the bedroom. It's farther away from Lady Benson and most of Sir William's bags are in there."

Taking his proffered hand, she followed him across the room and into Sir William's bedchamber. Robert shut the door behind her and set the candle on the side of the bed.

"We'll need some more light."

Lucy wondered why he'd decided to break in at midnight when it was hard to see anything, but kept her thoughts to herself as he lit another candle.

"Let's look through the cupboards and the tallboy just to make sure nothing has been left behind," Robert said.

"And make sure there aren't any secret panels or places to hide anything?" Lucy suggested.

"Seeing as this house is rented, I doubt that any of the furniture here would have that purpose, or that Sir William would know about it."

"Oh." Lucy nodded. "Of course not."

"That's not to say that we still shouldn't be on the lookout for anything odd."

Despite gently tapping every surface and running her fingers over the backs of the drawers, Lucy found nothing of interest.

Eventually, Robert turned his attention to the three pieces of luggage that Sir William had brought with him from Yorkshire.

"Which one do you think is most likely to contain a secret drawer or a concealed container?" Robert crouched down and Lucy followed suit.

"The biggest one." Lucy patted the huge trunk, which was about three feet high and three feet wide. "Is it locked?"

Robert undid the clasps and the top of the trunk opened easily. "No, thank goodness."

He held the candle up over the contents and grimaced. "Now I wish we *had* brought Foley with us. I have no idea how we're going to pack this all up again."

By the time they had taken everything out of the trunk and piled it up behind them, Lucy was beginning to agree with Robert. They'd spent precious minutes examining the inside lid of the trunk but had found nothing within the lining except a folded ten guinea note. She'd meticulously checked every pocket of each garment and gone through Sir William's potions and lotions, but to no avail.

"Wait . . ." Robert was feeling around the edge of the bottom of the trunk. "The lining continues beneath this piece."

He roughly measured the inside of the trunk with his hands and compared it to the outside. "I suspect this trunk has a false bottom. Let's see if we can remove it."

With both of them working together, they managed to lever off the thin wooden base to reveal what lay beneath.

Robert smiled at her. "I think we've found it." He carefully lifted out the ornate black lacquered box. "Let's put everything else back, and then we can take a good look at this."

*   *   *

"There appear to be some kind of barrels to turn to release the hasp over the latch," Robert murmured. "I assume this might be the code Peregrine was referring to." He looked up at Lucy. "Now all we have to do is work out what that is."

"How many letters or numbers do we need to find?" Lucy whispered.

"Six, by the looks of it." Robert moved the candle even closer so that he could see what characters were etched in the brass. "They look like all numbers except the first one, which is a letter." He sighed. "I don't even know where to begin."

"Start with the letter *A*," Lucy said. "It's the first letter of Arden's name."

Robert used his thumb to turn the dial until it reached the *A*, and heard a faint click. "Well, that was lucky. Now on to the rest of it."

"If it's only numbers, then it can't be any words from the actual text," Lucy mused. "I wonder if it's the numerical equivalent of the rest of Arden's name?"

"Too short," Robert said, "unless you repeat the *A*."

"Let's try that. *R* is the eighteenth letter of the alphabet."

"Which won't work as the numbers go from nought to nine."

"Then maybe it is a one, followed by an eight, followed by four for the *D*, five for the *E*, and fourteen . . . That's too long, isn't it?" Lucy sighed.

"Then what else can it be?" Robert asked. "Was there any particular pattern to the puzzles Sir William and Peregrine liked to play?"

"They did use a lot of Shakespearean quotes," Lucy said slowly.

"In what context?" His leg was starting to hurt from sitting on the hard floor. "And can you relate it to a series of numbers?"

"I wish it was that simple." Lucy sighed. "Perhaps we

would be better off taking the box back to our house and dealing with it there."

"I'd rather not steal anything from the Bensons," Robert demurred.

"Then what are we doing here if you don't intend to find the will and use it to solve the mystery?" Lucy hissed. "If we take the box, we can give it to Peregrine and get *him* to open it!"

"What if he's the murderer?" Robert countered. "Do we really want to merrily hand over everything?"

"For goodness' *sake,* Robert—"

He pressed his hand over her mouth, as a familiar voice spoke from the dressing room next door.

"I have to search again! I cannot allow all these terrible things to happen to my family!" Lady Benson wailed. "If we could only recover the *will.*"

Robert met Lucy's gaze and slowly removed his hand from her lips. There was no door to the servants' stairs in the master bedchamber. He took Lucy's hand and drew her to her feet. She scooped up the box in her arms and held it against her chest.

"Please, Miranda, do not distress yourself. You and Edward have already agreed to go to court to split the money fairly between you."

That was Dr. Mantel's calm voice.

"But how can I *trust* him? Look what happened to *Peregrine!*" Miranda cried. "I can't trust *anyone.*"

"You can trust me, my darling."

Robert's gaze clashed with Lucy's startled one.

"Well, of course I can, but I still don't think you are telling me *everything.*"

"If I am keeping things from you, there would be a very good reason for it. I love you and cannot bear to see you upset."

"You are so *good* to me, so *kind . . .*"

Miranda went silent, and Robert imagined she was probably being kissed.

"Now, come back to bed and I will endeavor to keep you occupied until morning when everything will look much brighter," Dr. Mantel murmured.

Robert shuddered. She'd definitely been kissed.

Robert backed toward the door that led out onto the landing and fumbled behind him for the latch. If Miranda did decide to ignore her lover's pleas and come through the door, he would make sure he and Lucy had an escape route.

The next thing he heard was the click of Miranda's bedroom door and Dr. Mantel's low, satisfied laughter. After slowly counting to five hundred and keeping one hand in Lucy's, Robert set off back to the dressing room. He didn't draw breath until they were both safely within their own four walls.

While Robert spoke to Foley, who had waited up for them, Lucy placed the lacquered box on the desk and studied it. She couldn't believe that they had been at the Bensons' for an hour, and how close they had come to being discovered. She opened the volume of Shakespeare at the page where the Forest of Arden first appeared, and considered all the numbers on the page.

"Act One, Scene One," Lucy murmured, and then moved her finger down the side of the column of prose to the exact line of text where the forest was first mentioned. "Line . . . one hundred." She frowned. "Peregrine did say something about turning letters into numbers, and that was the key. And this is a device he used in many of his puzzles to his father. Could it be that simple?"

"Could what be that simple?" Robert asked as he came in and closed the door behind him. He carried a bottle of brandy under his arm, and two glasses in his right hand. "I thought we deserved a drink after that scare."

"You have one, but I'm wondering about the code. Sir William often used numerical references for particular lines of Shakespeare that he wanted Peregrine to look up to solve the cipher."

He took a seat beside her. "You don't want to discuss Dr. Mantel's presence in Miranda Benson's bedchamber?"

"We'll need to discuss that, too, but what about the code?" She tapped the open page of the book. "If Peregrine was suggesting we substitute numbers for letters, maybe the *A* is not a clue for Arden, but for Act One?"

Robert leaned closer and studied the list of numbers she'd made. "Act One, Scene One, line one hundred? Where did you get the one hundred from?"

Lucy showed him the text of the play and pointed at the relevant line containing the word *Arden.* "See?" She moved her finger across to the tiny printed *100* on the right-hand side of the column directly next to the printed words. "It's mentioned right here."

"Ah!" Robert nodded. "One zero zero. That makes five numbers plus the letter *A.* Shall I try it?"

"A, one, one, one zero, zero." Robert spun the brass tumblers, and there was a definite click. "Good Lord, Lucy. I think you might have done it."

He eased the box open and stared down at the pile of documents within, one of which bore many seals and was tied with a red ribbon.

"*The last will and testament of Sir William Benson, Baronet,*" Lucy read out, and then looked at her husband. "Now what on *earth* are we going to do with it?"

Chapter 20

"To what do I owe this honor?" Peregrine inquired as Robert and Lucy came into his bedchamber. He was sitting up in bed and had obviously felt well enough to consume the bowl of gruel that sat on his nightstand. "Are you kicking me out?"

"Not quite yet."

Robert laid the black lacquered box on the bed. He and Lucy had argued for quite a while about what to do with all the information they had uncovered. Seeing as they now believed there might be a different reason for the murder of Sir William, he'd argued that Peregrine was their only chance of solving the rest of it.

"How on earth did you find that?" Peregrine exclaimed.

Lucy smiled at him. "With your help, and a little luck."

"When I was delirious with fever? You are an incredibly devious woman, Lady Kurland."

"You thought you were dying," Lucy pointed out. "You *begged* me to find the box and break the code."

"I don't remember what I did." Peregrine sighed. "But it sounds like the sort of ridiculous thing I *would* do, so I can hardly blame you for my sins." He eyed Robert. "Why have you brought it to me, and not Mr. Carstairs?"

"There is the small matter that we were trespassing

when we found it." Robert crossed one booted foot over the over. "And we thought you might help us understand exactly what is going on before we proceed any further."

Peregrine opened the box and took out the will. "I've already seen it."

Robert nodded. "We suspected as much, which begs the question of why you didn't destroy it, but put it back where your father had hidden it?"

"I thought it was amusing. The idea that they were all frantically looking for it and that not one of them thought to ask me—the favorite son." Peregrine shrugged, and then winced as if suddenly aware of his wounded side. "My father told me about his latest version over breakfast the day he died. That's why I followed him to the baths and argued with him. I stole it out of his pocket when he went off with Dr. Mantel to get in the baths."

"You didn't approve of his decisions?" Robert asked.

"Hardly. He was intending to leave everything to me."

Lucy blinked at him. "And you didn't approve of *that*?"

"How *could* I?" For once Peregrine wasn't smiling. "Firstly, I doubted it would stand up in court, and secondly, much as I dislike my brothers, I *did* think he was being rather unfair to them. The thought of them *all* coming whining to me when they went into debt was also quite fatiguing. I'm already wealthy in my own right, and while I like money, I don't need *all* of it."

"Do you know who witnessed the new will?" Robert asked.

Peregrine grabbed the will and leafed through the many pages to the end where there was a lengthy codicil. "You can read it for yourself. Mr. Tompkins and Dr. Mantel witnessed the damned thing."

"Dr. Mantel did?" Robert glanced at Lucy. "Was Lady Benson left nothing?"

Peregrine grimaced. "A pittance that would make her totally dependent on remaining in my good graces."

"Which explains a lot." Robert nodded. "I wonder if you

would be so good as to look at the other documents Sir William kept in there."

"Of course." Peregrine set the will aside and took out another bundle of letters. "These are related to the Hall brothers and their father, Dennis. I haven't seen them before." He sifted through them, his eyes widening. "It appears that there was no reliable evidence that Mr. Hall was dead, which means that Miranda is probably a bigamist." His smile widened. "Good *God,* how deliciously *scandalous!*"

"One has to assume that this was why Sir William decided to cut his wife out of his will," Lucy said. "She wasn't really entitled to *anything.*"

Peregrine stacked up the papers. "This is all well and good, but it still doesn't tell me who murdered my father, does it?"

"Actually, we think it does." Robert looked at Lucy, who nodded for him to go on. "We believe Dr. Mantel killed him, and Mr. Tompkins."

"Dr. *Mantel?*" Peregrine said. "*Why?*"

"Because he is involved in a love affair with Lady Benson. If he discovered that she had been written out of Sir William's will, don't you think he would've done something about it?"

"And he would know, seeing as he was one of the witnesses," Peregrine said slowly. "Why didn't I think he might be guilty of murder?"

"Probably because like us you believed he was a physician who took a solemn vow to *first do no harm,*" Robert said. "Our own physician is so trustworthy it blinded us to the obvious truth."

Peregrine nodded. "Dr. Mantel was also at the baths on that fateful day."

"The only thing we aren't clear on yet is how much Lady Benson knew about all this," Lucy added. "And that's why we need your help. . . ."

*   *   *

"Be careful!" Peregrine scolded the two footmen who were carrying him. "I don't want yet another injury."

Lucy and Robert followed a complaining Peregrine into the Benson house and up the stairs to the drawing room. Edward, Augustus, Lady Benson, Arden, and Dr. Mantel were all gathered there awaiting his return. While Peregrine settled himself in a chair with as much drama as Lady Benson usually brought to the proceedings, Robert went down the stairs again to make certain that Mr. Carstairs had also arrived.

He escorted the solicitor up the stairs, ignoring his muttered comments about the disorderly conduct of the Bensons and his desire to never do business with them again. When he reached the drawing room, Robert ushered Mr. Carstairs in and remained by the doors, blocking the exit.

Peregrine caught his eye and Robert nodded.

"It is good to be back with my family," Peregrine said, raising his voice sufficiently to drown out everyone else. For the first time, Robert could imagine him on a stage. "I thought that I was going to die, and that made me rethink my past choices." He sighed heavily and beckoned to Lucy, who brought the box over to him.

"I have a confession to make."

Edward scowled at him. "What have you done now, Peregrine?"

"I . . . stole Father's will."

A cacophony of noise filled the room, making Robert wince. When they all settled down again, Edward was the first to recover.

"*Why?*"

Peregrine shrugged. "I didn't want you all to see what was in it."

"Had Father finally disinherited you?" Edward asked hopefully.

"No. He disinherited you lot."

Edward visibly rocked back on his heels, and Lady Benson pressed a hand to her mouth.

"You mean . . . he left everything to *you?*" Edward said faintly.

"Yes." Peregrine held out the will to Mr. Carstairs. "You might wish to take hold of this before anyone in my family destroys it." He continued. "It's a good job I *did* steal the damn thing before someone decided it was better if it remained hidden. Mr. Tompkins was one of the witnesses, and he's dead, and dear Dr. Mantel was the other, and he was set upon by scoundrels along with me." He paused. "It's almost as if *someone* didn't want anyone to know there had been a new will."

Edward glared at his brother. "I do hope you're not suggesting it was *me*, Peregrine."

"I suppose it could've been you, or Augustus, or even my dear sweet stepmother, who would *hate* having to come and beg me for money."

Robert winced at the malice of Peregrine's tone, but for once he didn't blame him. Knowing the volatility of the Benson family and their propensity for open strife he was hoping everything would soon boil over in a satisfactory manner.

"Now, I say." Dr. Mantel stood up. "Leave Lady Benson out of this. She has done nothing wrong."

Peregrine raised his eyebrows. "Well, that depends on whether you believe *bigamy* is a sin or not, doesn't it? What do you think, Miranda?"

Lady Miranda's mouth dropped open and she drew in an audible breath. Dr. Mantel grabbed hold of her elbow.

"You do not have to answer him, my lady."

"Oh, I think she does," Peregrine retorted. "Did she fool you with her tears and protestations, too, Dr. Mantel? Did she promise you that if you helped her get rid of her ailing husband you could be her new one?" His laugh was unkind. "What a *shame* that she can't marry anyone because she is still a wife."

"My father is dead," Arden insisted. "He died when we were children."

"I'm afraid that isn't true." Peregrine held out the documents to Arden. "I assume this is what Brandon was searching for at your mother's behest when he came across Mr. Tompkins and killed him."

"Balderdash!" Arden shouted. "Brandon didn't kill *anyone* and my mother *never* asked us to search for the documents!"

"Then who did?" Robert finally intervened, and caught Arden's furious attention. "Was it Dr. *Mantel* by any chance?"

"Yes, he *did* suggest it because he cares about my mother's health and knew she was distressed by the matter." Arden glowered at Robert. "What's wrong with *that*?"

"Perhaps Dr. Mantel can answer you." Robert looked across at the tight-lipped doctor. "Although one does have to wonder whether the *title* of doctor is actually yours by merit, or merely something you acquired so that you could get close to Sir William and Lady Benson. According to my physician your skills are *abysmally* lacking."

"I'm not sure what you are implying, Sir Robert." Dr. Mantel raised his eyebrows.

"He's *implying* that you murdered my father so that you could marry Miranda, and have now found out that she's actually of no use to you at all," Peregrine drawled.

"He *is* of use!" Lady Benson jumped to her feet and rushed over to Peregrine, her finger pointing at his face. "And I would *not* be a bigamist!"

Dr. Mantel briefly closed his eyes as everyone stared at Lady Benson.

"Are you . . . suggesting that Dr. Mantel is in fact your first husband?" Peregrine asked slowly.

Lady Benson raised her chin. "Yes, he is! Dennis *loves* me, and *everything* he has done is because of that!"

Robert stiffened as Dr. Mantel made a run toward the door, and stepped forward to stop him. The doctor lowered his shoulder and rammed his head into Robert's chest, sending him sprawling backward onto the floor. Behind Robert, Lady Benson screamed, and Edward and Arden shouted.

Lucy appeared at his side. "Are you all right, Robert?"

"Yes, I think so." He stood up with her help and shut the door, blocking the Bensons' pursuit. "He won't get far. I have some men positioned downstairs to take Dr. Mantel into custody."

He walked over to Peregrine, who was smiling at him. "Perhaps now that we have established that Dr. Mantel is a murderer, we might sort out some of the other pertinent details. I assume Dr. Mantel killed Mr. Tompkins because he was the only other person apart from Peregrine who knew what was in the new will."

"*And* he got me stabbed by footpads," Peregrine added.

"Precisely." Robert nodded. "It was clever of him to receive minor injuries of his own."

Robert deliberately half turned to Lady Benson, who was sobbing her heart out while Arden attempted to comfort her and raised his voice. "If Dr. Mantel *did* murder both men then perhaps you might drop the charges against Brandon, Mr. Benson?"

Lady Benson's head shot up. "What charges?"

Arden took her hand. "Brandon's being held in Bath Gaol on suspicion of murdering Mr. Tompkins."

"Why didn't anyone *tell* me?" she wailed.

Lucy spoke up for the first time. "Perhaps Dr. Mantel intended to blame Peregrine for both murders after he died from his wounds, and thus set Brandon—who presumably is his son, free?"

"If Dennis did that to his own *son* . . ." Lady Benson bared her teeth. "I will kill him *myself*! He wasn't *supposed* to murder Mr. Tompkins! I knew *nothing* about that. I just asked him to help me make certain Sir William would not suffer anymore. He *hated* being old."

"You think my father would've thanked you for putting him out of his misery?" Peregrine's voice was full of scorn. "You disgustingly self-centered *harpy*!"

Robert had to step in front of Lady Benson as she

launched an attack on Peregrine. It took Arden to calm her down and restrain her.

Eventually Lady Benson was escorted up to her bedroom and locked in. Robert received word that Dr. Mantel, or whatever his name was, had been apprehended and was on his way to Bath Gaol. Edward went down to his study in somewhat of a daze with Augustus in tow to write a letter releasing Brandon from all charges and presumably to compose a new one accusing Dr. Mantel.

Mr. Carstairs picked up the will and put it in his case. "This family is an abomination. As soon as I get back to my office in Yorkshire I am going to pass the whole circus on to another partner."

"An excellent idea, sir," Robert commended him. "Perhaps Mr. Peregrine Benson will soon sort the sorry business out with you and make sure all the Bensons are happy again."

"Indeed I will." Peregrine grinned at the sour-faced solicitor. "I can't wait!"

"So let me get this straight," Dr. Fletcher said as he stood in front of the fireplace in the drawing room. "Dr. Mantel wasn't qualified to be a doctor, and was an *actor*?"

"*That's* what worries you?" Robert asked. "The fact that he also murdered two people is rather more important."

"I know that." Dr. Fletcher waved an impatient hand. "And he is, or was, Lady Benson's husband?"

"Correct." Robert nodded. "He came back to her at some point after she married Sir William—I'm not sure if she *knew* he was alive when she got married again, but that might come out at the trial. She did encourage Dr. Mantel to pretend to be her physician and do away with her husband when they came to Bath. They probably reckoned that fewer questions would be asked than if he'd died at home where everyone knew him."

"They didn't reckon on you and Lady Kurland and your nose for murder, did they?" Dr. Fletcher said. "From a medical standpoint I assume Dr. Mantel might have stabbed Sir William as he helped him into the baths, shoved his head under the water, and then walked away assuming nature would take its course while he was far away bargaining for herbs."

"Which is exactly what *would* have happened if you and Sir Robert hadn't been at the baths that morning," Lucy added. "No one would have noticed a thing if Sir William's own doctor certified that his client had drowned after suffering heart failure."

"Lady Benson also confessed that she and Dr. Mantel tried to get the will by bribing the servant you spoke to, Lucy," Robert said. "That's probably why Miranda went through all the clothes so thoroughly when you brought them back to her. I'm still not quite sure how involved she was in the planning or whether Dr. Mantel kept her in blissful ignorance."

"What a mess," Lucy sighed. "And if *Peregrine* had died . . ." She shivered. "Then we would not have been able to solve any of it."

The door to the drawing room flew open to reveal Penelope looking rather perplexed. She pointed down at her gown.

"I am all *wet*! What on *earth* is going on?"

Dr. Fletcher started stuttering while Lucy rose to her feet, went over to Penelope, and took her hand.

"Your baby is coming. Let's go up to your bedchamber while Dr. Fletcher remembers what he's supposed to be doing and joins us."

Later that evening, Robert looked up as Lucy came into his study.

"How is everything?"

She beamed at him. "Penelope and Dr. Fletcher have a fine, healthy son."

He raised his glass of brandy to her. "How wonderful for them."

"And, of course, Penelope had the easiest and quickest birth I have ever seen, and is boasting that she doesn't understand what women complain about. She will be insufferable now." Lucy sighed as Robert pulled her down to sit on his lap.

"Did Anna assist you?"

"Yes, and thank goodness she was there because Dr. Fletcher suddenly became an indecisive, bumbling fool." Lucy paused. "Although I *do* think it did Anna good to see such an easy birth. She confided to me that she is considering writing to Captain Akers and asking him to visit her in Kurland St. Mary."

"Well, that *is* good news. Have the Fletchers decided on a name for the child yet?"

"They were still arguing it out when I left." Lucy struggled not to smile. "Dr. Fletcher wanted to call the child Robert Declan, and for some reason Penelope was *quite* against it."

Robert chuckled and wrapped an arm around Lucy's waist, his fingers spreading over her rounded stomach. "I do hope that when *this* one arrives, you won't object to adding a Robert in there somewhere if it is a boy?"

She put her hand over his. "You *knew*?"

"My darling girl, I am a trifle unobservant, but not about such an intimate matter as what goes on in my own bed."

"Why didn't you say anything?" Lucy asked.

"Because I assumed that you would tell me in your own good time." He looked up at her. "Which I hoped would be before I had to stay in Bath for another six months."

"I was too afraid," Lucy confessed. "I'm not sure I even want to talk about it *now*."

"Then we will not speak about it until we get home." He kissed her very carefully and held her gaze. "Let's talk about something else."

"The Bensons?" Lucy suggested.

Robert scowled at her. "Good Lord, no! I've had quite enough of that family to last me a lifetime!"

INDIGO

A VALENTINO MYSTERY

INDIGO

LOREN D. ESTLEMAN

THORNDIKE PRESS
A part of Gale, a Cengage Company

GALE
A Cengage Company

LIBRARY OF CONGRESS CIP DATA ON FILE.
CATALOGUING IN PUBLICATION FOR THIS BOOK
IS AVAILABLE FROM THE LIBRARY OF CONGRESS.

ISBN-13: 978-1-4328-8417-8 (hardcover alk. paper)

Published in 2021 by arrangement with Tor/Forge

Printed in Mexico
Print Number: 01   Print Year: 2021

In memory of Richard S. Wheeler,
an immortal writer; a lifelong friend

I think I'm in a frame. . . . I'm going in there
now to look at the picture.

— Robert Mitchum, *Out of the Past* (1947)
written by Geoffrey Homes
(Daniel Mainwaring)

I think I'm in a frame. . . . I'm going in there
now to look at the picture.

— Robert Mitchum, Out of the Past (1947)
written by Geoffrey Homes
(Daniel Mainwaring)

■ ■ ■ ■

I
APPOINTMENT WITH DANGER

■ ■ ■ ■

Harriet said, "But you've seen it a thousand times."

"A gross exaggeration," said Valentino.

"Okay, nine hundred and ninety-nine. On TV, on silver nitrate, celluloid, VHS, Beta —"

"Enough about Beta. Haven't you ever made a mistake?"

"— LaserDisc, DVD, Blu-ray, digital HD; you even followed it frame-by-frame and line-by-line in the pages of the Film Classics Library. Val, during intimate moments you shout out, 'Play, it, Sam!' Why would you want to watch it again on such a special occasion?"

"Everyone should see a classic film at least once on a full-size screen in a public theater, with an audience. That's how it was intended originally."

She jumped on that. "You've seen it that way too, in that art house in Glendale. You

geeked out when one of those two girls sitting in front of us whispered to her friend, 'I bet she doesn't show up at the train station.' "

"Well, I want to do that again tonight. Seeing *Casablanca* with someone who's never seen it before is like watching it for the first time all over again."

Harriet Johansen stood in the middle of The Oracle's auditorium, sweeping her arms to encompass the motion picture palace's gilded and velvet-swagged trim, its mythic statuary and plush brocade. "Why not here? You've spent a fortune restoring this barn. Save it for the grand opening. That's what you and I are celebrating, after all: the butt of the last contract laborer on its way out the door, after five years."

"Nearer six. We met here, remember."

"How could I forget? You, me, and a forty-year-old corpse in the basement. Could it be more romantic?"

"Beats hooking up on a dating app."

She smiled, removed her short silk cape, baring her shoulders, slung it around his neck, and went up on tiptoe to kiss him. Then she pulled back to study his face. "Seriously, what's wrong with here?"

Valentino shook his head. "It'd be anticlimactic after Grauman's screened the same

film. Who'd bother to see it again so soon?"

"You, for one." She stopped smiling. "Val, are you putting off actually opening this place to the public?"

"Think you know me, do you?"

"I know I know you. Answer the question."

"Okay, I'm a little nervous. What if no one comes?"

"You built it. They'll come."

His eyes rolled. "That's terrible."

"Now you know what it's like to hang out with you."

"I just need a little more time — to plan the campaign, I mean. You can't just throw open the doors and expect people to come pouring in like Black Friday at Macy's."

"Okay, you win." She retrieved her cape and put it back on. "But as long as we're all dressed up, let's stop someplace for a drink on the way."

"I'll get my wallet. They're still carding me in my thirties."

"Stop complaining. Your youthful good looks are what attracted me to you in the first place."

"You know, deep down, you're quite shallow."

He took the hidden stairs to his apartment in the projection booth. For years Valentino

13

had lived among the wreckage of old Hollywood, commuting between The Oracle and UCLA, where he supervised the hunt for and restoration of lost motion pictures for the Film & Television Archive. The rest of the time — that time he didn't spend with Harriet — he fought with painters, plasterers, plumbers, electricians, inspectors, and his prima donna of an architect. At long last the work was finished — most of it, anyway — and they'd planned this night on the town to commemorate the event.

Harriet was parked in a tow-away zone in front of the theater. The sun visor was tipped down on the driver's side, showing the word POLICE in block letters. "Shame on you," Valentino said. "You're a forensic pathologist. What's the hurry? All the people you make appointments with are dead. Anyway, you punched out two hours ago."

"Oh, like you never snuck into the screening room at work to watch the Three Stooges on company time."

"Their contribution to slapstick cinema —" He fell back against his seat as she peeled away from the curb.

They went east on Broadway. Vintage movie houses rolled past, their names spelled out in neon and incandescent lights: The Mil-

lion Dollar, The Orpheus, The Pantages, now advertising Spanish-language features for the largely Hispanic local population. By some miracle, a city of restless bulldozers had overlooked this slice of old California. He went there often for architectural inspiration and nostalgia; but much of the neighborhood was crumbling. He'd turned to point out that they had missed Grauman's Chinese Theatre by many blocks when she drew up before the terra-cotta façade of a five-story building older than most of its neighbors and cut the engine.

"Seriously?" he said. "Aren't we a little overdressed for a mugging?"

"Need I remind you, Merton of the Movies, that more classic films and TV shows have been shot in the Bradbury Building than almost any other place in town? Especially crime stories, which are your favorite."

"But it's no place to order a drink! It's all offices."

"Well, maybe we'll find a bottle of Old Grand-Dad in some shamus's desk drawer." She opened the door and swung her feet to the ground. He got out and followed her to the entrance, feeling more than usually self-conscious in a well-pressed suit and polished shoes.

But he looked forward to revisiting the

Bradbury. In his younger days, before Harriet, before The Oracle, before he had any standing in the university, he'd gone there with a sack lunch just to sit in the foyer and watch ghosts. Thanks to the casting departments of Warner Brothers, Paramount, and RKO, generations of hard-boiled detectives and sadistic racketeers had prowled its halls, leaving their shimmering silver essence behind.

Its exterior was unobtrusive, almost anonymous; practically the only note of character was a plaque assigning it to the National Register of Historic Places. But inside lay a breathtaking display of Gay Nineties splendor: tessellated floors, ceramic fixtures, filigreed stairs that climbed up and up a series of railed balconies, the iconic cage elevator, all visible from ground level because of the air shaft that shot straight to the skylight, prisming California sunshine into old-time Technicolor.

Was it still pristine, or had the carrion-birds of Civic Improvement gutted it to attract orthodontists, CPAs, and designers of web sites? Valentino opened the door for Harriet, feeling as he did so a chill of anticipation mixed with dread.

"Surprise!"

The lobby — ornate and unchanged —

16

was packed with familiar faces. Professor Kyle Broadhead, the venerable director of the film preservation department, shared space with his young bride, Fanta; Henry Anklemire, the high-pressure PR rep in charge of UCLA's Information Services; some technicians Valentino had befriended in the lab where films were rescued and restored; and Leo Kalishnikov, the genius (and didn't he know it!) architect in charge of returning The Oracle to its Roaring Twenties glory.

Harriet applauded. "Perfect!"

"Keep quiet, wait till the door opens, yell 'Surprise,' " Broadhead said with a shrug. "Pretty hard to screw that up; although I did worry that Val might overhear Kalishnikov's getup from a block away."

The architect beamed, as if he'd been paid a compliment. Silver-haired and gaunt, he stood apart from the party-clad crowd in a white double-breasted tuxedo, borsalino hat tipped low over his left ear, and a full-length velour cape, red to match his hatband and shoes. "I made a special trip to my tailor in London just for this occasion." The Russian's accent today was pure Sergei Eisenstein; it came and went according to his fancy.

Broadhead said, "And still they let you

back in the country."

Valentino turned to Harriet. "So, no *Casablanca*?"

"We'll always have *Casablanca.*" She turned. "How long have we been planning this, Fanta?"

The younger woman rested a hand on Broadhead's arm. She was his former student and now his wife — against all odds, given the professor's long solitary widowhood and the age gap. They were unabashedly devoted to each other. "We started talking about it the first time Val threw the main switch. We were interrupted by the fire engines."

"The blaze was not unexpected," her husband added. "What *was*, was me still being around to attend this soiree. The Great Wall didn't take as long or exceed the budget by as much."

Henry Anklemire, his chubby little frame swathed in a faded purple smoking jacket, snorted. "Baloney. You'll bury us every one. You're an excrement of the university."

"*You're* an excrement of the university," said Broadhead. "I'm an ornament. By the way, which long-dead thespian is responsible for that horse blanket you have on?"

"David Niven. Wardrobe department at United Artists will never miss it. This was in

18

one of the pockets: Bonus." He pointed to his obvious toupee.

"I didn't know Niven made a Davy Crockett movie. Ouch!"

Fanta squeezed Broadhead's biceps. "Down, Kyle. This is Val's night."

"Yes, dear." He pried himself loose, rubbing the sore spot, and turned to a rolling cart laden with bottles and trays of hors d'oeuvres. From a gleaming copper ice bucket he plucked a magnum of champagne, swaddled the neck in a linen napkin, and began untwisting the wire that secured the cork. "No celebration is complete without dehydrated gray cells and toxic acetaldehyde surging from your liver."

"A hangover, to the non-biologist," Harriet said. "You've been stepping out on your specialty, Yoda."

"Purely in its interest. I've come to the chapter in my magnum opus on the history of cinema where I dissect *The Lost Weekend, The Thin Man,* and *When a Man Loves a Woman.* Our esteemed dean has suggested the title 'A Dissertation on Dipsomania,' but rather than induce coma among my dozens of readers I shall call it 'You're Out of Scotch.'" The cork shot out with an ear-splitting pop and struck a chord off an iron railing. He stanched the flow of bubbly with

19

the napkin, filled a series of crystal flutes, passed them around, kept one for himself, and lifted it. "To the *Titanic,* the *Hindenburg,* New Coke, and The Oracle: four disasters in declining order of casualties."

"Kyle!"

"Very well, my dear. I raise my glass in honor of bold enterprise and devotion to lost glamour, however misdirected."

"Better, lover. Still not good." She drank.

The film archivist sipped, raised his eyebrows. "This is fine. I thought you bought all your liquor in Tijuana."

"Too much trouble now that a passport is required. Mine expired while I was in a cell in Yugoslavia. Anyway, the occasion is stellar. How often does a man manage to outrun *all* his creditors?"

"The jury's still out on that; but thank you."

Broadhead set down his drink. "Reserve your gratitude for when it's appropriate." He walked around behind the cart, drawing everyone's attention to a sheet-covered rectangle resting on an easel; Valentino had been only half aware of it, dismissing it as part of a repair project, common to old structures of historic importance.

Fanta leaned in close to the guest of honor. "He's been busting to show you this

20

for days. I had to promise him sexual favors to hold off."

Valentino grimaced. "Thank you for that image."

A tasseled cord hung alongside the drapery. Broadhead, standing next to it, took hold of this, paused, and tugged hard. The cloth slid to the floor without interruption.

A hush followed, shattered by spontaneous applause.

"Oh, my." Valentino stared. "Oh, my."

2

It was an oil painting in a Deco frame, a portrait of a stunningly beautiful woman, rendered by an artist of rare talent. Her cascade of raven hair caught the light in haloes as if she were standing directly across from Valentino. A naked shoulder was opalescent. The eyes — part defiant, part fragile — were a bewitching shade of hazel; they lacked only the addition of a green scarf to turn them to jade. The lips were full and exquisitely shaped. It was a face without flaws.

There wasn't a sound in the room. Even Anklemire, far from the most sensitive soul in attendance, stood mute, his glass raised halfway to his lips and motionless.

"Laura." The name came out in a whisper, as if Valentino had spoken in church.

"The same," said Broadhead, "yet different. When Rouben Mamoulian was signed to direct, he commissioned his wife to paint

this picture. Gene Tierney posed for it in person. But it isn't the one everyone remembers from *Laura.* When Otto Preminger came on to replace Mamoulian, he rejected it. I gather it had something to do with her gaze set in the wrong direction; wrong, I suspect, because it wasn't directed at Preminger. Anyway he had a studio photograph blown up and air-brushed to resemble a painting. That one's unavailable, and if it were, it would be beyond most people's means. This one is dear enough, but because it's less well-known, the price was far more reasonable."

"Even so, Kyle, you can't possibly afford this."

"Right you are. We ornaments of the university are vastly overrated and notoriously underpaid. But *he* can."

Valentino turned to follow the direction of Broadhead's pointing finger. From a corner he'd have sworn was deserted only moments earlier stepped an elegant-looking old man, with white hair fine as sugar combed back from his forehead, very brown skin, and eyes the color of mahogany. His thin build created an impression of height; in fact he was only slightly taller than Anklemire, but a creature from an entirely different species. His evening clothes were silk, the jacket and

trousers midnight blue, the shirt snow-white, and his black patent leather shoes glistened like volcanic glass. He was ancient, but erect, and his smile was both genuine and modest.

"*Señor* Bozal!"

The smile broadened. "You remember me. Swell!"

Valentino took the slim brown hand that was offered him. Although the fingers were bony, his grip was firm and dry.

"How could I not? The party you threw to commemorate your gift to my department was almost as lavish as the donation itself. Wherever did you find a cache of George Hurrell's studio stills no one had seen in eighty years?"

"No comment. An old mug like me needs his secrets."

Ignacio Bozal's habitual use of forties-era urban slang, so much in contrast with his Castilian accent, surprised and amused everyone who met him for the first time: He looked like a Spanish grandee and talked like a combination of Allen Jenkins and Broderick Crawford.

Twenty years before immigrating to the United States, he'd suddenly appeared in Acapulco with a bankroll big enough to buy and renovate a broken-down resort hotel

24

and open for business just before the birth of the Mexican Riviera. His American investors accepted his claim that he'd been a silent partner in a gold mine somewhere in the Sierras; but then they'd profited too greatly from the association to press for specifics.

Valentino, whose department was so much richer for Bozal's contributions, was similarly inclined.

"The minute I heard about this shindig, I decided to crash the gate. But I ain't so rough around the edges I'd come empty-handed." The old man gestured toward the painting.

"It's too generous," Valentino said. "I've done nothing to justify such a present."

"Maybe not. But you will, if we can come to a deal."

The old man's gentle appearance was reassuring; it was his underworld vernacular that lent a sinister interpretation to the remark. On a soundstage, the camera operator would dolly in for a close-up of his enigmatic expression just before fading out.

Harriet, who had stopped at one glass of champagne and made free with the canapés, drove. Laura, cocooned in the sheet that had veiled her, rode in the back seat. The

theaters were dark at that hour, and the streetlamps, spaced farther apart there than in the busier neighborhoods, illuminated Harriet's profile in flickers.

"How old do you think Bozal is?" she said.

Valentino came out of a half-doze; he'd stopped at one canapé and made free with the champagne. "Based on what little is known of his history, my guess is he's approaching the century mark, not that you'd know it to look at him."

"How much *do* you know about his history?"

"I told you where he says he got his capital. Personally, it sounds a little too close to *The Treasure of the Sierra Madre*. Did you notice the way he talks?"

"How could I miss it? It's like Dick Tracy marinated in Cesar Romero."

"When he came to this country, the TV airwaves were jammed with sports, soap operas, and old movies. He didn't follow sports, and the soaps weren't his cup of tea, so he learned his English from films Hollywood considered too old to re-release to theaters, so they dumped them on television. His preference happened to run to gangster movies. Anyway, that's his story."

"What's yours?"

"I don't have one, but any man who

comes out of nowhere with a bundle is bound to attract rumors: He made his stake harboring Nazi war criminals in Brazil, or was a member of the Perón government in Argentina, where he looted the treasury."

They entered West Hollywood, where the glow of the thousands of bulbs that illuminated the marquee of The Oracle were visible for blocks. After decades of darkness, it pleased him to come home to a dazzling display. Kyle Broadhead, less romantic, referred to it as "a human sacrifice to the gaping maw of Consolidated Edison."

"You don't think there's any truth to the rumors, do you?" Harriet said.

"Of course not. In the absence of evidence, people will go to any lengths to provide a substitute; and they never gossip about the basic goodness of Man."

She smiled. "I like that you believe that. So why do you like crime thrillers so much?"

"When I feel blue, I watch Fred Astaire dancing with Ginger Rogers. When I feel naughty, I watch Lawrence Tierney plotting a murder with Claire Trevor. The first cheers me up; the second keeps me from acting on my baser instincts."

" 'Baloney,' to quote Henry Anklemire. What's this deal Bozal was talking about, in return for the painting? You were off in a

corner together, whispering like a couple of heisters."

He laughed, hiccupped; excused himself. "Two minutes with him and you sound like Bonnie Parker. He's invited me to his house tomorrow morning."

"That sounds like more of a favor for you than for him."

"He was cagy about it, but from some broad hints he made I gather he's come into a film that shouldn't be screened except by someone who knows how to manage old stock. Of course he has a home theater, and of course it will make The Oracle look like an all-night grindhouse in San Diego."

"Doubt that."

"I wouldn't rule anything out where Bozal is concerned. He's one of the biggest private collectors in the business. If I play my cards right, I'll pick up some tips on how he manages to find such treasures without the resources of a major university behind him."

"Greedy. You've already got Laura."

"Told you I have baser instincts."

They pulled up in front of the Baroque/ Italianate/ Byzantine pile of sandstone, with bulbs chasing up, down, and around the towering marquee: GRAND OPENING SOON, read the legend in foot-high letters.

"How are you feeling tonight?" Her brows

28

were arched. "Blue or naughty?"

"Inebriated as a North American mammal of the weasel family." He got out, stumbling, opened the back door, and leaned in to retrieve the portrait.

She alighted from her side. "You'd better let me carry that. You're liable to trip and put your head through it, and then you'll feel like Abbott and Costello."

3

Court Street was old town, wop town, cook town, any town. It lay across the top of Bunker Hill and you could find anything there from down-at-heels ex-Greenwich-villagers to crooks on the lam, from ladies of anybody's evening to County Relief clients brawling with haggard landladies in grand old houses with scrolled porches, parquetry floors, and immense sweeping banisters of white oak, mahogany and Circassian walnut.

That was how Raymond Chandler, the great (and unabashedly politically incorrect) detective-story pioneer had described the place in his own time. His works had poured the foundation for film *noir,* Ignacio Bozal's crash course on English as a second language, and incidentally Valentino's guiltiest pleasure. Some of these dark forays into the abnormal psychology of crime had been

based on Chandler's novels and stories, others were filmed directly from his screenplays; most of the rest bore his influence.

Although Valentino knew the neighborhood well — and as recently as last night's celebration in the Bradbury Building — he looked forward to returning as a guest of its most famous resident.

There's nothing rarer than an East L.A. millionaire. That paradox was enough in itself to pique the film archivist's interest, without the added incentive of an invitation to screen some mysterious property possibly lost for generations. Together, they'd compelled him to cancel his day's appointments and brave the gangs and carjackers who preyed upon the honest residents to pay the old man a visit.

There, scorning the mansions of Bel-Air and Beverly Hills, Ignacio Bozal had bought a city block of modest houses in the largely Mexican-American suburb of Los Angeles. A wall went up around it, sheltering his middle-aged children, grown grandchildren, and great-grandchildren under his benevolent eye. He'd kept the largest home for himself and converted it to make room for his various collections; an example of one of which boated into the curb in front of The Oracle and blew a horn that played the

first four notes of the *Dragnet* theme.

"Boated" sprang to mind the moment Valentino pushed through the brass-framed front door to the sidewalk: The car was more than twenty feet long, most of its length belonging to the hood, which resembled the visor of a medieval knight's helmet. The cup-shaped headlights were encased in gleaming chromium to match wheel covers the size of hula hoops, and the paint was two-tone, liquid black and royal purple, baked on in so many coats it made a man dizzy staring into the depths of his own reflection.

The next surprise was the driver. Such a rig suggested a chauffeur in livery. Instead, Bozal himself leaned across the front seat from behind the wheel to swing open the door on the passenger's side. He was dressed casually in an old rust-colored suede jacket, threadbare at the elbows, faded jeans, penny loafers, and a billed cap bearing the logo of what his guest suspected belonged to a Mexican baseball team: a rattlesnake coiled around a bat, with a cigar in its mouth.

"Bugatti Type 'forty-one," he said as they peeled away from the curb, the motor churning like a powerful dynamo beneath the country block of hood. "The Royale.

Only seven ever made, back in 'thirty-one. The kings of Spain and Belgium each had one. That year I had a bike that blew a tire before I rode it the distance from the rear bumper to the front; not that I ever saw one of these babies then."

Valentino felt swaddled in rich aromatic leather. The old man was a skilled driver, careful but confident. The white-enamel elephant attached to the radiator cap remained rock-steady in the center of the lane. The scenery slid by precisely at the speed limit, according to the gauge in the padded dash. This was what it must have been like to ride in a first-class cabin on the Twentieth Century Limited.

Nearing Bunker Hill, enough of the Victorian homes were still standing to help Chandler find his bearings, but he'd have been nonplussed by the high-rise buildings that had sprung up to cast their shadows on the spires and turrets. They crossed into East L.A., passing Mexican restaurants, corner markets, and long stretches of cinder block sporting gaily colored murals, then purred to a stop before an iron gate in a stucco wall sprayed all over with graffiti. Bozal tilted his head toward the peace signs, hallucinogenic images, and aerosol text in two languages.

"Kids, they gotta have whatchacallit artistic release. I don't mind it, 'cause I'm behind it." He punched the horn.

After a short interval the gate opened and a young Hispanic man in a tailored gray uniform stepped outside. Blue-white teeth shone in a brown face. "Hi, Grandpapa!"

"We have a guest, Ernesto."

"*!Sí!* Welcome, *señor.*" He stood aside and they cruised through the opening.

The compound reminded Valentino of a barrio scene in *Border Crossing:* tawny children in baggy swimsuits frolicking in the spray from an open fire hydrant, substantially built women in light summer dresses sitting on porches, sleek-haired *hombres* in bright sport shirts smoking cigarettes and conversing in rapid Spanish on the sidewalks. There was plenty of family resemblance to go around. His host had established a colony of his own north of the border, a modern-day Cortez expanding his influence deep into gringo country.

At the end of the block they turned into a circular driveway paved with limestone around a gushing fountain. A motionless parade of exotic automobiles parked bumper-to-bumper formed a horseshoe around the edge. The guest knew little about makes and models, but he was aware

that the low-slung convertibles, bus-shaped sedans, high-centered horseless carriages, and slab-sided hardtops covered the history of the motorcar from early days to the Kennedy years. They were enameled in canary yellow, emerald green, candy-apple red, cerulean blue, and gunmetal gray, and all glistening as if they'd been run through a gigantic dishwasher and dipped in molten wax.

"Overflow," Bozal said, pulling up behind a seven-passenger touring car straight out of the original *Scarface* (it might well have been in the movie, at that) and setting the brake. "I knocked down five bungalows to make room for a garage and it still wasn't big enough. I'm waiting for my granddaughter next door to get hitched, then I'll doze her place and build on. Her fiancé's got a job waiting in Omaha, for cat's sake. Maybe I'll get some good steaks out of the deal."

The house was the biggest in the compound, although it was by no means palatial; its owner seemed to have had more interest in obtaining room to display his treasures than to loll in the lap of luxury.

"Hello, Grandfather." A woman in her twenties, pretty but pouty-looking, opened the front door. She wore a red dress, mod-

est in design, but her trim figure, lustrous black hair, and healthy flush under olive-colored skin made it provocative.

Bozal introduced Valentino. "Esperanza, my granddaughter. Not the one who's deserting me for the Nebraska wilderness. I offered to put her through college, but she insists on working her way to a master's; in communications, no less. She could be head curator of the Motion Picture Hall of Fame, but she wants to produce a news show on cable."

"CNN," she clarified. "C-SPAN would be my next choice. Movies are my grand-father's thing, not mine; but he's forgiven me so far as to pay me three times the go-ing wage for answering the door and taking visitors' coats." Despite her solemn expression, a merry light glimmered in her eye. Valentino saw something more than idle mischief when their gazes met; but he was off the market: a mantra worth repeating. She swiveled aside for them to pass.

"What's your poison?" Bozal took up a post behind a sleek white bar with a wall-size mirror at his back. The glittering display of liquor bottles and stemmed glasses slung upside-down from the ceiling might have belonged to a gangster boss's lair on a 1940s soundstage.

36

"It's early for me, thanks."

"You ain't had practice." He poured amber liquid from a cut-glass decanter into a tumbler, squirted in seltzer, and carried his drink down into a sunken living room.

The room was done in neutral tones, a sharp contrast to the warm, vibrant colors that decorated the rest of the neighborhood. It was like stepping from bright glare into shade. The chairs and sofas were uphol-stered in cushy leather. Above the mantel hung a portrait of a woman with the proud features of a Spanish patrician. She wore jet buttons in her ears and a plain blouse cut low to show off her shoulders. It was as haunting as the painting now in Valentino's possession, the original centerpiece for the film *Laura*.

Bozal saw the cast of his glance. "Estrella, my wife. I lost her fifty years ago. Damn careless, if you ask me."

"I'm sorry."

"Don't be. She wouldn't know regret if it bit her on the nose. She's responsible for everything you lay eyes on here. All I did was supply the juice. Wasn't for her, I'd be one of them parasites you see in the country clubs, palling around with cheap broads in expensive perfume." He lifted his glass to the image and sipped.

"But why East L.A.?"

"Might as well ask why Beverly Hills? There, I'd be just a spick with money, probably earned pushing drugs; a racist neighbor with unlimited credit is still a son of a bitch in a sheet. Here, I'm part of the community, something bigger than me."

They sat facing each other in matching armchairs.

"I can't thank you enough for Laura," Valentino said. "It will occupy the place of honor in the lobby of The Oracle."

"Just don't fall in love with it. That gag only works in movies, and then only through the closing credits. The audience rips it apart on the way home."

"Not *Laura*."

Bozal aimed a porcelain smile over the edge of his glass. It was as vaguely sinister as his eccentric use of the English language. "Okay, sure. But lay off the thanks till you see my end of the deal. You may want to give it back."

4

Harriet was wrong.

Partially, anyway. While the theater Bozal had installed in the lower level of his home didn't make The Oracle look like a dump tailor-made for showing barely acceptable features, it outstripped the grandest screening rooms commissioned by major movie stars and most neighborhood picture houses.

He'd taken a larger-than-average basement, extended it under his multi-car garage, and hired a team of contractors to turn it into something Valentino could describe only as an underground mall: what seemed miles of tiled hallway passed a replica of a 1930s automobile showroom, complete with Depression-era models in mint condition on display, brightly gleaming, a mid-century-type service station built of white glazed brick with a black 1955 Porsche pulled up to the pumps — waiting,

it seemed, for James Dean to bring the engine to life and speed toward his date with destiny — and a men's haberdashery stocked with mannequins decked out in vests, double-breasted suits, and snappy fedoras, decorated with patriotic posters advertising war bonds to fight the Axis.

Their way led at last to the theater itself, a plush Art Moderne palace lit by wall sconces, with stadium seating to accommodate two dozen viewers and gold velvet curtains cloaking a screen with a stage for live performances between shows.

"It's magnificent," was all the visitor could find to say.

"You should've seen it when I bought the place. The previous owner hosted cockfights down here. His neighbors turned him in. He needed quick money to pay his lawyer, so I got it for a song. 'Course, more excavation and the retrofitting ate up the difference. Let's go see the projection booth."

A door concealed in the molding led up a short flight of stairs into a square chamber with walls of plain concrete. It contained an ultramodern laser projector mounted to the ceiling and a black steel giant resembling a locomotive. It had reels the size of platters and a threading system as complicated as the Gordian knot.

Valentino goggled at this. "Is that a 'forty-four Bell and Howell?"

" 'Forty. I scored it in a junk shop in Tehuantepec, where it'd been busy collecting dust and mouse turds for sixty years. Took me another ten to track down replacement parts from all over the world. I had to buy a shut-down theater in Prague just to get the lens assembly. Outfit in Detroit made the arc lamp from scratch; Bausch and Lomb the reflector mirror. I lucked out on the mechanic. He was retired, living right down there in the Valley. He'd never worked on a projector before, but it's just a series of simple machines, going back to the Greeks."

"How big is your silver-nitrate collection?"

"Big enough. But I went to all that bother for just one."

Bozal turned and took a pizza-size film can off a steel utility rack. "Ever hear of a mug named Van Oliver?"

The abrupt question surprised Valentino. Plainly the old man had little patience for small talk. "Old-time picture actor. He was murdered, supposedly. Another one of Hollywood's unsolved mysteries."

His host jerked his chin, approving. Aged and slight as he was — his gold Rolex and cuff links looked too heavy for his fragile wrists — all his movements were steady and

41

his eyes bright as a bird's. "That's refreshing. Most people don't know Van Oliver from Oliver Hardy."

"We can't all be buffs. Most people wouldn't know him. He only made one movie, and it —" He stopped, looking at the can. He felt the old familiar thrill.

Bozal's smile was wicked. It was the privilege of rich men to carry suspense to the brink of cruelty. "Officially, he just disappeared. My bet is they buried him up in the hills, or rowed him out past Catalina and dumped him overboard in a cement overcoat. In those days, you couldn't convict anyone of murder in the state of California without a corpse. I guess the law didn't want to fry someone just because someone else decided to take a powder and forgot to tell anyone, but it sure sold a lot of shovels and quicklime."

"It was almost a double murder, if you can apply the term to a movie studio," said Valentino. "He'd been getting the kind of star treatment they reserve for major properties: elocution lessons, tailors, a big flashy car, dates with glamour queens, and an army of press agents, so he could make a splash during interviews and premieres. Only he couldn't, because he died before the film was released. They shelved it. That

was the end of RKO."

"Helped by that nut Howard Hughes. Sooner or later he drove everything he owned into the ground. You can't keep hiring and firing and quadrupling budgets and stay in business. Lucy told me the best day in her life was the day she bought the studio, four years after RKO fired her."

"You knew Lucille Ball?"

"Through Desi. In those days the Spanish colony in Hollywood was thick as thieves."

Valentino had never met anyone closely connected with *I Love Lucy,* Desi Arnaz, and the birth of Desilu Studios.

"That was in 'fifty-seven," Bozal said. "They might have re-cut and reshot the picture to build up one of the other players and brought it out later, but the *noir* cycle was on its last legs. Welles's *Touch of Evil* came out the next year and tanked."

He snarled out the side of his mouth. "Universal butchered *Evil* in post-production; shoved Welles right off the cliff, so of course it under-performed. Nothing's changed in sixty years except the suits. Anyway, the Oliver vehicle went the same way as its star. Nobody gave a rat's behind about preservation then. Re-release was strictly for proven properties, the studios had already sold their old libraries to

television, and there was no video. Desilu edited down the script to an hour for TV, but none of the networks would touch it, even with a new cast. In this town a bad rep has a half-life of a hundred years. You know the title?"

"*Bleak Street,*" Valentino said. "Oliver played a racketeer loosely based on Bugsy Siegel. Only he didn't play him the way pioneer actors played gangsters in the thirties. The few insiders who saw the dailies said he had an entirely new take on the character. If the movie had been allowed to open, it would have revolutionized the crime film the way *The Godfather* did fifteen years later."

"Not just crime pictures. Acting; only it didn't seem like acting. Edward G. Robinson was nasty, Paul Muni a goon, Jimmy Cagney was like a bomb about to go off. Oliver was entirely natural; you wouldn't know he was reading lines. Also it's clear no stunt doubles were used for his fight scenes. It wasn't like watching a movie, more like something happening right in front of you, that you might be sucked into any time: disturbing, which was ideal for the form. There was even a rumor he wrote the screenplay himself under a pseudonym, or at least made changes in the text. The plot

had all the usual clichés, but I'd stand the production up beside anything else out there."

As he warmed to his subject, Bozal's speech shifted away from street lingo toward more formal language, using jargon familiar to any story conference. Clearly the old man's passion outstripped his affectations. What was more to the point, he wasn't parroting something he'd read or heard; he spoke as someone who'd seen the evidence firsthand. The shock of hope Valentino had felt settled into a cozy hum. He had little doubt now what was in the can.

He wondered if he was a latent masochist. He put off asking the question that was foremost on his mind. Instead he drew out the excruciating pleasure of suspense.

"What made everyone so certain he was killed? Sudden success can be terrifying. Maybe he just dropped out of sight because he couldn't take the pressure. It was easier then to relocate and make up a new identity."

"His kind thrives on pressure; enduring it as well as applying it. How do you think he did such a good job capturing a gangster's personality? He came here from New York to work for Mickey Cohen, the local mob boss."

"Doing what?"

"Bodyguard; not that the little twerp needed one. He already had an army on the job. He thought surrounding himself with muscle made him look like a bigger shot than he was. Some folks said Oliver got bored with sitting around Mickey's house in Brentwood watching Roy Rogers and started making hits on the side."

"Sounds like typical Hollywood hokum."

"Probably. That last part anyway. But he'd been seen around town with Mickey, shooting golf and picking up dames in nightclubs. When the *Bleak Street* hype started, the attention got to be too much for his employers. They were camera shy after so many big-time operators got themselves deported or shut up for tax evasion. They cut their losses same way they did with Bugsy Siegel back in 'forty-seven, only by then they'd learned not to be so public about it."

Valentino banked his fires. His profession had taken him close to criminal territory before, and he hadn't enjoyed the experience. "How much of this is likely and how much gossip?"

Bozal tented his shoulders, let them drop. "In this town, who can say? Is there any other place so visible, yet so frequently out of focus?" He drummed his fingers on the

46

edge of the film can.

His guest couldn't hold out any longer. "Where'd you find it?"

5

"Retired film editor died last year; he was there when RKO changed hands. I bought his estate."

"Don't tell me. You bought it all just to get that one item."

"No, there were some outtakes from a couple of Astaire-Rogers musicals and six minutes of the original *Untouchables* nobody's seen in fifty years; also a Movieola machine in cherry condition and a box of cutting and splicing tools. I sold the tools to a collector for five times what they were worth. I usually make money on these deals. Heck, I unloaded that theater in Prague to Hilton."

"I can't believe I missed a sale like that. What was the editor's name?"

"You wouldn't recognize it. He was out before the industry gave negative cutters screen credit. It was a private deal in Europe."

Valentino was certain this rapid-fire response was a lie. Shrewd as he was, Bozal lacked the imagination to make up a name for his mysterious source that would convince a fellow traveler. Most likely he was protecting a favorite fishing hole.

"You have the negative?"

"No such luck. Studio security never let those out of their sight, even when the high exalted muckety-mucks decided against release. He probably remastered the film, made a fresh positive, and smuggled it out in the confusion during the change in management. When you think of how much contraband managed to walk off those lots over the years —"

Valentino broke under pressure. "Just to be clear, sir; it's *Bleak Street* we're talking about?"

The old man showed no offense at the interruption. He smiled and scooped a telephone handset from its niche in the wall. "Esperanza."

Minutes later the attractive young Hispanic woman entered the booth. Her simple red sheath and modest heels accentuated the contours of her muscular (but by no means unfeminine) calves. She directed another brief appraising glance at the visi-

tor, then shifted her attention to her grandfather.

"Mr. Valentino will show you what to do."

"Grandfather, I know how to handle film stock. On top of what you taught me, my teachers gave me a thorough grounding in all aspects of communications technology, even obsolete —"

"*Handling* is precisely what I *don't* want you to do, *niña*. Pay close attention to everything this man says and does. If he isn't satisfied that you can be trusted to carry on in his absence, I'll have to be a rotten host and keep him at work."

However irked she might have been by Bozal's lack of faith in her abilities, she slid her eyes toward the archivist in a way that harbored no animosity; quite the reverse.

Bozal seemed not to notice. Still holding the large flat can, he turned to the archivist. "Is there anything you need that you didn't bring?"

"Depends on what condition the film is in. I have a kit in the car, but if the integrity is compromised in any way, I wouldn't take a chance on screening until the techs have had a chance to examine it back at the lab."

" 'Compromised.' The way you guys talk. You'd think it's a dame instead of a movie." Bozal chuckled. "No vinegar stink, no yel-

lowing. A little rust inside one of the original cans, so I had the reels taken out and put in these." He thumped the can, which was made of brushed aluminum and rust-proof.

"Molecular sieves?"

"Yup."

"How about the reels?"

"You tell me. I wouldn't let anyone unwind and rewind the stock onto fresh ones except an expert."

It was Valentino's turn to smile. "Someone's been doing his homework."

"Sure. I didn't just fall off the turnip truck."

"Then I'm ready." Valentino slid a pair of latex gloves from his inside breast pocket.

There were five cans on the rack, each containing a reel. Esperanza was a keen student and a fast learner — all the better for her tutor, who was relieved to break free of her spell early. Throughout the lesson she stood closer than seemed necessary.

He wasn't flattered. There was something impersonal in her frank interest; calculating, as if she'd set herself a challenge, either to annoy the family patriarch or to win some kind of bet, perhaps only with herself. No, there was nothing flattering about the situation. He was spoken for, and had no inten-

tion of becoming a notch on someone's belt.

If getting Grandfather's goat was her purpose, it seemed to have failed. He showed no interest in her behavior, or for that matter in the process of managing fragile film. Valentino suspected he knew more about silver-nitrate etiquette than he cared to let on.

So why had he been so eager to invite the film archivist to this private premiere? The man was (in a phrase borrowed from Kyle Broadhead) "a riddle wrapped in a mystery inside an enigma — with a chewy chocolate center."

But this sense of unease fled before the prospect ahead. This was how an archaeologist must feel upon discovering an ancient civilization long thought lost. Descending the steps to the theater, he leaned heavily on the handrail; more so than his elderly host, whose gait remained steady. Valentino had gone rubbery in the knees.

They took center seats facing the curtained screen. Bozal tilted back the top of an armrest, exposing a row of switches and a gridded speaker. "Refreshment? Popcorn, a soda, something with more of a kick? I like to match the drink to the movie, like the right wine with supper. Rum with Fairbanks, champagne with Garbo, beer

with Brando."

"And with Oliver?"

Out came the porcelains. "Scotch, straight up."

"Still too early, but thanks."

"You'll never get to be as old as me if you don't start pickling your innards." He flipped a switch. *"?Sí, Abuelo?"* came a youthful male voice from the speaker.

"Can it, Eduardo. You speak English better than all your teachers. Pour me a Dewar's."

Presently a trim, dark-complected boy of twelve or thirteen entered from the hall carrying a tall tumbler on a tray. His blue-black hair was cut close to the scalp and he wore a white tunic buttoned at the shoulder over black chinos, orange Reeboks on his feet. Bozal scooped the glass off the tray and made a sort of magician's gesture with his other hand. A folded twenty-dollar bill had appeared on the tray.

"Thank you, Grandfather."

When he'd left, Valentino asked the old man how many grandchildren he had.

"Eduardo's a *great*-grandchild; and I don't know how many of *them* there are either."

"But you know all their names?"

"I'm lousy at math."

Another switch spread the heavy curtains with a hum, exposing a high-quality screen wide enough to display *Lawrence of Arabia* in all its original glory. He raised the top of the armrest on his other side and lifted a telephone receiver. Valentino overheard Esperanza's voice.

"Ready when you are, I.B.!"

"Cut the comedy and roll the film." He hung up and closed the armrest. "You got any kids?"

"No."

"If you ever do, first time they tell a joke, smack 'em in the kisser."

"That sounds like something from a movie, but I can't place it."

"It's in the second reel. Shush, now. If there's one thing I can't stand it's mugs that yak during the movie."

Bozal threw yet another switch. The lights went down. Valentino's excitement level went up.

6

A square beam of light shot through the aperture in the booth and splashed across the screen, followed closely by the clickety-click of celluloid frames clattering through the gate; is there any sound more sweet?

There were a few seconds of blank footage, the lead-in, and then the old familiar countdown began, the letters and numerals jumping due to broken sprocket holes (not enough to damage the film):

10
NINE
8
7
SIX
5
4
3
2

A broadcast tower appeared, sending out animated concentric circles from atop the curvature of the earth, accompanied by Morse code beeps: the RKO Studio logo, in razor-sharp black and white and shimmering silver, illuminating the image as if from behind; an effect missing from features printed on modern safety stock. The picture was square, conforming to the original aspect ratio, the blank screen on both sides masked by the gold velvet curtains.

Now the title pounced onto the screen, with a plosive from the string section, the letters standing out dramatically in pseudo-third dimension, like blocks in a prison wall:

BLEAK STREET

With a sigh, Valentino settled in for seventy-nine minutes of voycuristic bliss.

His host had been right about the elements of cliché. All the allegorical tropes were in place: the revenge-driven anti-hero, the implausibly patient Good Girl, the poisonous Femme Fatale, the Psycho Villain, and the hapless Squealer, shot to death in a telephone booth whilst informing on his colleagues. *Bleak Street* had, in fact, every disadvantage of a sub-genre on the verge of extinction.

However, superior performances, edge-of-the-seat tension, and a cloying miasma of dread made it anything but run-of-the-mill. Even the gutter dialogue, boiled as hard as a ten-minute egg and too glib for ordinary conversation, came off as naturally as infection settling into a neglected wound.

Van Oliver was the keystone. From the moment he made his entrance, stepping down off a train from New York and pausing, only his eyes moving as he stood on the platform with one hand hidden inside the breast of his trenchcoat, searching for friends or enemies (possibly both in one package), the movie became unique, and all his. He was a lean man in his early twenties, with dark Mediterranean features under the turned-down brim of his fedora, piratically handsome. When he opened his mouth to deliver his first line, Valentino half expected an exotic accent. Pure American came out instead, in a casual baritone that took on a dangerous edge when he met resistance. He acted balletic rings around the veteran cast. It was impossible to take one's eyes off him. Even the scenes in which he didn't appear crackled with tension, actors and audience alike anticipating his return. He seemed to have *star* tattooed on his forehead.

The action scenes — Oliver disarming a

rival with one hand, punishing him with a backward swipe of the other, retreating into a pitch-black doorway from the approach of a cruising police car — again with one hand out of sight beneath his coat, ready to commit cold-blooded murder in his obsession with his grim purpose — were exciting and fresh. There was little on-screen violence, however. One of the hallmarks of this school of filmmaking was its sardonic compliance with the stern Hays/Breen censorship code, averting graphic scenes of bloodshed by casting the action in shadow on an alley wall. Like the offstage murder of King Duncan in *Macbeth,* the device compelled the audience to supply the gory details from its imagination, creating a tableau far more disturbing than any special-effects team could create.

This was the form, pure and simple: Spun by writers, directors, actors, and cinematographers from the whole cloth of wartime angst, released in an unbroken chain of mostly second features to feed an insatiable appetite for gritty realism. It was dismissed by critics, censors, and sometimes the creators themselves as pulp, melodrama, sordid trash; even subversive anti-American propaganda. It took a colony of French reviewers, exposed all of a sudden to this

fare in one undigested lump at the end of World War II, to give it a name: *cinema noir* (black film). Like so many of America's native contributions to world culture, it could be traced back to foreign lands, smuggled onto our shores by refugee directors from Fascist Europe, introducing the look of German Expressionism, French existentialism, and the nihilistic view of a world gone terribly wrong.

Pools of harsh cold light. Cameras tilted at precarious angles. Shadows cut out as if by a shiv. Rain-slick streets stuck in perpetual midnight. It was all conspiracy, wrought by *auteurs,* scenarists, studio electricians, and second-unit crews to create a nightmare that was still there when you awoke. Desperate characters speeding headlong toward destruction, like a sedan careering down a mountain road with a roadblock at the bottom and the audience riding in the back seat.

The ending riveted. Oliver's death scene was defiant, not contrite, and bore all the earmarks of a life actually expiring on camera, not at all play-acting. His curtain line — "You and what army?" — belonged in any reference book on great movie quotations. It could not have occurred during the gangster cycle of the Depression — the

powerful Catholic Anti-Indecency League would never have allowed it — and its lack of inner conflict was a slap in the face to the standard view of 1940s *noir*. Had the picture been released, this drastic departure might have revitalized the genre, extending its existence another twenty years. Valentino found himself applauding when the closing credits appeared.

The lights came up. Ignacio Bozal, lounging now in the adjoining seat with legs crossed, observed his companion's expression with a smirk. "Quite a show, eh? Paul Newman would never have got a shot at *The Left Handed Gun* if Oliver had hung around: All that Actors Studio bunk would've stunk like cheap aftershave next to the real deal. That's why I buy into all that hype about mob connections. You don't pick up that stuff mawking over your little dog getting run over when you were six."

"I don't know if I agree about Paul Newman, but *Bleak Street* could have jumpstarted the revolution of the sixties ten years early."

"It would also have buried the studio system that much faster. The red-baiters in Washington jumped on any excuse to denounce a picture as pro-Communist; it meant headlines and re-election. The studio

60

moguls didn't know it at the time, but Oliver getting killed was the best thing that could've happened to them. It saved their butts from unemployment and probably indictment."

Valentino pointed to where the credits had faded from the screen. "Whatever happened to Madeleine Nash, the bad girl? She looked familiar."

"She had bits as wisecracking secretaries in a couple of programmers before she landed this part. Her real name was Magdalena Novello; she was Puerto Rican. She could turn the accent on and off. After the picture was shelved, RKO didn't renew her contract. Columbia offered her a long-term deal, but that meant sleeping with Harry Cohn, so she turned it down. I heard she married some joker and moved to Europe."

"Too bad; for moviegoers, I mean. She held her own against Oliver."

"She'd've been out of work in a couple of years anyway. Can you see her as June Cleaver in *Leave It to Beaver,* or teaching a bunch of teenage brats in *Our Miss Brooks*? TV wouldn't have let her play anything else; the FCC was worse than Hays and Breen. Mustn't warp the morals of the little rugrats in their parents' living rooms."

"For someone who came here late in life,

you know a lot about inside Hollywood."

The old man blew a raspberry, loud enough for Esperanza to call and ask if he was okay. He said something terse and hung up. "Everybody who was anybody wintered at my joint in Acapulco. You hear a lot of gossip when you play the obliging host. See a lot, too. Marilyn Monroe went skinny-dipping in the pool." He leered.

"Is that how you heard about Van Oliver?"

"Some of it down there, some up here. It's part of industry lore. If there's anything folks in the profession like to talk about, it's scandal, and the nastier the better. He was just what you saw on-screen, though I don't know if there's anything to that rumor about him bumping guys off. He ran errands for the Five Families back East, everyone seemed to agree on that. Maybe he was tagged to babysit Mickey Cohen, or maybe to muscle in on the guilds. Anyway he got his picture taken at the Brown Derby and the Coconut Grove, usually with some hot-to-trot starlet on his arm. Howard Hughes liked his looks and offered him a screen test. Well, you can see the impression he made. The studio changed his name from Benny Obrilenski and signed him for three pictures."

"And the mob saw that as a threat?"

"Maybe they didn't approve of moonlighting, or maybe Oliver fell for his own publicity and told them to go climb a rope. Anyway, when the picture wrapped, so did he."

Valentino pondered. From the direction of the booth, he heard the rapid clicking of reels being rewound. He knew the sound better than the beating of his own heart. Like her grandfather, Esperanza knew more about the proper treatment of volatile silver-nitrate film stock than either would admit. The hospitality of the Bozal household was genuine enough; but as friendly as its residents behaved, inside those walls lurked unspoken thoughts, hidden agendas, and secrets to the ceiling.

7

Bozal picked up the telephone handset, which appeared to be a direct line to the projection room. "Finished rewinding?"

"*Sí, Abuelo.* Just putting the last reel in the can."

She was teasing her grandfather. Obviously she'd overheard him upbraiding Eduardo for his Spanish conceit; but he didn't rise to the bait. He seemed to be more permissive with his granddaughter. "Bring 'em all down."

A tense silence — tense for Valentino — fell while they waited. Presently the young woman descended the steps with cans under both arms and at a nod from Bozal stacked them on the vacant seat beside him.

He scowled up at her. "I don't expect the eggheads in that high-dollar school to teach you anything, but don't my lessons count?"

Red spots showed on her dusky cheeks, the first sign she'd given of embarrassment.

She muttered an apology and rearranged the cans so that they stood upright, braced by the armrests.

He said something in a flood of Spanish too rapid for even one fluent to keep up; thus did he deliver a rebuke for her earlier impertinence and display his superior vocabulary in one stroke. Lips pressed tight, she nodded and made her exit.

He waited until the door closed, then tipped a hand toward the film. "Do with it how you like; give it to your bosses or use it to re-open your playhouse with a bang."

The remark, off-hand as it sounded, shook Valentino head to toe. He was ashamed of all the unworthy things he'd been thinking. He was even prepared to forgive Esperanza for her relentless flirting.

At first he thought he'd misunderstood. At the risk of changing the old man's mind, he said, "You're offering me *Bleak Street,* free of charge?"

His host smiled wearily.

"Please. What would I do with the money, stuff it in my mattress? It's lumpy enough as it is. I don't sleep as good as when I was ninety."

"A rediscovered classic of this quality, and a mysterious disappearance? I can hear our man in Information Services rubbing his

hands over the publicity. These days, just unveiling a priceless property isn't enough. You've got to have a brass band and the lead story on Fox News."

"These days, my aunt's fanny. I told you nothing's changed in this town. MGM spent a cool million in 'thirty-eight scouring every beauty pageant, finishing school, and Campfire Girls jamboree in the country looking for an actress to play Scarlett O'Hara, when it had already signed Vivien Leigh; that's a million in *Depression* dollars. Then it was newsreels and fan magazines, now it's a continuous crawl on the bottom of a TV screen. I guess that's what they call progress."

"This gift is beyond generous, *Señor* Bozal. There may be an honorary doctorate in it for you and a seat on the board of regents."

"*Muchacho,* a spick with a buncha letters after his name is just a wetback with a diploma, and I stopped going to meetings before you were born. Nothing ever gets finished except a lotta pastry." The old man's snicker carried traces of Dan Duryea and Torquemada. "There *is* something you can do for me, and it won't cost you a cent."

Valentino was back on his guard. When someone promised something that

66

"wouldn't cost you a cent," you better be sure you can afford it.

This time he wasn't kept in suspense. "I got some Vatican bigshots stalling over a theme park I want to open in Tuscany, dedicated to classic Italian cinema; I need the Pope's okay to bring the authorities in Rome on board, on account of some of the steamy scenes in *La Dolce Vita* and *Eight and a Half.* I'm this close to swinging a visit by a delegation of Cardinals." He pinched the air. "I know I can win 'em over with a face-to-face on my own turf. An exclusive screening of *Greed* could seal the deal. The flick drips with Old Testament justice; they lap that up. The fact that it was lost for eighty years is a bonus.

"I'll pay for the dupe," he added, when his listener hesitated.

But the brief silence was from shock and relief, not doubt.

"You'll have a print if I have to bootleg it myself," Valentino said.

"God, I love foul play!"

Henry Anklemire leapt up from behind his desk next to the boiler room. As always, "Our man in Information Services" resembled an evil cherub in a toupee a shade too dark for his vintage and a checked suit (size

67

portly), polka-dot tie, and striped shirt that made a cataclysmic statement Valentino thought could not have been coincidental. The little flack had an arrangement (perhaps sexual, perhaps mercenary) with most of the wardrobe mistresses in the industry that kept him supplied with costumes reaching as far back as the slapstick comedies of Hal Roach. His face glowed as from a strong shot of whiskey. So far as the film archivist was aware, he was no lush; he got his highs from the prospects of a successful hype.

"We'll keep that angle between ourselves until we spring it on the public," Valentino said. "The dean thinks Sherlock Holmes was a sociopath."

But there was no stopping Anklemire once he was on a roll.

"Look at Marilyn Monroe; not one-tenth the talent of Billie Holiday, but she had the good sense to get murdered by the Kennedys. You ever see Billie Holiday on a T-shirt?"

"From time to time. It's *Judy* Holliday you're talking about; and the answer is no. In any case you wouldn't know Judy from Jumbo if I hadn't forced you to watch *Born Yesterday* on DVD. Also, there's some question about whether the Kennedys were involved in Marilyn's death."

Anklemire had offered his expertise to the university after a year of retirement on top of forty years of advertising cigarettes, automobiles, and feminine hygiene products for a venerable agency on Madison Avenue, on condition that his salary wouldn't threaten his retirement benefits. Even when the government changed the law to allow unlimited compensation from the private sector without penalty, he hadn't applied for a raise; twelve months of shooting golf and playing canasta with his next-door neighbors in Tarzana had made him desperate for any activity that didn't involve listening to anyone's blow-by-blow account of his prostate operation. The department director had assured him that low pay was no obstacle to his employment.

Most of the academic community loathed the little caricature of a man, for the very reasons the archivist liked him. He was an aggressive promoter who knew the common denominator that shook loose money from every corner of society, and he had no patience for objections based on propriety or prestige. Give him a salable commodity and he'd sell it. He knew nothing about movies or their heritage, but he knew how to turn silver nitrate into gold.

Even Kyle Broadhead, who tolerated him

at best, acknowledged that one crass little garden gnome like him was worth twenty "ornaments of the university," as the professor himself had been ordained.

"*Born Yesterday,* great flick. They ought to colorize it." Anklemire's face grew solemn, or as close to it as it ever came. "What you want to do, you want to send the pitcher on tour, book the revival houses, pass the hat for donations. Hey, invite the FBI! They could sponsor the whole *schmear,* tack on a documentary feature about how crime don't pay."

"Henry, J. Edgar Hoover's been dead almost fifty years."

"Sure. I don't just read the trades. Right now, the Bureau can use a boost more than us. You don't win no friends slapping the cuffs on folks just for telling fibs; who'd be left?"

"Not you." Valentino smiled.

"Okay, it's a long shot. Nobody ever gained nothing by not trying. After it's finished the circuit, this — what's it called again?"

"*Bleak Street.*"

"Stinko title. Change it. No? Okay, we'll work around it. After it's made the rounds, we lease it to TCM, then bring it out on DVD: Two-disc set, buncha talking heads

70

yakking about what the movie really meant to say, how the lab rats saved it from ruin, yada-yada, that stuff everybody says they care about but nobody watches all the way through, only they buy it, 'cause who'd settle for one when he can have two? This outfit sure can use the cash."

He raised his voice above the banging of the water pipes next door. "What we do to get the media to cooperate is play up the mysterious-disappearance angle, especially the mob connection; pound it into the ground. That didn't hurt Geraldo one little bit, even if he did come up with bupkus from Al Capone's secret vault."

Watching "Angle-worm Anklemire" work himself up to orgasm was always entertaining, but as Valentino saw it, part of *his* job was to keep him from flying off the rails. "We found a ground-breaking movie that's been missing for six decades. Isn't that worth anything?"

"Boring. Strictly third paragraph, bottom of the hour after the weather. Nobody cares."

"Nobody but the people you and I work for. They're what's keeping you from sitting around watching *Matlock* with your fellow inmates in an assisted-living community in Oxnard."

"Which is where'd I be, if I followed that line of reasoning." His face was grave. When you least expected it, the court jester took off his cap and bells and assumed all the dignity of a Supreme Court justice. "Tell you what, Professor; you do what you do best and leave me to mine."

To this little man, who liked to brag that he'd been making his way in the world since dropping out of school at sixteen, everyone else at the university was a tenured Ph.D.

Valentino was too cowed by this solemn display to put up an argument on behalf of film history. "What do you need from me?"

"You're the archaeologist. Start digging. I can't write copy without material."

"Archivist, not archaeologist."

"What's the difference? Do some homework. Interview people. Get me color: big hats, gun molls, armor-plated Cadillacs, rat-a-tat-tat!" He mimed firing a submachine gun.

Here he was again, the living video arcade; and for the first time his visitor realized that the buffoonery was a mask. He used his antics to distract people from the fact that he was as serious about what he did as anyone else at UCLA, Valentino included. It made people underestimate him and drop their guard just as he moved in for the kill.

"I can't promise much, Henry. *Bleak Street* was shelved in post-production, before the publicity mill could warm up. All I've got is rumors and some inside stories Bozal overheard. Without corroboration, they're useless. The public isn't as ignorant of hype as it was sixty years ago; it wants sensation — dirt, to be blunt. You've got a star with possibly sinister connections who dropped off the face of the earth just as the underworld was consolidating the power it drew from Prohibition. A pro like you could build a campaign as tall as the Watts Tower on a foundation like that. What else could you possibly need?"

Ignacio Bozal had nothing on Henry Anklemire when it came to blowing a juicy raspberry.

"That's prologue, the kind of stuff they used to blow off in whatchacall expository text after the title card and the bill. Nobody goes to the movies to read, for Pete's sake. They want faces, sex, action, the bloodier the better. Forget the on-set baloney. Find somebody who was there and make 'em dish up."

"You're forgetting how long ago this was. Whatever happened to Oliver has found its way to everyone else connected with the picture. There's no hit man like Old Father

Time. Wait." An image leapt into the foreground of Valentino's brain. He'd been only vaguely aware of it at the time of exposure. He took out his phone, into which he'd entered all the information he used to keep in notebooks, tapped keys, scrolled.

"Roy Fitzhugh's still with us," he said; "or was when I entered his name here. I saw him in the film, playing a mob henchman. It was an early role, and he had only one line, so he didn't make it into the end credits. I was overwhelmed with the whole package, so it didn't register at the time."

"Fix that. Save being a fan for after quitting, when you're sitting at home with a bowl of popcorn in your lap. Be a working stiff when you're on the clock."

"I interviewed him last year about a bit he had in *M Squad.* Here it is." He stopped scrolling.

"He must be a hundred."

"Not quite that bad. He always played older than he was. He had one of those faces. I hope his memory's still good."

"Go see him. I'd send a photog with you, but the flash might stop every pump in the joint. Try to keep him on topic. We want to know what happened to this monkey Oliver, not how many football teams Jayne Mansfield slept with."

74

Valentino laughed. "What do you want me to do, solve his murder?"

"If you can squeeze it in."

Valentino laughed. "What do you want me to do, solve his murder?"

"If you can solve it in"

8

The archivist was still shaking his head when he dropped by the lab to see how the technicians were coming with the film he'd brought back from East L.A.

"Why are you shouting?" Jack Dupree, an uncommonly handsome young man with a gleaming shaven onyx head, squinted as if against bright sun. He wore a yellow Haz-Mat suit, minus the sci-fi hood and latex gloves, which he'd don before approaching fragile, volatile celluloid.

"I'm not shout—" He remembered then that Dupree had been present at his surprise party in the Bradbury Building. Without doubt he hadn't taken in enough paté and crackers to absorb the champagne. Valentino lowered his voice to a hush. "Talk to Kyle Broadhead. He came back from the Adriatic with a killer hangover cure."

"I talked to him. Killer's the word. Where do you even find hog thistle? You're tenth in

line; and that's only because the board of regents think Broadhead's the Golden Goose and you're his fair-haired boy. Normally we assign priority according to the age of the print. Right now we're duping footage from the 1906 San Francisco earthquake."

Valentino, who had a good layman's knowledge of what went into making a new negative from an old positive, then a new master from the negative, kept his impatience to himself. "Okay. I'd appreciate a heads-up when you've started."

Dupree pressed his temples. "Don't say 'head.' "

From there Valentino went to his office in the university's old power plant, where Ruth, the gargoyle who guarded the gate, sat at her computer in the doughnut-shaped reception desk. Her long, red-lacquered nails rattled like sleet against glass as she manipulated her computer keyboard.

"Is Professor Broadhead in?"

She didn't look up from the screen. Her pulled-back, implausibly black hair and white-on-white face wore a coat of varnish as impervious as the one on her nails, and the legs of her heavy steel-rimmed bifocals hugged her temples so tight he thought they must leave grooves when she took them off.

If she *ever* took them off; it was Broadhead's opinion that she slept in the building's attic, upside-down, like a bat. She was a motion-picture industry veteran whom, it was rumored, the tyrannical old studio CEOs had been too afraid of to fire. She'd occupied this particular bunker when Valentino came to work on his first day and would likely still be there when he retired in twenty or thirty years.

"If he isn't," she said, "he climbed out the window."

This reference to her alertness was no idle boast. He'd never known her to go out for lunch or take so much as a bathroom break.

He left her to continue clattering away and tapped on Broadhead's door.

"It's unlocked. I lost the key years ago."

Valentino entered just in time to see a feathered dart bury its point in a corkboard attached to the faux-wood-paneled wall opposite the door. The board was a new feature in the Spartan office. Its concentric rings were colored individually, and numbered from five to ten, working from the outer circle to the bull's-eye. The prospect of Broadhead taking exercise of any kind was good for the front page of the faculty newsletter.

"Let me guess. Fanta's been after you to

get in shape, and this is your answer."

"Don't be a loon. I address that by taking the stairs instead of the elevator the third Wednesday of each month."

"Why the third Wednesday?"

"It's the day my Social Security check is deposited. That way I never forget, and have become the fine physical specimen you see before you as a result."

The pot-bellied academic, in a corduroy jacket worn shiny at the elbows, ill-advised horizontally striped sweater vest, frayed collar, baggy slacks, and scuffed Spectators, stepped up to the board and retrieved the dart.

Valentino held his tongue as regard to his mentor's self-description; Broadhead's infamous iconoclasm did not extend to remarks directed against himself. "In that case, I can only conclude that you intend to turn this place into an Irish pub."

"English. The Irish need the extra room for drunken brawls. I can say that without incurring the wrath of HR, because my grandfather on my mother's side came from County Sligo. He disinherited Mom for marrying a Brit." He returned to his mark — it was there on the floor, an actual chalk line — and took aim.

"Where are the other darts?"

79

"Budget cuts." The projectile struck the target dead center. "Blast!"

"What's wrong? You hit the bull's-eye."

"Don't offer an opinion until you understand the rules. This infernal enterprise represents my work ethic."

"You call this working?"

Broadhead cocked a polished elbow toward his computer, a battleship-gray antique as big as a pizza oven. "It's how I warm up. The part of the board I hit determines the number of pages I'll write that day."

"So today it's ten."

"As on every other day, it's best two out of three. I can manage the five pages represented by the outer perimeter standing on my head — if I use fifteen-point type and three-inch margins."

"Blocked?"

"No, I just suck at darts. Blast and double-blast!" Ten again. He left the dart there and slouched behind his desk. "I can't seem to finish the damn chapter on drinking in the movies. It makes me thirsty, and I swore off liquor a year ago."

Reflecting on last night, Valentino realized he hadn't seen Broadhead do more than lift his champagne glass in salute. "Why? I've never seen you drunk."

"Nor will you. My age is the time to quit

bad habits for good. That way I won't have to keep it up for long."

"So put the chapter aside and move on."

"Not an option. In addition to being a recovering alcoholic I'm an obsessive compulsive. I cannot 'move on' to Chapter Four until I've completed Chapter Three."

"You've only written three chapters? You started the book two years ago."

"Thank you for pointing that out. Something tells me you didn't come here to cause me torment. When I need that, I can always call out to Ruth."

His visitor pulled up the only other chair in the room and sat. He told him about his trip to Bozal's house and the old man's gift and what he'd asked for in return.

"You both profit," Broadhead said. "He winds up with the director's cut of the most eagerly sought Grail in our profession, and you get yet another feather to stick in a cap that already resembles a Sioux war bonnet."

"Actually, *Bleak Street* and *Greed* are equals, in terms of being fellow victims. They were both considered to be casualties of attrition and neglect, destroyed probably to make storage room for more commercial properties."

"Like *Francis the Talking Mule*." Broadhead stabbed a fistful of tobacco into his

dilapidated pipe from the Taster's Choice can where he kept it; his disdain for the aesthetics of his vice stood shoulder-to-shoulder with his disregard for university rules and state law. He struck a match and filled the room with smoke the color of dirty cotton batting and the odor of burning tires. Valentino tipped his chair far enough back to crack the door.

"So what troubles you, sprout? Conflicted over whether to keep this latest windfall to yourself or pass it along to the university that keeps you in Milk Duds and Big Gulps?"

"No. I resolved that issue by turning it in to the lab. Maybe you can use your influence with the dean to loan it to me for the premiere. You're teacher's pet; I got that on the authority of Jack Dupree."

"And who in thunder is Jack Dupree? Sounds like a riverboat gambler."

"He's only run the lab as long as I've been here. You just gave him your hangover cure."

"Oh, yes, the black youngster with the bowling-ball dome. Did it help?"

"Never mind that. You should make an effort to learn the names of your staff."

"I'm an educator. I don't *have* a staff. That sign on my door was a gift in lieu of a raise."

"There isn't any sign on your door."

"I misplaced it along with the key. My position as head of the Film and TV Preservation Department is strictly honorary, a title to impress would-be donors in the endless round of cocktail parties I'm obliged to show up at and pretend apple juice is bourbon. I made it clear at the outset I would attend no meetings and make no decisions."

"Kind of the way you teach class."

"I never miss the first day or the last. I provide the sturdy bookends between which the teaching assistants mold young minds. Many of those moldy young minds have gone on to respectably mediocre academic careers." He took the pipe from between his teeth and let it smolder in the jar cover he used for an ashtray. "Cut to the chase, lad. Those five pages aren't going to write themselves."

"Ten."

"Speak!"

"Henry Anklemire wants me to close the case on Van Oliver's vanishing act."

Broadhead's expression was as bitter as his tobacco. "That little imp of the perverse has gotten you in Dutch more times than his closet has moths. I wouldn't complain,

except sooner or later I always get sucked in."

"You always volunteered. I never asked you to do anything that would put you in danger or in trouble with the police."

"That's what I meant when I said 'sucked in.' Any muddling about in real-life crime, no matter how remote and how much dust has collected on it, is a slippery slope; and Anklemire's the banana peel. Have you ever seen even one Mack Sennett comedy in which the peel got hurt?"

"All I want is your advice."

"Tell the little troll to strap a refrigerator to his back and swim up the coast. Chances are he'll meet Oliver on the way."

"You know his heart won't be in the publicity campaign if I don't at least make the effort."

"Why ask me if your mind's made up?"

"Because I knew you'd do just what you're doing: make faces, apply a colorful metaphor in reference to Anklemire's lack of physical stature and excess of *chutzpah,* and eventually come around to give me grudging approval."

"I haven't come around."

Valentino rose, walked to the corkboard, jerked loose the dart, took up Broadhead's late position, toe to the mark, took aim, and

pierced the target in the No. 5 ring.

"Days of Wine and Roses," he said, dusting his palms. "The drying-out scene, with Jack Lemmon screaming in restraints. If that one doesn't kill your taste for booze, you're better off eliminating the chapter altogether."

The professor's scowl deepened. He stuck his pipe back between his teeth, drew a gnawed yellow pencil from the plain white mug on his desk, and scribbled a note on his blotter. Then he raised the pencil to make the sign of the cross. "Go with God, my son. You'll need Him."

9

After his department's screening room, the graduate library was Valentino's favorite place on campus. Thanks in large part to Kyle Broadhead's talents at squeezing blood (donations of cash, private collections, and above all, cash), UCLA maintained an impressive, although incomplete, archive of fan magazines. It spanned the industry from the silents through Cinerama, when the voracious competition from television lured readers in droves from *Photoplay* to *TV Guide,* demolishing a publicity machine that had existed for half a century. In those pages — some slick and sturdy, others pulp and crumbling — a surprising amount of authentic Hollywood history could be found among the studio hype. It was like panning a stream for nuggets; all it required was someone who knew how to separate the genuine article from fool's gold.

Efforts to commit the material to micro-

film were ongoing, but it was an expensive and tedious process, and far down the list of priorities; any major university is a honeycomb, with many bees to sustain, the drones last of all. For every drawerful of microfilm spools, there were hundreds of periodicals moldering in stout storage cartons. These last stood in rows on steel utility shelves from floor to ceiling, like the anonymous antiquities in the government storeroom at the end of *Raiders of the Lost Ark.*

Guided by the dates in card slots (and with the help of a ten-foot stepladder), Valentino made some likely selections and carried them to a carrel and a vacant microfilm reader. Sitting, he looked forward to his chore with almost the same anticipation he brought to a screening; for him, what seemed toxic to a civilian was an adventure in time travel: Thread the film onto the pegs, switch on the glorified slide projector, crank forward, and leap ahead, days, weeks, months, years at a turn; crank backward, and enter the past. Same thing depending on which way you fanned through musty-smelling pages, the world speeding past at sixty frames a second.

There, among advertisements for Packards and Lucky Strikes, he found some produc-

tion and pre-production material on *Bleak Street*. Most of it was photographic: stills of the actors in and out of costume, horsing around on the set, pretending to menace one another in tableaus similar to the scenes they'd shot. Few people studying such pictures in modern film books realized they were looking at fake publicity stills and not actual frames from the movies. By and large they were posed and shot by house photographers. Valentino, for one, sometimes wished the movies themselves looked as good as their advertising.

In our cynical time, the burlesque teasing among the players was stagy and anything but spontaneous, an attempt to show the world how well everyone got along and that even major stars didn't really take themselves seriously. In their own time, the scheme backfired, convincing outsiders that "Hollywood people" were shallow, facetious, narcissistic parasites, when in most cases they were dedicated professionals, working inhuman hours under conditions of near-slavery.

Van Oliver, it appeared, was quite chummy with Roy Fitzhugh, who played the gangster hero's bodyguard until he was killed in the first reel during an attempt on his boss's life. The pair were photographed with their

arms around each other's shoulders, trading mock punches and grinning, and messing each other's Brilliantined pompadours with impudent hands. The archivist knew that such carryings-on were often a ruse to disguise deep mutual dislike, similar to the one that had led to fisticuffs between George Raft and Edward G. Robinson on the set of *Manpower*. However, there were rather more of them than the average, despite the brevity of Fitzhugh's part in the picture. Valentino was inclined to believe the two were close.

Which was a break; provided the elderly actor retained the wits necessary to remember events from so long ago. Many a promising trip to the Motion Picture Country Home had dashed itself to bits on the rocks of Alzheimer's and senile dementia. They were crueler even than the pernicious decay that had sentenced ninety percent of world film to oblivion.

Bleak Street vanished from the puff columns in June 1957 — its announced month of release — as thoroughly as its star had dropped from sight weeks earlier. Under normal circumstances, the feature would have been mentioned everywhere at that time, with cover articles on its leading players in *Modern Screen* and *Liberty,* billboards

splashed throughout Los Angeles and its suburbs, press kits sent out in flocks like carrier pigeons, and advertisements in newspapers in key cities across the country. Instead, the story moved to the city section of the *L.A. Times,* where burly detectives assigned to Missing Persons and Homicide were photographed grilling hapless suspects raked in from the local underworld. Almost overnight, a routine campaign intended for the Entertainment section decamped to the crime pages.

Studio clout had managed to squelch any negative publicity concerning its chief commercial property of the season; in those "factory town" days, the police commission took its marching orders from Louis B. Mayer, Howard Hughes, Harry Cohn, Darryl Zanuck, and the Brothers Warner (none of whom realized how quickly their influence would evaporate in the face of the competition from TV). But when Hughes's people dropkicked the production, the Oliver case became open season. As his sinister background became public property, the focus of the investigation shifted from Where is he? to Where is his body? Racketeer Mickey Cohen reported to police headquarters with his attorneys, disavowing any knowledge of the missing man's fate, or

90

for that matter the man himself: "Oh, sure, we was seen places, but I go lots of places and meet lots of people I don't remember after. I'm like the Queen that way."

"Which queen might that be?" sneered one of the reporters who'd swarmed around him on the steps of City Hall. (This from *Confidential,* the controversial scandal sheet that at the time had violated all the unspoken rules that prohibited seamy speculation.)

The obligatory sweep of known local offenders harvested a bumper crop of newspaper photos of men hiding their faces behind their hats and jut-chinned detectives subjecting pale-faced suspects to the third-degree; generations of exposure to Hollywood hype had taught the LAPD a thing or two about public relations, but the yield in solid leads was negative.

As in every successful drama, there was comic relief. A plainclothes sergeant flew to New York City to interview Mafia kingpin Frank Costello, who assured him he'd never heard of anyone named Van Oliver *or* Benny Obrilenski, and in any case Costello was a legitimate businessman, currently engaged in supplying jukeboxes to neighborhood bars. A front-page picture appeared of the sergeant emerging from a well-known

91

brothel said to belong to Lucky Luciano, who'd been deported to Sicily for running a prostitution racket. The sergeant came home to find himself back in uniform, directing traffic at Hollywood and Vine.

The entire affair was precisely the kind of publicity the studios paid millions to avoid. The ghosts of William Desmond Taylor, a director whose murder had exposed a sordid 1920s landscape of drugs and sex, Fatty Arbuckle, a silent comic accused of involuntary manslaughter at a wild party, and sundry other figures caught up in sinful boomtown excess, had haunted the industry throughout its history, threatening it each time with stepped-up censorship and congressional investigation. No wonder *Bleak Street* was pulled and buried as deep as Oliver himself.

If he *was* buried. Once again, the "film detective" had been saddled with the unpleasant task of turning over old bones, churning up ancient secrets, and making himself equally unpopular with the people who were paid to investigate crimes and those who profited by committing them. It was like stepping from the safety of a climate-controlled auditorium onto the silver screen, and square into harm's way.

10

"Tell me more about this flirting," Harriet said.

They were dining in The Brass Gimbal, a hangout that favored behind-the-scenes personnel connected to the movie industry: Foley operators, script supervisors, set decorators, wardrobe and makeup specialists, electricians, cinematographers, laboratory technicians, and sometimes second-unit directors, provided they minded their manners and weren't overheard using terms like *auteur, mise-en-scene,* or *day-for-night;* the management valued craftsmen above artists. On occasion an A-list movie star would ask for a table, but although the establishment turned away no one, a chilly reception and indifferent service discouraged a return visit.

It was far from Harriet's favorite meeting place (iceberg salad was the only item listed under "healthy choices"), but since it stood

approximately halfway between the UCLA campus and LAPD headquarters, they often met there for lunch; on this day, more particularly supper. Four hours had slipped out from under Valentino unnoticed as he was convening with Old Hollywood in the undergrad library, and Harriet was due back at work in an hour. A bus transporting prisoners from the Riverside County jail to San Quentin had gone off the Pacific Coast Highway in a fiery crash near Long Beach, claiming the lives of half a dozen convicts, and the entire CSI unit had been recruited to help out with identification.

Notwithstanding her pressing schedule, she'd taken time to change from her smock and sweats into a sleek sleeveless dress that displayed her well-developed biceps to advantage; turn over just a few more cadavers and she could out-arm-wrestle him ten times out of ten.

"Flirting, that's what you took from what I said? I'm more or less under Anklemire's orders to plunge headfirst into a sixty-year-old police case, and all you heard was a girl batted her eyes at me?"

She poked her fork at a pile of bleached pasta topped with black squid ink — the weekly Monochrome Special — like a farmer trying to skewer a trespasser hidden

94

in a haystack. "She batted her eyes, seriously? That's the kind of detail I'm after. As for the other, you were up to your chin in disgruntled cops when we met, and many times thereafter. Who was it who said that beyond a certain point all risks are equal?"

"The captain of the *Lusitania*. She didn't exactly bat her eyes; that was just an expression. I'm not even sure she was coming on to me. Maybe she's that way with everyone and just doesn't realize what it looks like."

"You're sweet." She smiled. "And worse than blind. When you do manage to see something that isn't on cold celluloid, you talk yourself out of it."

"Are you saying you're jealous?"

"Not of you. You I trust. This girl, this Appasionetta —"

"Esperanza."

"Even worse. How do parents know? They look at one baby through the glass in the maternity ward and say, 'Esperanza.' They look at another and say, 'Harriet.' "

"You don't have to fish for compliments. You know very well you're attractive."

"Anyone can manage attractive. I want to be drop-dead gorgeous, like your Spanish *señorita*."

"I never said she was drop-dead gorgeous. I didn't even describe her."

"You didn't have to. Vixens all run to a type at that age, regardless of their nationality. My father always said if you want to know what a girl will look like in twenty years, take a look at her mother."

He put down his triple-decker burger — the BCU ("big close-up") half-eaten. His eyes had been bigger than his stomach after missing lunch, and in any case the turn the conversation had taken had squelched his hunger. "Apart from being sexist and possibly racist, there's no evidence to support it in this instance. I never met her mother, but I've seen a portrait of her grandmother in Bozal's living room. Even allowing for artistic license, she was stunning." Belatedly, he added: "Not that any other woman's looks interest me."

She laughed, instantly dispelling the gloom. "I'm teasing, Val. Any serious rivals I ever had for your affections have been dead for years. Hedy Lamarr, for example. She was brilliant *and* beautiful."

He changed his expression by force of will. He suspected he'd been pouting. "Torture isn't teasing."

"You're right, of course. It's just that it's always been a mystery to me that you never raise a fuss when I work late with those young studs in the lab."

96

"You dissect corpses for a living. It's not exactly soft music and candlelight." He picked up his burger. His appetite had returned. "You're just as much of a detective as the suits in Homicide. What do you make of this Van Oliver angle?"

She sat back with her Perrier (she was on duty, after all). "I'd say the danger's minimal. He's been missing since Eisenhower, and all the dese, dem, and dose guys he associated with are either six feet under or sucking oxygen from portable tanks in stir."

He stifled a smile. He couldn't imagine her using "stir" in that context before taking up with a fan of crime films and prison flicks.

She didn't notice, or feigned not to. "The police shouldn't be a problem. All the cold cases that need to be transferred to hard drive are backed up as far as the Pet Rock, so the Oliver file will go on feeding silverfish in the sub-basement at HQ through the Second Coming, or until the *L.A. Times* is hard enough up for a Sunday feature. Even if you crack the case, any egos you might bruise in the CID are on pension; worst they can do is block your parking space with their walkers."

"Oh."

"You sound disappointed."

97

"I was sort of hoping you'd talk me out of it. Kyle was right when he said I shouldn't have had 'film detective' printed on my business cards. I never meant it to be taken seriously."

"You should've known. Henry's been a promoter all his life. He thinks artistic license is a permit to shoot painters and poets." She looked at her watch, laid down her napkin, and slid out of the booth. "Gotta go see a man about some stiffs. Stay here and have dessert. The 'Key Light Pie' doesn't look too terribly lethal." She stooped and kissed him on the cheek. "Give my regards to the fossils."

"I didn't tell you I'm going to the Country Home."

"You didn't have to. It's your version of Google." She breezed on out, trailing admiring male gazes all the way to the door. *Drop-dead gorgeous,* Valentino thought.

Woodland Hills, site of the Motion Picture Country Home — a facility operated by the Screen Actors Guild to keep dues-paying members in comfort and dignity during their declining years — wasn't far, but figuring in rush hour, Valentino would likely find the doors closed to visitors when he got there. He went back to The Oracle instead

98

and did his homework.

The climate-controlled basement housed his huge store of DVDs, opposite his smaller collection of master prints in approved aluminum containers. He selected a number of titles on disc and took them up to the projection room, which doubled as his apartment. There, a laser projector mounted to the ceiling shared space with the massive twin Bell & Howells he reserved for screening movies on celluloid. He switched on the laser unit, fed a DVD into the player, and settled in for an evening filled with paranoid crooks, sadistic cops, wicked women, and lonely men pushed to the limits of human endurance.

Laura first: Murder victim Gene Tierney's portrait, haunting detective Dana Andrews from the grave; Clifton Webb's effeminate intellectual snarking his way toward double-murder; Tierney's sudden emergence from beyond the pale; and weak playboy Vincent Price, no doubt watching Webb's performance closely for future reference as his own career took a new turn shortly thereafter. The differences between the portrait that director Otto Preminger eventually chose to replace the one now in Valentino's possession were marked, but both bore a resemblance to something the film archivist

could not quite place. He knew this would vex him until he found the missing link.

Double Indemnity next: Cocky insurance peddler Fred MacMurray, caught in the web spun by restless housewife Barbara Stanwyck, following his male member to homicide and eventually his own death.

Pitfall. Bored suburbanite Dick Powell, derailed from marital fidelity by Lizabeth Scott's beauty and victimized innocence, threatened by the hulking jealousy of Raymond Burr (pre–Perry Mason) and cornered into the fatal shooting of another victim, a confession to the police, and the destruction of his family life.

Out of the Past. Perhaps the granddaddy of them all. Robert Mitchum refuses to send Jane Greer over for ripping off racketeer Kirk Douglas and pays for it with all three of their lives.

Each was different, but it followed a universal theme: Guilt, flight, regret, resignation, oblivion, either one's own death or the end of all that was good in his (and sometimes her) life. "Once," went the confession, "I did something wrong."

It was said these films had no color, only black, white, and gray; but he saw a deeper hue, one that blended light and shadow into a melancholy wash of fear, despair, tragedy,

and regret: midnight blue. No, darker yet. Indigo.

Still in a mood to be moody (but also in the interest of laying groundwork for tomorrow), he surfed his way through a string of low-budget B-thrillers showcasing Roy Fitzhugh in brief but memorable roles, doing the hatchet work for criminal superiors, swapping one-liners with fellow fast-talking newspaper reporters, driving cabs, and ratting out his underworld colleagues. Most of these activities led him directly to his doom. From film to film he honed the dying scene to perfection, executing a mortally wounded swan dive off a rotting pier, dancing a macabre jig in step with Tommy-gun rounds slamming into his torso, smacking both palms against a pane of glass with bullets in his back. He was the Astaire of the alley, the Caruso of canaries, the Garbo of the gutter. In his best year he earned scale, the Screen Actors Guild minimum.

Valentino fell asleep during *Corpse and Robbers* and woke up to the sound of the overture, informing him the movie had ended and the disc had returned to the menu. He switched everything off and crawled into bed without undressing.

He dozed off quickly, but heard himself saying, "Am I doing something wrong?"

and regret: midnight blue. No, darker yet. Indigo

Still in a mood to be moody (but also in the interest of laying groundwork for tomorrow), he surfed his way through a string of low-budget B-thrillers showcasing Roy Kilhugh in brief but memorable roles, doing the hatchet work for criminal superiors, swapping one-liners with fellow fast-talking newspaper reporters, driving cabs, and ratting out his underworld colleagues. Most of these activities led him directly to his doom. From film to film he honed the dying scene to perfection, executing a mortally wounded swan dive off a rolling pier, dancing a macabre jig in sea with Tommy-gun rounds slamming into his torso, smacking both palms against a pane of glass with bullets in his back. He was the Astaire of the alley, the Caruso of cadavers, the Garbo of the gutter. In his best year he earned scale, the Screen Actors Guild minimum.

Valentino fell asleep during Corpse and Robbers and woke up to the sound of the overture, informing him the movie had ended and the disc had returned to the menu. He switched everything off and crawled into bed without undressing.

He dozed off quickly, but heard himself saying, "Am I doing something wrong?"

■ ■ ■ ■ ■

II
MURDER,
MY SWEET

■ ■ ■ ■ ■

11

He turned over in his sleep. Something slid off his hip and struck the floor with a bang like a gunshot. He sat up straight, his heart bounding off his breastbone. He dove for the pistol under his pillow, then remembered that he wasn't one of the *noir* heroes he'd been watching all night and that he didn't own a gun.

Sunlight had found its way into the chamber, gradually dispelling his jumbled dreams and reflecting off the plastic DVD case that had fallen from the bed: Tyrone Power's cruelly handsome face with a cigarette dangling from his lip and the title, in blood-red letters gnawed around the edges: *NIGHTMARE ALLEY.*

Appropriate.

He climbed out from under the covers, spilling several more cases from the bedspread like shards of fallen plaster; wondered for a moment why he was still fully

clothed, then remembered.

He was worse than an alcoholic; he was a bijou binger. Any day now he'd be checking himself into the Harrison Ford Clinic to get straight.

Harriet had given him a countertop cook stove for his last birthday. It performed the services of both a traditional and a convection oven, a toaster, and a microwave; he wasn't quite sure, but he suspected it was a prop from a *Transformer* film. Operating it was a good deal more complicated than threading film through a projector, but he'd mastered the basics. Moving like a sleepwalker, he placed an English muffin on the toaster grate, twisted the dial, started a cup of water heating in the microwave, and opened a jar of instant coffee. He promised himself to install the usual kitchen appliances in the projection booth. His own creature comforts had taken second place behind putting the theater back on its Prohibition-era feet. It was bad enough he'd been forced to close the mezzanine men's room to the public in order to install a shower for his own use; he couldn't help feeling he'd turned his back on his customers. But he felt grungy in yesterday's clothes, and his welcome in the Bruins locker room at UCLA had long since worn out.

While he waited to eat, he retrieved his phone from a pocket and dialed a number from memory. It rang several times before Kym Trujillo answered. She sounded out of breath.

"Valentino!" she said. "Ready to check in? I can't think of anyone else your age who could hold his own in the conversation in the cafeteria."

Valentino had called the Motion Picture Country Home.

He said, "You sound like you should check in yourself. Should I call back when you're through moving furniture?"

"I wish. I just helped two nurses hoist a resident from the floor in the TV room. You know how much weight those stuntmen put on after they retire?"

"Is he all right?"

"He's fine, but the serving cart he fell on will never be the same. I'm okay, too, just a couple of cracked ribs and a ruptured spleen. Thanks for asking."

He knew this for an affectionate dig. She'd been Admissions director long enough to have faced every issue connected with caring for the elderly and egocentric, and she enjoyed her work every bit as much as he did his. "I'd like to arrange a visit with one of your residents."

107

"If it's the stuntman, you'll have to wait until the doc finishes pulling a twelve-piece tea service out of his belly button."

"It's Roy Fitzhugh."

Her tone warmed; her breathing had returned to normal, as he knew it would. She was five-two and ninety pounds of pure energy. "I know Roy. I admitted him myself. He's a hoot. Hang on." She came back on the line three minutes later, sounding subdued. "I talked to one of his nurses. He has his good days and his bad. Today's not so good. You might try later, after he's had his afternoon nap."

"He was sharp as a tack last time."

"Still is, if you catch him during his window."

He thanked her and said he'd call back. The exchange had sobered him. With age came wisdom, but it could steal back all it gave.

The toaster oven dinged, startling him; he'd forgotten all about breakfast. Through the glass in the microwave door, he saw that the cup of water was boiling, and for a confused second he didn't know which to address first.

The odor of burnt toast made up his mind. He tipped down the oven door, transferred the blackened English muffin to

the typewriter stand he used for a dining table, fished out the steaming cup, and stirred in powdered coffee. The breadbox contained only an empty package; he'd used the last of the muffins. He scraped off the worst of the char and broke his fast crunching incinerated carbohydrates and burning his tongue with molten brew.

Not his best morning. He had a sinking feeling worse was yet to come.

He swallowed the last crumb of charcoal and let his coffee cool while he made his way by phone through a succession of robotic voices — some of them computer-generated, others just bored — arriving finally at one he recognized.

"West Hollywood Homicide, Clifford." A contralto voice, perfectly in keeping with its owner, a flame-haired, six-foot-plus Elle Macpherson type who had scorned the runway for the Los Angeles Police Department.

"Sergeant, this is Valentino. Do you remember me?"

"How could I forget? It isn't every day I crack a fifty-year-old murder case with nothing to work with but a skeleton and an amateur Columbo hopped up on Orville Redenbacher."

In that case, he thought, *you're in for a treat.*

Aloud he said, "That's getting to be a long time ago. I'm planning the grand reopening of The Oracle soon. Look for your free pass in the mail."

"Kind of you, but you didn't have to call. The mail room staff here is almost as efficient as the Criminal Intelligence Division."

"Actually, that's not the reason I called."

"Why am I not surprised?" Her tone of guarded goodwill had begun to evaporate.

It was gone entirely when he finished explaining what he wanted.

"You're worse than just in a rut; you're going backwards. The mainframe hard-drive has enough to remember without a murder investigation as old as Sputnik. The only file would be in hard copy in the bowels of City Hall, deep and dark in the center of the earth, fastened with gates and bars."

Valentino remembered his Sunday-school lessons well enough to appreciate her grasp of Biblical text. "But it *is* there?"

"Unless it went into the incinerator under LBJ. Why should I send a uniform down there to dig through the boxes with six new complaints on my desk this morning, and eight left over from last week?"

110

"Have someone show me where they are and I'll do the digging. It's what I'm trained for."

"There was something in *my* training about not letting civilians monkey with open cases."

"Records are public property, aren't they?"

"So file a request under Freedom of Information. You'll have it by Christmas."

"It's just research, Sergeant. I'm not looking to bring anyone to justice, even if whoever killed Van Oliver is alive and getting around on hip replacements. There's an acknowledgment in it for the LAPD when we go public. Your chief's pretty hot on shaking loose personnel to provide technical advice on movie sets; a story like this would get your PR department off *Entertainment Tonight* and on CNN."

"If you're threatening to go over my head, I've already got a permanent part there from all the traffic that came ahead of you."

"Sergeant, you know I'd never do that." But his heart was back playing handball against his ribs. The last thing he wanted to do was raise her ire.

She fell silent long enough for him to hear telephones ringing on her end, more bored voices asking for names and addresses.

"Well, I'm not letting you into the basement. I'll send a man down when I can spare him. Next week, maybe."

"If you could do it today, I'll credit you as a consultant. I'm hoping to interview a surviving witness this afternoon. I'd like to go in with all the information I can get."

The line got muffled, as if she'd cupped a hand over the mouthpiece in order to release a string of oaths. When she came back on, her tone was chilly but calm. "If you're asking me would I like to be in pictures, the answer would be 'Over my dead body,' but we don't sling that one around in Homicide. You'll get it when you get it; if you get it."

"I'll be in my office at the university till noon. Do you still have the addr— ?"

He was talking to a dial tone.

12

In his office, Valentino cleared a stack of old press kits, newspaper cuttings, and lobby cards from his desk and returned to a project he'd been pursuing on and off for months: trying to guess what went into a gap in the last reel of *M*, Fritz Lang's sound masterpiece; the long-missing U.S. release dubbed into English, using the standard subtitled version in an all-in-one DVD player and monitor to guide him. The first had come his way from an impound lot in Düsseldorf, where a Swiss-born cinema buff had been appointed to catalogue personal effects seized from a recently convicted Nazi war criminal.

His intercom buzzed while he was comparing Peter Lorre's impassioned plea for mercy with the original. (Disappointingly, the anonymous actor who'd provided the child-killer's voice had made no attempt to imitate Lorre's sinister inflections.) Al-

though the ancient print had been transferred to safety stock, he switched off the Movieola to prevent the bulb from overheating and causing it damage, then answered the call.

"Cheese-it," was Ruth's only remark.

By which means he wasn't surprised to find a uniformed officer standing outside his door. The visitor shoved a fat insulated mailer as big as a king-size pillow into his arms and stuck out a clipboard.

"You have to sign for it. Sergeant Clifford said to come back for you with the siren if you don't return it by six o'clock."

Someone had scribbled *B.O.* on the big envelope with a thick black felt-tip. The archivist, who was still stuck in Germany between the wars, took a moment to realize the initials stood for Benny Obrilenski and not body odor; although the bundle was aromatic enough. It smelled like old newspapers left to gather years of mildew in some outbuilding. He balanced it under one arm and signed the receipt with the ballpoint the officer had handed him. "Why the rush? No one's looked at it in sixty-three years."

"Buddy, you're the one that woke up the bureaucracy." The officer sneezed violently and blew his nose in a handkerchief. Valen-

114

tino noticed then a smear of dust on his blue trousers, and felt a twinge of sympathy. This was the luckless grunt who'd been tagged to rummage through the heaps in some sub-sub-basement in search of this one item. He wondered what mistake the officer had made to draw such duty.

After he closed the door, Valentino rewound the German film, put it and the commercial DVD away in separate containers, and made room on the desk. The mailer was new, fastened by only a brass clasp; file material so old would be too dilapidated for safe travel without a sturdy container, and of course while it was being packed up, Clifford would make at least a perfunctory search of the contents before letting them out of her sight. She'd have made time for that, despite her workload.

The envelope was stout enough to stand upright on the floor beside his chair. He reached inside with both hands and hauled a thick sheaf up onto the desk. As it thumped down, dust billowed out in all directions. Bits of brittle rubber bands clung to the cardboard folders. Still, the files held their shape after all those years in snug confinement.

The task ahead wasn't unfamiliar. Since the dawn of Hollywood, ream upon ream of

115

paper had accompanied each studio project: shooting scripts, inter-office memos, production notes, etc. Pawing through repositories in both hemispheres, he'd ingested enough dust, mold spores, and wood-fiber to shock a physician specializing in black lung disease. He knew enough to crack his door for ventilation, hydrate himself from time to time using the water cooler in Reception, and apply gallons of lotion to his hands to keep them from drying and cracking.

He read dozens of police reports and witness statements typewritten on yellow sheets, none of which added anything significant to his knowledge of the Van Oliver disappearance; the miasma of exasperation shared by the detectives who'd assembled them was nearly tangible. He found two photographs sandwiched between pages: a publicity shot of Oliver, smiling cautiously in a beautifully tailored suit with wide lapels, and a front-and-profile mug of Benjamin Obrilenski, not smiling, taken at the time of his arrest in Brooklyn, New York, for questioning in an election-year sweep of known or suspected offenders. On the evidence in the packet, it was the only arrest on his record, and he'd been released for lack of evidence. His physical

description, printed beneath the mug, revealed he was shorter than he appeared on-screen, a mere five-foot six.

Bleak Street's director, a studio hack named Melvin Fletcher, told police he'd last seen the missing man "tying one on" at the wrap party Fletcher threw at his house on Sunset Boulevard after the end of principal photography, but didn't see him leave, and never saw him again. The officers spent considerably more time interviewing Madeleine Nash, Oliver's co-star, but she, too, claimed to have lost him in the crush at the party. She dismissed rumors of an off-screen romantic involvement with Oliver as "PR hooey." Valentino was inclined to accept this, as Bozal had told him she'd married not long after and gone to live abroad.

Roy Fitzhugh told detectives he'd accompanied Oliver out to the curb and put him in a cab that was waiting there. He'd assumed the star had called for it, as he was too drunk to drive and had declined Fitzhugh's invitation to take him home. When Oliver failed to report to RKO the next day to discuss publicity, a flunky was sent to his apartment, where he found the door unlocked and his bed made. There was no sign of disturbance, but also none to

indicate he'd gone home after leaving the party.

That made Fitzhugh the last person known to have seen Van Oliver/Benny Obrilenski alive. Everyone, the host included, denied ordering the cab, and none of the local taxi companies or gypsies had any record of the fare. Consequently, Fitzhugh had been interviewed twice more, the second time at police headquarters after it was discovered he'd been detained in Mexico in 1936 on suspicion of smuggling firearms across the border from the U.S. He told detectives he'd been with his late father, a member of the Abraham Lincoln Brigade, and that the guns were intended for Republican rebels fighting in Spain. No firearms were found in their possession, and they were escorted out of the country. Roy had been only eight years old, but he could never return to Mexico.

He stuck to his story, however, and since in those turbulent days there was no shortage of Americans eager to defeat Fascism, he got the benefit of the doubt.

Clipped to this report was an eight-by-ten photo, probably from Fitzhugh's résumé, of the actor in his prime. He looked more respectable than most of his movie roles, with no cigarette-burns on his lapels or soup

stains on his tie. His heavy jaw and chronic five-o'clock shadow had typecast him as mugs, lugs, and pugs in dozens of programmers; he'd shuttled from soundstage to soundstage, often without changing clothes.

Robbery was considered as a murder motive. Oliver had been paid $2,500 per week for twelve weeks of shooting, and since he had no bank account under either of his names and no cash was ever found, it was possible he had the entire $30,000 — a fabulous sum then — on his person when he left the party. But the prevailing opinion, stated in memos, was that the mob, or some old rival from New York, had abducted him in a phony cab and taken him for the well-known ride. Bodies disposed of under such circumstances rarely surfaced.

Even the most high-profile criminal investigations lost steam for lack of a lead. In time the Van Oliver case slipped off the inside pages and into oblivion. For a while it would return, zombie-fashion, when feature editors ran out of material for the Sunday supplements, but eventually it was forgotten. The current generation had no patience for backstage documentaries and paperback accounts of unsolved Hollywood mysteries, leaving such fare to buffs like Valentino.

The fates of the others involved, he remembered, were varied. Madeleine Nash, *née* Magdalena Novello, quit show business, presumably for wedded bliss; Fitzhugh went on to play a one-man repertoire company of second-tier hoods, weary desk sergeants, and truck drivers until his retirement; other cast members appeared in various features, some successful, some not; director Fletcher was yanked early from his next assignment over "artistic differences" and replaced, to take his own life sometime in the early sixties when the only work he could get was directing second-unit crews for TV westerns. Valentino could only speculate what might have happened to all of them had *Bleak Street* ever seen the light of day.

He finished his coffee and called Kym Trujillo's extension. Roy Fitzhugh, she reported, was in fine fettle, having awakened fresh from his nap. He was looking forward to Valentino's visit.

13

On his way out, he opened the door to find Kyle Broadhead standing there. The professor was holding papers.

"As much as I try to maintain a policy of never expressing gratitude — on the theory that sooner or later the party involved will require a *quid pro quo* — I've come to thank you for *Days of Wine and Roses.* Behold: five pages."

"I'm glad, but I can't claim all the credit. You should talk to Blake Edwards."

"God, no! I already owe him a favor for writing me out of *S.O.B.*" He saw the bundle under the other's arm. "Off to the bank? You may now thank *me* and we'll call it even. I'm the one who said you were wasting your time on film preservation when you're sitting on a gold mine in blackmail material."

"Nothing so felonious. I'm off to Woodland Hills, but first I have to stop by the

West Hollywood police precinct and return something I borrowed from Sergeant Clifford."

"The big red dog? Good Lord, you're already in her debt for agreeing not to throw you in the hoosegow."

"I think the statute of limitations has run out on that one. I really must be going; the brain I want to pick at the Country Home has a sell-by date."

Broadhead's face went flat. "You're doing it, aren't you? Jumping in up to your neck in another police case." He held up his hands in a defensive gesture. "Include me out. I let my membership in the Junior G-Men expire after the last time."

"What about that *quid pro quo?*"

"I knew it! What did I tell you?"

"Relax, Kyle. I'm kidding. I already owe you more than I can ever repay."

Broadhead lowered his hands. "Who are you going to see?"

"Roy Fitzhugh."

"Isn't he dead?"

"Not yet; but that's no reason to waste time." Valentino pulled his door shut. On the way to the stairs he heard Broadhead saying: "I could've sworn I went to his funeral. If I don't start making a record of these things I might wind up going to the

122

same one over and over."

The old character actor had a cheerful room with a fine view of the Santa Monica Mountains and a TV set with a forty-eight-inch screen, where an all-female talk show clucked away in merciful silence. He wore a crisp flannel shirt buttoned to the neck, navy sweats, comfortably worn loafers, and the chirpy air of a man ready to spring out of his wheelchair and dash around the neighborhood.

Valentino did a double-take when he saw him. From Kym Trujillo's assessment of his precarious mental condition, he'd expected the man to have aged significantly since his last visit; but although he was bald except for a white fringe of hair, he was instantly recognizable from his many screen appearances. A few wrinkles and sags did nothing to detract from his trademark bulldog jaw and bright Irish blue eyes.

"I remember you!" Fitzhugh said. "You grilled me for an hour on *Home Sweet Homicide.* Last September it was."

Valentino himself couldn't have told what month he'd visited. He wondered if Kym had been thinking of someone else when she'd expressed doubts about his mental health. "I tried to talk you into doing the

commentary on the DVD. You wouldn't, so I had to pump you for everything I could get. You've brought me a great deal of happiness over the years, Mr. Fitzhugh. I've seen all your films."

"Not all."

The old man's lips pleated when he smiled. His dentures did the rest of the work, in a glass by his neatly made bed.

"Every one." Valentino looked him straight in the eye. "*Bleak Street* included."

This drew no reaction. "I got a new one opening next week at Sid's."

"Sid's?"

"Sid Grauman. I'll have him hold two tickets for you."

The founder of Grauman's Chinese Theatre had been dead for many years; and there hadn't been a new Roy Fitzhugh film since before that.

"Some screwball comedy thing," he went on. "I forget the title. Jim Stewart's in it, and that dish Kim Novak."

He understood then. Memory was a strange creature. It could leave a man shaky about things that had been said or done a few minutes previously, and razor sharp when it came to events a half-century in the past. To confuse it with the present wasn't unusual in the Home. It was the policy of

124

the establishment to humor the victim rather than try to correct him and cause distress.

That suited Valentino's purposes down to the ground.

"You're very generous, sir. I can't wait to see it. But it's *Bleak Street* I wanted to talk about."

When Fitzhugh frowned, that famous chin bunched up like a pile of rocks. "That swish Fletcher. Said I talked through my schnozz, I should take elocution lessons. I said, 'Mr. Hughes has been paying me for a year to talk through my schnozz. If it's Ronnie Colman you want, try MGM.' "

"You were pretty friendly with Van Oliver."

"Benny's swell." For him, the production had just wrapped. "From the beginning he tells me to lay off that 'Van Oliver' stuff. He wasn't any more of a crook than my dear ol da', smuggling guns to the freedom fighters. Also he fixed it so my two scenes in the picture got scheduled on the first day of shooting and the last; that way I was on the payroll all the way through." Suddenly his eyes narrowed. "What's a college egghead want with an old dropout like me? I ain't worked since they canned me from *Barnaby Jones* for blowing my lines. That never hap-

pened before."

Valentino adjusted to the time shift. "We found a print of *Bleak Street.* The university's planning a big publicity campaign to honor the film and fund our Preservation department. Anything you could tell us about it would be a big help."

"That swish Fletcher said I talked through my schnozz. Know what I told *him*?"

He fired his next question before the conversation settled into a continuous loop. "What was Madeleine Nash like?"

Fitzhugh's face was fascinating to watch. The clouds cleared and the years fell away as if a veil had dropped.

"Maggie was a doll. She wasn't anything like the bad girl she played; that's how good an actress she was. And she had a beautiful voice: Sang old Spanish songs on the set. She was Puerto Rican, but you'd never guess it except when she sang or got tired and forgot her voice coaching. She died too young."

Valentino stiffened.

"I heard she got married and moved out of the country."

"Who we talking about?"

He'd lost him again. Time for a subject change.

"You were the last person known to have

seen Van — Benny — before he vanished. Did you tell the police everything you knew?"

"Mister, they came after me with everything but a rubber hose, and they only didn't use it on account of all them reporters hanging around. You'd of thought the reason my old da' and I went down to Mexico was to raise an army to invade San Diego. Did I tell 'em everything I know!" He leaned over in his wheelchair and spat on the rug; this was the Roy Fitzhugh of *Corpse and Robbers, Cell Block, The Big Noise:* one tough gorilla with a mad-on against the world. "They'd have to beat me to jelly before I'd give 'em the time of day; then, of course, I wouldn't be able to."

That old sixth sense kicked in; the flush the film archivist felt in a bazaar in Cairo or a Culver City junk shop just before he turned and found a treasure that had sat collecting dust and no interest for years, waiting for him to come to its rescue.

He spoke carefully, afraid to startle the old man out of lucidity, yet keenly aware that he might tire at any moment and be of no use as a source of information. "Mr. Fitzhugh, do you have any idea who might have been involved in Benny Obrilenski's disappearance?"

The man in the wheelchair stared. He held this attitude so long his visitor worried that he was experiencing a seizure of some kind. He was thinking of calling for help when Fitzhugh opened his mouth. For a moment nothing came out, although he was working his lips. Then: "Talk to Ivy. If she wasn't behind it, she sure as hell knows someone who knows who was."

"Ivy?"

"Ivy Lane." A toothless grin cracked the simian jaw. "Here's where you tell me you seen all her pictures."

A plump, bouncy nurse in a floral smock knocked and entered with a blood-pressure cuff. Valentino tamped down his annoyance, ashamed at himself for resenting the Home's scrupulous attention to the residents' health. But he could hear the clock ticking. There was no telling when the window would slam shut on Roy Fitzhugh's recollections.

"One-thirty over eighty. I wish mine were as good." She undid the cuff.

"Sister, I wish more'n that." He winked and smacked her on the bottom.

Unfazed, she left them with a cheerful smile.

"Ivy Lane." Valentino jogged the actor's memory.

"Yeah. We had a name for her kind, but we didn't bandy it around like they do now. The French come up with something more polite later: *femme fatale.*" He pronounced it "femmy fataly." "Could she act? Search me. What you got on-screen was what you got off it. Made Dracula's daughter look like Suzy Sunshine."

Valentino had seen her menace Cornel Wilde in *Switchback;* a statuesque ash-blonde with the ruthless beauty of a sorceress from Greek myth and the tongue of a serpent.

"But she wasn't in *Bleak Street.*" He suspected Fitzhugh's mind had begun to wander again.

"Thanks to that swish Fletcher. He said I talked through my schnozz."

He leapt in before the other could return to Square One. "The director had something to do with why she wasn't in the film?"

Fitzhugh was back on track. "She was cast opposite Benny, but Fletcher nixed her on account of she was too tall for the leading man. That was bull. It went back to *The Big Noise,* when she got Fletch fired before he'd even shot one reel. I had a bit in that one, driving a getaway car. She and him never did hit it off, and she was running around

129

with Mr. Hughes at the time, so she got her way."

That checked. In his days as the owner of RKO, before he became a recluse, Howard Hughes had been infamous for his dalliances with his female players. "In that case, her complaint was with the director, not the star."

"You'd think. But she didn't see it that way. She thought Benny'd rigged it so he wouldn't look like a midget. She threw a hissy right there on the set; said she'd get square with Benny if it was the last thing she did. Fletcher had to threaten to call security to get her to leave."

"There must have been other witnesses. Why didn't anyone else come forward?"

"It was just us four. Benny and me was shooting close-ups to insert in post-production. Ivy just showed up, to have it out with Benny."

"What did he do?"

"Nothing. You don't know him. He never turned a hair no matter what you said or done to him. That's one of the reasons I liked him."

"Why didn't Melvin Fletcher tell all this to the police?"

Fitzhugh's face went sly. In the old days that expression had lent extra weight to his

heavies. "I told you he was a swish. She called him a queer to his face during *The Big Noise*. He sure as shootin' wasn't going to come clean with the cops. It was a jailable offense, and what was worse, he'd never work in this town again."

"Still, it's a long way from there to accusing Ivy Lane of murder."

"Oh, she'd never get her hands dirty; not with her connections."

"Connections?"

Fitzhugh raised a finger and pushed his nose to one side.

"Wise guys. Back then you couldn't walk two blocks in any direction without bumping into a silk suit or one of his goons; they had the unions, the agencies, cash investments everywhere in the trade. Ivy used to date one till the spooks from the Breen office put on the pressure to break it off. I forget his name; it'd be Big Vinnie or Joey the Hippo, Little Augie Vermicelli, something anyway out of Dick Tracy. See, it was okay to *play* a bad girl, but not to be one on your own time. That don't mean she didn't stay in touch."

Valentino was seized with a double-emotion he knew well: the heady sense of having moved closer to his quest than anyone who'd gone before him, and the

stark fear of what that would mean to the authorities who'd failed to make that same leap.

And the gangster angle kept coming up. No due process there, just a short trip and a sure place in Hollywood lore.

"Do you know if Ivy Lane is still alive?"

Fitzhugh stared at him, blinked. "Hitch, I didn't get those new sides. How'm I going to work if I don't know my lines?"

The actor, he'd remembered, had been cast early in Alfred Hitchcock's *The Wrong Man* before the part had gone to someone else; it was no wonder he'd never received the script changes.

The window had closed; there would be no more new revelations that day. The archivist thanked the old man for his time and left him to his past.

14

As was so often the case when it came to digging up long-ago events, the interview with Roy Fitzhugh had left Valentino with as many questions as answers.

Was Ivy Lane a murderess, if not directly, then by proxy? A spat over a casting decision seemed a flimsy motive for taking a human life; but then, the motion-picture industry was ruled by ego, and what would seem ludicrous in every other society was a matter of survival in the precarious business of entertaining a fickle public. At the time *Bleak Street* was in production, barely a generation had passed since the talkie revolution had carved a bloodbath through Hollywood royalty. The image of John Gilbert, the brightest star of his era, scraping along playing bit parts on stages he'd commanded only a few years before, was etched indelibly in memory.

William Goldman, the late great screen-

writer, had said it best: "Never under-estimate the insecurity of a major star."

Or:

Could the old man have deliberately misled Valentino with well-timed displays of false senility? He had by his own admission withheld crucial evidence from the police, despite the stone-age methods of interrogation in those pre–Civil Rights days. Since then he'd had decades to perfect his act. A man stuck in the unchanging routine of assisted living might exploit a young visitor's gullibility for no reason other than his own amusement.

And what of Madeleine Nash? Ignacio Bozal had provided a bucolic sketch of a gifted player who had turned her back on stardom for marriage abroad, while Fitzhugh had said she'd died "too young." How young was too young? What, precisely, did those two words mean to a man pushing ninety?

In the end, Valentino trusted neither man not to have sent him on a wild-goose chase, just because he could. Eyewitness testimony was reliable only when it was confirmed, and the Grim Reaper had swept his sickle through the population of witnesses who could corroborate or contradict their stories. When it came to cold cases, Van Oliver's was forty below zero.

He crossed the city limits and turned onto Ventura, which had been transformed into a parking lot. Police barricades blocked the lanes in both directions. Two stuntmen were fighting on the roof of a four-story building in the next block, their fists swishing an inch past each other's face, with a stack of mattresses and empty cardboard boxes reaching from the sidewalk in front to the second floor. One of the men at least would plunge into that safety net eventually.

It was a familiar disruption in L.A., but that didn't stop the natives from blowing their horns. This one would go on for a while; the camera crews on the roof and on the street were seated in canvas chairs, drinking bottled water and punching buttons on cell phones while their equipment stood idle. When the rehearsal would end and the actual filming would begin was anybody's guess, including the director's. Valentino switched off his ignition. He was nursing his domestic compact along until such time as the revenue from The Oracle laid his worst debts to rest, and the tired motor stalled whenever it idled longer than a minute.

He tapped his own horn for the sake of the brotherhood of the boulevard, then picked up his own phone and hit speed dial.

One fought fire with fire, and old men with old men.

"That's never a good sign," Kyle Broadhead said.

The sign read CLOSED BY ORDER OF THE LOS ANGELES COUNTY BOARD OF HEALTH, and it was stuck to the glass entry door to The Brass Gimbal.

Valentino caught the attention of a man in a black polyester suit, white shirt, and black knitted necktie, a bureaucrat straight from central casting. He'd just finished smoothing the adhesive border to the glass.

"Is this temporary?"

"Not up to me; at least until the board sends me back for a compliance visit and I see what's what. I found a whole colony of cockroaches playing leapfrog in the salad bar."

"The Green Screen?" Broadhead said. "I *told* Fanta there's a reason rabbits don't live long."

"Where do we go now?"

Broadhead waved an arm, taking in the Starbucks on their side of the street and its double on the opposite corner. "Take your pick."

The one they chose was crowded, with a long line, but the barista in charge was ef-

ficient. Ten minutes after they entered, the pair took their tall high-dollar waxed-paper cups, a cruller, and a lemon-filled long john to one of the stand-up tables and rested their elbows. Valentino had bought, as he'd suggested the conference. While waiting in line he'd filled in his mentor on what he'd learned.

"Roy Fitzhugh," Broadhead said. "They built this town on his back. He never starred, went unbilled often as not; just showed up on time every day, sober and on his mark, lines down pat, and made ten pictures to Clark Gable's one. No Oscars, not even a nomination, but he lent money to some who won."

Valentino blew steam off his cup. "I didn't realize you knew so much about him."

"I don't; yet I do. He represents an endangered species. Movies are technically better than ever, and their top-notch talent are almost worth their confiscatory salaries, but the industry will never again have the deep bench of supporting players it had in the old days. As soon as one gets more than a just a mention in the trades, the studio builds a feature around him, and lets whatever other project that might have benefited from his contribution collapse under its own weight. And so Adam Sandler winds up car-

rying the film on his hydrocephalic head."

"Stirring speech, Kyle, although if you're planning to address a Guild meeting you'd better be sure Happy Gilmore isn't in attendance."

"I don't give speeches; it's in my contract. I'm quoting chapter two of the new book."

"I'll be sure and pick up a copy. Right now it doesn't solve my dilemma."

"It's not *your* dilemma. Go back to Henry Anklemire and tell him he'll have to work with what he's got. He'll whine a spell and kick a cat out a window, then put his nose to the stone." He shook his head. "All this time you've spent around old crocks like me and you still haven't learned you don't have to do anything you don't want to."

"I do if I want to keep on paying my bills."

Broadhead dunked his pastry in his coffee and twirled it like a swizzle. "They call me an ornament of the university. You know what an ornament is? A strip of colored paper you throw out after a party. It's the pillars that stick."

"I'm a pillar?"

"Shut up. I don't know why the sky pilots call pride a sin. Modesty's worse. Every time you snag a rare film and give it to the program, you dig your toe in the dirt and say your reward is in serving the cause of

cinema history. You've accomplished more than all your predecessors put together."

"I wouldn't say —"

"Sinner! Damn it, man, you need to cash in on your reputation! You could strangle the dean's wife live on TMZ and he'd have Anklemire spin it so it came out you were giving her the Heimlich maneuver. You're bullet-proof, and you're afraid a Nerf ball will shatter a rib."

Valentino watched him rescue the sodden doughnut from ruin. It seemed to require all his concentration. "I guess I could just walk away."

"You *guess*? Were you this clueless when I had you in my class, or am I the only one here who's getting smarter?"

He let Broadhead have that one. It was preferable to the reaction he'd get if he told him he didn't *want* to walk away. He had the scent now.

He took a last bite of his cruller and a swig of coffee. It was still hot enough to poach an egg. "Let's blow."

Broadhead stared. "How many of those hard-boiled flicks have you been watching?"

They bussed their table and stepped outside. The sun had dipped below the smog, tinting its normally brown underside an eerie shade of copper. Like the green sky

that warned the Midwest of a tornado, it promised a major ozone alert by morning, and with it the standard official admonition to avoid going outside, which few locals obeyed. Valentino was parked across the street. He offered Broadhead a lift.

"I'll walk. It may be my last fresh air for a spell. Also I enjoy the look on the faces of Angelinos when they see a man using his feet for something other than the gas pedal."

They shook hands and the archivist stepped off the curb.

"Look out!"

A black, slab-sided town car with shuttered headlights sped straight at Valentino. He leapt back onto the sidewalk just as it swept past, close enough to snag the hem of his jacket in the slipstream. Braking, its tires shrilled, slewing the vehicle into the curb.

The window hummed down on the passenger's side and the driver leaned across the seat, framing his face in the opening. Teak-colored eyes in a nut-brown face caught Valentino's gaze. "Sorry, buddy. Didn't see you. I will next time."

The car slammed into gear and was gone around the corner before Valentino could react.

Broadhead seized him by the shoulders from behind and spun him around. "That

maniac! Are you okay?"

"Did you hear what he said?"

"No. What?"

Somehow it sounded even more suggestive when he repeated it.

"Huh." The professor looked at the little haze of dust still settling in the car's wake. "I guess this would have been a good time to get a license number."

maniac! Are you okay?"

"Did you hear what he said?"

"No. What?"

15

"Do you think I should report what happened to the police?"

In the passenger's seat, Broadhead
frowned at the windshield. After the close
call with the town car he'd changed his
mind about walking back to the office. "I
can't advise you there. You're the one who
almost wound up a hood ornament."

"It could have been an accident. What did
the man say that was really suspicious?"

"You're right. This old-time mob angle is
turning us into nervous Nellies."

"On the other hand, what does 'I won't
next time' mean? What's the population of
L.A., anyway?"

"Three and a half million, give or take a
dress extra."

"So what are the odds there'll be a next
time?"

"Good point. It was a veiled threat."

"But if it was deliberate, he could have

142

clipped me anyway. All he had to do was bump up over the curb. I've done that by accident, turning a sharp corner."

"Me, too. He was just shook up and said the first thing that came to mind."

"Still, the way he said it. In a monotone, like a hoodlum in a B movie."

"Now that you mention it. Better report it."

"They'd laugh me out of the station, and they'd be right. These things happen a hundred times a day. Nobody in southern California goes anywhere except on wheels, and the speed limit's a joke."

"Yup. Just forget it."

"Thanks, Kyle. Talking with you always clears my head."

"What I'm here for."

Dusk wasn't just gathering; it was coming in on the gallop. The shadows cast by the Sierras pushed hard toward the Valley under a low ceiling built of coastal fog and auto exhaust. Homeward-bound traffic clogged every major artery and most of the minors, but Valentino swam against the current. He dropped Broadhead off to collect his own car and went back to his office in the old power plant, to return the dubbed *M* to the secure storage vault next to the lab and to

143

think about his next move.

He hadn't been fooled by Kyle's performance in the car. The wily old lecturer had used that Socratic ploy hundreds of times in his class, leading a skeptical student around in tight circles until he came to reject his own pet theory as ludicrous. In this case, the object had been both to prevent Valentino from paralyzing himself with panic and to keep him on his guard. How often had the old pedagogue said it? "Just because you're paranoid doesn't mean someone isn't out to get you." The trick was to shelve one's fear until he could confirm the reason for it and act on what he'd learned.

However, Valentino had withheld something from his mentor that might have changed the object of the lesson; had Broadhead seen *Bleak Street,* he might have noticed what he had.

He'd glimpsed the face in the open car window for less than two seconds, but everything about it — the shape, the coloring, the set of the features — bore so close a resemblance to the young Van Oliver that he might have been his double.

Of course, it was just fantasy, fueled by shock; which was why he hadn't bothered to share the observation. A crime from the

past, a dangerous woman, and now a seeming resurrection from the grave: This whole adventure was veering too close to the plot of a *noir* film to be anything but illusion.

Ruth, a fixture as always, looked up from the memorandum on her desk; she was crossing out entire passages in red pencil, like a teacher grading a term paper. It might have been written by Broadhead or anyone else in the department who shared her services. Nobody connected had ever summoned up the courage to challenge her right to edit their communications. She pointed the stiletto blade of her pencil toward the door of his office.

"Visitor."

"And you just let him in?"

"This is a public-funded institution of learning, not Area Fifty-one. Do you think anyone could smuggle so much as a stolen paper clip past me? Also it isn't a him." She stuck out a business card.

He took it. An impressionistic pen-and-ink sketch in the corner limned a gaunt vulpine torso and face with baleful eyes, brows that soared like raven's wings, and neon-red lips: Theda Bara, silent star of *Cleopatra* and many other man-eating roles during the early silent period (all gone now, an entire career lost to attrition and neglect):

the first *femme fatale.* She was touted as the daughter of a Middle Eastern potentate, her name an anagram of "Arab Death." In truth she'd been born Theodosia Goodman in Ohio. The Hollywood propaganda machine hit the ground running as early as 1917.

To the right of the drawing and below, engraved in shiny black letters, was a legend, followed by several contact numbers:

TEDDIE GOODMAN
CHIEF CONSULTANT
SUPERNOVA INTERNATIONAL

No, it wasn't the legendary Theda, although in person it was an easy assumption. Valentino suspected the name was an alias, adopted to catch the eye of her employer, Mark David Turkus, billionaire founder of Supernova, UCLA's fiercest competitor in the business of locating, restoring, preserving, and marketing lost cinematic treasures. Valentino suspected further that she'd taken the idea from his own name, coincidentally the same as another legendary silent star's. He could prove his identity from his birth certificate, but not having seen hers, he could only speculate based on her long record of manipulation and underhanded practices.

She could give lessons to Theda's predatory dames in the arts of bribery, subterfuge, and seduction.

"Teddie," he greeted, pulling his office door shut behind him. "How nice of you to show up without the bother of a satanic rite."

She was sitting behind his desk, her pencil arms spread and her white hands braced palms down on the top, forming an indestructible triangle. Today she had on a sleeveless dress of some shimmering green metallic material that fit her as tightly as the skin of a snake; it looked as if she'd need a can opener to get out of it. She wore her enameled black hair smoothed straight back from her high pale forehead, and her jet-trail eyebrows drew a *V* (for vampire) above a long straight nose and scarlet slash of mouth.

"Not funny," she said.

"Not meant to be." He hiked a hip onto the corner of the desk and rested a hand on his thigh. It was never bad policy to affect a casual attitude in her presence. The room temperature always seemed to drop ten degrees when she walked in. "It's been a while. The Augustine murder case, wasn't it?"

"As you know full well. If it hadn't been

for me, there'd be four fresh plots in Forest Lawn. While the rest of you eggheads were running this way and that, splicing useless clues like it was one of your precious movies, I got the drop on the worst mass-killer in this state since Charles Manson." Films to her were commodities only.

"No argument; but what have you done lately?"

Twin streaks of crimson appeared on the polished-pearl skin that covered her cheekbones, to fade as quickly as desert blossoms after a rain. Teddie Goodman's goat could be gotten, but never for long. She pointed a bare shoulder at the file cabinet where he'd stashed *M.* "Congratulations. Where's the rest of it?"

"Someplace with a better lock. Seems to me the last time you went snooping among my stuff, a couple of apes threw you down a flight of stairs. Most predators learn from their mistakes."

"Mark wanted to take you to court for that. You know he'd win; even if the university stood behind you, he'd have buried it under a pile of Tiffany-class lawyers. I told him if he did that, you'd just get fired. It'd take us a week to find out who replaced you and a month to figure out his working method, whereas with you still on the job

all I had to do was follow you around until I found out what you were after, then sprint past you to the finish. He'd seen me do it often enough."

"I tripped you up a couple of times," he said. "Anyway, what's past is past. What's brought you slumming around the halls of academe this time?"

"How far are you along on putting *Bleak Street* into circulation?"

He slid off the desk, to avoid falling, and cleared a heap of yellowed press releases off the other chair in the office in order to sit down. This gave him time to recover. "Who's your pipeline into the LAPD?" There was no use denying anything where Teddie was concerned. She never struck until she was sure of her information.

"What makes you think I have one?"

"Only a few people know I have anything to do with the film. I'm sure of the ones I've known for years, and the most recent is an unlikely informant based on his health and living arrangements. That leaves the police, who I asked for the files on the Van Oliver disappearance. They run a tight ship, but it's been known to spring leaks."

Her expression didn't change; but then it would take a jackhammer to crack her features. "If you repeat that in front of wit-

nesses, I'll sue you for slander. Any tank-town shyster could win that one. I asked you a question."

"Give it up, Teddie. It's a donation, acquired legally by its former owner, and it's in a secure facility even your high-tech skeleton keys can't crack. Tell the Turk he's barking up the wrong tree this time."

"How it was acquired remains to be seen; but it wouldn't matter."

"And why is that?"

"Because possession and ownership are two different things when it comes to intellectual property. Say you have a letter addressed personally to you by Brad Pitt. You can sell that letter to someone else, but you can't publish its contents without the permission of the copyright owner; Brad Pitt, in this hypothesis. You can't release *Bleak Street* for public viewing and charge a fee unless the owner of the copyright agrees."

"RKO ceased to exist sixty years ago. Who could the owner be?" But he had the sinking sensation that he knew the answer.

When Teddie Goodman smiled, he could hear the hissing of a fuse. "Must I say it?"

He didn't reply.

She rolled a polished shoulder. "Super-nova International bought out the entire

150

RKO library last month, as well as all properties belonging to the studio's successors, Desilu and Lorimar: Everything from *Cimarron* to 'Who shot J.R.?' The minute you open *Bleak Street* anywhere, you and your employers will be up to your neck in subpoenas. But I like you, Valentino, and so does Mark. We have no interest in exposing you to public humiliation."

From her lap she drew a clutch purse made of glistening black leather trimmed with the same metallic green fabric as her dress and opened the clasp. It was just large enough to contain the No. 10 envelope she placed on Valentino's side of the desk. This bore the embossed return address of the District Court of the County of Los Angeles.

"This is a judicial order restraining you from engaging in any public exhibition of the property known as *Bleak Street* until such time as you can show cause in court how such exhibition would not infringe upon the rights of the owner of the said intellectual property. The formal language is more involved, but I'll leave the whereases and hereinafters for you to work out in private." She snapped the purse shut.

Valentino didn't pick up the envelope. "You're devious, but I've never known you

to lie. If you say that's what this is, I'm sure it's genuine."

"I like you too."

"Hear me out. With us in possession of the film and Supernova in control of the copyright, I'm sure we can work out a deal that's beneficial to us both. There might even be a substantial corporate tax benefit involved. I'm sure Mr. Turkus's attorneys will be able to work out the details."

She pursed her lips, collapsing her cheeks so that they appeared even more cadaverous than usual.

"We can come to a deal, but I doubt you'd like it."

"I'm listening." He braced himself. He knew this was going to be bad. Later he would have to admit that he never dreamed just *how* bad.

"It's my employer's intention," she said, "to see that *Bleak Street* is never released. In order to guarantee that, he's prepared to invest as much of his resources as are necessary to buy all existing prints and negatives of the property and then destroy them."

Valentino stared. Her face gave no indication that she was joking. In fact he knew from long association that Teddie Goodman was incapable of either expressing humor or appreciating it.

152

She smiled for the second time in one visit, breaking a precedent. "I forgot to congratulate you on The Oracle's grand opening. How soon can Mark and I buy tickets?"

She smiled for the second time in one visit, breaking a precedent. "I forgot to congratulate you on The Oracle's grand opening. How soon can Mark and I buy tickets?

16

After she left, Valentino called Smith Oldfield with the university's legal department and made an appointment for the next morning. Then he went home, turned off his cell, and unplugged his landline. His sleep was uninterrupted, but he dreamed of close encounters with speeding automobiles, cunning old men with pliant memories, and slinky vamps luring callow young men silently to their doom.

In the morning, Oldfield, ever the gentleman, opened the door of his office personally to admit him. The New England–born attorney, who traced his ancestors back to the *Mayflower* (not that he was ever crass enough to mention it), rarely kept anyone waiting for long.

The office might have been constructed in Boston and transported across the country to a soundstage, all ready for Lewis Stone or Sidney Blackmer or Louis Calhern to

cloud the air inside with phrases like *habeas corpus, amicus curiae, voire dire,* and *actus reus;* terminology that Kyle Broadhead liked to dismiss as "body-snatching from linguistic graveyards, sanctioned under the law." It was all leather and oak, cream-colored bindings, fox hunts and diplomas.

The lawyer, tailored comfortably in well-seasoned wool, stepped to a paneled cabinet. "Coffee? I promise I can improve upon the supermarket blend they serve in the break rooms." He swung open a cabinet containing a black-and-silver Keurig coffee-maker and something else that caught the visitor's eye: a sleek gold statuette a little over a foot tall, with what looked like a strip of black electrical tape masking the engraving on its base. Oldfield took the appliance out quickly and swung the door shut.

"Was that an Oscar?"

The attorney placed the Keurig on a credenza and plugged it in, taking more care than seemed necessary for the operation. "I'd rather you hadn't seen that. My office cleaner failed to put it back in its proper place. I can't tell you whose name is on it."

"I didn't think it was yours. I doubt the bar association would look kindly on a lawyer winning an award for acting."

"I performed a service for a friend. I told

155

him he didn't owe me anything, but he insisted I hold the, er, item until he can pay me for my time and expenses."

"Do you think he will?"

"Yes. And not just because he wants to put that thing back on his mantel."

"May I ask how long it's been?"

Oldfield's face was a blank wall. "He'll be back for it."

There was no use pursuing the subject. This particular officer of the court would carry a confidence to the grave.

Valentino declined coffee with thanks. Oldfield looked disappointed; clearly he was proud of his brew, and the other regretted his decision. They repaired to a cluster of deep club chairs and sat down facing each other. Everything about the host, from his crisp gray temples to the shell-rim glasses he held in his lap, suggested that he'd made the transcontinental trip along with the smoky Ivy League furnishings.

Valentino knew all this for set-dressing. Oldfield was as thoroughly grounded in show-business psychology as anyone else in town. The opposing counsel who on first impression expected him to enter the ring with reticence, reserve, and old-school decorum was quickly disillusioned. He was a tiger in tweed.

"How *is* Miss Goodman?" he said, once the nature of Valentino's business was explained. "She should have recovered from her injuries by now. I envy you young people your resiliency."

"She's resilient; some might say she's positively reptilian. She grows a new limb for every one lost." Valentino handed him the court order.

Oldfield donned his readers and unfolded the stapled-together sheets. He read them with close attention, as if he were alone in the room. For all his genteel manners, when it came to the nuts and bolts of his profession, he made no concessions to cheery optimism: His clients were left to draw what they might from his "Hms" and headshakes. To all appearances, were he a physician studying a patient's chart, he was preparing to deliver a fatal diagnosis.

Finally he refolded the papers and his glasses. Cleared his throat. Valentino prevented himself from leaning forward only with effort.

"I'm afraid it's more than a nuisance suit," Oldfield said.

"That comes as no surprise. A five-car pileup on the freeway is a nuisance. Teddie's a natural disaster."

"Hm. If Supernova is indeed in sole

ownership of the RKO library — and based on what I know of the judge who signed it, I cannot imagine anything has been over-looked — the corporation is within its rights to enjoin you from exhibiting the property in question. To do so would constitute an assumption of ownership."

"But I do own it. Or rather, UCLA does now."

"In a case involving intellectual property, to possess is not to own."

"Can we fight this?"

"One can *always* fight; that's the spirit behind the rule of law. The *letter* is some-thing else again. I could not counsel pursu-ing the matter with any assurance that the result would not be as it stands at present."

Valentino nodded. He felt as if he'd been given a straight answer to the question, "How long have I got?" He rose and held out his hand for the papers. "Thank you, Mr. Oldfield."

"Perhaps you could meet with Mr. Turkus and come to some kind of terms outside the legal arena."

"Doubtful. Teddie made it clear he intends to prevent the film from ever being shown to anyone, anywhere, under any circum-stances."

"That seems extreme."

"I can't fathom it myself. Our entire history has been one of us determined to beat the other to a property and then bringing it out in the public arena. This new wrinkle has me scratching my head."

"To put it mildly." The lawyer gave him back the court order. His expression was illegible. Years of experience with judges and juries had gone into the construction of that poker face. "It's none of my business, I suppose; but assuming you'll take my advice and avoid going to court, may I ask what you intend to do?"

Valentino hesitated. "If I answered that question, could I be assured it won't leave this room?"

Oldfield frowned. "Client confidentiality doesn't extend to committing an illegal act before it takes place. I cannot withhold prior knowledge of a crime."

"Thank you, Counselor." Valentino shook his hand again and let himself back out into a morning that anywhere but in southern California would pass as twilight.

17

"Valentino?" said the woman on the other end of the telephone.

"Valentino," said Valentino.

"Seriously?"

"Unfortunately."

She chuckled. The distinctive husky voice had been further roughened by sixty years of cigarettes and aging vocal cords. "I was told you died seven years before I was born."

"I'm glad I didn't. I'm a fan."

"You needn't flatter me, Mr. Valentino, or whatever your real name is. What can you want of an old relic like me?"

Ivy Lane had proved remarkably easy to locate. Decades after her last appearance on film — one scene in an episode of *Ironside* — she was still a paid-up member of the Screen Actors Guild, where a contact had passed along her address and phone number, swearing him to strictest confidence.

He'd decided to play it straight. To one of

his temperament, laying his cards on the table came more easily than subterfuge, and usually led to better results.

"I'm with the Film and TV Preservation Department at UCLA. I'd like to interview you about your involvement with the filming of *Bleak Street.*" He held his breath. If his interest made her suspicious enough to refuse, it would at least indicate that Roy Fitzhugh hadn't made up the story of a confrontation on the set.

Did he hear a slight gasp? It was difficult to tell over the wire. When she spoke, her tone was unchanged.

"Great heavens. I haven't heard about that one in many, many years. I'm sorry to disappoint you, but I *had* no involvement in the production. I had to leave the cast because of a scheduling conflict."

He fudged a bit (but then so had she, if what Fitzhugh had said was on the level). "That was my information. It's what I wanted to ask you about."

"It's a filthy day. Would one o'clock tomorrow be convenient?"

He hesitated, then said it would be if it was for her, and they broke the connection.

Her invitation, coming so quickly, had been unexpected; but if this turned out to be another bum steer, he'd at least have the

161

pleasure of adding another personal meeting with a silver-screen icon to his collection.

Valentino had no idea why Teddie and Turkus wanted to suppress *Bleak Street;* but he was just as determined to crack the Van Oliver case. He could no more stop what he'd started than he could throw a projector into reverse in the middle of a showing, breaking the film beyond repair.

The scenery outside the power plant was depressing. The smog lay now on the rooftops, causing school closures and warnings to the elderly and the very young to remain indoors. There was an advantage to Valentino that the dip in senior-citizen shuttles and school buses made the rush hour less harrowing than usual. He reached Santa Monica in record time. There a retired Foley mixer had promised him a lead to the missing courtship scene from the Judy Garland/James Mason *A Star Is Born;* for years, restorers had been forced to use production stills to bridge the plot gap under the existing soundtrack. The film's popularity suffered: Moving pictures were expected to move. But once he got there, the old man tried to hold him up for a bribe in return for information that was patently a bluff.

"Thanks for your time," he said, turning toward the door; *and for wasting mine.*

He was disappointed, but not devastated. Most leads led nowhere, through deliberate misdirection or faulty memory or mistaken notions of the worth of the item in play; it was part of the game, and one reason that a true discovery tasted so sweet. On this smutty day, however, the return trip stuck him in the slow-moving sludge of hometown traffic, with nothing to entertain him on his AM-S/M radio but gas-bag talk show hosts, a college basketball contest for dead-last in the standings, ads pitching cures for erectile dysfunction, and rap marathons that left him with a pounding headache and despair for the future of the human race.

" 'The Man that Got Away' my foot, Judy," he said aloud. "Make that my career."

"No one said it'd be all gala premieres and your footprints on the Walk of Fame, Val."

This voice, the only other one in the car, made him jerk the wheel. The driver of a Land Rover passing him on the right blasted his horn, sending him back over the line.

He wrestled his cell phone from his pants pocket and glanced at the screen. He'd butt-dialed Kyle Broadhead, who'd overheard every word. Valentino hit END without replying.

■ ■ ■ ■

Overnight the wind shifted to the southwest, blowing the noxious clouds out over the Pacific. A freshly minted sun in a clear sky shone on pink stucco, yellow adobe, red ceramic tile, and swimming pools like bits of sparkling blue glass. It was one of those mornings the Chamber of Commerce chose to roust photographers from bed in order to take the postcard shot for the tourists. With no pressing issues awaiting him at work, Valentino took his toasted bagel and fresh-squeezed orange juice out onto the rear terrace to read the trades and spend the morning admiring Max Fink's neighborhood: the place as it had looked in 1927, when the box-office baron broke ground on The Oracle.

Afterward, its new owner put on a pale blue shirt and his best summerweight suit. He debated with himself over whether to wear a necktie, then selected one of the handful he kept for excursions east. The old Hollywood and the new had different standards. He wanted to make a good impression.

Driving, he split his attention between the rearview mirror and the road, looking for

black town cars with shuttered headlights. When none materialized, he relaxed. A steady diet of crime movies was bad for the imagination.

He drove among convertibles with their tops down, waving at clever-faced youths selling maps to the stars' homes (the scuttle-butt they sometimes sold him was a good deal more reliable than the maps them-selves, dozens of which crammed his glove compartment with their out-of-date infor-mation), entered Laurel Canyon, and pulled into a scooped-out parking area at the base of a stupendously long flight of flagstone steps. His watch read 12:45 P.M. He hoped he wouldn't be late; he hadn't counted on having to scale the Matterhorn.

The house was one of those stately sprawl-ing old Spanish villas pegged to the side of the canyon, a fortunate survivor of the wildfires that visited the place almost annu-ally. Heavy rain in the spring created lush undergrowth, to be turned into kindling when the Santa Ana winds blew hot and dry from Mexico; all that was required was a spark from a backyard grill or a carelessly flung cigarette butt or just a heated argu-ment to turn the place into an inferno. (Broadhead: "Fires, hurricanes, mudslides, earthquakes. God threw us out of Paradise

165

once. When will we get the message?")

The steps staggered up and up and up the geological ages, literally a stairway to the stars: When Beverly Hills ran out of room for private palaces, the glitterati had fled this direction. Climbing with the aid of an iron handrail, Valentino felt a niggling sense of *déjà vu.* He wondered where he'd seen the place before. He was sure this was a part of the canyon he'd never visited.

Then he remembered: It was the house where Ivy Lane had shot Cornel Wilde in *Switchback.* These were the very steps where Wilde had stumbled and then rolled down, tumbling end over end, bouncing off stone and iron, finally landing on his back in the street. Blank, staring eyes turned toward a heaven too far beyond his mortal reach, captured in extreme close-up as sirens approached, growing louder and louder until THE END came up and the orchestra drowned them out.

Fade to black.

Co-star Ivy Lane had either lent her own home to the production or formed some kind of attachment to it during filming and bought or rented it later; years later, perhaps, in a fit of nostalgia. It looked less forbidding, almost cheerful, in color on a sunny day than it had in black-and-white.

Someone had removed the sinister hedges and planted flowers in boxes under the windows.

Had he come there after dark, when the jagged stone steps and the pale-stucco house at the top would be lit only by the streetlamps strung out along the base of the cliff, leaving the rest in indigo shadow, he might have made the connection immediately. As it was, he had the eerie sensation of having stepped directly into a frame from a motion picture.

The house itself was typical of the regional culture, an *hommage* to the haciendas that had been brutally bulldozed to make room for an earlier generation of bungalows and motor courts. On the expansive front porch, Valentino leaned against a post of piñon pine and waited for his breath to catch up and his heart rate to slow to normal. It had been a long ascent even for a young man, and part of it through Cornel Wilde's ghost. Finally he pushed away from the post, straightened his tie, and pressed a coral button in a verdigris copper setting.

Instantly the door was opened by a man whose broad bulk filled the opening as thoroughly as a second door. Valentino had the uneasy feeling that he'd been tracked all the way from the floor of the canyon, like

an intruder wandering into an ambush. The man wore a tan poplin sportcoat over a white tailored shirt, open at the neck to display his smooth tanned muscular throat. His hair started two inches above the bridge of his flat nose and grew so close to the skull it left the bony structure exposed. Black, tiny eyes under a rocky outcrop of brow and a blue-coal chin suggested a direct line to Cro-Magnon man. In Ivy Lane's day, he'd have been the man who stood behind the man barking the orders, wearing tight-fitting chalk stripes and a white tie on a black shirt.

The first words out of the man's mouth were even less encouraging than his monolithic demeanor.

"Are you with the police or the coroner's office?"

18

The voice was a deep drum roll. Stepping back, Valentino stared up into a pair of nostrils like ship's funnels. The line he'd been fed (he thought it a tasteless joke) sounded rehearsed; once again he had that sense of Been There Before. He knew this man from somewhere.

"Neither," he said. "I have an appointment with Miss Lane. The name is Valentino."

The man-mountain rumbled. The noise seemed to indicate amusement. "Yeah, sure."

He suppressed a sigh. Establishing his right to a name so well known in the entertainment world presented an obstacle almost daily. One generation remembered the star of *The Sheik* and *Blood and Sand,* avatars of the silent era; another compared him to a fashion designer of international renown. So far as he knew, he was related

169

to neither. Experience had taught him to keep his business cards handy. He gave one to the ogre, who glanced at it and poked it into his handkerchief pocket.

"All her appointments are canceled, sorry." The door started to close.

A female voice called from the other side of the poplin sportcoat. "Who is it, Vivien?"

Vivien?

"Someone who says his name is Valentino. He has cards." He sneered the last sentence. "I told him —"

"Yes, I heard that part. Show him in."

When at last the giant stirred, it was like tectonic plates shifting. He moved to one side, leaving just enough space for Valentino to enter the house sideways. Coming from bright sunlight, he was blinded temporarily by the dim illumination inside. From out of the gloom came a hand, trapping his in a solid grip. As his pupils caught up, he found himself facing a woman nearly as tall as he. She wore large red-framed glasses and a tailored red suit without a blouse. This did wondrous things for a figure that didn't seem to need to have much for it. Her honey-colored hair was caught loosely behind her neck.

"I'm Georgia Tanner, Miss Lane's legal

representative. She mentioned your conversation."

"Then I won't have to explain myself."

"Something about one of her films."

"*Bleak Street;* except it really wasn't one of her films. She dropped out before the cameras rolled."

"What business are you in again?"

Vivien retrieved the card from his pocket, looked at it again, and presented it.

" 'Valentino,' " he said, as if she couldn't read what was on the card. " 'Film Detective.' A dick. I said it the second I saw him."

Looking at him again, Valentino felt a shock of recognition. Now that there was some distance between them, he could take in the huge man's blunt features and heavily muscled build in perspective. He was older than he looked; splinters of silver in his stubble suggested he dyed his hair. In the early eighties, under the name "Bull" Broderick, he'd been interviewed in *TV Guide* as Lou Ferrigno's stunt double in *The Incredible Hulk.* The foyers and pantries of Greater Los Angeles were littered with more half-forgotten faces than a cutting room floor.

Valentino told Georgia Tanner where he worked. "Calling myself a detective gets

more attention in the entertainment industry than archivist. My job is to locate and acquire rare motion pictures so they can be preserved for future generations to see and appreciate."

"Goodness, you *are* a detective."

"In a way. Some films seem just as determined to stay lost as any fugitive from justice." He was suffocating from the lack of a change of subject. "May I see Miss Lane?"

"I don't see what help she could be, since as you say she wasn't in — what was it, again?"

He repeated the title. He was pretty sure she hadn't forgotten it. At this point in her career, she had yet to develop Smith Oldfield's impervious mien. "So far as I know, she's one of only two surviving actors who had anything to do with the production. Forgive me, but I didn't think I'd have to jump through hoops just to ask your client some friendly questions."

The professional smile left her face. "Miss Lane is dead. She committed suicide late last night or early this morning."

The news came as a physical blow. He was struck by the thought that he'd never lived in a world that didn't contain Ivy Lane. She

had sounded so lively over the phone, so much more like herself than the dozens of starlets who had attempted to imitate her in roles patterned after her iconic image.

"Have the police definitely established suicide?"

"We're waiting for them now," Georgia Tanner said. "She always came down promptly at eleven for lunch. Today, when she was more than a half hour late, Vivien went up to look in on her. He tried to wake her, but her skin was already cool. He called me at my office and I came straight over. I found an empty prescription bottle on her bedside table. It was Seconal."

"Vivien is the butler?"

"Bodyguard," said the giant.

Valentino looked from him to the attorney. "Why would an eighty-seven-year-old woman need a bodyguard?"

"She didn't. She hadn't since she quit being Hollywood's Bitch Goddess when Cinemascope came in." She smiled tightly. "Does my language shock you?"

"I'm familiar with all the euphemisms: femme fatale, bad girl, vamp, harpy, bitch goddess. They predate the rating system."

"Yes." She seemed disappointed. "Anyway, she was accustomed to having one around. She played so many spider women, you see,

173

and some moviegoers in those innocent days had trouble separating the image from the reality. That was over long before Vivien came. In his ten years here he's been more of a companion. He was absolutely devoted to her."

"Still am."

Did the big man's voice break? Valentino looked at him again. His eyes were pink around the edges and slightly swollen. He felt a little more kindly to him then. They were both fans of Ivy Lane.

"Can either of you think of a reason she'd want to end her life?"

A glance passed between attorney and bodyguard. She shook her head. "That's up to the police, I suppose."

"May I see her?"

She was startled. "Whatever for?"

"I've only known her on-screen. This may be my last chance to see her in — well, person."

"Creep." Vivien spoke under his breath.

Georgia Tanner consulted the floor. It was blue and white Mexican tile, the same shining squares William Demarest had dropped his cigar ashes on when he came to investigate the armored-car robbery at the center of *Switchback*'s convoluted plot.

She looked up. "I don't suppose it would

174

do any harm, if you don't touch anything."

"I go too." It was a line Vivien never got to use in his non-speaking *Hulk* role.

They passed through large, sun-splashed rooms and up an open swirl of staircase with a brass banister like the railing of an ocean liner. Original paintings for posters advertising Ivy Lane's movies lined the staircase wall: Ivy locked in steamy embraces with Wilde, Dick Powell, John Payne, Robert Mitchum, Alan Ladd. Invariably, a shadowy figure lurked in the keylit background, gripping a gun; Peter Lorre, Elisha Cook, Jr., Steve Brodie — a pictorial *Who's Who* of heavies from Central Casting's exhaustive inventory. One of the great Dark Ladies of the uncertain postwar period, Lane was the stereotypical seductress who lured the ambivalent hero to the wrong side of the law, and eventually his doom — and hers as well, as dictated by the code laid down by the censorship offices of Will Hays and Joseph Breen. Her silver-blond mane and hoarse, predatory purr had furnished an insidious antidote to the bright-eyed, perky heroines who had dominated the industry before Pearl Harbor. This, according to the subtext, was what had become of the "gentler sex" while the men were away at the front.

The bedroom, done entirely in cream and black and as big as a warehouse, was scarcely large enough to contain the enormity of death.

Fresh flowers bloomed unaware in a vase on a low dresser forested with unposed family pictures in silver frames. A pair of fuzzy pink slippers on the floor beside a bed shaped like a sleigh, and a pale pink silk dressing gown draped over the footboard, awaited their mistress. Here the only item pertaining to the movies was the honorary Oscar presented to her years before by the Academy as an apology for having passed over her finest performances in favor of ponderous costume dramas and glossy musical extravaganzas; in the world of pompous prestigious showboaters, no "melodramas" need apply. The award looked lonely on its corner of a mirror-topped vanity table. A framed certificate commemorating her efforts on behalf of the World Hunger Foundation occupied a much more prominent position on the wall just inside the door.

Was this a woman who could have arranged Van Oliver's murder, merely because she suspected him of edging her out of the *Bleak Street* cast? But a realist like Kyle Broadhead would have reminded him of the

good deeds performed by the worst offenders, and the worst transgressions committed by the most celebrated humanitarians. Stereotypical casting existed only on the soundstage; people were invariably more complex and inexplicable than they were represented in screenplays.

The three were not alone with the deceased. As they entered, a man and woman seated next to the bed looked up at them with barren eyes. The man was gray-haired, dressed somewhat flashily in stacked lapels and a yellow silk handkerchief, and might have been considered large in any company that didn't include the hulking Vivien. The woman was a few years younger and wore plain slacks and a sweater and no makeup. Her brown hair was cut short.

"Dale Grant, Miss Lane's nephew," said Ms. Tanner. "His wife, Louise. This is Mr. Valentino."

"Valentino will do," said Valentino.

Grant rose and offered a listless hand. "Are you a policeman?"

He shook his head. That made twice in half an hour he'd been mistaken for the law. "Just an admirer. With your permission I'd like to pay my respects."

"Don't tell me it's on the news already," said Grant. "I wouldn't have thought Aunt

Ivy was such good copy. It's been so long since she was in the public eye."

Ms. Tanner said, "Valentino is here by invitation."

Grant's brow puckered. "That's odd. She was scrupulous about keeping commitments. Even despondent as she must have been, she'd have thought it rude. I know that sounds fatuous, but —" He spread his hands, at a loss to complete the sentence.

Valentino finished it for him. "— a person like that would be more likely to put off her plans in order to accommodate an expected visitor; even plans for her own death."

He was acutely aware that four pairs of eyes were staring at him; but his own were fixed on the small still figure in the bed.

19

Valentino forced himself to be objective, to see an elderly woman and not a figure of glamour created by experts in makeup, lighting, and filters.

True, age had scored and lengthened the face that had seduced half the second string of leading men; yet the features were girlish in repose. Her hair, tinted a lighter shade of yellow now to conceal the gray, was arranged in a demure braid over her left shoulder. She wore a plain flannel nightgown and her slim hands, the veins coarsened by time, were nearly as pale as the cream-colored spread upon which they rested.

"Did she leave a note?"

Georgia Tanner shook her head. She, too, was watching the inert face, as if waiting for the eyes to open and the expression to change: *Don't count me out yet.* "She wasn't much for writing, notes or letters. When a

man came from AFI asking if she'd consider donating her papers, she said, " 'What papers? I'm an actress, not a scientist.' "

"I'm still not buying this," Grant said. "I just saw her last week. She was as chipper as ever."

"These decisions are often made on the spur of the moment, Dale," said the attorney. "I don't think she ever forgave the industry for tossing her on the scrapheap when she turned forty. There's talk of remaking *Carlotta,* with Cameron Diaz, of all people. That was Ivy's signature role. It must have eaten at her, though she wouldn't show it. I was here last night, and she seemed fine then; but let's not forget she was an actress."

"Perhaps you're right. Well, maybe she'll have her moment back in the spotlight now. Too bad she can't enjoy it. She only pretended to be a recluse in order to attract attention." Grant's throat worked. "If you'll excuse me." He hurried out. His wife remained in her seat for an undecided moment, then got up and followed him.

"He loved his aunt very much," Georgia Tanner said. "He came here to have brunch with her. He took the news badly. I think he's only in denial because he's afraid he'd be furious with her for what she did. You

never know what form grief will take."

"Is he a bitter man usually?"

"Only with himself. I understand there was a row when he dropped out of medical school and went into business. Things were never the same between them after that. Not that they ever spoke of it when I was around. Louise let it slip once. She doesn't say much, but when she does it's usually indiscreet."

"Was his aunt as vain as he said?"

"Not among friends and family, but she enjoyed putting on a show for strangers. She said people who came to see Ivy Lane expected an event, and she wasn't about to disappoint them. That would explain why she agreed to see you."

"I wonder what changed her mind."

From far down the canyon came the sound of a siren. It echoed off the cliffs, which distorted it into a bone-chilling howl. It seemed to go on a long time, then suddenly whooped around the corner and growled to a halt at the base of the steps.

At least ten minutes passed before the doorbell rang. Valentino and Georgia Tanner followed Vivien to the foyer, where the big man opened the door on a pair of uniformed officers and more than six feet of equal op-

181

portunity employment in the person of Sergeant Lucille Clifford of Homicide.

She was wearing her sunset-red hair above the shoulders now, but retained the stern towering air of an ambulatory Statue of Liberty. She stood straight as a pike in a powder-blue blazer cut long enough to conceal her service revolver, a black knee-length skirt, black-and-white pumps with modest heels, and her gold shield on a folder clipped to an outside pocket.

If the film archivist had hopes she'd mellowed since their last encounter, her first words dashed them to pieces.

"Glad I'm not with the coroner. I'd hate to be the one to carry a stiff down those stairs." She spotted Valentino. "You."

"Sergeant. Isn't this outside your beat?"

"We don't pound beats anymore, Boston Blackie. Don't carry Roscoes or pinch apples neither. In cases of sudden death — suicide, trip and fall, an alien in the belly — it's any Homicide detective in a storm. But since you brought it up, this one's a little fresh for you, isn't it? You usually don't come in until forty years after the body heat ran out."

"This time it's coincidence — maybe. I'm still working on whatever became of Van Oliver. He and Ivy Lane had a history."

"Of course they did. I've been waiting for the other shoe to drop ever since you borrowed the file."

A paw like a steam shovel landed on Valentino's shoulder.

"Kind of chummy with L.A.'s finest, ain't we? What're you, one of them pervs gets his jollies browsing the morgue?"

"Vivien!" snapped the Tanner woman.

"I don't trust this bird." But the hand was withdrawn.

"Pardon my glove, Sasquatch." Clifford slid in past him. To Tanner: "If I were you, I'd trust your big friend's instincts. Are you the one who called?"

"Yes." She made introductions. Dale and Louise Grant had joined them.

"Vivien; seriously?"

The bodyguard clenched his jaw. "My friends call me Bull."

"Okay, Mr. Broderick." The sergeant identified herself and the officers. One's surname was Howard, the other's Harold. Harold was black, Howard white; or was it the other way around? To Valentino they were as alike as opposite pieces on a chessboard.

Tanner filled them in on the way to the bedroom. There, Clifford glanced at the body with no show of interest, then made a

silent signal. She and the officers split up to examine the room. The inlaid ebony dresser was full of extravagant evening gowns, the walk-in closet a riot of rainbow silk and satin negligees on padded hangers. Some still had price tags. Howard and Harold wrote in pads.

Returning to the bed, the sergeant slid a gold pencil from an inside pocket, inserted it in the empty prescription bottle lying on its side on the nightstand, and lifted it to eye level. She read aloud the physician's name printed on the label. Harold and Howard recorded it. She put it back in the original position.

"Mr. Grant," she said, "were you her only living relative?"

Georgia Tanner spoke. "Yes. There was a son by her first marriage, but he was killed in Iraq."

This met with a stony look. "Impressive. His lips didn't even move."

The attorney flushed. "Force of habit, sorry. I represent the family."

"This is an informal interview, Counselor. Nice house. Does it go with the inheritance?"

Grant answered this time. "I've no idea. I haven't seen a will. I don't even know there is one."

184

"Ms. Tanner?"

She nodded. "There is. At the behest of my client, I can't disclose the details until the reading."

"Uh-huh. I suppose you come in for a commission."

Vivien stepped in front of Clifford. He had two inches on her and at least sixty pounds. "That ain't no way to talk."

She didn't twitch a muscle. "What's a bodyguard's devotion worth in dollars and cents?"

It might have been Valentino's imagination, but it seemed to him the man had begun to swell and turn green. Officers Harold and Howard took a step in Vivien's direction; but Clifford remained immobile, her smoky blue eyes fixed on Vivien's face as if she were looking at a sample on a microscope slide.

Ms. Tanner crossed her arms. "For your information, Lieutenant —"

"Sergeant. I work for a living."

"Noted. Ivy's third husband went through what was left of her fortune thirty years ago. Aside from this house and property, her Social Security pension was all she had, and most of that went into taxes and upkeep. I charged her a minimal fee to manage her affairs. As an officer of the court, I under-

stand it's your job to eliminate all the pos-sibilities, but —"

"I'm glad you understand. Where's a good room where I can conduct interviews?"

To his surprise, Valentino was her first subject. They sat on a pair of floral-print chairs in a small sun room, rattan blinds shielding them from the strong light coming through the west-facing windows. She crossed her legs and rested her hands in her lap. "Give me all of it."

He took that literally; always a sound policy when dealing with her. He began with Ignacio Bozal's bargain, *Greed* in return for *Bleak Street,* Valentino's interest in the Van Oliver case, the near-miss outside Starbuck's, and the morsel of information he'd gotten from Roy Fitzhugh that had brought him to Ivy Lane's house. He with-held nothing, not even the detail he'd kept from Kyle Broadhead to avoid ridicule. Finally he recapped his conversation with the others in the bedroom. She listened without changing expression and took no notes.

"People step off curbs into traffic every day," she said. "Sometimes they don't get run over. I think your friend the professor's right. It's probably nothing."

"He argued the other side, too."

"He should run for governor. So you think the guy looked like Oliver. Even if he's still around, he wouldn't look like himself. This state's rotten with bad drivers. We've cornered the market on sunny-ots."

"What's a sunny-ot?"

"An idiot that follows the sun till it sets in California."

"But what are the odds Ivy Lane would wind up dead the very day I was to ask her about her fight with Oliver?"

"This isn't Vegas. There are no odds."

"But —"

She uncrossed her legs, leaned forward, and patted his hand. She couldn't have astonished him more if she'd asked him out on a date. "Listen and learn."

At her instruction, the two men in uniform conducted the others into the room one at a time. Valentino stood in a corner trying to be unobtrusive as each took his old seat and answered questions. He couldn't tell which were significant and which were just to establish a pattern, like the innocuous queries posed during a lie-detector test. Clifford's was a highly specialized art. The sessions were brief and took place only minutes apart.

She saved the bodyguard for last. When he sat, his platter-sized hands resting on his

thighs, the chair disappeared. Throughout the interview he kept casting suspicious glances Valentino's way.

"Was Grant here last night?" Clifford asked.

"No. This is the first time him and Mrs. Grant have been in all week."

"Does he have a key?"

"Sure. He's her nephew. But nobody comes in or goes out without me knowing."

"Where do you sleep?"

"Other end of the hall from Ms. Lane."

"Did she know about your record?"

He turned his face, black with rage, toward Valentino, who met it with blank shock.

"I'm clean," he said, turning back. His hands closed on his thighs, the knuckles white. "I paid my debt."

"I know. I'm the one who booked you. I might forget a face, but not sitting on that body, and with the name Vivien. I was on road patrol then. You blew four-point-oh on the Breathalyzer. You'd had your license yanked what, three times?"

"Twice. I ain't had a drop in ten years."

"That'd be just about the time you came to work for Ivy Lane."

"Yeah. I told her all about it. She said it was nothing to her so long as I kept my nose

clean, and that I done. I might not of done it for anybody else, but I done it for her."

"Okay."

He kneaded his thighs. Valentino doubted those wrinkles would come out. "Okay?"

"Do I need to spell it? You're off the hook, Bull. Send Grant back in, will you?"

The nephew came in, but he didn't sit. "Did you forget something?" he said.

"One question, Grant. How'd you do it?"

20

"Do what?" Grant's big heatlamp-tanned face was flat.

"Don't say anything more, Dale." Georgia Tanner came in, practically sprinting. Clearly she'd been eavesdropping from outside the door. She glared down at Clifford. "You won't get far boosting your arrest record when you have no chance of obtaining a conviction. Weren't you listening when I said Ivy's estate wasn't worth committing murder to acquire?"

"You're the first one to bring up murder, Counselor. I'm tempted to think there's a reason it was on your mind; but that would look like I *was* only interested in making a bust. But since it's on the table, a house this size on two acres in one of the most exclusive neighborhoods in a town with the highest property values in the world? How much was the last offer?"

The attorney's eyes dilated behind her

glasses. "I didn't say —"

"It's California, sister. Everyone wants to live here, even Republicans."

"Twelve million. She told the agent she'd burn the place down before she'd let some Arab potentate house his harem in her garden."

"Was Grant present when the offer was made?"

The nephew's face darkened. He took a step toward her chair. A hand squeezed his shoulder, stopping him. Valentino knew what that grip felt like. Vivien had entered, followed closely by Louise Grant, as silent as ever.

"I know how you did it," Clifford said. "I just wanted to see if I could jolt you into blurting it out, but you've got a smart lawyer. Did you think I wouldn't know what to look for in an O.D. case? Did you think even if I missed it, the medical examiner would too? The skin around even the tiniest punctures discolors and swells as a body's temperature goes down."

Valentino said, "But you barely glanced at the body."

"I knew what to look for, and where to look. In most cases of this type, it's in the jugular." To Grant: "Last night, after Georgia Tanner left and you were sure your aunt

191

and her watchdog were asleep, you let yourself in, using your key, and dissolved a lethal dose of Seconal into a solution. It's my guess you came here already loaded for bear. We'll search your place for any pills you may have left behind. You'd know how much to use from your med-school training, and anyone can get hold of a hypodermic."

Vivien chimed in. "I'm a light sleeper. Seems to me I'd of heard something."

"Not unless there was a struggle. Being family, Grant knew where she kept the pills. He smeared his prints, because to wipe them off would've ruled out suicide, and dumped the pills down the sink. A million dollars for ten minutes' work is good wages even by Hollywood standards."

Grant boiled over. "This is pure guesswork! Worse, it's slander! I'll —"

Tanner shushed him.

Clifford looked at her. "You should take your own advice, Counselor. We'll be asking you again whether you disclosed the terms of the will to Grant."

Flushing again, Tanner said, "I may have mentioned something; to Mrs. Grant. She confided to me that she was worried about her husband's business. I — I sometimes think I'm part of this family. Louise is the

worrying type. I wanted to comfort her. I swore her to secrecy," she added, with a glance Louise Grant's way.

"You can trust a spouse to keep a secret, if one of them is dead." The sergeant returned her attention to Grant. "You forgot one thing: Ivy Lane's nightgown. Tanner said she liked to put on a show for strangers, and you said yourself your aunt enjoyed being the center of attention. She had a closet full of beautiful negligees. The woman you both described would never have taken her own life in plain flannel."

A bellow shattered the tension in the room; it was the cry of a mortally wounded grizzly. Vivien reached down from his great height, snatched Grant's stacked lapels in his enormous hands, and lifted him off the floor. Grant gulped for air.

"Put him down!"

Four heads swiveled toward Louise Grant. The nephew's wife had an open purse in one hand and a hypodermic syringe in the other. She held the needle in an underhand grip like a switchblade. The point glittered.

"Put him down or I'll stick this in your kidney." Her thin, drawn face was feral.

Harold and Howard, who'd been hovering inside the doorway, stepped toward her. They stopped at a gesture from the sergeant.

The bodyguard lowered her husband to the floor and let go. Grant clawed the yellow handkerchief out of his pocket and mopped his face.

Clifford's head moved less than a hundredth of an inch. In less time than that took, one of the officers had Louise Grant in a chokehold and the other wrested the weapon from her hand before she could react.

The sergeant repeated the movement. The arm was withdrawn from the woman's throat, but the officers remained at her side, muscles flexed.

"She wouldn't die."

Everyone else was silent, watching Louise Grant. Her face now was drained of energy, her voice entirely without emotion.

"She was going to outlive us all. Dale's business was failing. She could have sold the house, bailed him out, and had plenty left over, but she refused. I pleaded with her. She said he should have considered the consequences when he dropped out of medical school."

"Louise." Grant twisted his handkerchief between his fists.

"I knew you'd never do it. She made you dance to her tune, the same way she manipulated all her leading men. It was no act. I

was a registered nurse when I married you. Remember how refreshed you felt this morning? I spiked your tea last night with Seconal. I was gone for over an hour with your key to this house and you slept right through it."

"Cuffs," Clifford told the officers. "Miranda. There's a lawyer present, remember."

The forensics team came — Harriet wasn't with it, but it was a big detail — and the sergeant's work was finished for the time being. Valentino offered her a lift back to West Hollywood. The unmarked car she'd come in was crowded with Harold, Howard, and their prisoner. Clifford frowned at the compact's tires, but climbed into the passenger's seat.

He drove. "How'd you guess it?"

" 'Guess'? Just for that I should issue you a citation for those baldies we're rolling on. You think we dumb flatfeet can't crack a case without Inspector Pinchbottom and the Little Rascals? We flag more killers in a week than Ellery Queen did in his whole career. Plus we're real."

"I don't suppose I could ask you to crack mine."

"And spoil your fun? One thing." She looked straight ahead. "What I said before,

about coincidences; don't bet the farm on that. If Van Oliver was killed under contract — even if Ivy Lane did arrange it — the statute of limitations doesn't apply. As long ago as that was, there may be someone still around who knows enough to be dangerous."

He guided the car a block in silence. "Thank you."

"Well, don't get all mushy about it. I didn't cross my fingers when I swore to serve and protect. That means everyone, even walk-ons billing themselves as detectives. We should've trademarked the name a hundred years ago."

They were at the station. She said, "Don't get dead, okay?"

"Well, thanks, Sergeant. I didn't know you cared."

"Sure I do. I got corpses stacked six deep, a husband who thinks I threw him over for the M.E., and a kid who half the time calls me by my sister's name. If you do get dead, try to do it on the sheriff's time." She got out.

Like mad dogs, Englishmen, and the sun, Angelinos rarely miss an opportunity to enjoy a starry night. Valentino's quarters, in the concrete bunker of a fireproof projec-

196

tion booth, had no windows, so after dark he went to the terrace to howl at the moon; or at least to look at it.

As he did so, his silhouette showing against the light spilling out the open door, a movement across the street below caught his eye. A figure that had been standing under a streetlamp turned into a dark doorway. In the process, Valentino saw a face lifted to the spot where he stood gripping the wrought-iron railing. There was no doubting it this time: The man wearing a trench coat and snapbrim hat could have doubled for Van Oliver in his prime; a dead ringer in every sense of the phrase.

tion booth, had no windows, so after dark
he went to the terrace to howl at the moon;
or at least to look at it.

As he did so, his silhouette showing
against the light spilling out the open door,
a movement across the street below caught
his eye. A figure that had been standing
under a streetlamp turned into a dark
doorway. In the process, Valandno saw a
face lifted to the spot where he stood gripping the wrought-iron railing. There was no
doubting it this time. The man wearing a
trench coat and snapbrim hat could have
doubled for Van Oliver in his prime: a dead
ringer in every sense of the phrase.

III
OUT OF THE PAST

21

That Saturday had been set aside for months: Harriet wanted to take in the annual Renaissance Fair in Agoura's Paramount Park. Valentino, who preferred as a rule to limit his theme-park experience to the Universal Studios tour, had agreed, but only because a tent showing had been arranged there for the newly restored *Black Shield of Falworth,* a prize he'd narrowly lost to Supernova International.

"Tony Curtis as a medieval knight?" she'd asked. " 'Yonder lies the castle of my fadda'?"

"He never said that; it's just another myth, like Cagney saying, 'You dirty rat.' But, yes. Mostly I like Torin Thatcher as the master of knights. I think Alec Guinness took notes when he was prepping for Obi-Wan Kenobi."

"What costume will you wear?"

"Do we have to? I mean, isn't that for kids?"

"What are we, Ma and Pa Kettle?"

So he put on a leather jerkin and a hat with a feather in it, courtesy of the wardrobe department at Warner Brothers; the outfit had faded from its original Lincoln green and smelled of moth flakes, but the sewn-in label bore the name of Errol Flynn's stunt double. He felt a little less foolish when Harriet came to her door in tights and a laced corset. At least nobody would be looking at him.

They walked out on *The Black Shield of Falworth* before the end of the first reel. He was steaming. She laced her arm inside his.

"Sorry, Val. I blame social media. Parents need to teach their brats to keep their opinions to themselves during the campy parts, at least in public."

He patted her arm. "It's okay. I guess it is kind of a dumbed-down *Ivanhoe.*"

"You've got it on DVD, right? We'll watch it in The Oracle."

"If that isn't true love, I don't know what is."

She laid her head on his shoulder. A knock-kneed jester with a neck tattoo scowled at them and said, "Hie thee to a room!"

In the commissary they dined at a trestle table on a mutton joint (Valentino; actually

202

a lamb shank) and roast boar (Harriet; actually a BLT), while jugglers and tumblers performed to the lively strains of a trumpet and lute. After the entertainers exited, he filled her in on his investigation, finishing with the mysterious stranger he'd spotted across from the theater.

"A trench coat and fedora?" she said. "You're kidding, right?"

"It didn't seem so funny last night."

"Did you notify the police?"

"I just did."

"What am I going to do, track him down, dissect him, and weigh his brain?"

"Thanks." He put down his knife and fork and pushed away his plate.

"You know what I mean."

"What could they do? This morning I checked out that doorway. It belongs to a restaurant closed for renovation. There weren't any Egyptian cigarette butts or darts dipped in African frog venom or bits of clay that can only be found in Argentina. I think someone's just trying to scare me off the case."

"You're an archivist, Val. You don't *have* cases. What do you think he'll do if he *can't* scare you off?"

He took a spoonful of mint jelly, testing his stomach's powers of recovery. "I'm no

danger to anyone. Whoever's responsible for Oliver's vanishing act — if anyone is — he's either dead or too old to pose any kind of threat."

"Still, you should report it."

"They'd laugh me out of the station."

She bit into her sandwich, chewed, swallowed. "You're probably right. A guy dressed like a character out of Oliver's movie, in the last place in the country that needs a coat and hat of any kind? Who just happened to look up just as you stepped outside, so you could see his face clearly in the light? No one who meant you any harm would do that. You're right: Someone's just trying to spook you."

"It's working. That thing downtown was a close call."

"Yes, and I was about to drop a piano on you for keeping that from me when you got to that business across the street. I still might."

"I didn't want you to worry in case it turned out to be nothing."

She pushed away her plate, the BLT unfinished. "Val, if we're not in this together, what are we?"

"You're right."

"This isn't the first time we've had this conversation."

"I know. I just —"

"What if some jerk almost ran me down and I kept it from you? How could I know it was an accident? Could be it was someone who knew I was connected with the police. It's open season on every department, the way the press plays it up every time someone accuses a cop of stepping out of bounds."

He watched an ogre climbing off the bench belonging to the neighboring table. His green mask was still peeled up from his mouth so he could eat. "I never thought of it that way."

"I can't keep walking you through the steps of a relationship. You can't just jump-cut to another scene when it suits you."

He smiled. "I love it when you talk dirty."

"Don't even try changing the subject that way. You're not Kyle." She plucked a chick-pea (the chalkboard menu referred to it as "grapeshot") off his plate and ate it. "You think Fitzhugh was right and Ivy Lane had something to do with what happened to Oliver?"

"You know what?" He brightened. "I'm going to go with that: The circumstances of her death are sure to be public knowledge by tonight. *Access Hollywood* thrives on that stuff. It's just the kind of publicity angle Henry Anklemire can run with."

"Accusing someone who isn't here to defend herself, on no evidence but an old man's suspicions? That's not like you."

He chewed morosely. "You're right, of course. Well, I'm through with it. I've taken the thing as far as I can. Whoever my ghost is, he can haunt someone else. Meanwhile we'll finish duping *Bleak Street* and hope Turkus will change his mind about releasing it."

"Let's drink a hearty quaff of mead in honor of that decision." She lifted her tankard.

He clanked his against it and sipped. "I never knew ye olde knights of olde drank anything that tasted so much like Diet Pepsi."

Waiting for her outside a portable restroom, Valentino saw something that stirred the mutton in his stomach. He crossed a long line waiting in front of a food truck and laid his hand on the epauleted shoulder of a figure in a trench coat with a hat pulled low over his forehead. The figure started and turned. It was a boy of seventeen or eighteen with a pearl in his nose that looked like a giant zit. Valentino turned his palms up in apology and walked back the way he'd come. America's youth had a lot to learn about what constituted Renaissance wear.

■ ■ ■ ■

On Monday, he dropped by the lab. Jack Dupree, sporting a white smock in place of his heavy-duty chemical wear, came out of the restricted area, looking less greenish under his dark pigment than he had the day after the celebration in the Bradbury Building.

"Looks like Dr. Broadhead's Elixir cleared away the alcoholic clouds," Valentino said in greeting.

"That, and the ice-cold beer I had for breakfast."

"Any progress on *Bleak Street*?"

The smile evaporated. "You know, we moved it up on the schedule as a favor to you and Broadhead. Practical jokes don't fly in cases like that."

"What kind of practical joke?"

Dupree studied his expression. "Let's go to the movies."

Gone was the old screening room with linoleum floors, folding chairs, a roll-up screen, and a projector on a squeaky cart. Thanks in no small part to some high-profile discoveries made by Valentino, alumni donations had paid for a soundproof chamber with blackout walls and ceiling,

graduated seats, interchangeable high- and negative-gain screens, noise-absorbing carpeting, a ten-channel stereo receiver, concert-class speakers, and acoustic diffusers that reflected sound evenly in all directions. This was no plush theater like Ignacio Bozal's or The Oracle, but a room intended strictly for the scientific study of film, as up-to-the-minute as a NASA control room. Equipment designed to project both digital and analog images made it possible to view either Julia Roberts or Greta Garbo at the top of their form, in sharper focus than the originals.

Some things never changed, however. At Kyle Broadhead's insistence, the university kept a certified projectionist on permanent retainer, not to please the union so much as to ensure the proper handling of his department's most valuable properties. This one kept sentry in a booth above the top row in back.

Dupree sat down beside Valentino in the center sweet spot. "Roll 'em, Sid!" To the archivist: "The can said '*Bleak Street,* Reel One.' "

Minutes later they watched a lively figure whistling as he steered a boat, spinning the spoked helm and tugging a steam whistle. The character was instantly recognizable in

the most remote corners of the world, and had been seen by more people than George Washington, Napoleon, Shirley Temple, Mao Tse-Tung, and Oprah Winfrey combined.

"*Steamboat Willie,*" Valentino whispered. "What — ?"

Dupree said, "I prefer to call him Mickey. I've been on a first-name basis with him since I was ten. That's when my parents took me to Disneyland the first time. Okay, Sid!"

The film stopped fluttering through the gate and the screen went white. The lab technician turned to Valentino. "Is there anything you want to tell me?"

22

"Kyle, I need your help."

"Does it have anything to do with Van Oliver?"

"It has *everything* to do with Van Oliver."

"Can't do it, sorry."

"Kyle —"

"Can't, son. My gat's in the shop. The guy offered me a loaner but I said I'd be better off without it for a while. I made a New Year's resolution to give up gambling and stop shooting people."

"You don't gamble."

"Then I'm halfway there. Call your buddy Anklemire. He's a smaller target."

"All I need is some advice."

"Give it up. How's that?"

"Kyle, I'm coming over. You can turn me down to my face."

"Nope. I'm on a fishing boat in Catalina."

"No, you're not. I called you at home. You don't own a cell."

"Nuts. I won't answer the door."

Something clicked. Valentino thought he'd hung up. Then Fanta's voice came on. "Come on over, Val. I'll put on coffee."

Broadhead said, "Get off the extension!"

Valentino said, "I didn't know you were home."

"The defense wants to settle the copyright infringement case I was working on. I got the day off."

"Blast you, woman! I'm going to the club."

"Shut up, old man," she said. "They kicked you out for nonpayment of dues before I was born."

Valentino said he was on his way.

Kyle Broadhead seldom went to his office on Monday. He'd lived in a Wilson-era clapboard bungalow in a neighborhood that had gone downhill after the motion-picture colony moved to Beverly Hills and Malibu, then came back when the population swelled between world wars, then slid again during the era of sex, drugs, and rock-and-roll, but had commenced to climb up again with gentrification. In Valentino's experience the professor had always kept it up, painting it a cheery yellow every few years, replacing the roof and windows, and over-paying a succession of youths to cut the grass; but since his marriage to Fanta, lilac

211

bushes and beds of iris and poppies the bright orange of crepe paper had transformed it into a modest showplace. Valentino parked in a driveway the couple shared with the house next door, wiped his feet on a crisp new welcome mat, and pushed the bell.

Fanta, tall and tan in a sleeveless white top knotted at her midriff, yellow shorts, and flip-flops, gave him a hug and dragged him over the threshold by the hand. "Welcome, stranger. This is the first time you've honored us since the wedding. I was afraid you'd dropped us when I made an honest man out of Kyle."

"I'm —"

"For the love of Mike, don't apologize!" came a voice from the little den off the living room. "The whole reason I gave H.R. only a P.O. box for my checks was to keep the university away from my door. If it gets out we invited anyone from work, everyone but the janitor will follow the trail and the next thing you know we'll be throwing Christmas parties."

"This is what I live with, Val."

"I warned you, as I recall." He followed her into the den.

Broadhead was sitting in the dilapidated overstuffed chair that had held court in the

212

living room from the time he'd moved in until Fanta arrived. He wore a dingy gray cardigan blown out at the elbows, baggy slacks, and heelless slippers on his feet. In front of him, a portable TV set with rabbit ears sat on a combination TV, radio, and phonograph in a console the size and shape of a coffin. Both sets were on with the sound turned down. A baseball game made up of all Japanese players took place on the larger screen, with what looked like a curling competition on the portable, both in silence.

"I didn't know you were into sports," Valentino said.

"Not since the introduction of the designated hitter and the reviewed play. I only turn on a game because people keep interrupting my reading." He marked his place in the book in his lap with a finger.

"He's talking about me," Fanta said. "He's formed the conclusion that if he pretends to be watching, I won't disturb him."

"You agreed to that?"

"Humor him in the things that don't count, so I can nag him into the things that do; like not blowing off friends when they come to him for help."

"That's not settled," Broadhead said.

She leaned down and kissed him on the

213

top of his shaggy head. "Coffee's almost ready." She went out and drew the door shut.

Valentino took in the den. It was cluttered with items that had occupied the living room during Kyle's widowerhood, including a large pewter urn on the mantel of a small gas fireplace. "Is that — ?"

"The late Mrs. Broadhead, yes. I wanted to move it out before the honeymoon; I even looked into reserving a space next to her favorite stars in Forest Lawn; by-the-by, Marilyn Monroe's booked for blocks. Fanta wouldn't have it. Some nonsense about not erasing my past just because I've discovered the future."

"That sounds like the kind of advice you give your students."

"Turn those things off, will you? They didn't come with remotes."

Valentino switched off the TVs. The pictures imploded and the screens went black. He sat on the arm of a love seat that faced Broadhead's chair at an angle; the cushions were piled with framed pictures, a loose collection of briar pipes, and ashtrays banished from around the house since it had turned into a place of cohabitation. Somehow it all seemed of a piece with the professor's lifestyle: Stark and organized at work, chaotic

at rest. He listened to the latest development with his lids lowered and his hands folded across his middle, Buddha fashion.

"*Steamboat Willie* wouldn't fill five reels," he said.

"I only saw part of one, but Jack Dupree says the others were a hodgepodge of comedy shorts, newsreels, and out-of-date travelogues. Batista's Cuba sounds like a fun place to spend a weekend, but only if you're a *Yanqui.*"

"You're sure the film cans were never out of your sight from the time Bozal gave them to you until you put them in storage?"

"I am; and department security has never been compromised in the past."

"The conclusion being that Bozal switched the reels sometime between the private screening and when he gave you the cans."

"To state the obvious, yes."

"There's nothing so obscure as the obvious, boys."

Both men looked up at Fanta, who had managed to open the door while carrying a loaded tray without drawing attention. Valentino sprang up to clear rubble off a square ottoman, took the tray, and placed it on the leather seat. The room would not sit three, but she waved off the visitor's offer to clear the love seat and lifted the steel carafe

to pour.

"The trouble with you academic types is you see everything as up and down, left and right," she said, handing out the steaming mugs. "If you ever spent any time in a courtroom you wouldn't be so sure. Motive's everything. Bozal wanted to trade *Bleak Street* for *Greed,* correct?"

"That was the arrangement." Valentino sat back down with his coffee.

"Then why renege? From what you've told us about him, he's not the kind to take foolish chances. He had to have known you'd screen the film again before you delivered on your end."

"Nothing obscure about that." Broadhead's tone was dry.

"Any judge in the district would throw your case against him out of court during the preliminary." She looked at Valentino. "Did you actually *see* Bozal put the reels in the cans before he gave them to you?"

"No. As a matter of fact —" He fell silent.

"What?" This in unison from Fanta and Kyle.

"Just a thought." He stood and set his coffee on the tray un-tasted. "Thanks, both of you."

Fanta said, "You're going out there, aren't you? East L.A."

"I'll call first."

She smiled. "When I invite myself to someone's house, I always bring a gift."

When that sank in, Valentino smiled too.

As arranged over the phone, Jack Dupree met him at the door of the secure storage facility next to the lab with an oversize gym bag in his arms. The technician's face asked a question. Valentino shrugged an answer, thanked him, and slung the bag over his shoulder by its strap. It was heavy.

A female voice answered the phone at Ignacio Bozal's house: low-pitched, with a slight Hispanic accent. He recognized it.

"My grandfather's napping, Mr. Valentino. May I take a message?"

"I'd like to visit, if he has time this afternoon. I have something for him. He'll know what it is."

He wished he could see Esperanza Bozal's face. Her tone was hard to interpret over the wire. "I'm sure he'll be happy to see you."

Outside, he started down the street to the north lot, where he'd parked. An automobile slowed and turned into the curb as if to let someone out. The driver's side door swung open, blocking his path. The man who stepped out stood well over six feet tall. His

charcoal-gray suit was tailored; had to be, to contain his chest and shoulders. Valentino looked from him to the vehicle. It was a black, slab-sided town car with shuttered headlights.

218

The driver, at least, bore no resemblance to the man who had nearly run him down and who had skulked in the shadows outside The Oracle; but his size and fierceness of expression weren't encouraging.

When he spoke, however, his voice was light, despite the echo chamber that was his chest. "Get in the car, please."

Please? Not a word in the vocabulary of the usual run of hood that kidnapped citizens on the street in broad daylight. But as Bozal had said, the mob had developed subtle methods since Prohibition. Their victims' bodies seldom showed up in ditches anymore, for instance, but in the foundations of skyscrapers and football stadiums.

"Another time, maybe. I'm in a hurry." He turned to go around the man, only to be stopped by a hand on his arm; not as big a hand as Vivien "Bull" Broderick's, nor the grip as punishing, but not one to be shaken

off easily.

What would Humphrey Bogart or Robert Mitchum say in this situation; or Woody Allen, for that matter? He had nothing to lose.

"I know someone who's bigger than you are."

The man nodded. His face was grave. "I believe you. I was two months' premature. Thirty-one ounces at birth. There's no telling how far I'd have developed if I'd gone full term." He dropped the hand. "Five minutes. I promise."

Valentino was pondering just how much damage could be inflicted on a person in five minutes when the window belonging to the rear passenger's seat hummed down and the man seated there leaned his head out the window. "I'll drop you off anywhere you want, and send the car back for you when you're ready. Please." A latch clicked and the door opened.

He'd feared this was Van Oliver's ghost — or at least his double — but recognized the face from another time. It belonged to the man who'd once sprung him from police custody on an obstruction case over a property both men were in competition to acquire. Mark David Turkus, the man who'd built a teenage hobby he'd started in his

parents' home into the biggest entertainment vendor in the world, had aged a bit — his trademark do-it-yourself haircut showed traces of gray, and creases had appeared around his plain black-rimmed glasses — but his face retained the *naïf* quality that had lulled so many of his competitors into underestimating his gift for ruthlessness. "The Turk," as they came to call him, *was* Supernova International, as surely as Johnny Weissmuller was Tarzan, Sean Connery James Bond, and Pee-wee Herman — well, Pee-wee Herman.

Turkus slid to the other side of the seat. The driver grasped the handle and swung the door wide.

Valentino climbed in and rested his hands on the bag in his lap. As soon as his body made contact with the buttery leather seat, he knew this wasn't the car that had nearly crushed him downtown. It was like comparing a dinghy to an ocean liner. There was room to stretch his legs without coming into contact with the front seat, and a complete portable bar straddled the upholstered hump above the transmission. Characteristic of his host's juvenile tastes, among the fifths of premium vodka, bourbon, and single-malt Scotch stood a two-liter bottle of Diet Dr Pepper.

The door snicked shut and the driver returned to his seat behind the wheel. Turkus tipped open the top of a built-in cooler and plunged a silver scoop into the ice. "Libation?" When Valentino declined, he filled a crystal tumbler with cubes and poured soda-pop inside slowly to control the fizzing. "My doctor says that if I insist on soft drinks, I should go with the full-leaded; sugar's more healthy than artificial sweetener. I'm used to it, though, and I make enough decisions without adding another. What's your position?"

"I don't have one."

Valentino realized then the car was moving; the motor was nearly silent, the suspension of the sort not to be found in any factory. Los Angeles slid past the tinted windows as smoothly as back-projection.

"He's head of surgery at the Mayo Clinic; but don't let that intimidate you." Turkus sipped at the effervescent beverage and belched discreetly into his fist. "A physician who carries five million in malpractice insurance is no one to fear, unless you're his patient. Where to?"

"Just circle around and drop me off at my car. That shouldn't take any longer than five minutes, even in this town." Valentino's knuckles whitened on the bag in his lap. A

man with Turkus's resources and business savvy posed as much of a threat as a thug with a tommy gun.

"What've you got there? You're holding it like it's the key to Fort Knox. There's no gold there, by the way; the chairman of the joint chiefs of staff conducted me on a personal tour last year. The actual bullion is stored someplace ten stories underground; can't tell you where. The fort itself is just diversion: spray-painted wooden blocks surrounded by marines in dress blues. Don't breathe a word of that to anyone," he whispered, leaning close. "It's a state secret."

"It's *Greed*."

"I'm sorry?"

Valentino patted the bag. "The von Stroheim film. I promised it to a friend. It's in general release now. *Bleak Street* is in secure storage, if that's what you're getting at." There was no sin in lying to the competition.

Mark David Turkus laughed; a juvenile laugh, not at all the sinister chuckle of the megalomaniac that Valentino had come to associate him with. It ended in a burp. "Excuse me. I don't want the film; for myself, I prefer musical extravaganzas, lots of glitz in bright high-key lighting. But I

understand the appeal of the dark stuff. It's why Adolf Hitler's autograph is worth twenty times Winston Churchill's. My attorneys assure me *Bleak Street* is as safe from public viewing as if it were socked away with all that gold in —" He burped again. "Whoops. I almost spilled the beans. Anyway, ironclad doesn't signify. I make sure everything's in steel surrounded by concrete; am I right, Sean?"

The driver answered without looking away from the windshield. "Yes, sir."

Turkus's smile was boyish. It was one of his most lethal weapons. "Sean's one of my attorneys."

"He's not a bodyguard?"

"That'd be bad for my image. Only gangsters need bodyguards. I selected him on his academic record. He got into Harvard on a football scholarship. When he blew out his knee, he started reading Blackstone. Turned out he had a knack for the law. I asked him to drive only because I just found out today I forgot to renew my license." Turkus's face went serious then. "That film must never be exhibited."

For no reason that Valentino could identify, he sensed he was being asked for help. He pressed the point before he could talk himself out of it.

"If you've tied it up so tight, why talk to me?"

"You don't let things go, that's why. You'll appeal the court ruling, and when it holds up you'll take it to the next court and the next, and even though you're bound to end in failure, the press will lap it up every step of the way. In this country, and especially in this town, when someone who's even marginally connected with the entertainment industry pushes an issue, the media take note. As a result, the thing someone has spent hundreds of thousands of dollars to keep quiet — and manages to do so legally — has a way of finding its way to the public, whether or not there's any evidence to support it. The result's the same. Someone's reputation is destroyed, along with thousands of lives that depend on it."

"Whose reputation are we talking about?"

Turkus pressed a toggle switch in his armrest. A Plexiglas shield slid up between the front and back seats. No doubt it was soundproof, but he lowered his voice anyway.

"Lawyer-client privilege is just a concept," he said. "You know it exists only when it's been violated. If you repeat this conversation to anyone and it gets back to me, as I assure you it will, you won't be able to get a

job delivering pizza anywhere in this country. The same goes for your entire staff. Your girlfriend, Miss Johansen? Unemployed and unemployable; thanks to the anonymous donor who made it possible to replace all the onboard computers in the LAPD fleet with next year's model.

"Not enough? Okay. Everything you brought to the university will become the property of Supernova. Your entire department — the archives, the film library, the laboratory, and the screening facility — will cease to exist."

Valentino experienced the same chill he'd felt when he saw the phantom outside The Oracle. He swallowed — silently, he hoped. "I take it not telling me what you're about to tell me is not an option."

"No, because without an explanation you'd never give up. Even if you failed to find out what happened to Van Oliver, your meddling would revive enough interest to reopen the investigation, if not by the police then by the press. Regardless of whether anything definite comes of it, the muck they'll rake up will cling to everyone involved with what happened sixty years ago, however remotely. The stock in Supernova will plummet. Who'd place any faith in a business everyone is convinced is founded

226

on murder? The board of directors would have no choice but to force me to resign."

The car stopped for the light at Hollywood and Vine. A mob of pedestrians in straw hats and loud sportshirts crossed the street in front of them, holding cell-phone cameras at arm's length trained on the signs identifying the historic corner. Valentino found himself lowering his voice as well.

"What does Supernova have to do with the Oliver case?"

Turkus subsided in his seat, hands dangling limp between his thighs. "My uncle, Constantine Venezelos Turkus; Connie, to his friends. His enemies called him something else. He was the original Turk. You know that saying, 'He knows where all the bodies are buried'? According to family lore it was Uncle Connie who buried them."

The car glided through neighborhoods Valentino knew intimately, but he could not have identified any of them. As Mark David Turkus spoke they seemed as foreign as craters on the moon.

The tycoon might have been retelling the plot of a movie he'd seen; but then that was the nature of this entire episode in the film archivist's life. No other quest had so closely resembled the grail he sought.

"Uncle Connie" had perfected his trade while serving with the U.S. Navy Shore Patrol during the First World War, rounding up AWOL sailors in New York City gin mills that had been declared off-limits by the local base commander and smashing the establishments to pieces. Eventually his superiors had decided that he was taking his job too seriously; he was court-martialed and given a dishonorable discharge.

With that stigma on his record, most

legitimate employment was denied him. Just what kind of work he'd found to support himself was something the family preferred not to dwell upon. When he suddenly took the train to California, it seemed logical to assume it was either to avoid arrest or retribution on the part of his associates.

Official disgrace presented no obstacle to the employment he found on the coast. There, during the Great Depression, he founded a freelance security firm that hired itself out to all the major studios.

"The operatives were known as the Blackbirds," the billionaire said. "Maybe you heard of them."

"Strikebreakers, weren't they?"

"Not right away. They were hired originally to protect the stars from blackmail. In those days gangsters threatened to throw acid in their faces if they didn't pony up. A lot of those goons suddenly took to greener pastures, so it stands to reason the Blackbirds were longer on offense than defense.

"When that crisis ended, the firm branched out. The contract players were forming labor unions. Fair wages and acceptable terms cut into the studios' bottom line, so the Turk's men broke up meetings, shanghaied union organizers across the state line, and waded into picket lines with

blackjacks and brass knuckles. They wore identical black suits to avoid roughing each other up by mistake; hence the nickname."

"They failed in the end," Valentino said. "The Screen Actors Guild is one of the most powerful in the country."

"Uncle Connie was no quitter. Kicking him out of the navy didn't stop him from doing the same work on the other side of the law. Having to flee the heat back East didn't scare him straight. When the mob backed off and the union survived, the Blackbirds went deeper underground, taking jobs the industry didn't dare do in-house."

"Such as?"

"Don't be naïve. What's it take to go from assault and battery to murder? Just a slight turn of the screw."

Twenty grim years passed, during which the elder Turkus passed in and out of police headquarters as through a revolving door. The last time during his career was in connection with the questionable "suicide" of George Reeves, TV's Superman, in 1959.

"There were others that didn't make the front page, of course," said Mark Turkus. "Too many, I think, for him to be involved in most of them. The police even called him out of retirement to ask him about Bob

Crane's murder in nineteen seventy-eight."

The *Hogan's Heroes* star. Valentino remembered the sordid details of a crime that was never solved.

Turkus went on. "The Black Dahlia case doesn't sound like him; but whenever powerful forces were involved, there was Connie's M.O., as big and fat as he himself got to be. As who wouldn't, on his commissions?

"I doubt he shared them all the time either," he added. "A man who worked himself up to the top doesn't mind getting his hands dirty."

There was more. In 1950, the Turk was arrested on suspicion of smuggling illegal aliens into the U.S. The theory was he delivered them to the studios to perform as extras, pocketing their wages in return for bringing them across the border. He spent three days in custody, then was released for lack of evidence.

"That was tame for him," said his nephew. "But he seems never to have passed up the chance to turn a fast buck."

"Wow."

"My legacy, I'm afraid. It's one of the reasons I always conduct business on the up-and-up. Even my fiercest competitors agree that at my most aggressive I've never

violated any law. That would include you, I suppose."

Valentino had to give him that much, however much rope the system of free enterprise offered to pitiless entrepreneurs with unlimited funds.

"Was he ever brought to justice?"

The billionaire's smile was grim. "Only the Old Testament kind. He was diagnosed with terminal cancer in nineteen eighty-six and blew his brains out with his old service pistol. By then he'd been retired for twenty years."

"How well did you know him?"

"I only saw him once, at a family funeral. By then he was as big as a house. Here." He slid a flat wallet from an inside pocket, took out a creased Polaroid photograph, and handed it over.

It had been taken from a distance, on a plot of ground dotted with headstones in tidy rows. He was easy to spot in the soberly dressed crowd. The pinstripe suit did nothing to disguise a parade-float of a man whose jowls and multiple chins stood out from the shadow of his felt hat.

"I found it in my mother's collection of family snapshots," Turkus said. "I doubt she realized he was in the frame or she'd never have kept it. I carry it around as a reminder

not to get too sweet on myself.

"He was my father's brother. They hadn't spoken in years, and they didn't on that occasion. No one was more surprised than I was when Uncle Connie left me twenty thousand dollars in his will."

"Why you?"

"Good question. I can't think he was driven by generosity. Maybe he did it to thumb his nose at the rest of his family. That was the seed money I used to start Supernova."

He raised his hands from his knees and spread them. "Now you know why I can't let you market *Bleak Street.*"

"Does Teddie Goodman know?"

"She's my employee, not my confidante. I wouldn't have told *you* if I thought there was any other way of stopping you."

"What do you know about your uncle and Van Oliver?"

"Only that he was questioned along with a lot of others. I can thank the length of the list of suspects for keeping him off center stage. That won't be the case if the story gets raked up again. My name alone will put him square in the spotlight and the company with it." He lowered his hands, linked the fingers, and stared down at them. "It's not just me that would suffer. A public-

relations blow like that would put thousands of people out of work and possibly trigger a national recession."

"But what was his motive?"

"Who knows? Maybe a mob contract, for whatever purposes. Like I said: anything for a buck."

"I wish you'd told me all this at the start."

"Would it have made any difference?"

"We'll never know now."

The car ghosted along for blocks, its occupants silent. Then Valentino said, "What if Constantine Turkus is cleared of any implication in the Oliver case? Would you lift the restraining order and allow UCLA to distribute the film?"

Mark David Turkus turned his attention from his hands clasped as in prayer to his fellow passenger. "No one can prove a man *didn't* do something. That's a basic law of nature."

"Of U.S. law too; that's why the prosecution has to prove guilt. In order to clear your uncle, I'll have to identify the real killer."

"After all this time, when all the experts have failed? And they called *me* a cock-eyed dreamer."

"You haven't answered my question."

"But what if it turns out Connie is the killer?"

"He's dead. It isn't as if sitting on the evidence would let a guilty man go free. No one would have to know."

They'd circled the campus and were approaching the spot where Valentino had been picked up. Turkus tapped on the Plexiglas and signaled the driver to pull over to the curb. He twisted in his seat to face the archivist. The corporate mask was back in place, rendering his face unreadable.

"Just so we're clear," he said. "If you manage to name the party behind Van Oliver's disappearance and it isn't Constantine Venezelos Turkus, you'll go public with it, closing the investigation for good. If it is my uncle, you'll suppress the information."

"That's what I'm offering."

"It's a gamble. Your silence alone would guarantee that the speculation will continue. It's bound to come around to him."

"I didn't say it wasn't risky. But apart from adopting Blackbird tactics, you won't stop me from seeing this through to the end. If it comes out in your favor, you'll never have to worry about Oliver again. And there's something else to be gained."

The eyes behind the glasses shone flatly, like plastic discs. So far as the man could be read at all, Valentino suspected he knew what was coming.

He didn't keep him in suspense. "You'll have peace of mind. If no capital crimes can definitely be laid to your family's door, you'll never have to wonder if your career was built on murder."

"Okay."

"Okay?"

"If you find out what happened to Van Oliver and who was responsible, Supernova will withdraw its suit and you'll be free to do what you want with *Bleak Street;* sell it, distribute it, burn it. The film is yours." He held out his hand.

Valentino grasped it. *Now if only I had it,* he thought.

25

Valentino gathered up the gym bag containing all twenty-four hours of Erich von Stroheim's *Greed.* He held up the photograph. "May I keep this?"

"Please do. If everything works out as I'd like, I won't have to ask for it back."

"I'll be in touch." He opened the door and stepped out.

Mark David Turkus leaned over and took hold of the handle. "Mind you, I don't expect anything."

The archivist watched the sleek car sliding down the street. The motor made little more noise than when he'd been riding inside. By comparison, his compact sounded like a cement mixer starting up.

It was another day of brilliant sun, bringing out the green grass and red, yellow, and blue wildflowers in the Hollywood hills like bright scraps of construction paper. The vivid hues in the murals and graffiti in

East L.A. were bolder yet, looking as if they'd been slapped on that morning with a brush dipped in a rainbow. He coasted to a stop before the gate in the parti-colored wall that enclosed the Bozal estate, and tooted his horn. The asthmatic bleating sound was a poor substitute for the virile blast of the old man's Bugatti.

The gate opened far enough for the young Chicano in the uniform to poke his head out.

"Hello, Ernesto. Your grandfather's expecting me."

A dazzling white grin split the medium-dark face. He spread the gate the rest of the way.

Everything was as before: children playing in shorts and nothing else, stout women minding them from their porch seats, young Antonio Banderas clones bent under open automobile hoods with heads cocked to keep the smoke from their cigarettes out of their eyes. It was as if four square blocks had drifted free of Guadalajara and come to rest a hundred miles north of the border, carrying with it several generations of Bozals.

Here again was the limestone turnaround at the end of the block, a half-century of classic cars drawn up bumper-to-bumper

238

like circled wagons in a western, and beyond it the large plain house, like anyone might see in one of the better neighborhoods in Mexico: well-tended, unpretentious, and hinting at the cozy life under its roof. He found a spot behind a glistening cherry-red 1936 Cord, the emblem between its hidden headlamps and the historic plate establishing its make and vintage for the visitor.

The door was opened by the master of the house himself, his slight form dressed as casually as before in a rumpled sweater, flannel shirt buttoned to the neck, corduroys shiny at the knees, and scuffed slippers. His head of fine white hair was bare. At sight of the bag his guest was carrying, he exposed his perfect dentures all the way to the eye-teeth.

"I'd hoped," he said. "That's the dingus, right?"

Valentino laughed. The old man seemed to have been brushing up on his hard-boiled slang. "I wouldn't advise you to try watching it in one sitting. It's ten hours long."

"At my age I'm lucky to make it ten minutes without getting up to pee." Before Valentino could react, Bozal grasped the strap and pulled it from his grip.

His ninety-year-old constitution was remarkable. Leading his visitor toward the

bar, he carried the bag as if it were a bundle of beach towels.

"Can I corrupt you, fella? Sun's not down past the yardarm." He stepped behind the bar, set down his burden, and picked up a cocktail shaker.

Valentino was about to decline; then he realized he hadn't had a drop of alcohol since the Bradbury party — was it only days ago? — and that he could use a drink. He was as far from an alcoholic as could be without becoming a total abstainer, but he understood the craving then.

"White wine, if you have it."

"Do I have it. Was W. C. Fields a lush?" He traded the shaker for a bottle with a Mondavi label and inserted a corkscrew. "You know he had more than fifty grand worth of booze socked away in his attic? This was during the Depression, when three bucks would get you a bottle of good bourbon."

"I never heard that about Fields."

"Take it or leave it, considering the source. I got it from Groucho Marx. Fields showed him the stash, he said."

"You knew Groucho?"

"Nobody did, really, except his brothers. I ran into him in the Brown Derby; we were with friends who knew each other. He was

240

hosting *You Bet Your Life* at the time." He pulled the cork, filled a stemware glass, and slid it across the bar. Then he retrieved the cocktail shaker and mixed a vodka martini for himself.

Valentino took a healthy sip of wine. It was good Gewürztraminer, slightly sweet and pungent. He swallowed and waited for his inhibitions to leave. "I screened *Bleak Street* again back at the university. I couldn't resist." He studied Bozal's face closely over the top of his glass.

The old man seemed to be engrossed in balancing a twist of lemon on the edge of his own glass. "Knew you would. It's just like chili."

"Like chili?"

"When you got the taste for it, it's all you want to eat till it's gone. You won't need it again for a long time, you're sick of it, but when you want it, nothing else'll do. It's that way with sex, too; till you find the right woman. Then you can't ever get your fill."

Was it a bluff? Did he think Valentino was bluffing? The man was the Sphinx. Was everyone involved in this thing a champion poker player except him?

It would take at least another drink to press him outright, but Valentino didn't want to call attention to his unease. He

241

wandered around the room, carrying his wine; stopped before the portrait above the mantel.

Estrella, Bozal's wife, dead these fifty years. Her beauty reached across the decades as if she were standing in front of him. He sipped again, barely conscious he was doing so. It wasn't for courage.

"Forget it, kid."

He coughed, dribbling wine over his chin. Bozal's voice was almost at his ear. He hadn't heard him coming up behind him. Apologizing for his clumsiness, he brushed at the droplets on his shirt.

"It's jake. Find myself doing it myself when I'm looking at her. Forget it, I said. She was gone before you were born. She won't come walking in on you from the rain like Laura. You're a good-looking lad, but you're no Dana Andrews. Neither was he, when the camera wasn't cranking. He was a bad drunk off-screen, worse than Fields; when he took it on the set, he was through."

"You knew him too?"

"Hmm?" Bozal was looking at the painting, his martini un-tasted.

"You knew Dana Andrews?"

He turned away from the mantel with a jerk. "He came out of retirement for a bit in *The St. Valentine's Day Massacre:* Nineteen-

sixty-seven, it was, but Roger Corman wanted it to look like 'twenty-nine. I rented him some clunkers from my fleet for the city exteriors. Andrews was on the set when I took charge of delivery. He was recovering then. Spilled it all to me, his battle with the bottle; me, a complete stranger. One of the twelve steps, I guess. Anyway it seemed to take. As far as I know he never touched another drop."

At any other time Valentino might have pressed the old man for more details, but he was scarcely listening. Something had begun to grow in his mind; something that had little if anything to do with whatever had happened to *Bleak Street.* It was absurd, fantastical, the stuff of a *noir* movie; but just what about this episode had not been? In any case it was too tentative to broach the subject just yet.

"Thank you for the wine. I'm sorry I can't finish it. I have a lot of work to do."

His host seemed surprised. "Shame to come all this way just to turn around and go back. I could've sent Eduardo to pick up *Greed.*"

"It isn't that pressing," he lied. "But I need to show myself at the office now and then or they might think I'd defected to USC."

Bozal took the glass before the other could return it to the bar. "No need to explain, son. I'm grateful as all get-out. Them dagoes from the Vatican are sure to come across with what I need when I give 'em a private screening. You can't ever go wrong dishing up one of the Seven Deadlies to the clergy."

"Is Esperanza home? I'd like to see her before I go."

"Sure. She's on spring break. Your girl know about this?" He looked sly.

"It's not like that. I want to tell her what a good job she did in the projection booth." He assumed a pained look that wasn't all manufacture. "Sir, I thought you were a little hard on her at the time."

Bozal showed no trace of resentment. "She's known me all her life. If she's looking for the doting grandpa this late in the game she's got me miscast. Her room's at the top of the main staircase, on the right. Can't miss it: smells like a Tijuana cathouse clear down to the ground floor." The old man shook his hand, picked up the gym bag, and started in the direction of the door to the basement theater.

He felt oddly light-headed as he climbed the stairs from the tiled entrance, passing

framed watercolors of the sun rising over the Gulf of Mexico and adobe walls in the moonlight. Confrontations were never his long suit, and beautiful women always brought out the awkward teenager he'd never quite outgrown, even when the women were not much more than half his age. Standing in front of the dark paneled oak door, he felt mad panic, like little Margaret O'Brien preparing to throw flour in the face of the neighborhood curmudgeon in *Meet Me in St. Louis.*

Get over it, Val. She's a college freshman, not the Spider Woman. He raised his fist and knocked.

The door opened almost instantly, as if the person on the other side were waiting just for him. The face he saw there emptied his head the rest of the way. He'd seen it twice before, but had never stood this close to young Van Oliver.

26

Valentino had come face-to-face with a ghost; but he needed no mirror to know what his own face looked like. The man at the door stared, his eyes as big as pancakes.

"Who is it, Emiliano? Oh." Coming up behind him, Esperanza stopped, paling under her natural coloring.

In that moment Valentino was sure who it was who had substituted random footage for *Bleak Street,* and that Bozal knew nothing about it.

She touched the stranger's arm. *"Está bien, hermano."*

He stepped away from the door. Valentino entered and pushed it shut behind him.

Emiliano looked less mysterious than he had across the street from The Oracle. Gone were the hat and trench coat. He wore a black T-shirt with the AC/DC logo on the front, faded jeans artfully ripped at the knees, and flip-flops. Still, his facial resem-

blance to the young Van Oliver was uncanny.

Esperanza had changed from her red sheath to a tank top over pleated slacks, and from heels to pink high-top sneakers. Her abundance of blue-black hair, high coloring, and bare brown shoulders were just as striking without the slinky outfit.

The room reflected her personality, with bright pink-and-black striped wallpaper, a rumpled bed with a canopy supported by minimalist black iron uprights, and posters of glamorous female pop stars of Spanish blood on the walls. There was a strong odor of night-blooming jasmine that Valentino recognized from their first meeting. It wasn't nearly as overpowering as Bozal had described it, except psychologically.

"I think you know why I'm here," he said.

"Who is this man?" said the Oliver clone.

Esperanza snapped her tongue off her teeth. "Don't pretend you're stupider than you are. Valentino, this is Emiliano, my brother."

At close range, the other was close to his sister's age; it was the air of intrigue that had made him look older. His features could be taken for Hispanic or Italian or Middle Eastern, as could Van Oliver/Benny Obrilenski's Semitic ones. The skin wore a slightly olive cast.

"You almost killed me with your car."

"I don't know what you're talking about." His expression was sullen.

"Oh, stop it," Esperanza said. "He knows it was you both times." She turned to Valentino. "He rented the car. If he'd borrowed one of Grandpapa's, it would have given us away. You'd have spotted it following you all the way to that Starbucks."

" 'Us'? Why would you want to have me run down?"

"I never wanted that. I told him not to pass too close, just close enough to scare you."

"It scared me. So did what he said afterwards: 'Sorry, buddy. Didn't see you. I will next time.' "

She glared at Emiliano, who shrugged. "I thought it up on the spot. I couldn't be sure just letting him see my face would do the trick."

Valentino wanted to ask about that face; but it could wait. "Why would you want to scare me? And why did you switch the films?"

She lifted her chin, and in that moment looked exactly like the portrait of her grandmother. In fact, seeing that haughty beauty in the flesh reminded him of someone else, someone he'd seen recently; or had

248

he? Too much had happened in too short a time for him to sort out all his impressions. It was like trying to recall the details of a dream that faded faster the more he tried: fleeing him.

"No one else must ever see that film," she said.

"Why?"

"I can't tell you."

"You might as well. I've figured out the rest. You've seen *Bleak Street*, or at least a photograph of Van Oliver. When you realized your brother looked enough like him to serve as his imposter, you sent him out to frighten me away from the project. Almost running me down wasn't enough. I had to have thought I was being stalked by a ghost. Just to make sure, you dressed him up like Oliver and had him show himself outside The Oracle, where you knew I lived. All that was necessary so I wouldn't press the issue when I found out you'd switched the films."

"That was his idea, the thing at the theater. I told him it was too risky, but he grabbed a coat and hat from Grandpapa's closet and did it anyway."

"I should've done more," Emiliano said. "He didn't scare as easy as you thought." He looked at Valentino. "What she says

goes. You can't have that movie."

"Have it your way, then. Don't tell me why. Maybe your grandfather can shed some light." He turned to the door and grasped the knob.

Esperanza dashed across the room and took hold of his arm, tight enough to cause pain. He reacted automatically, seizing both her wrists. All his frustrations went into that grasp. Pain and terror twisted her face. Her brother stepped forward, raising a fist.

"¡Alto!" His sister's shout startled him. He stopped. She made no resistance to Valentino's manhandling; she was a rag doll. He let go, ashamed. She rubbed each of her wrists, marked vividly by his fingers. "I can't explain now why we did what we did. That would cause as much harm as if we'd done nothing. If I give you the film, will you promise not to do anything with it and to say nothing to Grandpapa until I can?"

"Why can't you explain now?"

"Not in this house. I'll come to you whenever and wherever you like, and then all will be clear. Maybe it will even change your mind about distributing *Bleak Street* at all." Once again the chin came up and she balled her fists at her sides. "If you refuse, no one will ever see it again. I'll destroy it."

The room filled with silence. Valentino broke it.

"Congratulations."

A crease marred the smooth brown expanse of her forehead. "For what?"

"You finally succeeded in scaring me."

She smiled then; the way she had on his last visit. It unnerved him nearly as much as the certainty that she intended to make good on her threat. This girl — no, this woman — was dangerous, and more to be feared than any ghost.

From under her bed she pulled a cardboard carton containing six unmarked film cans. He didn't wait for her to bring them to him. He swept past her brother, scooped one off the top, opened it, and took out the reel. He unspooled more than a foot of glistening black celluloid and held it up to the light. The first thing he saw was Van Oliver's face, in its proper place and time at last. Hands shaking with relief, he returned everything to the carton and hoisted it under one arm.

At the door he turned back to face Esperanza Bozal. "One week," he said. "It will probably take that long to make a copy. If by then I don't know what this was all about, I'll put the film into general release. Is that understood?"

Brother and sister nodded in unison.

Outside the house, Valentino began to shake again, this time in every limb. He'd managed to run the first successful bluff of his career.

For it was a bluff. He had *Bleak Street,* but could not follow through on his threat to release it if Esperanza didn't hold up her end of the bargain. If he in his turn failed to deliver on his promise to Mark David Turkus and wrap up the Oliver case, he might as well be carrying an empty box.

And then, during the relatively mindless activity of driving back to the secure storage vault at UCLA, it came to him just like that, the answer to everything. It raced through his brain, a surrealist montage of images flashing across his vision like sped-up frames in a film designed to mystify and disturb. It confused, it deranged; it enlightened. When it was finished, he knew what had happened to Van Oliver. Knew it for a certainty.

Now all he had to do was prove it.

27

Kym Trujillo came out to see him in the entryway of the Motion Picture Country Home. She was petit in a no-nonsense gray pantsuit that gave her free range of motion when pitching in to help nurses and attendants support the weight of ailing residents. She wasn't a dramatic figure like Esperanza Bozal, but with her dark hair piled atop her head and sharp, intelligent features she was as impressive as any beauty from a Spanish opera. Today she was flushed and out of breath.

"I wish you'd called," she told Valentino when he'd explained the reason for his visit. "I might have saved you a trip. We think Roy Fitzhugh had a stroke. We're waiting for the EMS team to come and take him to Cedars of Lebanon."

He felt a stab of concern, as much for the old character actor as for himself and his mission. "Is it bad?"

"There are no good strokes, but it seems to have been mild. It's important we get him into treatment as soon as possible. Every minute counts."

"Could I see him?"

She pursed her lips.

"I shouldn't let you. The regulations are clear about visitors in emergency situations; family only. But he's outlived all his family. You may be able to help keep him calm. He mustn't be upset." Her strong brows drew together. "I mean that. If he shows any sign of agitation, you'll have to leave."

"I promise. I just want to ask him about something he said the last time I was here, information he volunteered. His mind wandered before he could finish."

"I can't tell you if he's lucid or not. It depends on what part of his brain is affected."

"If he isn't, I'll leave. I don't want to be in the way."

"He's in his room. I'm coming along. When the emergency crew comes you'll have to clear out, regardless of his condition."

He thanked her and went with her to Fitzhugh's room. The old man looked small and frail lying under the blankets on his bed. It was difficult to distinguish the

outlines of his face from the white pil-
lowcase where his head rested. His pale blue
eyes were open and he was breathing evenly
with the help of an oxygen tank by the bed
and tubes in his nostrils, but he was shaking
slightly. Valentino, whose profession placed
him frequently in the company of the
elderly, recognized it as palsy rather than
the effects of a chill. A nurse he'd met
before sat in a chair nearby, wearing one of
the cheerful floral smocks that had replaced
the stark white uniforms of old. She looked
up from her cell phone screen, recognized
him, and greeted him with a tight smile.

He remained standing, conscious of Kym
Trujillo hovering behind him. He kept his
voice low. "It's Valentino, Mr. Fitzhugh. Do
you remember me?"

The eyes rolled his direction. A weak smile
parted the lips. He wasn't wearing his
dentures. "Of course, son. I may be at
death's door, but I ain't senile."

Kym said, "Nonsense, Roy. You're as mad
as a hatter, but you've got some good years
left."

The man in the bed made a dry chuckling
sound. It was the kind of banter that existed
between a health care professional and a
patient who knew better than any doctors.

"Last time we talked about Van Oliver,"

Valentino said. "You became friends while you were together in *Bleak Street.*"

"He made up for a lot. That swish Fletcher said I talked through my schnozz."

They were back in the groove, but he had to prevent the old man from constantly repeating himself and keep him on topic. "You said something about Madeleine Nash, the female lead."

"Maggie. A doll. She used to sing old Spanish songs on the set."

"You said she died."

The eyes misted. Valentino couldn't tell if he was in mourning for an old colleague or in pain. "Yeah. Damn shame."

"I was told she married soon after the film wrapped and left the country."

"Yeah."

Valentino wanted to press it; but he was acutely aware of Kym's eyes boring holes in the back of his neck. He waited. He'd never waited so long for anything, but only a couple of seconds passed before a gray tongue slid along Fitzhugh's pleated lips and he spoke. "I meant after, long after. But still too soon. She never got to see her grandchildren."

"She had grandchildren?"

"Her *grand*children had grandchildren. She missed 'em all. That shouldn't happen

256

to anyone. I hung on this long, and what've I got to show for it? Not a soul to carry on my blood." Something glistened and slid down his cheek, a rivulet tracing the course through a crease.

"You stayed in touch after she went to Europe?"

"Europe?" The old man turned his head a half-inch the visitor's way. The tear had pooled at the corner of his mouth. No others followed it. "Who said she went to Europe?"

Valentino tried to tamp down his excitement. The patient might sense it, become alarmed, and cause him to be ejected.

He realized now he'd had only one source for the Europe story. Everyone else had merely said Madeleine Nash, née Magdalena Novello, left the United States. At that point her vanishing act had been as complete as Van Oliver's, if not as dramatic. All the scattered pieces of a mystery sixty years old were coming together, fitting as snugly as Legos.

He stepped closer to the bed. "Where did she go, if not Europe? Who did she marry?"

"Val." It was Kym.

He stepped back, took a deep breath and let it out. When he spoke his voice was even. "The night Oliver disappeared, you put him

257

in a cab outside Melvin Fletcher's house. Did you get a good look at the driver?"

"Who needs drivers?" Once again, the old man's eyes were as clear as glass beads. "I played one so many times I could drive anyone anywhere." He frowned. "Almost anywhere."

"You made up the taxi story. You drove him yourself."

"Not the whole way. I couldn't show my face in Mexico after that business with my da' when I was a kid."

"After you picked up Oliver you took Nash on board, or someone else did. Who was it? Who met you at the border to take them across?"

A fog slid across the aged eyes. Valentino was losing him. On an impulse he snatched out the photo Mark David Turkus had given him. He held it close to Fitzhugh's face, his thumb next to the obese figure in the background of the cemetery.

The fog cleared. The old man stared. "Holy crap! He got fat."

"Coming through. Out of the way, please."

A man and a woman in uniform with medical patches on the sleeves came in, trundling a stretcher with foldaway wheels. In his fevered state, Valentino hadn't heard the ambulance's siren approaching outside.

With Kym Trujillo's hand on his arm he made way, accompanying her out into the corridor.

She let go. "I hope that wasn't a mistake. It sounded pretty important or I wouldn't have let it go on. I guess I got caught up."

"I'm no expert, but I think he'll recover. He's a tough old bird; always was. That kind doesn't give up without a fight."

"I'm sorry he couldn't answer your last question."

"I'm not. I have the answer. All I needed was someone to lead me to it." He slid the picture back into his pocket. As his fingers left it, his eyes went to something in a corner, just past where the corridor opened into the entryway, a volume the size of a family Bible spread open on a wooden lectern. "May I look at the register?"

"Of course. It's open to everyone, you know that."

She left him to supervise Roy Fitzhugh's removal, and Valentino went to the book. He looked at the ruled pages where guests had signed in, adding the dates and times of their visits and occasionally a sentiment. Among them he recognized acquaintances, some of them famous; but none was the one he sought. He turned back the heavy gilt-edged leaves.

And there it was.

A few days ago, he'd have been shocked, then elated. Now he just felt drained. If he'd thought to look there the last time he visited, he could have saved everyone a lot of trouble, most of all himself.

28

A black sedan with a hood nearly as long as the Bugatti's (into which his own car could fit without scratching the fenders), narrow running boards, and blazing whitewall tires drifted into the loading zone in front of The Oracle. It was shaped like the spaceship in a Buck Rogers movie, sleek as a shark, every part curving gracefully into every other, with chrome so bright it caught cold fire under the sun of another brilliant day in southern California. Its plate and the insignia above the radiator grille — a gold-and-red enamel escutcheon — identified it as a 1948 Packard.

Valentino, standing in front of the theater's glass-and-nickel doors, was prepared to accept it as the one Van Oliver had driven in throughout *Bleak Street;* it was a graven image, as much as the man himself. At this point in the affair that had begun less than a week earlier in the lobby of the Bradbury

Building, he was inclined not to discount anything as impossible.

History repeated itself, never more relentlessly than today.

The rear passenger's door popped open and Ignacio Bozal leaned out, placing a small foot in a crisp brown-and-ivory wingtip onto the running board. The elderly collector had abandoned his shabby house wear for a dove-gray fedora with the brim tugged down rakishly over one eyebrow and a Burberry trench coat knotted rather than tied at the waist, the buckle dangling; the outfit looked more natural on him than it had on his grandson. Valentino caught a glimpse of blue pinstripes, black silk socks that hugged his ankles too snugly to have been held up other than by elastic garters, and a silk necktie decorated with red and black squares set at diamond-shaped angles. He touched the knot as if to secure it, and uncased his store-bought teeth in a neon grin.

"Get in the car."

He made it sound gruff, like a henchman in an old crime film. There was no trace of a Spanish accent.

Valentino asked him where they were going.

"For a ride, what else?"

The archivist didn't laugh. Knowing what he now knew of the man, the answer sounded less like a joke and more like a sinister promise.

Bozal sensed his hesitation. "Around the block a few times; as many as it takes to talk. You never rode in a car like this. I own more'n a hundred, and this one's my favorite. I'm not forgetting the Bugatti. It's got breeding, but this one's got flash." He withdrew his foot and slid to the other side.

It was the second time the archivist had been waylaid by a wealthy and powerful figure in a luxury sedan. As often as he'd seen the scene replayed on-screen, it had never gotten old: until now. Nevertheless he got in.

He recognized the driver. This time he was wearing a chauffeur's uniform. "Where to, Grandpapa?"

"Shut up and drive. I'm still sore at you. Your sister too."

"We were only —"

"Can it!"

Emiliano's face lost its eager-to-please expression. It looked even more like Oliver's; like Bozal's, stripped of the six decades that had taken place since *Bleak Street*. For they were one and the same.

Bozal shook his head. "Can't lay eyes on

that kid without feeling someone's walking over my grave. Like looking in a mirror that stopped sixty years ago. Genes are sneaky. They'll go into hiding for generations, then jump out and yell 'Boo!' That what tipped you? I knew it was you when the phone rang. I got the story out of the kids by then. You were smart enough to figure out the rest."

"Not as smart as you think. I should have seen it long before then, but I still didn't get it, not till I could put a little distance between us. The resemblance couldn't have been just coincidence. Neither did all the other signs: Estrella's portrait, painted years after Madeleine Nash left pictures to get married, but the features hadn't changed along with the hairstyle; Esperanza, who could double for Madeleine, except I'd only seen her in black-and-white, not in color or in person; your language — not learned secondhand from watching old movies on TV, but ingrained in you during your time with the New York mob."

They were moving now, cruising through East L.A. neighborhoods he'd never visited. The motor wasn't muted, like the one in Turkus's modern town car, nor did it rumble, like the twelve pistons charging up and down under the Bugatti's hood. It was a

powerful throb one could feel in the soles of his feet; the suppressed growl of a savage animal engaged in the stalk.

"Why Estrella, by the way?" Valentino asked. "Why not call her Magdalena?"

"That and Ignacio Bozal were the names on the papers we bought in Tijuana. There wasn't time to have fresh forgeries made. I got used to it. I never could call her Madeleine; that was some PR flak's brainstorm to make her more acceptable to a WASP audience, like when they changed Rita Cansino's last name to Hayworth. She died in Peru in 'sixty-five — Estrella, not Rita. Cancer. That's why I left Acapulco. We had eight good years, but there were too many memories there. The kids — Esperanza and Emiliano's parents and aunts and uncle — were my staff when I opened the hotel. They learned good manners and passed them on; even misplaced loyalty."

"You're Van Oliver. Or do you prefer Benny Obrilenski?"

They were passing down a narrow street walled by blank-faced buildings, *carnicerias* and laundries catering to the local restaurant trade, and probably an indoor *cannabis* farm or two under grow lights. They cast shadows in which only Bozal's bottom teeth showed in a shark's grimace. "I ditched it

265

when I quit the Outfit. Couldn't get used to Van Oliver, though; sounded like a dance-hall gigolo with greased hair and patent-leather pumps."

Valentino had the bizarre feeling he was riding with a stranger, yet one he'd known almost as long as he'd known Bozal. Sometimes — likely from years of careful habit — the man would lapse even now into the border accent, but for the most part it was pure Flatbush: "berl" for "boil," "goil" for "girl," peppered generously with dropped *g*'s and expectorated *t*'s. The clothes, the car, and especially the candor of their conversation had turned the clock back to 1957.

He said, "I knew you'd figured it out last night, when I called to see if Roy was up for a visit and they said he had one. It had to be you. No one else comes to see him these days."

"Did they tell you the rest?"

"Yeah. Call me Madame Zara, I guess. I had a feeling, which is why I called. This morning I was about to check with Cedars of Lebanon when the phone rang and it was you."

"I checked. He's stable. That's all they'd tell me." Valentino went on. "I'd have figured it out a lot earlier if I'd thought to

266

check the visitors' register the last time I was at the Country Home. There was your name, the one you're using now. You signed in three times this year, across from Fitzhugh's name. Ignacio Bozal had no reason to shoot the breeze with an old character actor. Van Oliver did."

"How much did he tell you?"

Valentino gave him part of it. Bozal nodded, his aquiline profile silhouetted in a crack of sunlight between buildings.

"He's slipping, all right. In the old days he wouldn't of said help if he was drowning."

"He's still cagy. All I got out of him at first was you and Madeleine Nash went to Mexico, and that only indirectly. You were the only one who said she went to Europe with her new husband. You misdirected me twice. You said you got *Bleak Street* from a private estate sale in Europe."

"I didn't lie about getting it from the editor, just that he was dead when I got it. I slipped him a grand back in 'fifty-seven. Just a sentimental souvenir. I met Estrella on that set."

"What about the rest of the money? RKO paid you twenty-five hundred a week all the time you were on contract. None of that ever showed up. In the end the authorities

concluded you'd stuck it in a safe-deposit box under an assumed name and never came back to claim it. That helped confirm the theory you were murdered."

"It'd just as easily meant I skipped with it; but by then the press was tired of the case and so were the cops."

Emiliano turned a corner into full sunlight. His grandfather's cheeks showed color for the first time; he never looked more like Benny Obrilenski, the mob bodyguard who'd struck Hollywood paydirt. "I earned that money! I wasn't about to kick back half to that sawed-off runt Mickey Cohen. He was raking in plenty enough from every racket in this burg without shaking me down for more.

"That's why we took it on the ankles, Maggie and me." He'd lapsed into Roy Fitzhugh's nickname for Madeleine Nash. "We'd go on making movie after movie, and half of what we got would go into the Mick's pocket. Our only way out was to skip and start over where nobody'd look for us. We sank dry shafts in every tank town and prairie dog hole in Central and South America, picked coffee beans right alongside the hired hands, till we scrounged up the case dough to buy that roach motel in Aca-

pulco and turn it around. You know the rest."

"Not quite. Fitzhugh couldn't cross you into Mexico because of that old smuggling rap. How much did you pay Constantine Turkus to smuggle you across the border?"

"Old Roy sure turned squealer at the end, didn't he?"

"Cut him slack. He was breathing bottled oxygen, waiting for the ambulance to take him to ICU. I ambushed him with a picture of Turkus. It got a reaction."

"I don't hold no grudge. He kept his trap shut all those years when it mattered. I didn't give the Turk much more than cab fare. I think he got a boot out of sneaking U.S. citizens into Mexico instead of the other way around."

"How'd you know him?"

"How do you think? Cohen got him his start busting heads for the studios. I had the lovely job of watching his back while he was doing it."

"That's terrible!"

"You won't get no argument from me. It's why I jumped at the chance when Howard Hughes offered me a contract. Son, you're looking at the only actor who didn't want to be a star. All I wanted was a way out. Maggie — my Estrella — she was a gift

269

from God: Maybe it meant I'd served my time in Perdition."

"You owed her a lot," Valentino said. "Magdalena Novello was a good Spanish tutor."

"She was, but she was raised Castilian. I got the local accent from the natives. I had the coloring to pass, at least with gringos. As far as Mexicans were concerned, it was *un asunto de no importa.* They'd been pulling the wool over gringos' eyes for a hundred years."

"Everyone here was satisfied he'd seen the last of Van Oliver. As long as you stayed in character, anyone who happened to recognize you years later might have doubted his own judgment."

It was too warm for a trench coat. The old man unbelted and unbuttoned it, spread it open, and took off his hat. He rested it on his knee and ran a brown hand through his white hair. "I had a couple of close calls, when some mugs came down for vacation. But by then Cohen was in stir for the long haul. I upgraded their rooms, tore up their bills, and they decided they'd made a mistake. Also by then I had some pull in Mexico City. It didn't pay to blow any whistles."

"You sound just like your character in

270

Bleak Street."

"You might say I was the first method actor. I started rehearsing it back in Brooklyn. But I've been playing Bozal so long, I had to climb into this getup to pull off Benny O. I figured you earned a second feature, that's why I offered you the film; getting *Greed* on a *quid pro quo* was just an excuse. 'Course I knew you'd dope out the rest. That's *your* M.O."

"But it's not why you agreed to see me today."

"No. If it wasn't for this phony town, I'd of wound up on a slab back East or making gravel in Sing Sing. I only done two things right in my life. You got to see what come of 'em both." He made his crooked grin. "How about them kids? They're smart where it's okay to be dumb and dumb where it counts to be smart. When I ran the picture for her, Esperanza spotted me in the first scene. She'll be a great TV reporter, or whatever it is she's training for. She's got the eye.

"Everything else she found on the Internet, all that bushwah about a great Hollywood mystery. When I let go of *Bleak Street,* she thought I was going screwy, setting myself up for some kind of rap, maybe even a pair of cement overshoes. She's sharp — sharper than Emiliano, for sure — but she

271

let her heart get in the way of her head, protecting me from mugs that were taking a dirt nap before she was born."

His tone dripped with derision, but there was a glint of pride in his eyes. With her brother as an accomplice, she'd nearly brought off a con job that Van Oliver and his old associates could have imagined only in their dreams.

Emiliano called out from the front seat. "The hat and coat were my idea, Grandpapa." His tone was indignant.

"Shut up and drive."

"What about the rest of your family?" Valentino asked. "Do they know?"

Bozal shook his head. "They're bound to, after I'm gone and the biographers nose around long enough to pick up the scent. It won't matter then. I worked a hell of a lot longer getting Bozal right than that character I played in the movie, and anytime you watch an actor put everything into a part and tell him what a good actor he is, it means he screwed up. I'd rather not get bad reviews from my own flesh and blood.

" 'Course," he said, "I won't hold you to anything. A deal's a deal, and you held up your end. You got clear title to *Bleak Street* and everything caught up in it."

The archivist made a decision.

"I've got a born-again classic, and an enduring Hollywood mystery to promote it. At this point, a solution would only gum up the works, like if they raised the *Titanic* or identified Jack the Ripper. It could squelch any interest in the film before it sees the light of day."

"You sure? Connie Turkus was camera-shy. If you showed Fitzhugh his picture, you must of got it from his nephew. He won't be too happy to see that can of worms spill out."

"Let me worry about Mark David Turkus, sir. It took me three times as long as it should have, but in the end I'm usually smart where it counts."

Ignacio Bozal — the name Valentino would always associate with him first and foremost — reached over and took his knee in a grip that would crack iron. "My whole film library goes to UCLA two minutes after I croak. There's some stuff there I bet even you never heard of."

Valentino was moved. "*Señor,* when that day comes, I'll make all the arrangements."

Van Oliver put his hat back on, tugging the brim over his left eyebrow, and buttoned and belted his trench coat. His grin was sinister.

"You and what army?"

29

The CEO of Supernova International kept his office in the penthouse suite of a former luxury hotel in Century City, where, local legend maintained, mega-producer Darryl F. Zanuck had kept his succession of mistresses during his reign at Twentieth Century Fox.

An armed man in uniform stood sentry before the entrance of the only elevator that went there, beside a white telephone on a fluted pedestal. He took Valentino's name, checked it against a steel clipboard, and lifted the receiver without dialing. He repeated the name to whoever picked up and cradled it. He pressed a button and the doors to the elevator slid open.

The car was done in green marble and red mahogany — invoking Christmas year-round — with the corporation's logo, the eye of a raptor in a circle like a camera lens, embossed on the paneling. As it climbed

with no effort on Valentino's part, the piped-in sound system played an orchestration without lyrics that the passenger quickly identified as "Saturday Night at the Movies (Who Cares What Picture We See?)." The illusion of purely emotional, non-commercial devotion to the lively art extended only as far as the room where the company conducted negotiations; that was where the raptor came out, talons first.

The doors opened directly into the suite. It took up the entire top floor without partitions. There was space enough for a vast and glossy desk, a huge table holding up a three-dimensional scale model of a resort on the Riviera, a Nautilus weight-trainer, a complete indoor putting green, and a bank of vintage pinball machines, restored to their original gaudy condition. Windows looked out on Los Angeles in every direction, with a Blu-ray–quality view of the Santa Monica Mountains to the west.

Inside this panoramic display stood a ring of seventy-inch plasma screens, blank at the moment, and inside that a bank of computer monitors on pedestals, a circle within a circle within a circle; this one affording a view of the globe from New York to London to Paris to Moscow to Tokyo to the parking lot at the base of the building, where a man

in a uniform identical to the one worn by the guard on the ground floor walked around taking pictures of license plates with a camera phone.

In the center of the last sat Mark David Turkus himself, at a potato chip–shaped desk with nothing on it but a yellow pad and a mechanical pencil, slurping something green through a straw from a tall glass tumbler. Somewhere a mobile phone or tablet hummed incessantly and without response; it could be the president of Pakistan or a pitch for a time-share in Florida for all the attention it got.

As Valentino entered, Turkus rose and came around the desk to offer his hand. He wore an old pullover, tan Dockers, and boat shoes threadbare at the toes; *GQ* had featured him on the cover as "The Man Who Invented Casual Friday."

His grip was tentative, representing years of practice. He'd learned the art of disguise from those ocean predators who camouflaged themselves as harmless creatures.

"I was surprised when you called me so soon," he said. "Does that mean you've made some kind of breakthrough?"

"Some kind."

Turkus indicated a pair of chairs that matched the desk, curved yellow plywood

with aluminum frames. "They're more comfortable than they look," he said.

"I'm sure they are, but I don't think this will take long."

"That's unencouraging. Bad news always does."

"That depends on what you consider bad. I know what became of Van Oliver."

The eyes behind the glasses were as flat as washers. "Did my uncle have anything to do with it?"

"Yes."

No change in expression. "And our arrangement stands? You will withhold the information, and *Bleak Street* will remain out of view, with no publicity attached?"

"For the time being."

The barometer in the room dropped. The man carried around his own climate.

"That's not what we agreed on. There was to be no time limit."

"Constantine Venezelos Turkus didn't kill Oliver."

A muscle twitched in the other's cheek; it was invisible unless one looked close. "But you said —"

"I can't give details. I promised someone I wouldn't during the party's lifetime. After that I'll be free to tell you the rest. At that time I'll expect you to honor your part of

our bargain and lift the restraining order. The film won't be exhibited and no mention of it will be made to the public until then."

"Can you throw me a bone of any kind?"

Valentino hesitated, as if thinking it over, then nodded. He'd made up his mind on that point before he'd asked for the appointment.

"Whatever else your uncle may have done, killing Van Oliver wasn't one of them. He had nothing to do with the disappearance that could damage your reputation or that of Supernova International."

"Now I'm more curious than ever." But he didn't look confused. Perhaps for the first time in his professional life, an emotion crossed "the Turk's" face; a look of profound relief.

"For some reason I get the impression we'll be meeting again soon," he said.

"Not too soon, I hope. This film's waited sixty years to premiere. A few more won't hurt it."

Something whirred. The elevator doors opened and Teddie Goodman stepped into the room.

She wore yet another of her outlandish outfits, part Theda Bara, part Jane Jetson, an angular metallic thing of scarlet and

278

black supported by eight-inch heels and crowned by a curving spiked comb of blackest jet angling along the part in her hair; for all the world it recalled the tailfin of a German U-boat. She stopped when she spotted Valentino, so abruptly she might have fallen on her face but for her catlike ability to stay on her feet. Her eyes flashed — quite literally — and went from him to Turkus. But she was too accustomed to self-survival — the law of the jungle — to ask the question that was obviously on her mind.

"Miss Goodman. I wasn't aware we'd scheduled a meeting."

Icy calm was restored. "We didn't. I had something to report, something I thought you should know right away. On second thought it can wait."

"If it has anything to do with Mr. Valentino's recent activities, I'm well aware of them. But thank you for your concern."

Her long black lashes lowered in what for her served as a bow. She turned, re-entered the elevator, and faced front. The doors slid shut on her frozen alabaster features.

Valentino broke the silence that followed. "I'll pay for that."

"Possibly. She frightens me, too, sometimes. The guard in the lobby is terrified of her, which is why she comes and goes as

she pleases. It can be a valuable property in one's representative. It can also be an intolerable annoyance." He rolled a shoulder. "I can't promise to call her off, short of firing her. She'd be a dangerous character set loose in the wild."

"I'll take my chances. I'd miss her, to be honest."

Once again, Turkus put out his hand.

"Thank you. On behalf of myself, my company, and my family. Thank you."

For the third time in two days, Valentino felt that deceptively mild grip. He'd heard there were close associates who hadn't shaken the billionaire's hand even once.

30

The Oracle was lit up as if for the 1927 premiere of *Wings,* the first feature to win the Academy Award for Best Picture. Light chased the LED bulbs around the towering marquee, left, right, up, down, and left again, technology's answer to man's quest for the eternal. Searchlights the size of trampolines tinted the bellies of clouds in cotton-candy colors, the shafts crisscrossing like swords in combat. Guests in full evening dress crossed the red carpet under the glittering canopy, admiring the barbaric splendor of ancient civilizations, mythic beasts, and pagan deities restored to life in gilt, plaster, and resin; all the illusionary, elusive, over-the-top art of the Hollywood Dream Factory.

Harriet Johansen was first to arrive, in a silver lamé gown that clung to her slim athletic frame and reflected the light in flat sheets. She kissed Valentino and pointed the

corner of her clutch purse at the man who'd taken her gold-bordered pass, in a tuxedo that could only have been cut to his massive measure. A black velvet band of mourning encircled one sleeve.

"Wherever did you find him?"

Valentino was standing next to the vacant ticket booth wearing a white dinner jacket.

"His name's Vivien, believe it or not. He came to me three days ago, saying he owed me a favor. He doesn't — I was just a catalyst — but I couldn't pass up the opportunity. He's already turned away a dozen people who thought this was a public event."

"I can't think how they made that mistake. The place only looks like the World's Fair." She looked at the man again. "He reminds me of someone."

"Only if you've seen *The Incredible Hulk*."

"The TV show? Loved it. In re-runs, I mean. Is he — ?"

"Not Lou Ferrigno. Leave it to a forensics expert to recognize a stunt double after all these years."

She beamed. "How can I help?"

"Stand beside me. That way no one will notice I borrowed this outfit from the Hallmark Channel."

"You look like Rick Blaine." She studied his face.

282

"Just by coincidence; it was the only thing available. I won't play it again, Sam. This time."

She was looking at the next arrivals. "I think I just got upstaged."

Fanta Broadhead approached, her arm linked with her husband's. She was a glittering mermaid in sparkling green sequins and a white wrap that would have passed for ermine if she didn't do *pro bono* work for the ASPCA.

The host kissed her on the cheek. "You look wonderful."

"This old thing?" She hugged Harriet. "You clean up well, too."

Valentino shook Broadhead's hand. "So do you."

The professor tugged at his starched collar. In a black tuxedo with onyx studs he might have passed for a truck driver at his daughter's wedding. "Third time I've worn the monkey suit, thanks to you. I should've suspected what Fanta was up to when she talked me into buying it instead of renting one for the hitching post. I thought she intended to bury me in it."

"We've heard it all before, old man," said his wife. "I told you when you proposed I wasn't going to spend the rest of my life in sensible shoes and a tailored suit like all the

rest of the faculty wives. That meant dressing you up so it wouldn't look like I checked you out of a hotel for transients. And just for the record, *I* proposed to *you.*"

"I said I'd think about it. I was still thinking when you dragged me to the cake-tasting."

"You forget a lawyer never asks a question she doesn't know the answer to," she said.

Broadhead turned to survey the small group lined up behind them. "Not much of a turnout. I warned you when this whole thing started you'll never lure people away from their living rooms and Netflix."

"Did you look at the invitation?" Valentino said.

" 'Admit two,' along with the lame tease of a sneak premiere. What part of 'grand opening' did you not understand?"

"It's the grandest company I could have wished for."

Fanta turned toward the centerpiece of the ornate lobby, an oil portrait of a hauntingly lovely brunette in its original Deco frame, securely sealed in a shadow box made of beveled glass. "It looks even better than it did in the Bradbury."

"I hoped it would. Mounting it in that case cost me four hundred dollars. Anytime someone offers you a gift, make sure you

can afford it."

"You know," she said, "I like it more than the one they used in the film."

"Meaning no disrespect to a beautiful actress, that's because the one Preminger had made looks like Gene Tierney. This one looks like Laura, the unachievable ideal. That's an impossible undertaking for any mortal casting director, no matter how talented. Vera Caspary preferred it to the other; but what did she know? She only wrote the novel the picture was based on."

"Will Bozal be coming?" Broadhead said.

"He declined. He's in Tuscany, scouting locations for a theme park he wants to build. It seems the Catholic Church liked the idea well enough to clear it with the authorities. Anyway, he's seen the picture."

Fanta said, "What *is* the picture, by the way? *Casablanca*? Harriet told me about that."

He smiled. "Not *Casablanca.*"

"He won't even tell *me,*" Harriet said.

Still smiling, he turned and opened the embossed bronze door that led into the auditorium.

Henry Anklemire was next in line, in his purple smoking jacket and a green-and-yellow-striped bow tie. "Snazzy joint, kiddo. You could put up the Lost Tribe of Israel in

a room this size and still have space for a pool table."

"Good of you to come, Henry. No hard feelings about what we discussed, I hope."

"What the heck. Don't take it the wrong way, but I didn't really think you could do it. Land on Mars, maybe, but rip the lid off a case the cops gave up on before you was born? Meshugana!"

"You can't win 'em all."

Anklemire patted his arm. "Better luck next time. Just let me know when I can go to work on the pitch. I'll come up with something."

"I will."

"Popcorn's free, right?"

"I hired a caterer. You can have shrimp and lobster if you like."

"Just so long as you don't rat me out to Temple Beth Shalom." He adjusted his toupee and strutted through the door.

Harriet smiled after him. "No one's *that* Jewish. I bet he's a closet Methodist."

"Nobody knows Henry," Valentino said. "He's entirely a creature of manufacture: Mr. Whipple out of Betty Crocker by way of Morris the Cat. They were all born on a drawing board on Madison Avenue."

"You're a puzzle yourself. For someone who was so determined to get to the bot-

286

tom of the Van Oliver case, you seem to have dropped it like a hot lightbulb. What'd I tell you about keeping secrets?"

"This one isn't mine to share," he said. "When it is, you'll be the first to know."

A new voice interrupted the conversation.

"I like what you've done with the place. Ditching the skeleton was a good start."

Valentino straightened at the sight of the tall redhead in the shimmering blue gown; it was part surprise, part force of habit whenever he found himself face-to-face with an old adversary. She looked more statuesque than ever in six-inch heels and pearls. For the first time it struck him that she was a remarkably beautiful woman, something she managed to camouflage through fierce intelligence and ruthless efficiency on the job.

"Sergeant Clifford. I'm so glad you came."

"I can tell. I haven't seen that look on anybody's face since I slapped the cuffs on a former child star with blood on his shirt. This is my husband, Ray. He's a criminal attorney. We only fight when he's cross-examining me in court."

He shook the hand of a stout, ruddy-faced man whose head barely cleared his wife's bare shoulders. "Don't listen to her. She was thrilled when she got the invitation. The

last time she got to gussy up, it was in dress blues with a black band on her shield."

"I object," she said.

"Overruled."

Valentino said, "Enjoy the show."

On her way past, Clifford bent to his ear. "When can I expect a signed statement? I'm not talking about Ivy Lane. The Oliver file's still open downtown."

Valentino hesitated. "I'll keep you posted."

Harriet said, "Did you do as I suggested and invite Teddie Goodman?"

"I decided against it, for reasons of delicacy. I'll tell you about it someday."

When everyone was seated, the lights came down and a bar of white light struck the screen.

Valentino had borrowed the UCLA projectionist for the evening, along with some footage from the secure storage vault. Following Bugs Bunny and a travelogue on the virtues of the Republic of Cuba came a black-and-white newsreel showing Queen Elizabeth II offering a gloved hand to President Eisenhower. Valentino, seated in the center balcony looking down on the screen, felt Harriet stirring restlessly in the adjoining seat. She knew he always insisted on matching the dates of vintage features with vintage films.

When the RKO tower went to black and the title card came on, she whispered, "I should've known."

She was a trained close observer, more so than he, for all his education in the visual arts. Halfway through the opening scene — the anti-hero's dramatic entrance, stepping down from the chair car of a westbound train — she tensed, shifted positions, turned her head partly Valentino's way, stopped, watched a minute more, then leaned across the armrest they shared.

"That looks like —"

He shushed her, whispered: "You know how I feel about talking during a movie."

When the RKO tower went to black and
the title card came on, she whispered, "I
should've known."

She was a trained close observer, more so
than he, for all his education in the visual
arts. Halfway through the opening scene —
the anti-hero's dramatic entrance, stepping
down from the chair car of a westbound
train — she tensed, shifted positions, turned
her head partly Valentino's way, stopped
watched a minute more, then leaned across
the armrest they shared.

"That looks like —"

He shushed her, whispered, "You know
how I feel about talking during a movie."

A WORD FROM VALENTINO

The images are iconic, and uniquely American: The pulled-down hat brim, the rumpled trench coat, the cigarette dangling from the corner of a lip; the feline creature in the tight dress, deadlier than the male; gigantic shadows on the brick wall of an alley, a piece of the city that has broken loose and lodged in a place of eternal night.

Like most native culture, this cinematic sub-genre (commonly bracketed between 1945 and 1958, although there are notable exceptions as far back as 1931 and as recent as 1967) came about through several influences: in this case, post-war disillusionment, the erosion of faith in governments and institutions, and men's concerns about women's independence earned during war-time employment in the defense industry. The final touch came from Jewish and dissident filmmakers in flight from the Holocaust, bringing with them the expressionistic

camera angles, Cubist sets, and themes outlawed as "decadent" by Nazi Germany. Ironically, the U.S. studios' strict censorship code, which prohibited overt violence, sexual situations, and sins unpunished, led to a subtlety of symbols and expression that still resonates today. Like the steam-engine, this was a development whose time had come. All it needed was a name.

That came from French critics who, when the embargo on U.S. films was lifted after the Liberation, saw the films back-to-back, observed the consistency of theme, and cried, film *noir*!;* literally, "black film." It was raw, it was unapologetic, and it told the truth: In the words of the narrator of *Detour* (1945), "Fate, or some mysterious force, can put the finger on you or me for no good reason at all."

Twenty-first-century audiences, accustomed to the frantic pace of superhero, sci-fi, and other hypermodern productions adapted from graphic novels (comic books, to an earlier generation) may lose patience with the oblique motives and slow buildup of suspense to be found in classic *noir,* but

* With help from French publisher Gallimard's "*Serie Noire,*" which brought translations of American crime novels to Europe.

a steady diet — excluding any movie whose special-effects credits run almost into the next showing — should convert all but the hopeless. These films were made for grown-ups, assuming intelligence on the part of their viewers, and an attention span longer than a high-five.

The effect of *noir* can't be described in words, only images: A man pushed out a high window, falling away from the camera; the orgasmic leer on a psychopath's face in the act of murder; the gold anklet worn by a scheming woman descending a staircase; a child-killer pleading for mercy on his knees before a jury of ordinary cutthroats; a cynical detective falling in love with the portrait of the woman whose murder he's investigating. These are not images you watch; you breathe them in like gas — odorless, colorless, inescapable, and lethal.

Then come back for another whiff.

a steady diet — excluding any movie whose special-effects credits run almost into the next showing — should convert all but the hopeless. These films were made for grown-ups, assuming intelligence on the part of their viewers, and an attention span longer than a high-five.

The effect of noir can't be described in words, only images: A man pushed out a high window, falling away from the camera; the orgasmic leer on a psychopath's face in the act of murder; the gold anklet worn by a scheming woman descending a staircase; a child-killer pleading for mercy on his knees before a jury of ordinary cutthroats; a cynical detective falling in love with the portrait of the woman whose murder he's investigating. These are noir images, you watch, you breathe them in like gas — odorless, colorless, inescapable, and lethal.

Then come back for another whiff.

CLOSING CREDITS

The list of *noir* films currently in circulation, previously overlooked, just plain forgotten, and dismissed as lost is constantly in flux, just as the material between covers that informs, analyzes, and educates the reader on this singular movement in cinema history is too vast to contain in the backmatter of one book. The revolution in home viewing that began with the VCR and exploded when DVDs came along has rescued thousands of features from storage vaults where many have remained for more than a century. Hundreds of *noir* entries have come to light, including titles previously unknown by accomplished film historians. The following sources are recommended (along with general works on film that were employed in researching *Indigo*):

BIBLIOGRAPHY

Alton, John. *Painting with Light.* Berkeley: University of California, 1995.

I can't praise this wonderful book too highly. The cinematographer whose use of contrast and composition gave *noir* its signature look shares with us the secrets of his genius. At a time when he and his colleagues were generally dismissed as mere technicians, Alton (*T-Men, Raw Deal, He Walked by Night, Border Incident, The Big Combo*) recognized the central part his craft played in the creation of this unique and powerful art. The chapter headings alone are enough to sell the book: "Hollywood Photography"; "Motion Picture Illumination"; "Mystery Lighting"; "Symphony in Snow," etc. It was first published in 1949, at the height of his career. The introduction to this new edition by film critic and documentarian Todd McCarthy is excellent.

Baker, J. J., editor. *Film Noir: 75 Years of the Greatest Crime Films.* New York: *Life,* 2016.

Decades after its demise as a weekly staple, this most American of magazine publishers remains current with its special issues examining single subjects. There's nothing new here, but I have to applaud this institution for bringing film *noir* back

into the spotlight, educating a new generation with this sumptuously illustrated primer.

Clarens, Carlos. *Crime Movies.* New York: Norton, 1980.
This is an early entry in the post-1970s renaissance of material on the crime thriller. The twelve-page chapter titled "Shades of Noir" alone contains tons of material on the evolution of the sub-genre from the novels of Dashiell Hammett, Raymond Chandler, James M. Cain, et al., through their screen adaptations, and films inspired by the adaptations, more than you'll find in many whole books.

Kaplan, E. Ann. *Women in Film Noir.* London: British Film Institute, 1978.
This study was heavily revised in 1980 and reprinted many times. The essays, including the title piece by Janey Place, establish *noir* as an empowering influence on behalf of womankind and actresses; evil these characters may be, but their superior intelligence and determination broke them out of the stereotypical roles of Good Girl, Tramp, Tomboy, Victim. None of *these* ladies stood by wringing her hands while a man took care of business.

Mainon, Dominique, and James Ursini. *Femme Fatale: Cinema's Most Unforgettable Lethal Ladies.* Milwaukee: Limelight, 2009.

From Theda Bara (the original Teddie Goodman) to Catherine Zeta-Jones, Mainon and Ursini provide a running tally of the Jezebels who have led their leading men (sometimes with their willing co-operation) to their doom. Exquisitely illustrated in glossy black-and-white and color plates, this one makes the descent into hell seem worth it.

Mordden, Ethan. *The Hollywood Studios: House Style in the Golden Age of the Movies.* New York: Knopf, 1988.

A general guide, essential in recognizing the trademark styles, business practices, and creative decisions of RKO, Warner Brothers, Universal, and United Artists; not forgetting those plucky independents whose B-movie budgets forced them to stay on point and make the best artistic use of the materials at hand, with results so impressive even their deep-pocket competitors co-opted their methods.

Muller, Eddie. *The Art of Noir: The Posters and Graphics from the Classic Era of Film Noir.* Woodstock, NY: Overlook, 2002.

Muller, a fixture on TV's Turner Classic Movies, frequent commentator on DVD releases, and a co-organizer of *noir* film festivals, knows his stuff. *The Art of Noir,* just one of his many books on this subject, is a coffee-table gem: 279 slick, folio-size pages of full-color reproductions of the advertising art that helped define the form, with capsule commentaries on the films themselves.

Silver, Allain, and James Ursini, eds. *Film Noir Reader, Vols. 1–3.* New York: Limelight, 1996, 1999, 2002.

Scholarly, but by no means pedantic, this series takes us from Raymond Borde and Etienne Chaumeton's seminal 1955 French essay "Towards a Definition of Film *Noir*" through Philip Gaines's "*Noir* 101," published in 1999. The third volume, co-edited by Robert Porfiro, provides illuminating interviews with period filmmakers.

Silver, Allain, Elizabeth Ward, James Ursini, and Robert Porfiro, eds. *Film Noir: The Encyclopedia.* New York: Overlook, 2010.

Fanatics have awaited this new edition for years; in the meantime we had to content ourselves with occasional "update" volumes. This one makes use of colossal numbers of

newly released DVDs, essays, and an expanded panel of experts to chronicle nearly every title in the *noir* canon (inexplicable snubs: *Murder, Inc.; Tight Spot*), along with production notes, period reviews, and modern commentary. You may not agree with them all the time, but you'll respect their dedication. A new section analyzes neo-*noir* remakes and originals. The word "indispensable" is overused, but if any source deserves it, this does. If it's not on your shelves, you're not one of us.

Silver, Allain, and James Ursini. *The Noir Style*. Woodstock, NY: Overlook, 1999.

Another coffee-table treasure, lavishly illustrated in black-and-white, tracing the evolution of the genre from *Scarface* (1931) through *The Silence of the Lambs* (1991), tying in the neo-*noir* movement that began in the 1970s. It makes a *prima facie* case against director James Spader's preposterous claim that this timeless school of moviemaking is a "historical" artifact, as dead as King Duncan.

Tuska, Jon. *Dark Cinema: American Film Noir in Cultural Perspective*. Westport, Conn.: Greenwood, 1984.

Treatises don't get more scholarly than

this. Tuska's exhaustive research draws a straight line from Euripides and Shakespeare to Clifford Odets, exhibiting a trend that explains mankind's fascination with the flawed heroes and heroines of tragedy. This historian's intimacy with many Hollywood idols enlivens his narrative, preventing it from sinking into a morass of cant.

FILMOGRAPHY

Here are some essentials; don't stop there.

The Big Combo. Directed by Joseph Lewis, written by Philip Yordan, starring Cornel Wilde, Richard Conte, Brian Donlevy, Jean Wallace, Robert Middlelton, Lee Van Cleef, Earl Holliman, and Helen Walker. Allied Artists, 1955.

This one rides on strong performances and John Alton's genius behind the camera. Wilde's detective sets out to nail mob boss Conte by tracking down the mysterious Alicia (Walker, as Conte's forcibly institutionalized ex-wife: "I'd rather be insane and alive than sane — and dead"). Van Cleef and Holliman's sadistic henchmen are patently homosexual; Lewis gets around censorship standards simply by letting them share a bedroom and some effeminate characteristics; who can object to that?

Brian Donlevy's death, mowed down by machine guns in eerie silence because Conte has taken away his hearing aid, is one of the iconic scenes in *noir*. Conte shone in gangster roles, managing to be evil and emotionally vulnerable at the same time (his final appearance, as Don Barzini in *The Godfather,* has touches of sardonic humor, and his slaying on the steps of a church echoes James Cagney's at the end of *The Roaring Twenties*). Censors decried Lewis's push-the-envelope love scene with Wallace and missed the homoerotic subtext mentioned above.

The Big Heat. Directed by Fritz Lang, written by Sydney Boehm (based on the novel by William P. McGivern), starring Glenn Ford, Gloria Grahame, Jocelyn Brando, Alexander Scourby, Lee Marvin, Jeanette Nolan. Columbia, 1953.

Lang, Billy Wilder's fellow émigré from Nazi Germany, is most often praised for his silent *Metropolis;* but even restored and remastered, that one creaks (and Blu-ray is wasted on productions that predate the technology), while *The Big Heat* grows stronger with each viewing. It's a simple revenge tale: Gangsters kill detective Ford's wife, so he quits the corrupt force and sets

out to destroy the mob. He seethes throughout, just under the boiling point. Marvin's
street soldier is a sadistic coward, deliriously
easy to hate, Nolan as the widow of a bent
cop is a heartless schemer, and Graham —
noir's best *femme fatale* by a league —
stands out as Marvin's kittenish, victim-
turned-avenger moll. (To Nolan: "We're
sisters under the mink.") McGivern was one
of the best of the postwar hard-boiled novel-
ists, and the film is faithful to the book.

Born to Kill. Directed by Robert Wise, written by Eve Greene and Richard Macauley
(based on the novel *Deadlier than the Male*
by James Gumm), starring Claire Trevor,
Lawrence Tierney, Walter Slezak, Audrey
Long, Elisha Cook, Jr. RKO, 1947.

Trevor's amoral, Tierney's a psychopath.
They marry: A match made in hell. Trevor
gave up A-list stardom at MGM for roles
she could get her teeth into, thanks be to
God. Tierney (no relation to Gene), whose
cruel good looks made him a convincing
remorseless killer (and whose off-screen
persona mirrored his screen image, as late
as 1992's *Reservoir Dogs*), was never less
human. Cook excels as his stooge, constantly trying to govern Tierney's rage (FYI:
He fails). The presence of one of these play-

ers in a crime movie screams *noir;* all three settle the point.

The Dark Corner. Directed by Henry Hathaway, written by Jay Dratler and Bernard Schoenfield (based on the story by Leo Rosten), starring Mark Stevens, Lucille Ball, Clifton Webb, William Bendix, Kurt Krueger. 20th Century Fox, 1946.

Ex-con P.I. Stevens is framed for murder; simple premise, diabolic plot. Future TV megastar Ball sparkles as the take-charge Girl Friday, and the process shot in which Bendix falls to his death away from the camera is a honey.

Detour. Directed by Edgar Ulmer, written by Martin Goldsmith, starring Tom Neal, Ann Savage, Claudia Drake, Edmund Mac-Donald. PRC, 1945.

The fatalistic premise, sharp use of light and shadow, and Ulmer's skill in whipping a Z budget into an A-minus production have made this a staple of the form; but for me, it's a prime example of what some call "dumb s**t noir." Hey, Einstein! Next time you want to stop someone (Savage, whose name fits this character) from incriminating you over the phone, skip the tug-of-war and rip the box out of the wall on your side of the door!

Double Indemnity. Directed by Billy Wilder, written by Wilder and Raymond Chandler (based on the novella by James M. Cain), starring Fred MacMurray, Barbara Stanwyck, Edward G. Robinson. Paramount, 1944.

The jewel in the crown. Insurance salesman MacMurray allows himself to be drawn by Stanwyck into a plot to murder her husband for his life insurance. A tale of seduction, betrayal, reprisal, and karma, with superior pace and some of the best dialogue in pictures, courtesy of Chandler, who made all the improvements on the overheated novella. MacMurray, Hollywood's textbook nice guy, retains our sympathy throughout, in spite of (and maybe because of) his complicity in homicide. Stanwyck's the ultimate *femme fatale,* cunning and ruthless, and Robinson's insurance investigator steals every scene he's in. The film was nominated for three Academy Awards: Best picture, script, direction. No other *noir* ever came close.

The Glass Key. Directed by Stuart Heisler, written by Jonathan Latimer (based on the novel by Dashiell Hammett), starring Brian Donlevy, Veronica Lake, Alan Ladd, William Bendix. Paramount, 1942.

Critics who dismiss Alan Ladd as a "pint-size tough guy" are probably compensating for their own inadequacies; he was taller than James Cagney and a better actor than John Garfield, who was just Paul Muni with angst. Study the emotionally charged scene with William Bendix, who last time he got together with Ladd beat him nearly to death: Try to keep your eyes off Ladd, delivering his lines through his teeth and playing with the whiskey bottle he's obviously planning to use to crown Bendix (he never does, making the tension all the more unbearable). The diminutive team of Ladd and Lake in several films set them apart as the Astaire and Rogers of *noir.* (Cheers also to Joel and Ethan Coen's 1990 *Miller's Crossing,* an un-credited remake that's more faithful to Hammett's vision, if not specifically to his plot.)

Kiss of Death. Directed by Henry Hathaway, written by Ben Hecht and Charles Lederer (from a story by Eleazar Lipsky), starring Victor Mature, Brian Donlevy, Coleen Gray, Richard Widmark, Karl Malden. 20th Century Fox, 1947.

How do you make a stool pigeon sympathetic? Easy: Cast Richard Widmark as his antagonist. Mature's solid, square build sets

him apart from the weasely squealers who are almost invariably whacked in phone booths ratting out his pals to the cops, while Widmark's slithery, jittery, giggling killer makes you want to squash him like a bug; if only you had the guts. For Tommy Udo (Widmark), shoving an old lady in a wheelchair down a long flight of stairs is like skipping rope, right down to the orgasmic giggle.

Laura. Directed (and produced) by Otto Preminger, written by Jay Dratler, Samuel Hoffenstein, Ring Lardner, Jr., and Betty Reinhardt (based on Vera Caspary's novel), starring Gene Tierney, Dana Andrews, Clifton Webb, Vincent Price, Judith Anderson. 20th Century Fox, 1944.

Glossy, glamorous, and psychologically ambiguous, *Laura* is the Tiffany of *noir.* Scintillating socialite Tierney, molded Pygmalion-fashion from common clay by catty columnist Webb (a tour-de-force performance by this second-string Claude Rains), murdered in her penthouse apartment, becomes the obsession of homicide detective Andrews, who falls in love with her through her backstory, personal effects, and above all her painted portrait. The hardbitten cop, who when asked if he'd ever

been in love replies, "A dame in Washington Heights got a fox fur out of me once," turns hostile when the "victim" reappears from the dead (the corpse isn't hers), and fixes upon her as the principal suspect, possibly in a fit of seeming betrayal. The cast is superb, with amusing and poignant support from cad Price and jaded *doyenne* Anderson. Unlike some suspensers that attempt to jam romance into the plot, *Laura*'s romantic subtext is both integral and inevitable.

The Maltese Falcon. Directed by John Huston, written by John Huston (based on the novel by Dashiell Hammett), starring Humphrey Bogart, Mary Astor, Peter Lorre, Barton MacLane, Sydney Greenstreet, Ward Bond, Jerome Cowan, Elisha Cook, Jr. Warner, 1941.

I confess I was disappointed the first time I saw this lodestone of the genre. Since it broke ground, its many imitators made it seem like nothing new. Later I came to appreciate it for Bogart's spot-on cynicism (armor to protect his firm integrity), Lorre's eel-like smarm, Cook's murderous adolescence, and Greenstreet's chortling villainy. Astor comes off too mature and sophisticated to convince us that Bogart's Sam

Spade is truly in love with her; but Huston's insistence on breaking with Hollywood tradition and actually filming the novel (two earlier attempts had strayed and consequently failed at the box office), set a precedent that, praise be, is still with us.

Murder, My Sweet. Directed by Edward Dmytryk, written by John Paxton (based on the novel *Farewell, My Lovely,* by Raymond Chandler), starring Dick Powell, Claire Trevor, Anne Shirley, Otto Kruger, Mike Mazurki. RKO, 1944.

Powell, after an unsuccessful bid for the part that went to Fred MacMurray in *Double Indemnity,* made a triumphant switch here from lightweight musicals to crime dramas. The neon-lit opening, with Mazurki's apish face reflected enormously in Powell's night-backed window, gave the genre its seductive look. (For a more direct interpretation of Chandler's novel, snag Dick Richards's 1975 *Farewell, My Lovely;* Mitchum, born to play Philip Marlowe, should have done it twenty years earlier — but, hey, it's Mitchum! opposite slinky Charlotte Rampling, who never evoked Lauren Bacall so closely again; nor, for that matter, did Bacall. But enjoy Powell's brash Marlowe, and yet another of Trevor's deli-

cious tramps.)

Out of the Past. Directed by Jacques Tourner, written by Geoffrey Homes (Daniel Mainwaring), Frank Fenton, and James M. Cain (based on Mainwaring's novel *Build My Gallows High*), starring Robert Mitchum, Jane Greer, Kirk Douglas, Rhonda Fleming, Steve Brodie, Virginia Huston, Dickie Moore. RKO, 1947.

This is *numero uno* on most aficionados' lists. I agree as to the players: Vintage Mitchum, that sleepy, dangerous panther; Greer's smoldering beauty; Douglas establishing his chummy-snake brand of perfidy early in his career; and Moore's eloquent silence as Mitchum's mute confidant. It was a mistake, however, to place Fleming's and Greer's scenes in San Francisco back-to-back, as two brunettes in updos (Greer's hair is down on her shoulders everywhere else), confusing these two scheming females in the viewer's mind and snarling the plot. That said, this is fine Greek tragedy, in which a single lapse in judgment leads to five violent deaths. This is what would have befallen Bogart's Spade had he refused to "send over" Brigid O'Shaughnessy in *Falcon* (although with due respect to Astor's

310

charms, I'd have a harder time dumping Greer).

Pitfall. Directed by André de Toth, written by William and André de Toth and Karl Kamb (based on the novel by Jay Dratler), starring Dick Powell, Lizabeth Scott, Jane Wyatt, Raymond Burr, Byron Barr. United Artists, 1948.

Powell's an insurance investigator and a restless family man trying to collect insured goods stolen by jailed thief Barr and given to girlfriend Scott. Powell and Scott begin an extramarital affair, to the intense displeasure of sleazy private eye Burr, in one of Burr's most threatening "heavy" (physically and figuratively) turns. To satisfy the Production Code, Powell must pay for his infidelity; but his penalty is the crux of a riveting and completely plausible plot. Wyatt, best remembered as Robert Young's faithful *hausfrau* in TV's *Father Knows Best,* excels as the dishonored wife: first furious, then defensively manipulative, finally resolved to pick up the pieces of a shattered marriage. (Powell's best, bitterest line: "How does it feel to be a decent, respectable married man?")

Too Late for Tears. Directed by Byron Haskin, written by Roy Huggins (based on

his novel), starring Lizabeth Scott, Don De-Fore, Dan Duryea, Arthur Kennedy, Kristine Miller, Barry Kelley. United Artists, 1949.

Scott and Duryea are the dream team. Her Jane Palmer will sacrifice anything, even her spouse (another solid contribution from the undervalued Kennedy), for the satchel of cash that accidentally falls in her lap. The magic moment comes when Duryea, whose screen persona has been aptly described as "a lady-slapping heel" — a nasty gigolo always out for the main chance — realizes that when it comes to pitiless determination, Scott is way out of his league.

Touch of Evil. Directed by Orson Welles, written by Welles (based on the novel *Badge of Evil* by Whit Masterson), starring Charlton Heston, Janet Leigh, Orson Welles, Joseph Calleia, Akim Tamiroff, Marlene Dietrich, Dennis Weaver, Mercedes McCambridge, Zsa Zsa Gabor. Universal, 1958.

Gloriously overheated, with enough deep-seared images to support a dozen *noirs,* Welles's best film after *Citizen Kane* makes full use of the innovations he brought to Hollywood (and for which the industry

never forgave him) to show this movement out with a bang. Heston's often ridiculed for playing a Mexican, but his dignified aspect and stony resolve to see justice prevail do more honor to the race than so many Hispanics habitually cast as moronic bandits and comic relief. This is a stunning double-play, with Welles bringing all his genius to the direction and also to the part of the loathsome Detective Quinlan. Leigh as victim is far from helpless, Weaver's bats**t motel manager is unique in cinema, and Dietrich's border-town madam provides the Greek chorus. Despite what's been said about the so-called "director's cut" — ostensibly based posthumously on Welles's production notes — watch the theatrical version first. That brilliant opening long take is more dramatic with the title crawl included.

White Heat. Directed by Raoul Walsh, written by Ivan Goff and Ben Roberts (based on a story by Virginia Kellogg), starring James Cagney, Virginia Mayo, Edmond O'Brien, Margaret Wycherly, Steve Cochran, Fred Clark. Warner, 1949.

Cagney's masterpiece. His Cody Jarrett, a Dillinger-type gangleader, albeit saddled with paranoid/schizophrenic tendencies and

the mother of all Oedipus complexes, is nevertheless charismatic and impossible not to root for; especially with undercover cop O'Brien worming his way into his confidence in order to betray him. This is what would have come of Tom Powers, Cagney's breakthrough role in *The Public Enemy,* had he survived Prohibition. Mayo is *fatale* as all get-out as his floozy wife, Cochran unforgettable as his rival for gang leadership. Raoul's past as a director of classic westerns soups up the action from the opening shot of a charging locomotive all the way to the explosive finish, leaving no place to go out for popcorn.

So many more *noirs;* and our running time is so short. Happy hunting!

ABOUT THE AUTHOR

Loren D. Estleman has written more than eighty books — historical novels, mysteries, and westerns. Winner of four Shamus Awards, five Spur Awards, and three Western Heritage Awards, he lives in Central Michigan with his wife, author Deborah Morgan.

that was about all he did. He didn't talk much to folks except in a whisper sometimes, and in school the teacher put him with the kids who were just starting. But Marcus sure could draw. Once he had drawn right on the back of the seat in front of them during the picture show. So now Lorraine had to take his drawing things away.

As they stepped inside, she was glad to see that there were still plenty of empty seats. It was a Saturday afternoon show, so almost everybody in the theater was a kid. The grown-ups would come to the evening show at seven o'clock.

Lorraine

There weren't so many boys here as usual. Probably because this movie was supposed to be a love story. *Kate of the Highlands* was the name of it. That was all right with Lorraine. Personally, she didn't understand why Nancy was so interested in boys. All they did was roughhouse and make loud jokes. Except for Marcus, of course.

Anyway, the star of *Kate of the Highlands* was Lorraine's very favorite movie actress—Nell Aldrich. Lorraine never missed one of her pictures. Once, when Nell's picture was on the cover of a movie magazine, Lorraine begged Momma for fifteen cents

MOTION PICTURE

AUGUST – 25 CTS

Do You Believe
in
Fortune Telling?
See Page 37

Hollywood's
Greatest
Love Story
See Page 20

The Thing That Makes Them Great

so she could buy it. She had the cover tacked to the wall over the bed she and Nancy shared.

The magazine had a long article about Nell. She lived out in California, where all the movie stars did. She was very rich, of course. The magazine said she got $100,000 for making a movie. Lorraine couldn't quite imagine that much money. She had told Daddy about it, and he laughed. "You could buy this whole town of Pickettsville, Georgia, with that," he said. "And have enough left over to tear it all down and build it up again."

According to the article, Nell lived in a big house with a swimming pool and a garden. Her house had twenty-six rooms in it—even though she lived by herself, except for the servants.

The house Lorraine's family lived in had only four rooms, if you counted the kitchen. That was big enough for five people. Lorraine thought it might be nice to have her own bedroom, but she had to admit she had no idea what she would do with twenty-six rooms.

Of course Nell had lots of parties. Lorraine had read about them too, and she thought she could imagine what it would be like to go to one. All the big stars would drive up in their fancy automobiles. They'd show off their gowns and jewels as they walked up the steps. Inside there would be musicians playing whatever you wanted all the time. Food too. Lorraine thought about the tables filled with cakes and ice cream and all those foods with French names. It seemed like food with French names must be better than regular food.

Lorraine and Marcus were able to get seats right in the front row. Lorraine leaned over and saw Mrs. Green, the piano player, sit down and get her sheet music ready. She played music that went along with each scene in the movie. If the scene was exciting, she played fast. If it was scary, the music sounded that way, too.

Marcus

Mrs. Green turned and looked up at the back of the theater. She gave a little nod. Lorraine knew that she was signaling Mr. Soileau that he could start the movie anytime. The lights started to dim and Lorraine settled back in her seat.

In this movie, Nell played a girl who lived in a farmhouse with her grandfather. Every day she went out with her collie dog and took the sheep up

JAFFREY GRADE SCHOOL
LIBRARY

on the side of a mountain. There were mountains all around. It was very beautiful.

Lorraine sat in the darkness and imagined what it must be like to live in such a place. She'd never seen a mountain, except in pictures. That was one of the best things about going to the movies: It was a way of getting out of Pickettsville. For a week afterward, Lorraine would live in the place she'd seen in the Saturday afternoon movie.

The mountains in the movie didn't stay peaceful for long. Nothing ever did in a Nell Aldrich movie. She always got into trouble of some sort. That was what made people like her so much, Lorraine thought. It wasn't just that she was beautiful and kind. It was that mean people treated her so badly.

And pretty soon, here came some soldiers marching into the valley where Nell and her grandfather lived. They had come to tax the people or take some of their sheep. Maybe both. It wasn't quite clear. But they were up to no good business, as Lorraine's grandmother used to say.

Nell had a boyfriend in the movie. He was a hothead, and joined a group of other young men to fight the soldiers. He reminded Lorraine a little bit of Daddy. Except that Daddy didn't have any group of people to meet with. But he was angry, like Nell's boyfriend in the movie.

Daddy had been a soldier in the Great War, back in 1918. Lorraine had only been two years old then, so she didn't remember. But Momma said he had come back changed from the war. He'd gone to France, where the fighting had been. The way Lorraine understood it, Daddy and the other American soldiers beat the Germans who had invaded France. Afterward, Daddy had stayed around for a while because the white soldiers got to go home first.

In France, the people didn't treat Negroes the way they did in Georgia. Once Daddy and some of his friends went into a restaurant. Not some lunch counter like the one where Moses Crandall served catfish sandwiches and home fries. A fancy one with white linen tablecloths and silverware. Daddy liked to tell the children about it.

"Three forks next to each plate," Daddy would always say. He ticked them off on his fingers: "One for the salad, one for the fish, and one for the pie." Well that was hard to believe, but not so much as the story that the waiters and the other customers were all white. And they never turned a hair when four black-faced Americans sat down to eat in the same room.

"That was when your Daddy went crazy," Momma told the children. She didn't really mean it, Lorraine knew. But it was probably crazy to come back to Pickettsville and think that it ought to be like France. Which is what Daddy did.

Lorraine was jolted out of her thoughts by a burst of loud piano music. In the movie, Nell had closed the door on a soldier who wanted her to be his girlfriend. He wasn't a good sport about it. He was the sort who wouldn't take no for an answer. So he came back with some other soldiers and set the house on fire.

Lorraine knew that things would get worse before they got better. And they did. Nell tried to get her grandfather out of the house, but he was weak and couldn't see. The soldiers broke inside and dragged her out, leaving him behind.

Nell was thrown over the back of a horse, and the soldiers rode off. Meanwhile, Nell's boyfriend saw the smoke of the burning house. He and his friends came running and managed to save the grandfather after all. He told them what had happened, and took hold of the boyfriend's arm. You couldn't hear what he said, but the words appeared on the screen: "She loves you, my boy. You must save her!"

Things got pretty exciting after that. The people who lived in the valley got out the guns and swords they'd been hiding. Now they rushed after the soldiers, who had gone back to their fort and locked Nell in a room in a tower.

Anybody else would have been a righteous mess after riding upside down on a horse. But Nell looked more beautiful than ever. She stood on a chair to look out the window. When she saw the men coming, she waved. Her boyfriend went right into action. He threw a rope up to the window and Nell tied it to the bars.

Just then, one of the soldiers came around and saw what was happening. He raised an alarm and a fight broke out. You couldn't hear the shots of the rifles or muskets. You just saw puffs of smoke that let you know the guns were going off. But Mrs. Green hammered that piano so hard that Lorraine felt she was right in the middle of the battle.

The daring boyfriend climbed the rope up to the window. He took a knife from his belt and dug one of the bars loose. Quick as a fish's tail, the boyfriend picked Nell up and slid down the rope with her. Lorraine had seen movie heroes do tricks like that with their sweethearts a hundred times. She wished she could talk some boy into trying that from the loft of old Mr. Ferris's barn. It seemed like the one thing that would make having a boyfriend worthwhile.

Well, the soldiers in the movie lost the battle. Nell and her boyfriend rode up into the mountains. Everybody in the theater knew what the last scene would be. The boys in the audience started groaning and hissing even before Nell and her boyfriend looked soulfully at each other and kissed.

It didn't last too long. The screen filled up with some more words. . . . "And so, the soldiers.

left the highlands, retreating before the stout hearts of brave men. Tyranny is driven out, as it must in every place where men yearn to be free."

Lorraine knew what Daddy would say to that. "Why not in Pickettsville?" He was always quoting from this newspaper he got in the mail. It said that Negroes ought to be standing up for their rights. Daddy even refused to go to the movie show because there was separate seating for Negroes and whites.

Just like there was everywhere else in town. "That's just the way it is," Momma would say with a shrug. But Daddy would reply, "It don't have to be."

T W O

Daddy on Trial

MARCH 4–MARCH 31, 1927

AFTER THE MOVIE ENDED, LORRAINE AND MARCUS waited for everyone to clear out. When Mr. Soileau had caught him drawing on the seat back, Marcus agreed to sweep up the theater as punishment. Since then, Marcus had been doing it every Saturday. Mr. Soileau was happy because he didn't have to pay someone. Marcus didn't mind because he discovered that he could pick up gum wrappers and empty popcorn bags. He used them as drawing paper.

The five-and-dime sold school notebooks and blank paper, of course. But Marcus filled those up so fast that Momma didn't have the money to buy him enough. Even at school the teacher had to limit him to five sheets of paper a week.

The teacher said that if Marcus worked as hard at writing or arithmetic as he did at drawing, he might make something of himself. When Daddy heard that, it sort of set him off. "What kind of talk is that?" he said. "Who's to say he can't make something of himself by drawing?" The family had just sat down to dinner.

"Where's he going to do that?" Momma asked.

"Anywhere they need drawings," Daddy replied. "Look here in this Sears catalog. It has hundreds and hundreds of drawings of the things they sell. Who do you think drew them?"

"Somebody not from around here," Momma said.

"Remember when I went off to fight in the Great War?" Daddy asked.

"We all remember that, John Henry, even the children because you've told us so often."

"I didn't know a thing about automobiles then, did I?" he went on.

"No, you didn't."

"But I learned how to fix trucks in the army," he said, poking a finger onto the palm of his left hand. He did that when he was explaining things. "And trucks are just the same thing. So when I came back here, I was the only person in Pick-ettsville who knew how an auto-mobile worked."

"And that's how you were able to get work fixing cars," Momma finished. "Yes, John Henry, we all know that story. But what does it have to do with Marcus?"

John Henry

Daddy poked his finger into his palm again. "It means that if he learns something that other people can't do, he can always find work." He nod ded his head firmly as if the argument was settled. "Please pass the sweet potatoes, Lorraine," he said.

So Marcus went right on drawing and paying little attention to anything else. Right now, he and Lorraine headed for home. Marcus was smooth-ing out the paper bags and candy wrappers he had picked up at the theater. He pointed to the little pocketbook Lorraine carried. "G'me," he said. She knew that meant, "Give me one of the things I draw with."

She reached into the pocketbook. He never used chalk on paper, so she asked, "You want a crayon or a pencil?"

19

"'cil," he replied, and she handed him one.

He stopped and sat down right at the side of the road. Nothing could budge Marcus when he got the urge to draw. Lorraine knew she could either go on home or wait for him to finish. She decided she might as well watch to see what he'd draw. She was curious.

He split open a popcorn bag and spread it flat, smoothing out the wrinkles as well as he could. He drew a rectangle in one corner of the paper, and then a long line leading all the way down to the opposite corner. He worked quickly. It was as if he had an idea and couldn't wait to get it onto the paper.

Lorraine soon saw what he was drawing. It was the scene from the movie when the boyfriend slid down the rope with Nell Aldrich. Marcus caught it just right. He didn't try to draw every single thing—just the important parts. He filled in just enough so that you could imagine the rest. At the end, he put in their faces. With a few lines, he captured the shape of their features. Anybody who had seen the movie would have recognized them.

"You're really good, Marcus," Lorraine told him as he held up the picture. "Can I have that for my wall?"

He shook his head a little. Turning the picture over, he pointed to the blank side. Lorraine laughed. She understood. He wanted to fill that up with another picture. Marcus didn't like to waste paper.

They turned onto the dirt road that led to the part of town where they lived. The houses here were smaller. Most of them needed a coat of paint, and some had their outside walls covered with tar paper. The yards were mostly plain dirt—no grass except some weeds. But there were flower beds aflame with bright red geraniums, yellow marigolds, and orange nasturtiums. Blue morning glories climbed up the sides of the houses. At night, you could walk along here and say hello to all the neighbors who were sitting on the front porches to catch a cool breeze. Lorraine thought it was a good place to live.

Their own house was like the others, except maybe a little prettier, Lorraine thought. Momma had hung gingham curtains in the front windows, and Daddy gave the whole house a coat of white-wash once a year.

As she and Marcus approached, the screen door suddenly flew open. Their older sister Nancy stood there, waving for them to hurry up. Something was the matter. All sorts of fears popped into Lorraine's head. Had Daddy gotten hurt at his job? Momma was always worrying that one of the cars would start up while he was fixing it.

Nancy all but pulled them into the house. "Now, shut up, now," she kept saying. That was the kind of thing Nancy told Lorraine and Marcus when she was in charge. Momma must have gone out.

"What's the matter?" Lorraine asked. "What's going on?"

"It's Daddy," said Nancy. She put her hands up to her face. "I don't know what we're going to do," she said. "The sheriff came and took him to jail."

Lorraine felt the way she had when she fell out of the big cottonwood tree in back of the house. She felt blood rush up behind her nose and she couldn't breathe. She managed to say, "What?" but it came out like a squeak.

Nancy

Lorraine took hold of Nancy's arms and pressed hard. "Why?" she said this time.

Nancy really didn't know much more. The sheriff had come in an automobile and taken Daddy away. Before they left, Daddy told Momma to go see Mr. Daniels. He owned the filling station where Daddy worked.

"Then let's go there," said Lorraine.

"No!" said Nancy. "Daddy told me to keep you and Marcus at home."

"But I want to find out what happened," Lorraine said.

Just then the front door opened. Momma stood there, looking the way she had when Grandmomma had died. Lorraine felt the blood behind her nose again. Something terrible was going on.

Frances

Momma sat down and told them what she'd found out. Mr. Daniels said that Daddy had been working on a car yesterday. "A regular old Model T Ford," Momma said.

"Oh, Momma, Daddy wouldn't make a mistake on a Model T," said Lorraine. "There isn't a thing he doesn't know about those cars."

"Wasn't a mistake," said Momma. "The man who owned it said he had left a wallet inside the car. When he picked the car up the wallet was gone. They say your Daddy stole it."

Lorraine and Nancy both shouted, "That's not so!" And Marcus shook his head as hard as he could.

"Daddy would never steal," said Lorraine. "He always taught us stealing was wrong."

"I know that," Momma said angrily. "Don't you think I know that?"

"The wallet must have gotten lost," Lorraine suggested. "Somebody will find it."

Her mother looked at her hard. "The man who says his wallet was stolen is Jefferson Willis."

The children thought about that for a second. Jefferson Willis was somebody they'd learned to stay clear of. Lorraine had seen him steer his car way over to the side of the road to make black kids jump into the ditch. Folks said he was the leader of the Ku Klux Klan in Pickettsville. One thing was sure: He was a nasty man who didn't mind telling people he didn't like Negroes.

"Well, I'll bet he's lying," Lorraine said.

"Hush up that talk," Nancy told her.

Lorraine paid no attention. "In fact, I'll bet you Mr. Daniels *knows* he's lying," she went on.

Momma just sighed. "He might, yes."

"So why doesn't he say so?"

Momma looked down for a minute, as if she were thinking. "Your Daddy is just too uppity for some folks," she said.

"But Mr. Daniels likes him. Daddy works for him."

"That's true," Momma said, nodding. "But no white man is going to take the side of a black man against another white man. Least, not in Pickettsville, Georgia."

Momma was right. They had a trial, but it wasn't much as far as Lorraine could see. She was up in the balcony of the courtroom with Momma and Nancy and Marcus. Jefferson Willis sat down on the stand next to the judge and said that his wallet had been stolen out of the car. The way he told it, his wallet had over fifty dollars in it.

Mr. Daniels came up next and said John Henry Dixon—Daddy—was the only person who'd been inside the car that day. Lorraine noticed Mr. Daniels wouldn't look at Daddy when he said that.

When they let Daddy speak, he said he never saw any wallet in or out of the automobile. Momma nodded as he spoke. But then he added something else. "I think everybody in this room knows that Jefferson Willis never carried fifty dollars in his wallet any time in his life," Daddy said. Momma just put her head down then and looked at the floor. Lorraine knew why. Daddy was foolish to say that, even though everybody knew it was true. A black man just wasn't allowed to say something bad about a white man.

Later on, they got to visit Daddy in jail. He'd already been found guilty. The judge had sentenced him to a year on the county work farm. That meant he would wear a suit with big black and white stripes and work at digging or paving roads or cutting down weeds and such. Lorraine had seen the work gangs along the roads sometimes. Their legs were chained so they could walk, but not run. She hated to think of Daddy that way.

Daddy kept his head high when they visited. He told them they mustn't worry about him. "I never minded hard work, and it's not going to hurt me," he said. "I'm more worried about all of you."

"We'll be fine," Momma said. "I can sew and cook for people. Nancy and Lorraine can earn some money, too. They're old enough to leave school."

"That's not what I mean," said Daddy. "I don't want you staying here in Pickettsville."

They were surprised. "Why not?" asked Momma.

"Someone warned me that Jefferson Willis isn't satisfied with sending me to the work farm. He's aiming to get at me by hurting you."

They sat in silence for a moment. Everyone knew that the Klan could do whatever it wanted. It had burned down houses, taken people into the woods and whipped them, even lynched a man a few years ago, Lorraine had heard.

"Where are we supposed to go?" asked Momma.

"Reverend Parish came by to see me," said Daddy. "He knows somebody up in Chicago who will give you a place to stay."

Chicago! The name sent a shiver down Lorraine's back. After dinner, Daddy would often read them stories about Chicago from a newspaper he got in the mail—the Chicago *Defender*. It was owned and written by Negroes, he said. It made Chicago sound like the best place in the world. But Momma always said you couldn't tell what was true until you saw it for yourself.

Well, now she'd get the chance.

Momma raised some objections, but Daddy had thought of everything. He had already put away money for their train tickets. "I'd been planning to move us all there anyway," he said. "I just waited too long. So now you all go on without me."

"We can't leave you, Daddy," Lorraine said.

"It's only for a year," he told her. "This time next March I'll join you in Chicago."

Lorraine looked at Momma, who was trying not to cry. "I'm going to hold you to that promise, John Henry," said Momma. "I'll come right back and get you myself."

But they all knew what she was really thinking. If Jefferson Willis could hurt Daddy some way, he'd still do it when Daddy was in the work farm.

He gave them all a big hug before they left.

THREE

A Long Ride

APRIL 2, 1927

THINGS MOVED FAST AFTER THAT. REVEREND PARISH said it was best that they leave right away. They packed two cardboard suitcases with all the clothes that would fit. The rest, they'd have to leave behind.

Lorraine took down the picture of Nell Aldrich and put it into a little box with some other things. A diamond ring that Daddy had won for her at a fair, a gold star that the teacher had given her for being the best speller in the school, and a four-leaf clover that she'd found and pressed. She hoped it would bring her good luck, but so far things hadn't turned out well.

Daddy being in jail was about the worst luck she could imagine.

They thought that Marcus would make a fuss when Momma said he couldn't take all his drawings. He had stacks of them under his bed. "Maybe a few pictures," Momma said. "But we haven't got room for all of them."

A funny thing happened, though. The night before they left, Marcus took all his pictures out in the backyard. Without telling anybody, he set them on fire. Lorraine smelled the smoke and ran outside. She couldn't believe what she saw. "You could have saved a few of them," she told Marcus. "You had drawings of lots of our friends." He just looked at her and shook his head.

Well, they were his drawings after all, she decided. She worried a little how Marcus was going to get along without Daddy. Daddy always defended him when people didn't understand the way he was.

They were up bright and early the next day. It was strange to think this was the last time they'd ever eat breakfast in their house. Lorraine couldn't remember ever living anyplace else.

Already the house seemed dull and empty without Daddy. Momma walked through the rooms, fretting and pointing to things. "Maybe we shouldn't leave that behind," she said.

They might have stayed there all morning and missed the train. But then they heard a horse and buggy stop in front of the house. It was Reverend Parish, come to take them to the station. He gave Momma a slip of paper with the name and address of the person they would stay with in Chicago. "You'll have to take a taxicab from the train station," he said.

Momma shook her head at the thought of it. "I don't know how we'll make it," she said. "Maybe we should just stay here after all."

But Reverend Parish told her Daddy was right. "John Henry will feel better knowing you're safe," he told Momma. He had brought them a basket with fried chicken that some ladies who belonged to the church had made. Momma just about cried when she saw that.

They arrived at the station with plenty of time to spare, and went into the colored waiting room. Momma went off with Reverend Parish to buy the tickets. Lorraine sat down and thought about the journey. She had seen trains go by every day of her life, and often wondered what it would be like to ride one. Late at night, she sometimes woke up to hear the

Valentino on the cover. He had died last year, when he was only thirty-one, but was still popular.

"Momma! That's so nice!" said Lorraine. Then she thought about it. "Where'd all this money come from? I thought Daddy had saved just enough for the tickets."

"Don't you worry where it came from," said Momma.

Lorraine still wondered, but she settled back in her seat and started to read the magazine. The trip to Chicago was supposed to take two and a half days, so there would be plenty of time for looking out the window.

In fact, after she finished reading the whole magazine, the view out the window looked exactly the same, except the sun was higher in the sky. There was still a farmer plowing his land, red and sticky clay that stretched as far as Lorraine could see.

Marcus had been hard at work, though. Lorraine saw that he had covered several pages with things she had barely noticed—a couple of crows pecking at something in a field, a mule straining to pull a plow, and even . . . Well! There was Lorraine herself!

She was hidden behind the pages of her magazine, but Marcus had drawn the dress she was wearing, pulled down over her knees as she crossed her legs on the seat. Just the top of her head peeped out from above the magazine.

Somebody else said what Lorraine was thinking. "Your little boy's quite an artist." Lorraine looked up to see a tall, heavy-set man standing in the aisle, looking at Momma. Lorraine was struck by how well he was dressed: a light tan linen suit, cream-colored shirt with a yellow-and-brown striped tie, and a straw hat with a yellow band. She wondered how he could afford such fine clothes.

"Yes, thank you," Momma said to him.

"Has he received any training?"

Momma seemed confused for a moment, unsure what he meant by "training."

"We sent all the children to school," she replied.

"But not a school devoted especially to nurturing artists?"

Momma looked over at Marcus, as if the thought startled her. "No, no," she said. "There aren't any schools like that around where we live."

"And where would that be?"

Lorraine was getting a little uncomfortable. The man was asking too many questions. She glanced at Nancy to see if she felt the same, but Nancy was just gaping at the man as if he'd been

Rudolph Valentino. Nancy couldn't see past the fancy clothes.

Marcus could, though. Lorraine saw him hunt through the crayons and pick out one that was the same color as the man's suit. While Marcus set to work, Lorraine turned back to listen to the conversation.

"Chicago?" the man was saying. "I hope you have someone to meet you at the station."

Momma nodded. "Yes, we do. We wouldn't think of going there otherwise."

"And of course, a place to stay."

"Yes, certainly," said Momma.

"You can't be too careful in a place like Chicago," said the man.

"Oh, yes, I know *that*." Momma said.

"I have an office in Chicago," he told her. He reached into one of his vest pockets. "Here's my card. Henderson is my name. Franklin Henderson. Should you need any help, you can call on me."

Momma hesitated, but took the card from his outstretched hand.

Franklin Henderson

"Our people must stick together," Mr. Henderson said.

"That's what my husband says," Momma replied.

Just then Marcus turned his notebook around so that Lorraine could see it. She covered her mouth to stifle a laugh.

Mr. Henderson noticed. "Have you drawn something else, my young man?" he said to Marcus. "Would you show it to me?"

With an innocent expression, Marcus tilted the notebook toward Mr. Henderson. Lorraine had already seen the drawing, so she watched the man's face. His big, hearty smile quivered a bit. It seemed to Lorraine as if his neck swelled and filled his shirt collar like a balloon.

The drawing showed Mr. Henderson—or at least a man dressed in the same color clothing. But his face was different from the real-life model. Marcus had given him a smile that stretched from ear to ear, and eyes that looked like a pig's when it's about to get a bucket of slops. It certainly was not flattering.

Mr. Henderson forced a smile anyway. He tipped his hat to Momma and said, "A very talented child you have. I'm pleased to make your acquaintance, Mrs.—?"

"Dixon," said Momma. "I'm Mrs. Dixon, and these are my children, Nancy, Lorraine, and Marcus."

The man gave them a nod and then moved down the aisle of the car.

"Momma, why'd you speak to that man?" Lorraine said as soon as he was out of earshot. "I thought you told us never to speak to strangers."

"Well, he was a bit forward, it's true," Momma said. "But he was probably raised in a city. Things are different there. People don't have the same manners that we do in the country."

"He kept asking you questions! You told him our names."

"Well, Miss Big Ears, since you were listening so close, you probably heard I told him someone was going to meet us in Chicago."

"Yes, why'd you do that?"

"So he wouldn't think we were alone and help-less."

Lorraine thought that over. Maybe Momma was more careful than Lorraine had thought. "What does it say on his card?"

Momma looked at it. "Says, 'Franklin Henderson. Real Estate, Insurance, Investigations.'"

"That's a lot of businesses. What do you think investigations means?"

"He finds things out," said Momma. "Maybe he finds things that are lost."

"Oh, I'd like to do that," said Lorraine. "Remember when I found Daddy's pocketknife? After he spent the whole day looking for it?"

"Yes, I remember," Momma said.

Lorraine had figured out that Daddy had sat down on the front steps to take his shoes off. And the knife had slipped out of his pocket and fallen under the steps. That would be pretty good work, if you could get paid for something like that.

Marcus leaned over and whispered in Momma's ear. She sighed. "All right, Marcus, you can go look for it. But don't you get in any trouble. Leave that notebook right here."

Marcus squeezed past Momma and went down the aisle.

"Where's he going?" asked Lorraine.

"Needs to use the privy," said Momma.

"They have one on the train?"

"'Course they do. What'd you think?"

"I figured you have to wait till it stopped at a station. I want to go, too." She stood up to see where Marcus was.

"You wait now till your brother comes back. I don't want you both running around the train."

A few minutes later, Marcus returned. Happily, he held up a roll of clean white paper. Nancy giggled. "Get rid of that, get rid of it," she said.

"What's that?" asked Lorraine.

"It's paper for the privy," Momma hissed. She snatched it out of Marcus's hand and gave it to Lorraine. "Put it back," she told her. "Don't let anybody see you."

Well, that was going to be a problem, Lorraine thought as she stepped into the aisle. Most of the seats were filled. As she walked to the end of the car, she felt like everybody was looking at her carrying the roll of paper.

But when she found the privy, she could see why Marcus had made a mistake. It wasn't like the privy back home, which was in a shed in the backyard. This one had a little sink that you could wash in. Two handles on top of it. She wondered why until she discovered cold water came out of one and hot from the other. At home the only way to get hot water was to pump cold water into a pan and then heat it on the stove. And of course the only paper they had in the privy was from old newspapers or the Sears catalog.

However, the privy turned out to be the only thing on the train that was better than home. They finished the basket of chicken the first day. After that they had to buy sandwiches. Food vendors came aboard for a few minutes at the larger train stations. They charged a lot—twenty-five cents a sandwich, but the bread was stale and the inside nothing but a slice or two of yellow cheese or peanut butter. The vendors sold iced tea, too, but when Momma heard it cost a dime a cup, she decided they'd get by without. There were paper cups in the privy, and the sink water didn't taste bad.

At night, the overhead lights in the car were dimmed. The passengers had to sleep in the wicker seats. For a long time Lorraine looked into the darkness outside the window. Once in a while she saw a light from a farmhouse or a little town. It made her feel lonely, and she wondered what Daddy was doing.

By the middle of their third day on the train, they were all feeling sticky and stiff. Lorraine had read her magazine so often that the pages were starting to tear. She decided she would never get on another train in her life. It was just like a prison, except that a prison couldn't crash and kill everybody inside. She almost wished the train *would* crash, so at least something different would happen.

At last, the conductor came through the car and called out, "Chicago! Illinois Central Station! Last stop! Take your belongings with you when you leave the train!"

This would be different, Lorraine thought. She had no idea how right she was.

FOUR

Making Money

IN THE MOVIE THEATER IN PICKETTSVILLE, SOME-times Mr. Soileau would speed up the movie. Or maybe the movie was made that way on purpose. So Charlie Chaplin or Harold Lloyd or one of the other comedy stars would begin to walk very fast. And all of the automobiles, streetcars, and the other people in the movie speeded up too.

Chicago was like that. Right from the time they got off the train, it seemed to Lorraine as if every-body was moving twice as fast as the people in Pickettsville. And you had to hurry just to keep up.

Lorraine asked Momma, "What's wrong with these people?"

"I don't know," said Momma. She was hurrying, too. They had to move along just as fast, or it seemed like they'd be run over.

When they entered the big waiting room at the station, it was even worse. Here, people were moving every which way—all tearing along with hardly a glance at anything around them.

There was a lot to look at too. Marcus touched Lorraine's hand and pointed up.

The ceiling was higher than any she had ever seen. Just looking at it made her feel like she was going to fall over backwards. There could have been two or three more floors inside this room without raising the roof any higher.

"G'me," said Marcus, opening his notebook.

Momma didn't notice. She was looking around, trying to figure out which way to go. Lorraine told her, "Momma, if we don't move, Marcus is going to sit right down here and draw."

Momma grabbed hold of Marcus's hand and started off toward one of the doorways. It was way bigger than it needed to be too. You could have driven a hay wagon through it. Lorraine and Nancy struggled to keep up, fighting through the crowd.

Outside was even worse. In the movies, Lorraine had seen big cities. She knew they had lots of automobiles. But she'd never seen a line of automobiles stretched in both directions with hardly a space between. She wondered how on earth people got across the street.

Chicago Train Station

Fortunately Momma had found a row of cars that had signs on top saying, "Taxi." Dragging Marcus along, she stepped up to talk to a driver. "Do you know how to get to East 32nd Street?" she asked.

He glanced up from the newspaper he was reading. "Cost you three dollars," he said.

Momma put her hand over her heart. "For each of us?"

The man laughed. "No, for the whole bunch," he said. He pointed down the street. "You could take the El for a nickel apiece."

They turned and looked. High above the street on giant steel pillars was a railroad track. Just then, a train came roaring past, its wheels screaming as it made a sharp turn.

Lorraine held her breath. She hoped Momma would take the taxi. Lorraine thought anybody who got on a railroad on tracks way up in the air had to be a crazy person.

Momma did too. "Get in the taxi," she told Lorraine and Nancy as she opened the back door.

There was only room for three in the back seat, so Lorraine sat in front next to the driver. As soon as he pulled away from the curb, she reached out for something to hold onto. She found a leather handle on the side of the door.

All the cars drove along so close to each other that Lorraine couldn't understand how they didn't collide. The driver would go forward as fast as he could and then push down on the brake just as the car in front of them stopped too.

When they reached the end of the block, the driver turned left. This street didn't have as many

Chicago streets

cars, so he was able to go even faster. But right overhead were the railroad tracks. They made Lorraine nervous, because she worried that the train would fall down and squash them flat.

The driver didn't seem worried about anything. He chewed on a toothpick and looked down at his newspaper on the seat whenever they had to stop. Sometimes Lorraine saw him looking at the newspaper even when the taxi was moving. Once she let out a cry when a car suddenly cut them off.

The driver gave her a look. "First time you ever in a car?" he asked.

Actually it was, but Lorraine said, "They don't drive like this where we come from."

He chuckled. "I'll betcha. All horses and mules."

Lorraine was stung. "My daddy *fixes* automobiles. He learned how in the war."

"Well," said the driver, "he can get plenty of work up here. Ford's paying fifty dollars a week now, and you only have to work eight hours a day. I don't know why I'm driving a cab when I could get work like that."

Fifty dollars a week! Lorraine was amazed. Daddy only got twenty at the garage. And he had to work from seven in the morning till six at night. "Where is the Ford factory?" she asked.

"Oh, it's outside of Detroit," said the driver. "If he wants a job in Chicago, tell him to try Pullman, making railroad cars. Just stay away from Armour's."

"What's Armour's?"

"The stockyards," he told her. "The slaughtering pens. Biggest and worst place in the world."

That made her curious. "Where is it?"

"Over there." He pointed off to their right. "You can't see it, but you'll be able to smell it all right. When the wind blows from that direction, the only place you can catch your breath is on the lake." He pointed in the other direction. "Over there."

Lorraine leaned her head out the window and sniffed. The air smelled like something old had burned up. "Is there a fire in the stockyards?" she asked.

"Nah, today's a good day," the driver told her. "The wind is coming from the lake."

She wondered what it must be like on a bad day.

After what seemed like a long time, the driver finally pulled the taxi to the curb. "This is the address you gave me," he said over his shoulder to Momma.

Lorraine looked out the window, amazed. "Momma, this can't be the right place," she said. The car stood in front of the largest and grandest house she'd ever seen. The only building this large in Pickettsville was the courthouse. "It looks like some rich family lives here."

"Used to be," said the driver. "Lots of rich people lived in this neighborhood. Marshall Field, the department store owner, lived not far away. But now the houses are all divided up inside. This is just a boardinghouse."

He was right. But it was pretty nice, all the same. Olive Waits, the woman who ran it, was expecting them. Reverend Parish had sent her a letter. She was a wiry woman who smiled a lot. "We're going to be just fine, yes sir," she kept saying.

She led them up a big circular staircase. Marcus kept poking Lorraine as they walked up to the third floor. He wanted her to notice the pretty stained-glass windows at each landing. You could tell that some rich family must have lived here once.

"I'm giving you two rooms," Mrs. Waits said. "But they're right next door to each other." Each room had two small beds in it, along with a chest of drawers and a chair. "The bathroom is down at the end of the hall," Mrs. Waits told them. Marcus started down there right away, but Lorraine caught him. "Leave the paper alone," she warned.

"Each room is six dollars a week," said Mrs. Waits. "That includes breakfast and dinner, which are served downstairs. No lunch."

Momma nodded. "Reverend Parish said you could help me find work."

"Oh, yes, we can do that, yes sir," said Mrs. Waits. "Can you type?"

Momma shook her head.

"Then housework of some kind would be best," said Mrs. Waits.

"I can cook, clean, and sew," said Momma.

"Would you be able to look after children?"

Momma smiled. "You see these three? They look all right to you?"

"I have some possibilities," said Mrs. Waits. She lowered her voice and leaned close. "If anyone asks, you should tell them your husband is dead."

Momma's eyes opened wide. "I can't do that! Why would I do that?"

"Because when you work in someone's home, you have to be trustworthy. If they know your husband is in prison—" Mrs. Waits shook her head.

"I see," said Momma.

"I'll leave you to settle in now. We're going to be just fine, yes sir," said Mrs. Waits.

As they unpacked, Lorraine asked, "You aren't going to tell anybody Daddy's dead, are you?"

"Heavens no," said Momma. "If you start something with a lie, it will never finish well. Remember who you heard that from?"

"Daddy."

"He's right too."

"But what if no one will hire you? How are we going to live if we run out of money?"

"Trust in the Lord, Lorraine," Momma said.

Lorraine knew that was right, but she could also remember Daddy saying, "The Lord helps those who help themselves."

After the long train ride, Lorraine thought she'd have no trouble sleeping. But there were a lot of strange noises here. Cars were going back and forth below their window, and people walked by talking loudly till late at night. Sirens woke her up a couple of times, and bright lights from a restaurant across the street shone through the flimsy curtains. It was exciting, but scary too.

For some reason, Lorraine remembered her four-leaf clover. She got up and tried to find it. But when she turned on the light, Nancy woke up. "What are you doing? Go to sleep, go to sleep," Nancy mumbled.

So Lorraine lay awake in the darkness for a long time. Maybe it was silly to think a four-leaf clover would bring you luck, she thought. "God helps those who helps themselves," Daddy said. But what could she do to help now? She still had not thought of anything when she fell asleep.

The next day, Momma was off bright and early to look for work. Nancy thought she might get a job too, so she went along. Mrs. Waits told Momma she'd keep an eye on Lorraine and Marcus.

But after breakfast she just shooed them outside. "Enjoy the fresh air," she said. "The wind's blowing from the lake. There's a park a few blocks over that way. Be careful and everything will be just fine, yes sir."

Lorraine didn't mind. Chicago had plenty of things to see, even if you didn't go very far. It was like Pickettsville in one way, she noticed. All the colored people lived in one part of town. There just were a lot more of them here.

And everything else was better than in any part of Pickettsville. She saw three movie theaters before they had walked two blocks. There was a candy store, two five-and-dimes, half a dozen fruit and vegetable stores, a butcher shop, and too many restaurants to count.

Some of the restaurants had counters right on the street where you could step up and eat. Every restaurant seemed to be named for someplace else—Louisiana Catfish, Kansas City Barbecue, Georgia Fried Chicken, Mississippi Chitlins. Maybe that was because people liked best the food from where they grew up.

Breakfast at the boardinghouse hadn't been very big, and the smell of all this food on the street was making Lorraine hungry. Trouble was, she and Marcus didn't have any money.

Of course that didn't matter to Marcus, because he could draw. He kept wanting to stop, so Lorraine finally let him sit right down on the sidewalk.

A boy selling newspapers stopped to see what Marcus was up to. Marcus quickly sketched a picture of him and the boy laughed. "That's pretty good," he said.

Lorraine saw a familiar face on the front page of one of the newspapers. "Can I see that?" she asked the boy.

"If you got a nickel, you can have it," he said.

"I haven't got a nickel. I just want to look at it."

"You can look at it under my arm." He thought this was funny.

"I don't mean that. I want to read it. I won't hurt it any. You can sell it to somebody else."

"Costs a nickel."

Lorraine was frustrated. It was Nell Aldrich's picture on the front page of the newspaper. The headline said something about her coming to Chicago.

"Look," said Lorraine, "How about this picture?" She pointed to Marcus's drawing. "I'll trade you the picture for a newspaper."

The boy frowned. "What am I going to do with a drawing of me?"

"Give it to your . . . girlfriend," Lorraine suggested.

"Haven't got a girlfriend."

"Well, give it to some girl you *want* to be your girlfriend."

"You think a girl would like that?"

"Sure she would."

The boy looked at the drawing again. "Could you make me look taller?" he asked Marcus.

Marcus sketched something in around the legs of the boy in the picture. It was a cloud with two birds flying through it.

The boy laughed, and handed a newspaper to Lorraine. "It's a deal," he said.

FIVE

The Best Food of All

APRIL 5, 1927

SCREEN STAR NELL ALDRICH TO FILM NEW MOVIE HERE

Hollywood movie star Nell Aldrich is scheduled to arrive in Chicago later this year. She will be shooting outdoor scenes for a new motion picture, *The Wicked Streets*. Victor Young, the director, said that the movie will portray a young girl's struggle against criminals who have ensnared her family.

Miss Aldrich's sister, Peggy Aldrich, has written the script for the movie. She will also supervise the photography and design of the production. The Aldrich sisters have worked together on many movies, with Nell in front of the camera and Peggy behind it.

59

Lorraine caught her breath as she read the article. She was going to be in the same city as Nell Aldrich. Of course Chicago was a big place, but maybe there would be some way Lorraine could go and see her. The newspaper didn't say when the movie was to be made. Lorraine wondered how she could find out.

Since Marcus had let her trade his drawing for the newspaper, Lorraine let him do what he wanted for the rest of the morning. They found the little park Mrs. Waits had told them about. Lorraine sat on a bench under a tree and read the rest of the newspaper while Marcus drew.

There were a lot of interesting things in the newspaper. In Massachusetts, two men named Sacco and Vanzetti had been sentenced to death for killing somebody. But a lot of people thought the two men weren't guilty. Those who supported Sacco and Vanzetti held big public meetings to protest the judge's decision. Not just in Massachusetts, but all over the country. Even in London and Paris.

Lorraine was fascinated. She didn't know you could get so many people interested in an unfair trial. She wondered how you got something like that started. Daddy's trial was unfair, that was for sure. But nobody cared, aside from the colored people in Pickettsville—and they were too scared to have a big public meeting. Of course Daddy had not been sentenced to death. But all the same . . . it was unfair.

She was jarred out of her thoughts when Marcus took hold of her hand. "What's the matter?" Lorraine asked, looking up from the newspaper.

He dumped a handful of coins in her lap. She stared at the money, mostly pennies, but two or three nickels too. She quickly put the newspaper on top of it so nobody could see.

"Marcus!" she whispered. "Where'd you get this money?" She looked around. "There isn't some place like that privy on the train, is there? Only with money instead of paper?"

He shook his head. "Gave me," he said.

"Somebody gave this money to you? Marcus, why would anybody do that?"

"For picture," he said, smiling. He showed her that some pages in his notebook had been torn out.

Lorraine didn't know what to say. People gave Marcus pennies and nickels for his pictures? The idea sent a chill through her. "I don't know what Momma would say about this," she said.

He pointed to the newspaper. "You did," he said.

"Well, I *traded* the drawing for the newspaper," she said. "Trading isn't the same as selling."

He shrugged and pointed to the money. "Hungry," he said.

That's right, Lorraine realized. Now we can buy something good to eat. "Georgia fried chicken?" she said.

He nodded.

They got back to the boardinghouse before Momma and Nancy did. After lunch, Marcus had sold some more drawings. This time, Lorraine watched. Mostly people liked pictures of themselves. But one lady paid him to draw a picture of her baby and an old man wanted one of his dog. Marcus didn't charge people a set price. He just took whatever they offered him.

Not counting what they'd spent on lunch, Marcus had earned thirty-seven cents by the end of the day. "Maybe we'd better not say anything about this to Momma just yet," Lorraine told him. "In case it's against the law or something."

As it turned out, Momma had her own surprise. "We're going to be moving again," she said. "I found a job. It's taking care of two children full time. Lovely little boys, age three and four."

"But why do we have to move?" asked Lorraine. "I like it here." She had already figured out that if Marcus could sell drawings at the same rate every day, he could make over two dollars a week.

"Well, they need me to watch these boys pretty much all the time," said Momma. "Their parents own a restaurant, and the mother does a lot of the cooking. So they want me to live in. They have a great big apartment above the restaurant."

"It's nice," said Nancy. "I saw it."

Momma continued, "I told them, I still got my own children to look after. I guess I might have lost the job right then, but they liked me. I told them about your Daddy."

"You did? Did they ask?"

"It just came up. These people . . . they're Italian. And the father is upset at the way Italians are being treated. I almost told him, you should see how we get treated in Pickettsville, Georgia. 'Course I didn't. Anyway, he told me about two Italians who got an unfair trial."

"Oh! Sacco and Vanzetti!" said Lorraine.

"That's their names. How'd you know about them?"

"I read their story in a newspaper."

Momma gave Lorraine a funny look, but went on. "So he kind of felt sorry for me, I guess, when I told him how Jefferson Willis lied to put John Henry in jail."

"Did he say how we could organize a committee to free him?" asked Lorraine. "They did that for Sacco and Vanzetti."

Momma shook her head. "I don't know about all that," she said. "But he went off and talked with his wife. Then they said we could have this apartment on the floor above theirs. I think they own the building, but they didn't want to tell me, so I wouldn't think they was rich. You know how people are. Anyway, let's pack up now."

When Lorraine saw the restaurant, she thought the people who owned it *must* be rich. It had a fancy sign with letters made out of glass tubes. Even though it was daytime, the tubes glowed red so you could see them way down the street.

✳✳✳ ROCCO'S FINE ITALIAN COOKING ✳✳✳

✳✳✳DANCING AND ENTERTAINMENT ✳✳✳

✳✳✳ NIGHTLY ✳✳✳

Inside, the restaurant was like a palace—at least, like the palaces Lorraine had seen in the movies. The ceiling was decorated with fancy gold-painted woodwork. Every wall had mirrors on it, making the rooms look even bigger. Marble statues and potted plants were part of the decorations.

Snow-white cloths covered every table. Waiters in black tuxedo jackets were setting the tables with crystal glasses and silverware. Lorraine looked and saw three forks next to each plate—just the way Daddy said they were in Paris.

A man came out of the kitchen. His tuxedo had a red carnation in the lapel. "This is Mr. Vivanti," said Momma. She introduced Lorraine and Marcus. Lorraine was a little disappointed. She had thought he might look like Rudolph Valentino, who had been born in Italy. Mr. Vivanti was as young as Valentino, but he was chubby and smiling. Valentino was razor-thin and always looked serious and soulful. When he died last August, *Photoplay* said that thousands of women waited all night to see his body. Nobody would do that for Mr. Vivanti.

The first thing Mr. Vivanti said was, "You must all be hungry." Lorraine smiled to herself, because the smells coming from the kitchen would

Rocco Vivanti

make anybody hungry. He told them to leave their suitcases upstairs and come back. "You can eat with all of us," he said. "Everybody has a little meal before the customers start to come in."

Mr. Vivanti's idea of a "little meal" told Lorraine why he was so round in the middle. Nobody in Pickettsville ever ate like this, she was sure.

At first, she thought that maybe he was just going to give them cold food. In fact, she didn't know the name of a single thing on the big platter one of the waiters set down on the table. "Just eat a little," Momma whispered. "Pretend you like it."

Lorraine picked up a very thin slice of meat with one of her forks and eyed it. It was too big to be sausage, but it had a lot of different things mixed into it. Mr. Vivanti came over to the table when he saw her looking. "That's salami," he said, and pointed out other things on the plate. "This is pepperoni, small because it's hot in the mouth. Those are artichoke hearts in olive oil, good for the stomach."

He turned to Marcus, who was watching everything with wide eyes. "You like an olive?" Mr. Vivanti asked. "These are stuffed with provolone cheese." Very slowly, Marcus reached out and picked up the olive. He put it into his mouth as if it might explode. Then his face lit up. He reached out and took three more. Mr. Vivanti smiled. "Try this," he said to Lorraine. "It's a fig wrapped in a slice of prosciutto."

It was strange but wonderful food, they discovered. Lorraine couldn't stop once she got started, and pretty soon the platter was nearly empty. She kept wondering why she smelled cooking from the kitchen. Then she found out. The double doors swung open and out came one of the waiters with a huge steaming plate of food. He set it down on their table. That was when Lorraine realized the cold food was just the beginning.

The hot food on the platter was called ravioli, little pillows stuffed with cheese and spices and covered with tomato sauce. Before, Lorraine had only eaten tomato sauce out of a can, and didn't like it much. But this . . . it was like eating something that God created and kept a secret because it was so good. She kept eating long after she was really full. And even when she just *had* to stop, she wanted to eat more.

Momma said, "That's wonderful sauce," and she wasn't just being polite.

Mr. Vivanti nodded. "You can't get it anywhere else," he said. "I grow special tomatoes to make it myself. I brought the seeds from Italy."

"You know," said Lorraine. "I always heard French food was the best, but it couldn't be better than this. Nothing could."

Mr. Vivanti smiled and his eyes twinkled. Lorraine could see that he was pleased. Then he asked, "Are you ready for dessert?"

Lorraine almost groaned, but she nodded her head. She knew that this was going to be the best of all. And it was.

SIX

Walk Through A Dream

LORRAINE WOULD ALWAYS REMEMBER THE DAY Nell Aldrich arrived in Chicago. It was the same day Charles Lindbergh landed in Paris. Everybody was talking about Lindbergh. The radio that played all day and night in the kitchen of the restaurant broadcast the news over and over. For the first time ever, a man had flown across the Atlantic Ocean alone. In the afternoon, people started to bring in newspapers with big headlines about Lindbergh's flight.

Lorraine was spending a lot of time in the kitchen by now. She helped scrape and wash the dirty dishes. Mr. Vivanti's wife, Teresita, gave her

the job. Teresita was just about the nicest white person Lorraine had ever met. She worked harder than anybody else in the restaurant, except maybe for her husband. Teresita spent about twelve hours in the kitchen every day cooking. Before that, she went to the markets to buy fresh food and planned the menu for that evening.

That was why she needed Momma to take care of the boys, Tony and Leo. They were awfully cute, but "a big handful," as Momma said.

Teresita was boss of the kitchen the way Mr. Vivanti—"Call me Rocco," he told Lorraine—was boss of the dining rooms. There were three dining rooms. One of them had a stage and a big floor where people danced after ten o'clock at night. Rocco wore a tuxedo and went from table to table, making sure people were enjoying the food and music.

"You know," Teresita told Lorraine one night, "when Rocco started, he had your job—washing dishes."

Lorraine smiled, thinking that Teresita was teasing her. "No, it's true," said Teresita. "It wasn't in this restaurant, of course. I was a waitress and he told me he would own his own place some day. I believed him. Who knows why?" She laughed.

Teresita Vivanti

"How did you save the money?" said Lorraine. She couldn't imagine how much it must cost to open a restaurant like this.

"He moved up to cook," Teresita said. "And then he used those tomatoes, special ones that he grew with seeds from Italy. He made a sauce and everybody loved it. Then another restaurant paid him more money to work there. We got married, we saved, we borrowed from a bank . . ." She shrugged. "Hard work, too."

Long before the restaurant closed each night, Teresita made Lorraine quit work and go to bed. But from her bedroom up on the third floor, Lorraine could still hear the music. They didn't play music like that back in Pickettsville. Late at night in their apartment, when Momma was asleep, Lorraine would practice the Charleston and the Black Bottom and some of the other dances she saw people do on the dance floor in the restaurant.

Lorraine could also lean out her bedroom window and see the people going in and out of the front door of the restaurant. Everybody famous in Chicago came here. The mayor ate here once or twice a week. All the singers from the opera came to Rocco's, because most of them were Italian, and sometimes they would stand up and sing after dinner.

One time, all the waiters came into the kitchen and began to whisper to Teresita. That meant somebody special had come in. She told them, "Go out and treat him just like everybody else." Then she wagged a finger at Lorraine. "You know who's here tonight?" she asked.

"Who?"

"The big gangster, Al Capone. He's got his own restaurant, so he usually doesn't come here. Maybe he's going to steal our food," she said with a smile. "You want to take a look?"

Lorraine shook her head. She'd read in the newspapers that Capone could have people killed

Al Capone

just with a snap of his fingers. Teresita just laughed. "Rocco doesn't like it when he comes in here," she said. "Maybe I should put a little soap in his food." She did that, sometimes, to get rid of rowdy customers.

Lorraine said, "Oh, you couldn't! If he found out . . ."

"He won't hurt you," Teresita said. "Gangsters only kill each other."

Lorraine was too curious, so she finally took a peek at Al Capone. The kitchen door opened enough so that she could see most of the big dining room. One of the waiters pointed him out. Capone was laughing with some other people at his table and smoking a cigar. She didn't look at him very long. Something about him made her afraid he wouldn't like being watched.

Today, when everybody was talking about Lindbergh, Lorraine asked Teresita if the air hero would come to the restaurant. "If he visits Chicago and likes to eat, he will," said Teresita. She glanced at one of the newspapers. "He's awfully thin. Somebody ought to make him a nice meal. But he's in Paris now. We've got to get ready for somebody else who's coming tonight or tomorrow."

"Who?"

"An old friend of Rocco's. She's a big movie star. You know—Nell Aldrich."

Lorraine dropped a plate and it smashed on the floor.

"What's the matter with you?" Teresita asked as Lorraine scrambled to pick up the pieces. She had never broken a plate before.

"I . . . it's just that Nell Aldrich . . . I've seen all her movies."

"All of them?" said Teresita, raising her eyebrows. "I don't think so. She's been making movies since before you were born. She doesn't look much older than you but she and Rocco were born on the same day. They get a big kick out of that. Rocco finally figured out he must be older than she is, because midnight in Italy is earlier than midnight over here."

"How did Rocco meet her?" asked Lorraine.

"Ask him sometime," replied Teresita. "I tell you what. When she comes in, Rocco will want to show her the boys. I'll let you know, and you can go upstairs and bring them down here."

Lorraine felt embarrassed. She was more afraid of Nell Aldrich than she had been of Al Capone. "Oh, I don't know," she said. "Maybe I could just peek at her."

"You'll be OK," said Teresita. "She's pretty nice to people, really. It's her sister who's the hard one."

Lorraine had read the same thing in a magazine. Nell's older sister Peggy was her manager. She wrote most of the scripts for Nell's movies and made all the decisions for her. She was always trying to keep photographers from taking pictures of Nell unless she approved them.

"Didn't the sister give up her own career because something bad happened?" asked Lorraine.

"I don't know if that was the reason," said Teresita. "But her husband was killed in the Great War."

Lorraine nodded. "That was it. My daddy was in the war. I don't know what we would have done if he'd been killed."

Teresita waved the thought away. "Listen," she said. "Nell may not come tonight anyway. Or she may come late. That's the way movie stars are. We've had others in here . . . Charlie Chaplin and Mary Pickford and Douglas Fairbanks. You're supposed to keep the kitchen open till they arrive, like you're a servant."

Something in Teresita's tone of voice surprised Lorraine. Teresita never complained about anything. Even after spending hours and hours in the hot kitchen, if somebody came into the restaurant late, she was always ready to fix another meal.

Lorraine must have shown her surprise, because Teresita suddenly turned away. "I'll tell you when she gets here," she said.

The rest of the evening, Lorraine felt like she was on pins and needles. All she could think about was Nell Aldrich. She wondered if Nell would be wearing the diamond necklace that the magazines said an Indian prince had given her. Or maybe she'd arrive in the Duesenberg car that had been a present from Felton LeFeu, the international playboy.

According to the magazines, Nell had turned down at least a dozen offers of marriage. Nobody knew why. Some said her sister forbade her to marry for the good of her career.

But would Nell really do whatever her older sister wanted? Lorraine couldn't imagine letting Nancy boss *her* around like that. Nell had plenty of money. She could leave her career and marry whoever she wanted.

Then Lorraine remembered a story from one of Nell's movies. She had played the role of a young woman who fell under the spell of an evil man. His name was Svengali, and he had the power to control her just through the force of his eyes. He turned her into a great singer, and she didn't have the mental powers to resist him. Nell was beautiful and rich, but maybe she didn't have strong mental powers.

By this time, the restaurant had gotten busy and the busboys were stacking plates on the sink. One of the other dishwashers yelled at Lorraine. She had to work harder and stop thinking about Nell.

By midnight, things began to slow down. Outside the kitchen, the orchestra was playing fast music and customers stopped eating to dance. This was when Lorraine usually quit work, but tonight she wanted to stay. What if Nell didn't come until two or three in the morning and Lorraine missed seeing her?

Lorraine sat down on an old wooden chair in the back of the kitchen. She yawned and closed her eyes. The next thing she knew somebody was shaking her gently.

It was Teresita. "Hey, I thought you went to bed," she said. "The movie star has arrived. You want to see her or not?"

Lorraine rubbed her eyes and nodded. "Go upstairs and bring Tony and Leo down," said Teresita. This wasn't such a strange request. Teresita sometimes woke the boys when she quit work so she could spend some time playing with them. "In a restaurant," Rocco once explained to Lorraine, "everybody keeps crazy hours."

When Lorraine went upstairs, the first thing she did was wake Marcus. She didn't know why she hadn't thought of this before. "Get dressed," she told him, "I want you to make a drawing for me."

He didn't complain. He was a light sleeper anyway, and knew that Lorraine must have something interesting to show him.

Meanwhile, she went to the boys' room. Momma had gone to sleep on a couch, and Lorraine didn't wake her. She decided Tony and Leo looked cute in their flannel pajamas, so she just put socks on their feet. "Your mama wants to see you,"

Tony   *Leo*

she told them. "She's going to show you a beautiful lady."

They met Marcus on the stairs. He had his notebook, but hesitated when he saw they were going into the main dining room. "It's all right," Lorraine told him, "we're invited."

The dinner lights had been dimmed, and blue spotlights shone over the dance floor. Aside from them, the only light in the room came from flickering candles inside red glass jars on each table. Lorraine stopped to look at the scene. Blue-shadowed dancing couples kicked their feet up and waved their arms on the dance floor. People seated at the tables around it sang along with the music and clapped.

Lorraine's eyes searched the room, and then she heard Rocco's voice. She saw him beckon from a table at the far side. There were several other people with him, and Lorraine couldn't see them clearly from this far away.

Walking through the room was like being in a dream, she thought. A dream that she was in a movie, passing through a crowd of glamorous people. People were turning to look at her. Lorraine imagined that she was wearing a daring flapper gown with a string of pearls and a sequined headband.

Just like the person she saw now, sitting next to Rocco.

Drawing
An Angel

MAY 21, 1927

WHEN NELL ALDRICH SMILED AT HER, LORRAINE
felt like she had stepped into a movie. Only she
knew that if she dared to reach out she could have
touched Nell. It was such an odd feeling.

Then Rocco took one of the boys away from
her and tossed him into the air. He caught him on
the way down, and everybody at the table
laughed.

"Your sons won't last long if you treat them
like that, Rocco," said Nell. Her voice was surprising to hear. Lorraine had thought it would be
higher than it was. Also, Nell spoke like a North-
erner, with a funny accent. Sitting in the movie the-

ater, Lorraine had always imagined Nell speaking just the way she did.

"These boys will last forever," Rocco said, picking up his other son. "Listen to you, Nell . . . telling me to be careful! Look at the way the people in your family live. How come Harry or your Uncle Georgie didn't cross the Atlantic before this fella Lindbergh?"

Nell

"Harry's not so wild now," Nell replied. "He stopped racing automobiles after he got married. And Uncle Georgie retired from flying too. He still walks with a cane from his last crash. Right now he and Freddy are working on some kind of invention that would put pictures on the radio."

Rocco nodded. "Oh, movies that talk. I read that one will be coming out by the end of the year."

"That's Al Jolson's movie, but it's not the same thing. Georgie and Freddy have something different in mind. A radio like the one in your home, only with pictures."

Rocco shook his head as if to say such a thing was impossible. "Anyway," he asked Nell, "are you going to make a talking movie?"

"We don't think her fans want to hear Nell talk," said a woman on the other side of the table.

Until she spoke, Lorraine hadn't even realized it was a woman. She was wearing a black beret and a man's dress shirt with an argyle sweater. Her hair must have been bobbed short because hardly any of it stuck out from under the beret.

"They don't?" asked Rocco. "Ask this girl here," he said, pointing at Lorraine. "She's Nell's number one fan."

The woman's eyes fell on Lorraine, who wanted to sink into the floor and disappear. Then she saw a corner of the woman's mouth turn up. It was her idea of a smile. "Who are you?" she asked.

"I'm Lorraine Dixon, miss. My mother takes care of Tony and Leo. I've seen just about all of Nell's movies."

This set everybody at the table laughing again. For a second, Lorraine didn't see what was funny. Then she realized that when she spoke it sounded like, "Ah've seen jus' 'bout alla Naill's moovies." They thought *she* had an accent.

Nell took Lorraine's hand. "Thank you," Nell said. "I would be nowhere without my fans. Don't mind what my sister Peggy says."

Lorraine could hardly breathe. Nobody in Pickettsville would ever believe she was talking with Nell Aldrich. She looked across the table at the other woman. Yes, she could see the resemblance between Nell and her sister. But there was

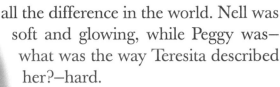

Peggy

all the difference in the world. Nell was soft and glowing, while Peggy was—what was the way Teresita described her?—hard.

As Lorraine watched, Peggy took a cigarette from a gold case that was enameled with a black design. She lit it with a matching lighter. Lorraine was shocked. She'd never seen a woman smoke before.

"What's *he* doing?" Peggy said suddenly, gesturing in Marcus's direction. He had sat down on the carpet and opened his notebook. He was hard at work and didn't even look up.

Lorraine looked at Nell. "That's my brother. He's drawing your picture. I hope you don't mind. He won't take long."

"Oh, that's cute," said Nell. "I think it's the cat's pajamas. Don't stop him, Peggy. Should I sit still or something?"

"No, he doesn't need that," Lorraine said.

"But should I look sad . . ." Nell brushed an imaginary tear off her cheek. ". . . or angry . . ." Now her mouth turned into a pout. " . . . or happy?" And her face blossomed into the nicest smile anybody could ever have.

"You'll need a director," said Peggy. "How about it, Victor?" she said to a man sitting on her right. He had dark curly hair and was wearing a formal dinner jacket with a black bow tie. Right at this moment, he was pouring something into a glass from a shiny metal flask he had taken from his jacket.

"Well, it depends on the situation," said Victor. "Is she in love or in danger?"

"I don't feel like I'm in danger," Nell said impishly.

Her sister spoke up. "You'd only be in danger if you drank some of that stuff Victor is pouring," said Peggy. "Rocco, don't you have something better you can serve us?"

Rocco shook his head. "Customers must bring their own," he said. "Unless it is wine. I serve wine because what would an Italian restaurant be without wine?"

Victor raised his glass. "Here's to the Eighteenth Amendment. Look around you, Peggy, and see who's obeying the law you wanted to pass."

Lorraine understood what he meant. The Eighteenth Amendment was a law that made all alcoholic drinks illegal. But almost nobody in Chicago paid any attention to it. At all the other tables, people either brought some liquor of their own or were sipping wine that waiters brought from a hidden storeroom in the cellar. Rocco's father grew the grapes for the wine—and the tomato plants—on a farm outside the city that Rocco had bought.

"It was the Nineteenth Amendment that we fought for," Peggy retorted. "That's the one that gave women the vote."

Just then, Marcus tapped Lorraine and showed her the picture. Nell noticed. "Let me see, let me see," she cried.

As Marcus handed Nell the notebook, Lorraine worried. What if she didn't like it? The man on the train hadn't liked the picture Marcus did of him.

And in fact, Nell looked at the drawing for a long minute without saying anything. Peggy whispered something to Victor, who chuckled. Rocco finally leaned over Nell's shoulder to see.

"Oh," he said, "he gave you wings."

That was right. Marcus had drawn Nell as an angel, with feathery wings and a smiling face. She was even more beautiful than in real life.

Peggy reached across the table and took the notebook from Nell, who still hadn't said anything. She looked at it with a frown and showed it to Victor. He raised his eyebrows. The two of them looked at Marcus. "Where did you learn to draw like this?" Peggy asked.

Marcus didn't say anything. "He just was born that way," Lorraine explained.

"Give it back to me," Nell said. She spoke in a different tone of voice. "I want to keep it."

Peggy handed it back. Nell started to leaf through the notebook. "Why, you've done a lot of drawings, haven't you?" she said to Marcus.

Marcus only responded by telling Lorraine, "Need book."

Lorraine took a deep breath. She needed courage. "He needs his notebook back," she said. "You can have the picture though."

"That's so lovely," said Nell as she carefully took the picture from the notebook.

Lorraine looked longingly at it. "If he does another, will you autograph it for me?"

Nell laughed. "I can do better than that," she said. "Victor, when do we begin shooting?"

"The day after tomorrow," the man on the other side of the table said.

"I want Lorraine and her brother to be my guests on the set," said Nell.

Lorraine's heart leaped as she understood. But then Victor frowned. "Oh, I don't know, Nell," he said. "You know how busy we're going to be. Kids just get in the way."

"Is that so?" Nell said. "What about Charley? Where's he going to be while we're shooting?"

Peggy snuffed out her cigarette. "Nell, I don't have anything else I can do with him. You know what a problem he is for me. Besides, he'll only sit in my trailer and read a book."

Nell shook her head. "He comes outside sometimes. Anyway, I can have guests on the set. It's in my contract."

Victor and Peggy looked at each other.

"In any case," said Nell, "if I don't see Lorraine and her brother—what's his name?" she asked, turning to Lorraine.

"Marcus."

"If Lorraine and Marcus aren't there, I'm not going to be happy."

Both Victor and Peggy looked unhappy to hear that. And right then, Lorraine knew that the magazines were wrong. When Nell wanted something, she was stronger than Peggy.

EIGHT

A Strange Boy

MAY 22, 1927

ALL THE NEXT DAY, LORRAINE'S MIND WENT BACK and forth. On the one hand, she was excited to think she would get to see Nell Aldrich making a movie. On the other, she worried that maybe Nell would forget all about her and Marcus. After Lorraine took Rocco's sons back upstairs and tucked them in bed, she couldn't sleep. Whenever she closed her eyes, she kept seeing herself with Nell in a movie.

When she told Momma she had met Nell Aldrich, Momma felt her forehead to see if she had a fever. "I'm not making it up!" Lorraine insisted. "Marcus was there too, and he drew her picture."

Momma nodded. "Well, he would do that, I'm sure."

"And she liked it so much that she invited us to come and see her make a movie."

Momma shook her head. "No, that's something you dreamed, Lorraine. I heard you tossing and turning in your bed."

But later on, Rocco told Momma it was true. "I got a phone call," he said, "from somebody who works for Victor. Victor's the director of the movie. Lorraine and Marcus have got to be ready early in the morning."

"Where are they supposed to go?" asked Momma.

Rocco shrugged. "To wherever they're making the movie. A car will pick them up and bring them home."

After that, Momma started to fret even more. "You behave yourselves, hear me?" she told them. "Lorraine, you'll have to watch Marcus like a hawk. There's probably paper lying all over the place."

"I don't think so, Momma," said Lorraine. "They make movies on film. Big rolls of it. We saw Mr. Soileau carrying them into the movie theater in Pickettsville."

"Uh-huh," Momma said. "And what about those big posters that they put up outside all the theaters? I guess those aren't paper? And Marcus would just scribble all over them if you let him."

When Lorraine came to work after dinner, Teresita teased her. "So I guess you'll be leaving us," she said.

"What do you mean?" asked Lorraine.

"You'll probably get in the movies now," said Teresita. "I'll have to pay a quarter just to get a look at you."

Lorraine's heart skipped a beat as she let herself imagine that might be true. "No," she said. "It's just for the day. We're supposed to watch some scenes being made, and come right back."

Teresita said, "Well, you better take off early so you can get up on time. We can get along without you for one night."

Lorraine and Marcus were standing outside the restaurant at seven o'clock the next morning. There wasn't much traffic, and Lorraine kept looking for a taxicab to turn the corner. That was the sort of car she expected.

So she didn't notice the long, dark blue automobile with a uniformed driver behind the wheel. Not until it rolled to a stop in front of the curb and the driver got out. The front seat of the car was open, with no roof, while the passenger part in back was all boxed in.

The driver opened the door to the passenger section and looked at her. She looked back, and swallowed. "Are you Miss Lorraine Dixon?" he asked in a voice that made her think of thick plum jam.

She nodded.

"I am here to transport you and your brother," he said, and looked at Marcus. Marcus didn't need any more urging. He popped right through the car door and sat down.

Lorraine wasn't quite sure what "transport" meant, but it looked like something she'd enjoy. She stepped across the sidewalk and into the car.

There was a lot more room in here than there had been in the taxi. The seats were covered with blue velvet. The windows had curtains that you could pull shut. She guessed that would be if you wanted to go to sleep. There was also a little wooden cabinet built into the back of the front seat. Before Lorraine could stop him, Marcus had opened it. Inside were bottles of soda pop and other drinks along with candy and little cakes wrapped in wax paper.

"You may partake of the refreshments if you like." The voice seemed to come out of nowhere. Lorraine froze, as if she'd been caught doing something terrible. Then she looked up and saw that the driver was speaking through a tube that connected to the passenger section. He could see the back of the car through a little mirror attached to the top of the windshield.

Marcus pointed to a speaking tube in their part of the car. Lorraine picked it up nervously. "Thank you," she managed to say. Marcus unwrapped one of the little cakes and offered her some. She shook her head. When he started to take a second cake, she slapped his hand. "Don't be greedy," she said. He opened one of the bottles of soda and gave her a look that said, "I can have one if I want."

They drove over to the lake and turned south. It was pretty here, a beautiful spring day with the sun shining on the dark blue water. Far out, Lorraine could see a sailboat. Other cars passed by, and the elevated railroad train roared past on the right. Beyond it, she could see the two brand-new Chicago skyscrapers, the Tribune Tower and the Wrigley Building.

The only thing different was that inside the car she couldn't hear any of the noises that the big city made twenty-four hours a day. It was like watching the world go by without having to be a part of it. I wonder what it would be like to live like this all the time, she thought.

Pretty soon, the car turned off Lake Shore Drive. They passed through streets that were lined with narrow houses built so close together that there wasn't any space between them. The car slowed, and Lorraine saw a barrier of wooden sawhorses in the street ahead. Some men there saw the car and moved one of the sawhorses to let them through.

On the other side, the street was filled with people. Not just on the sidewalks—everywhere. Lorraine saw three men in dark suits carrying machine guns, and her hair stood on end. Then she realized they were only actors getting ready for a scene.

Other people were moving a big platform, which held a camera attached to a folding metal arm that could raise it high into the air. Men and women were scurrying here and there, carrying costumes, film scripts, and all sorts of things that she could only guess what they were.

Alfred

The car came to a stop in front of several large trailers. Doors on each one were marked with names. Lorraine read one: NELL ALDRICH, with a star above it. The driver opened the door of the car to let them out. "I will be here to take you home at four o'clock," he said. "If you wish to leave earlier, you can ask for me. My name is Alfred."

Lorraine started toward the trailer marked with Nell's name, but Alfred stopped her. "You're supposed to wait in that one till you're called," he said. He pointed to a trailer marked with Peggy's name.

Inside, it was furnished with a desk, some folding chairs, and two comfortable-looking couches. A typewriter and a stack of white paper sat on the desk. A chubby boy wearing glasses and an oxford shirt with a tie sat on one of the couches. He was reading a book.

He didn't seem to notice them at first. Then Lorraine realized he was only finishing the paragraph he was reading. Finally he marked his place with a slip of paper and looked up.

"You must be Lorraine and Marcus," he said. "My name is Charley. Actually, it's Charles Norman Junior, but nobody calls me that. It reminds people of my father. He was, as you can surmise, Charles Norman Senior."

Lorraine put her hand over her mouth. There was something funny about the formal way the boy spoke, considering that he looked only about ten, no older than Marcus.

Charley

"If you'd like something to eat," Charley added, "I can order something. They'll bring us just about anything you might care for."

"Marcus ate in the car," Lorraine said. People must get awfully hungry making movies, she thought. They had food everywhere. "Can we see Nell?" she asked.

"Oh, we'd just be in the way," he told her. "Right now her trailer is full of people fitting her costume, fixing her hair, making up her face, and telling her what she's supposed to do in the next scene."

Lorraine thought all that would be interesting to see.

"Excuse me!" said Charley suddenly. "Please don't touch those papers."

Lorraine turned to see Marcus at the desk holding some of the sheets of paper that had been next to the typewriter. He put them down, and Lorraine pointed angrily to the couch. "You already have a notebook, Marcus," she said. "Momma bought you a new one just so you wouldn't mess with anybody else's paper."

Marcus sat down. "Paper had type," he said, shrugging.

"It's the script," Charley explained. "Really, as far as I'm concerned you could burn the whole thing, but Peggy would be quite angry."

"Isn't Peggy your mother?" Lorraine asked.

Charley nodded. "Yes, but she doesn't like me to call her that. It reminds her of my father."

"Why doesn't she like to be reminded of your father?"

"He was killed in the Great War."

Lorraine nodded. "But I'd think that would make her want to remember him."

"I don't remember him at all," said Charley. "But it makes my mother sad to remember him. They were only married for a year before he went to France and was killed."

Lorraine thought about telling him her Daddy had gone to France and come back, but she decided against it.

Charles Norman Sr.

"Anyway, we're just supposed to stay out of the way," Charley said. "I'm very good at that."

"But we came to see the movie being made," Lorraine replied. "Nell invited us."

"Not just yet," he said. He reached into his pants and pulled out a large old pocket watch. When he opened the case, it played a little tune. "The shooting isn't due to begin for another half hour," he said, snapping the watch closed again. "But I warn you, watching a movie being made is quite boring. You should have brought a book." He turned and pointed to a bookcase at the far end of the trailer. "I have most of the Tom Swift books," he said. "Even though Peggy says Aunt Zena wouldn't have liked them, I find them to be quite enjoyable."

"Who's Aunt Zena?" asked Lorraine.

"One of my numerous relatives. She's dead too, but her spirit lives on in the family."

Lorraine remembered reading about Nell's famous family. "Why don't you go stay with one of your other relatives?"

"Peggy wishes I would, actually," he told her. "She thinks I'm a bother. I go to a boarding school most of the year, but I got kicked out of the latest one. Peggy would prefer I spend the summer in Maine with my grandparents. They want me to become something, though, so I avoid them."

"Become something?" Lorraine asked.

"Oh, you know . . . or perhaps you don't. Cousin Harry builds race cars and Cousin Jack is a scientist—though no one can explain what it is he studies. I have another cousin, Polly, who's in Brazil searching for undiscovered insects." He made a face. "Imagine that! And my cousin Freddy knows all about radio. You see? They've all become something. I'm not any good at things like those."

"You must want to do something," said Lorraine. "Everybody has to."

"That's exactly what my grandmother would say," Charley replied. "If I had my choice, I'd want to be like my cousin Molly."

Lorraine thought for a second. "She's the tennis player."

"That's right. Everybody knows her, even you, because she's a champion."

Lorraine looked him over. "I don't know much about tennis," she said. "But I think you'd have to . . . lose weight if you wanted to play."

He nodded. "Exactly. I looked in the mirror one day and said, 'Charley, there is only one athlete who looks like you.'"

Lorraine tried to think of one. "Who?"

"Babe Ruth."

Over on the couch, Marcus laughed. It sounded like a flock of baby chicks at feeding time. Lorraine glared at him. She was embarrassed.

"He doesn't mean anything," she explained to Charley.

"Of course he does," Charley said. "Everyone reacts that way, more or less. So I've decided it's the ideal thing to say when people ask me what I want to be. That way, no one will take me seriously."

He pulled out the watch again. "Time to go," he said. "Remember, if you get bored, just tell me and we can come back here and read."

NINE

Good Luck or Bad?

LORRAINE DIDN'T THINK IT WAS BORING TO WATCH movies being made. There was a lot more to it than she had imagined. The director had to plan out each scene. Victor shouted through a big megaphone to give directions. The camera had to be set in place, the actors had to know where to stand, and everybody else had to make sure to get out of the scene.

Marcus almost slipped up once. He had sat down to draw as usual. There were a lot of new things for him to look at, so he didn't pay attention when the director called for everybody to move. Just before the film started to roll, the cameraman caught sight of him. "Who's that?" he yelled.

Marcus was sitting far behind the actors, but the camera would put him in the scene anyway.

Lorraine dragged Marcus away and gave him a good talking to. He stormed off and sat down in front of the trailers. The camera wouldn't be pointed in that direction. He should be safe there, thought Lorraine. After warning him once more about leaving any stray paper alone, she moved back to where she could see the scene.

Actually Nell didn't look nearly as beautiful today as she had in Rocco's restaurant. It was the makeup. "Why are her lips brown?" Lorraine asked Charley.

"So they'll look right on the black-and-white film," he told her. "Anything red looks very black on the film." He pointed to a man holding a big white screen. "He has to reflect the light into the actors' faces so they don't have shadows under their eyes," Charlie explained. "So if they didn't have tan makeup on their faces, they would look too pasty and white."

In the scene, three men with machine guns were threatening Nell and her boyfriend. Then they all got into a car.

When the scene was over, the director had them do it again. Then a third time. Finally, Victor yelled, "Print that."

All the actors started back to the trailers. Lorraine caught Nell's eye and she stopped.

"How do you like it?" Nell asked.

"It's the most interesting thing I've ever seen," Lorraine told her. "I didn't know movies were so complicated to make."

Nell said, "It's different from a play. In a play you hear the audience's reaction. Here, I never know what people are going to think. It's a shame I only get a chance to do a play once a year now."

"But everybody loves your movies," said Lorraine.

"I'm always afraid they won't like the next one," Nell said. "It all depends on other people—the writer, the director, even the makeup artist."

Peggy showed up then. "Nell," she said, "I want to go over the next scene with you."

"Coming," said Nell.

Peggy glanced at the two children. "Stay out of the way, Charley," she said.

"See?" said Charley when they were gone.

"I don't think she means anything by it," Lorraine told him. "It's the sort of thing mothers say."

"No, she means it," he replied.

They didn't get to see the actors again for a long time. The camera had to be moved and the director didn't like the new position. Then Peggy came out of Nell's trailer and began to argue with Victor about the script.

"See, nothing much ever happens," said Charley. He took out his watch again. The little tune played briefly as he opened it. "Almost time for lunch, though."

"That's such an interesting watch," said Lorraine. "What's the name of that song it plays?"

"I don't know," Charley said. "It originally belonged to my great-grandfather. He left it to my mother, and then when my father went to France she gave it to him. They sent it back after he'd been killed, but she didn't want it any more."

"If I were her, I would have kept it to remember him by," said Lorraine.

"Yes, but she *didn't* want to remember," Charley reminded her. "She only told me it's bad luck to listen to the song all the way through. Father must have done that. Do you believe in luck?"

"I guess," said Lorraine. "But my Daddy said God helps those who help themselves. Everybody has some good and bad luck. You just have to take advantage of the good luck and be careful during the bad."

"As long as you can tell which is which," said Charley.

"I don't think I'd have any trouble with *that*," Lorraine replied. "My Daddy got thrown in jail for something he didn't do. So then we had to leave Georgia and come up here. Seems like a lot of bad luck to me."

Charley thought about that. "None of that is luck, exactly," he said. "Luck is when something unexpected happens to you."

"Well, we didn't expect he'd be thrown in jail."

"No, I guess not. How long does he have to stay there?"

"A year."

"That's not so bad. I've been in boarding schools for six years, and they're *like* prisons. I think you probably get beat up more in boarding school than in prison."

Lorraine couldn't help laughing, even though she was sad thinking of Daddy.

"It's true," said Charley.

"You know what?" said Lorraine. "You're just lucky, but you don't know it so you aren't taking advantage of it."

He made a noise that sounded like a baby elephant snorting. "I wish you could trade places with me and you'd see," he said.

"Oh!" Lorraine exclaimed. "I'd like to see you . . . washing dishes!"

Lorraine was fed up talking to him. She walked over to check on Marcus. He was happy as a bug. He'd been drawing pictures of all the people who went in and out of Nell's trailer. He showed them to her.

Lorraine particularly liked the one of Peggy. Marcus had used a lot of black crayon and made her look like a spider. "Better not show that to anybody else," said Lorraine.

"Where's the one you drew of Charley?" she added. "I saw you start it when you were sitting on the couch."

Marcus gave her a sly look, and riffled through the pages of his notebook. Finally he turned it around for her to see. It showed a very fat boy chewing on a book. "Well, that's him," said Lorraine.

She closed the notebook quickly as the real Charley appeared. He was carrying a cardboard box and set it down next to Marcus. "I'm supposed to see that you get lunch," he explained. "I hope you like hot dogs."

Charley himself certainly did. He had brought a dozen of them, all slathered with yellow mustard. He went back for bottles of soda, warning them not to eat all the hot dogs while he was gone.

There was little danger of it. Two of them turned out to be enough for Lorraine, although three of them disappeared when they got too close to Marcus. Charley had no trouble finishing off the rest. He even looked a little disappointed as he realized he'd eaten the last one.

"It was nice of you to bring us lunch," said Lorraine. "I'm sorry I got angry at you before."

"Oh, it's all right," he said. "I was thinking about what you said, and it gave me an idea."

"What is it?"

"I'll tell you later. Right now, if you want to see it, they're going to shoot Nell's rescue scene."

"Are you coming, Marcus?" Lorraine asked.

He shook his head and rubbed his stomach. He was too full. "Be here," he told her.

"Don't get into trouble," she said.

When Lorraine and Charley went back, they saw that a car had been overturned and lay on its side in the street. "Isn't that the same car Nell and her boyfriend were forced into earlier?" asked Lorraine.

"Yes," Charley replied. He pointed to a police car that was nearby. "But in the movie the police car has chased it and it overturned while coming around a corner."

"How come we didn't get to see that?"

"Because they'll film it another day with professional race drivers. They don't shoot the scenes in order."

Just then, Nell walked onto the street. Lorraine gasped. Nell's face was scratched and smudged. Her dress was torn, and something brown was running down her arm.

"It'll look like blood in the movie," Charley explained. Lorraine understood. Nell was made up to look like she'd been in an automobile accident.

One of the crew brought a stepladder and someone else opened the door of the overturned car. Nell climbed up and stepped inside. Then another crew member set a match to some kindling sticks behind the car.

After the ladder was taken away, Victor yelled, "Camera," as the flames licked up the side of the car. Nell poked her head out of the window and screamed. At least she *looked* as if she were screaming. There wasn't any need for her to actually scream, since the movie had no sound.

Two policemen rushed up to the car and climbed onto it. They reached inside and pulled

Nell through the window. They dragged Nell out of the way, even though she struggled and pointed toward the car.

"Print that!" shouted Victor.

"Is that all?" Lorraine asked.

"Well, the car will explode after that," said Charley, "but they'll film that when everybody is out of the way."

"What about her boyfriend?"

"Whose boyfriend?"

"Nell's. He was in the car with her."

"Oh, Peggy got in a fight with the actor, so they're killing him off here. I think Nell's character will fall in love with one of the policemen who saved her."

"Do they change the story just like that?"

"Peggy can. Because Nell trusts her. It drives Victor crazy, though."

Seeing the rescue scene was a little disappointing, Lorraine thought. Now whenever she saw something exciting at the movies, she would wonder how it was made.

Suddenly there was a tremendous flash of light, followed by a loud boom. Lorraine raised her arms to protect herself. Everybody around them ducked or dropped to the ground. People started to scream, but they weren't acting now.

When the noise died down, Lorraine could see what had happened. The overturned automobile had exploded.

TEN

A Stolen Necklace

EVERYTHING GOT VERY CONFUSED AFTER THAT. Victor started to yell through his megaphone, "Who set off those charges?" Meanwhile, people who hadn't been watching the scene came pouring out of the trailers. Lorraine saw a crew member lying on the ground with blood—real blood—running down his face.

"Marcus!" Lorraine shouted. She looked around, and spotted him sitting in the same place she'd left him. He looked as if nothing had happened.

"Let's get out of the way," said Charley, tugging Lorraine toward the trailers.

Just then they heard sirens. Two police cars—real ones—came roaring down the street with their sirens on.

A man got out of one of the police cars and walked up to them. He was wearing a rumpled brown suit instead of a uniform. "What are you kids doing here?" he asked.

"Nell Aldrich is my aunt," said Charley. "She's in the movie."

"We got a call about an explosion here," the man said. "Did you see what happened?"

"No, we didn't see anything."

"All right, who's in charge?"

Charley pointed out Victor, who was still shouting orders. The policeman headed that way.

"Let's get inside the trailer," Charley said.

As the door closed behind him, Lorraine asked, "Why did you tell the policeman we didn't see what happened?"

He shrugged. "It's the best way to stay out of trouble. Just clam up."

Lorraine nodded. "Maybe Marcus and I should go home now," she said. "Can you find Alfred for us?"

Charley looked disappointed. "Wait a while. Tell me some more about your father and how he got in jail."

Lorraine was sorry she'd even said anything about it. But she related the whole story to him.

"Peggy might be interested in that," Charley said when Lorraine finished.

"Why?" she asked. Peggy seemed like the last person who might care what happened to Daddy.

"Oh, she's always looking for something to fight for," Charley told her. "When she was younger she helped to get women the right to vote. Lately she's been working to get Sacco and Vanzetti out of jail. Do you know who they are?"

"Yes. But why would Peggy . . .?"

"Be interested in them? Well, the trial was unfair, for one thing. Rocco was the one who got her interested. Peggy and Nell once helped Rocco when he was running from the police. Did you know that?"

Lorraine stared at him. She could hardly believe it. "Rocco's not the sort of person who would run from the police," she said. "He knows the mayor of Chicago."

"He didn't always," Charley told her. "Now he gives money to the Sacco and Vanzetti defense fund."

Lorraine thought about it. She remembered what Teresita had told her about the days when she and Rocco were poor. "Maybe you're right," she said.

"Oh, I've heard them talk about it," said Charley.

"Do you really think Peggy would help? I mean, is there any way they could get Daddy out of jail?"

Before he could answer, there was a knock at the door of the trailer. A policeman in uniform poked his head inside. "What are you kids doing in here?" he asked.

"Nothing," said Charley.

"Were you the two Lieutenant Reilly saw when he got here?"

"No," Charley said. But Lorraine added, "We saw a man in a brown suit, but he didn't tell us his name."

"Stay here, then," the policeman said. "He wants to talk to you. And here's another kid." He opened the door wider and Marcus stepped inside. "Is he related to you?" the policeman asked Lorraine.

"Yes, but he didn't do anything," she said.

"Who said he did?" replied the policeman.

Charley nudged Lorraine in the ribs. She knew he was telling her to clam up.

The policeman left anyway, and Lorraine asked Marcus what happened.

"Trailer," Marcus said. "Some stole."

"Somebody stole a trailer?"

He shook his head no. Quickly he sketched a picture on his pad and then showed it to her.

Lorraine recognized Nell's face. In the picture, she was wearing a necklace. Marcus put his finger on it. "Stole that," he said.

"Someone stole her necklace?"

"Oh, my," said Charley. "That must be the necklace she got from Prince Chaputra. We're going to be in real trouble."

"Stop that," said Lorraine. "None of us stole the necklace."

"You'll see," he replied. "They'll find a way to blame us anyway."

Lorraine turned back to Marcus. "How do you know about this?" she asked him.

"Heard police talk," he said.

Pretty soon, the man in the brown suit showed up and said he was Lieutenant Reilly. He asked them if they'd seen anybody going in or out of Nell's trailer. Charley told him no, and this time Nell agreed.

Lieutenant Reilly pointed to Marcus. "How about this one?" he asked. "He was sitting right there, so he must have seen people going into the trailer. But he wouldn't talk to us."

"He doesn't say much," Lorraine told him. She took a deep breath. "Marcus," she asked, "did you see anybody come out of the trailer with a necklace?"

Lieutenant Reilly

"Wait a second," Lieutenant Reilly said. "How'd you know about the necklace?"

Without thinking, Lorraine pointed to Marcus. "He told us," she said.

"I see," said the lieutenant suspiciously. "He was sitting there all day, right?"

"Yes, so he'd stay out of trouble."

"So he would know when the trailer was empty."

Charley was nudging Lorraine so hard that she slapped his arm away.

Lieutenant Reilly stood up. "All right, stay here," he told them. "There's a policeman outside if you try to leave. I'll be right back."

When he was gone, Charley put his face in his hands. "I *told* you not to say anything," he moaned.

"But he's got it all wrong," Lorraine said.

"Promise me one thing," Charley said. "Whatever you do, don't tell them your father's in jail for stealing."

Lorraine's face got hot. "He was innocent!" she said.

"Didn't stop him from going to jail," Charley replied.

In a few minutes, the lieutenant returned with a policewoman. She searched each of the children while Lieutenant Reilly watched. "None of them has the necklace," the policewoman announced.

Lieutenant Reilly looked around. "They could have hidden it here," he said. He motioned to the policewoman. "You take them outside and keep a close eye on them. I'll have somebody search the trailer."

Charley looked miserable. "Can I take a few books?" he asked.

Lieutenant Reilly's eyes flickered to the bookshelves. "You think I'm dumb or something?" he asked Charley. "That's the first place I'll look."

Serves you right, Charley, Lorraine thought. You didn't clam up.

However, as they stepped outside the trailer with the policewoman, Peggy appeared. "What's going on here?" she asked. "What are you doing with Charley?"

Lieutenant Reilly came to the door of the trailer. "We're just holding him for now," he said.

"For what?" Peggy demanded.

"We think they may have something to do with the theft," he replied.

"That's nonsense," Peggy said. "What reason do you have for suspecting them?"

"That colored boy was sitting by the trailer," Lieutenant Reilly said.

"Did you search him?"

"We searched all three of them, but—"

Peggy didn't let him finish. "Charley? You searched Charley?" Peggy gave a laugh that sounded more like a shout. "There's been an explosion," she said. "People have been hurt, a necklace stolen . . . and you searched *Charley*? No wonder people say the criminals are running this town."

"Now, see here, miss . . . " the lieutenant began.

Peggy turned to the policewoman. "Let those children go at once, do you hear me?"

The policewoman took a step back and then looked at the lieutenant. He said to Peggy, "If you insist, miss. But I can't be responsible if they get away."

"Oh, certainly," Peggy said. "If they rob any banks, you can tell your boss I unleashed a crime wave."

Lieutenant Reilly nodded to the policewoman. "But we're still gong to have to search this trailer," he told Peggy. Peggy gave him a look that Lorraine thought would have struck an ordinary person dead.

ELEVEN

An Unexpected Friend

MOVIE STAR'S NECKLACE STOLEN; REWARD OFFERED

Yesterday, a diamond necklace belonging to movie star Nell Aldrich was stolen from the actress's trailer dressing room. Miss Aldrich was in Chicago shooting a new movie, *The Wicked Streets*.

A short time before the theft, an explosion destroyed an automobile used in the making of the film. Lt. Brendan Reilly, of the 13th Detective Squad, stated that the explosion may have been intended as a distraction to allow the thief to enter Miss Aldrich's trailer. Lt. Reilly added that there may have been several people involved in the theft. He said that the police have questioned several suspects.

> Victor Young, director of the movie, has announced that Global Productions is offering a $1,000 reward for the recovery of the necklace.

Lorraine read the newspaper while she was eating breakfast. It was pretty clear that Lieutenant Reilly still thought she, Marcus, and Charley knew something about the stolen necklace. She wished she did. Lorraine thought of all the things she could do with a thousand dollars. First off, she'd find out how to get Daddy out of jail.

She thought about what happened yesterday. When the car exploded, everybody came out of the trailers to see what happened. From what the newspaper said, that must have been when the necklace was taken. Victor was shouting and everybody was looking at what was left of the car.

Except . . . Suddenly Lorraine realized how she might find out who the thief was. She was so excited that she bit down on the spoon she was using to eat her Quaker oatmeal.

Momma appeared just then. She had Tony and Leo with her. "Lorraine," she said. "Somebody called up from downstairs. There's a boy waiting to see you."

Momma said "boy" as if Al Capone himself were waiting for Lorraine.

"A boy?" Lorraine said.

"Yes. It's bad enough Nancy is seeing boys, without you starting too." Nancy had upset

Momma by staying out past ten o'clock last Saturday night with some boy she'd met.

"Momma, I don't even know any boys in Chicago."

"Says his name is Charley. You telling me that's not a boy?"

"Charley?" Lorraine was astonished. What could *he* want? "Come along, then, Momma. You'll see it's not a boy." Not the kind of boy Momma was thinking of, anyway.

They walked down the two flights of stairs. Tony and Leo squirmed away from Momma and ran. They were almost the same size, even though they were a year apart. They were forever racing each other, wrestling, and trying to be the first one to do something or other. Lorraine didn't see how Momma could put up with them all day long. At least Marcus was quiet.

Which reminded her. "Momma? Where's Marcus?"

"Oh, he's roaming around in that world of his," Momma replied. "He hasn't even asked me for notebooks lately. Has he stopped drawing?"

Lorraine shook her head. She didn't tell Momma that she suspected Marcus was still selling his drawings and using that money to buy paper.

As she stepped onto the last staircase, she got a surprise. There, at the bottom of the stairs, stood Charley. He wore yellow cotton knickers with brown socks pulled up to the knee, a blue shirt and tie, and a little cap like the kind baseball players wore. It was too small for him.

"Momma," said Lorraine, "this is Charley."

"Oh," said Momma. Charley smiled. He sure didn't look much like Al Capone. Momma said, "Where'd you meet him?"

"He's Nell Aldrich's nephew, Momma. What are you doing here, Charley?"

"Well," he began. "In all the excitement yesterday, I forgot to tell you."

"What excitement?" Momma asked suspiciously.

"Oh, nothing," said Charley. "Just the usual excitement of making a movie."

"I heard that there was a necklace stolen," said Momma.

"Well, we don't know anything about that," said Charley.

"Just why are you here?" Lorraine asked again.

"You remember when we were talking?" Charley replied. "About changing places? Well, I thought I'd come and take your place and wash dishes."

Lorraine stared at him. "Does your mo—, does Peggy know about this?"

"Of course."

"Charley," she said sternly. She knew by now that he stretched the truth.

"Well, she knows I'm gone," he said. "Alfred drove me here in the Pierce-Arrow. Peggy doesn't care where I'm going as long as I'm not in the way."

Lorraine shook her head. "Anyhow, you're too early. There aren't any dishes to wash."

"Oh," he said. He shifted back and forth from one foot to the other. "So what are you going to do today?"

Lorraine hesitated. With Momma right there, she couldn't very well reply that she was going to try to find the missing necklace. "I don't know," she said. "Maybe I'll go over to Seward Park. Marcus might be over there."

"Do people play baseball there?"

"Sometimes. Why?"

"I thought maybe we could practice baseball together."

Lorraine didn't know what to make of that. She realized that Charley probably had no friends, at least not in Chicago. On the other hand, having Charley as a friend was like having something stuck to your shoe.

"We'd need gloves, a bat, and a ball," she pointed out.

"Oh, Alfred will take us someplace where we can buy those."

Lorraine decided there was no sense arguing with him. "All right," she said. "But I've got to get something upstairs first. Wait here."

things." She showed Charley Mr. Henderson's business card. "I'm going to take the drawings to him."

Charley frowned. "Wellllll . . ." he said.

"What's the matter?"

"It would be more fun to do it ourselves."

"Suppose we know who the thief is. How would we get him to give us the necklace?"

"Oh, Alfred will help. Tom Swift has a giant assistant named Koku who is useful if any rough stuff is required. Alfred can be our Koku."

"I think we'll just let him drive, Charley."

In the car, Charley looked through the drawings Marcus had made by the trailer. "I recognize almost all the people," he said. "Here's Nell's hairdresser, her makeup artist, the people from wardrobe, Peggy, Victor . . . Now here's Curtis Mitchell. He's the actor that Peggy decided to kill off."

"It's more likely to be someone you don't recognize," Lorraine told him. "Someone who doesn't belong there."

"Why?"

"Because the thief couldn't be someone who works for the movie company."

"Oh, yes he could. That would be the way he would escape without being noticed."

Lorraine had to admit Charley was right. That ruined her plan. She thought they could just pick out the picture of someone who wasn't supposed to be there.

Alfred guided the car to a stop in front of a row of old houses that had been turned into businesses. ROOMS CHEAP read one sign. MEN'S SUITS $10 read another. FUNERAL HOME. And there it was: HENDERSON REAL ESTATE, INSURANCE, INVESTIGATIONS. On the sign was a hand pointing up, with the words, "Two Flights Up."

Lorraine, Charley, and Marcus got out of the car. Some men leaning against the building were eyeing them. "Where'd you all come from?" one of them said. The others whistled and laughed.

Alfred waved Charley over to the driver's side of the car and Lorraine followed. "Are you sure this is the right place?" Alfred asked. "I fear that this isn't a reputable business. Perhaps I should come inside with you."

"Maybe so," said Charley. "There might be rough stuff."

"There isn't going to be any rough stuff," Lorraine said. "Mr. Henderson is a gentleman."

Alfred raised his eyebrows, and she could see he didn't believe her.

Chasing the Thief

MAY 23, 1927

CHARLEY WAS HUFFING AND PUFFING BY THE TIME they reached the third floor of the building. Lorraine thought of pointing out that she had to climb two flights of stairs several times a day. But Charley looked so exhausted that she kept quiet.

They found a door with a frosted glass panel that had Mr. Henderson's name on it. A paper sign taped underneath said "ENTER." Alfred opened the door.

Inside was a room with a few shabby mismatched chairs and a dusty carpet. Lorraine wrinkled her nose. Somebody had left a fish sandwich in here and forgotten to throw it out.

"Who's there?" came a voice from an adjoining room. They walked through a doorway to find Mr. Henderson seated at a large oak desk. A telephone book had been stuffed under one corner, apparently because one of the desk's short legs was missing.

Mr. Henderson himself still looked as good as he had on the train. He was wearing a light green suit with a cream-colored shirt and lime-green tie.

He looked puzzled when they came through the door. Of course, Lorraine thought, it wouldn't be easy to explain what two colored kids, a rich white boy, and a chauffeur were doing together.

"Do you remember us?" she asked.

"Oh, no," he said. "I'm sure I would remember if I had seen you before."

"Not all of us," she said. "But on the train a few months back, my brother here drew your picture. You gave your business card to my Momma."

He snapped his fingers. "Of course," he said. "How is your mother? Do you think she'd be interested in any life insurance?"

"No," Lorraine said. "The truth is . . . we need an investigator."

Mr. Henderson frowned.

"It says on your card that you're an investigator," she reminded him.

He cleared his throat and looked at her. "Well, that's one of *several* lines of business enterprises I have."

"Well, we don't need those others, the real estate and insurance," she told him. "We want you to find something for us."

"What is it?"

"A diamond necklace that was stolen from Nell Aldrich."

He grinned, showing all his teeth—just the way Marcus had drawn his picture on the train. "I read about that," he said, "and believe me, if I could find it I'd already be collecting the reward."

"But we have a clue."

"I'm sure. Now if you don't mind, I have something important to do."

Charley stepped forward. "You don't believe her. But she's right. Nell Aldrich is my aunt and I think I've figured out who the thief is."

Mr. Henderson looked at Charley, and then at Alfred. "OK," he said. "Mind telling me who you are?"

"I am Alfred," Alfred said in a dignified voice that only added to Mr. Henderson's puzzlement. "I am looking out for young Charles."

Lorraine was afraid Charley had just told another fib. "We haven't actually figured out who the thief is," she told Mr. Henderson.

"You want me to do that," Mr. Henderson said.

"No, I *have*," Charley insisted. "In the car, Lorraine, you said it had to be the person who didn't belong. It took me a while to figure out who that is. Bring your notebook over here, Marcus."

Charley opened the notebook on Mr. Henderson's desk. As he leafed through it, he explained when Marcus had drawn the pictures. "So we know everybody who could have been the thief," he said. Then he put his finger on one of the pictures. "But *he* is the one who shouldn't have been in Nell's trailer."

They all leaned over the desk to look. "I recognize him," said Mr. Henderson. "He's that movie actor, Curtis Mitchell."

"But he belonged there," Lorraine objected.

"Not in Nell's trailer," replied Charlie. "He had his own trailer, and he had already shot his last scene of the day. He should have been getting out of his costume. And notice . . . this is the last picture Marcus drew. It must have been just after the explosion."

"All very interesting," said Mr. Henderson, sitting back in his chair. "But I can't do a thing about it. You should go to the police."

"The police won't believe us," said Charley.

"They think we probably stole the necklace," added Lorraine.

"Mm," said Mr. Henderson. He didn't sound encouraging.

"We have to act fast," Charley said. "Right now, Mr. Mitchell is probably planning his getaway."

"See, you have no proof," said Mr. Henderson. "You'd have to catch him with the necklace."

"It's probably in his room at the Palmer House," Charley said.

Mr. Henderson perked up. "The Palmer House?"

"Yes, that's where everybody in the cast is staying."

Mr. Henderson pinched his nose. "I happen to have a contact at the Palmer House. This is very confidential, you understand. He has helped me in past investigations. I could possibly get a look inside Mr. Mitchell's hotel room."

"Wizard. That's just what we need," said Charley.

"But first," said Mr. Henderson, "let's discuss this reward. Since I'm doing all the work, I should get . . . oh . . . three fourths of it."

Lorraine looked at Charley. She could see that he didn't care about the money. The excitement of finding the thief was enough for him. But she could not agree to give most of the reward money away.

All at once, Alfred spoke up. "You can have two hundred dollars as your share."

Palmer House

Mr. Henderson looked as if he'd stepped on a nail. "Oh, that's out of the question. In the first place, I have expenses."

"We will drive you there," said Alfred. "The car is in front of the building."

Mr. Henderson turned and looked out his window at what was parked down below. He whistled. "Even so," he said, "I will have other expenses regarding the obtaining of the key to Mr. Mitchell's room." He gave Alfred a wink.

"You'll have to pay off somebody," said Charley.

"There's a bright little fellow," said Mr. Henderson.

But Alfred wouldn't budge. They finally settled on $250 as Mr. Henderson's share. Lorraine was happy. Even if she had to split the remaining $750 with Charley, it would still be more money than she'd ever seen in one place.

They went downstairs and got in the car. The men outside the building made some comments about Mr. Henderson. He acted as if the car were his, but got in the front seat next to Alfred. "Passengers sit in the rear, sir," said Alfred.

"I like the fresh air," Mr. Henderson replied. As they drove down the street, he waved to people he knew. Lorraine smiled. She'd like to do that in Pickettsville.

They drove right up to the front entrance of the Palmer House, which was about the fanciest hotel in Chicago. A man in a uniform took the car away and they walked into the lobby.

Lorraine thought again how strange they must look. There was a hotel in Pickettsville, but she wouldn't even be allowed to go through the front door there.

But nobody stared or tried to stop them. Some black men carried luggage for the hotel guests, and

Lorraine saw a black woman in a maid's uniform go by carrying a stack of towels.

"Why don't you all wait here?" said Mr. Henderson. "I'll come back and tell you if I find the necklace."

"We'd prefer to accompany you," said Alfred.

Mr. Henderson nodded. "Good plan. Nobody would suspect burglars of bringing their kids along on the job." He stopped one of the men pushing a luggage cart and spoke to him in a low tone.

Mr. Henderson turned to Alfred. "Expense time," he said. "He wants $25 for lending us a house key."

Alfred frowned and took the money from his wallet. He handed it to Mr. Henderson.

To almost anyone else, it looked like Mr. Henderson and the luggage man were just shaking hands. But Lorraine saw the folded money and the key slide from one palm to another.

Calmly, Mr. Henderson walked toward the elevators. The others followed. "I hope you know his room number," Mr. Henderson told Charley.

"Sixteen oh four," Charley said. "He complained because it wasn't a suite, just a single room."

The hallway on the sixteenth floor was deserted. But a maid's cart outside one door indicated that the rooms were being cleaned. "We can't take long," said Mr. Henderson. "I'm supposed to get this key back in fifteen minutes."

"It's down this way," Charley said. They headed down the hall after him. Lorraine was starting to get a little worried. What if they broke into this man's room and somebody caught them? Worse yet, what if they were wrong and he wasn't the thief after all? If they got into trouble, how was she going to explain things to Momma?

Just then, she heard a door open. Up ahead, a man stepped into the corridor carrying a suitcase and a small black briefcase. Lorraine saw Charley stop dead in his tracks. He turned his head and whispered, "That's him."

As the man walked closer, Lorraine recognized him too. Looking at the luggage, she realized he was checking out of the hotel. And with him would disappear the necklace and the thousand-dollar reward.

The actor looked at Charley and gave him a funny smile. "Hey, kid," he said. "Tell your mother thanks for everything."

His tone convinced Lorraine that Charley was right. For some reason, she decided the necklace must be in the briefcase. As the actor passed by, she snatched the case out of his hand. He was so surprised that she was able to get it away from him.

Curtis Mitchell

But as she turned and ran, he gave an angry yell. She heard him start to run after her. "Trip him, Marcus," she murmured as she passed her brother.

All she needed, she thought, was a little luck. If she could open the briefcase before he caught her—and if the necklace was inside.

She heard a thud and a grunt as if somebody had fallen. Good going, Marcus, she thought.

Now she had two choices: run into the room the maid was cleaning and slam the door, or head for the elevators. The sound of a bell—meaning that an elevator was about to stop at this floor—made up her mind. She turned the corner toward the elevators and then. . . .

She ran straight into a heavy-set man wearing a brown suit that looked just as rumpled as it had yesterday.

Lieutenant Reilly stared down at her. "Hey," he said, "I know you."

"Would you look in this case, please?" she asked.

"Where are you going in such a hurry?"

She never got to answer because the actor, Mr. Henderson, Alfred, and Charley all came around the corner at once.

Lieutenant Reilly took out a wallet and showed his badge. "All right," he said. "Let's all go downstairs and straighten this out."

THIRTEEN

The Babe

SEPTEMBER 6, 1927

AS THEY SAT DOWN IN THE FRONT-ROW SEATS AT Fenway Park, Lorraine caught her breath. She couldn't imagine all these people had come just to watch a baseball game. There were more people in the stands than lived in the whole town of Pickettsville.

Pickettsville seemed very far away now. Lorraine had wanted to go back there when the lawyer Peggy hired went down to get Daddy a new trial. But Peggy said it might take months for that to happen. "Maybe the judge will rule against him anyway," Peggy said. "In spite of all our efforts, we weren't able to save Sacco and Vanzetti. Things don't always turn out the way we hope."

145

That was the only bad thing that happened that summer, though. After the necklace had been recovered, Nell and Peggy invited Lorraine and Marcus to visit their family's house in Maine. Lorraine was a little disappointed, because she wanted to see Nell's house in Hollywood. But the Aldrich family went to Maine every Fourth of July to put on a play. "The tradition was started by our grandfather," Nell told Lorraine, "and we don't want to give it up."

Momma wasn't sure she wanted to let Lorraine and Marcus go to Maine. But Peggy talked her into it. "It will be good for Charley," she said. "He never has had anyone his own age around. And the three of them get along so well."

Lorraine wondered if Peggy knew Charley was looking in the newspaper every day for more crimes they could solve. Maine sounded like it might be too peaceful for him.

Really, Lieutenant Reilly had tried to take credit for capturing the thief who stole the necklace. He was coming to question the actor when Lorraine ran into him. And of course Lieutenant Reilly opened the briefcase before anybody else. But Alfred told the newspaper reporters how Lorraine, Marcus, and Charley solved the case.

The Chicago newspapers played up the story with big headlines. Charley was overjoyed when one of them called him "the boy sleuth." The newspapers even printed Marcus's drawing of the thief. Nell was glad to pay them the $1,000 reward. Charley turned down his share because he said it was a family favor to Nell. At last, he'd made a name for himself in his family.

In return, Peggy and Nell wrote a play in which Charley's character was remarkably like Tom Swift, boy sleuth. They offered to put Lorraine and Marcus in the play too, but they were too shy.

It was more fun to watch, Lorraine thought. She and Marcus had seats right in the front row. Not in the balcony—right up in front of the stage. The theater was crowded too, because a lot of people wanted to see Nell Aldrich act in person.

The audience was a little disappointed, because she had given herself the role of the villain. She played a spy who was trying to steal the plans for a new kind of flying machine. The boy sleuth discovered the plot and after a series of adventures managed to capture Nell.

Lorraine, Marcus, and Charley spent the rest of the summer at the Aldrich estate. Despite what Charley told her earlier, it was far from boring. They rode horses, swam, and sailed on the lake, and learned how to play tennis from Charley's cousin Molly.

Charley demanded that they play baseball pretty often. Clearly, he was still planning to become captain of his school team, as soon as Peggy found a school he hadn't yet been kicked out of.

Lorraine discovered that she had to be pretty careful playing baseball with Charley. The first time she threw him a ball, he raised his brand-new leather glove to catch it. Only somehow he missed it completely. They had to take him up to the house to find ice to put on his bloody nose. Then there was the time he hit himself on the ankle with a bat, and couldn't walk for a couple of days.

You had to say this for Charley, though. He didn't give up. Lorraine thought he'd be a lot better off sitting and reading under a tree. A good sturdy tree that wouldn't fall on him.

But he kept at it. And when Peggy returned at the end of the summer and asked what they all wanted to do before school started, Charley had an answer. "I want to see Babe Ruth play."

So here they were, on Labor Day weekend, sitting in the front row of Fenway Park in Boston, where the Yankees were going to play a doubleheader against the Red Sox. Lorraine was going to miss the Aldriches, she thought, because they always seemed to have front-row seats.

In fact, they were right near the Yankee dugout. Before the game started, Babe Ruth himself stepped onto the field, just a few feet away from them.

As soon as he appeared, everybody in the front row of the stands held out their programs, balls, gloves—anything for him to autograph.

The Babe gave them all his famous smile and started to sign. Lorraine saw that he really was as chubby as a barrel, like Charley. But he had very thin legs. You could see how slim they were from the tight stockings below the knees of his uniform.

Charley held out a baseball and a pen, pleading for the Babe to take them. He finally did. When he got right up close, Lorraine noticed his heavy shoulders and thick arms and realized where he got the power to hit home runs.

She glanced down at Marcus in the seat next to her. He was the only person in the whole front row who wasn't holding up something for the Babe to sign. Of course that was because he was making his own drawing of the world's most famous baseball player.

As Babe started to write his name on Charley's baseball, he noticed Marcus too. "Hey, kid," he said. "Is that me you're drawing?"

Marcus nodded, hardly looking up from his notebook.

"Want me to sign it?" asked the Babe.

Marcus shook his head no. "You didn't draw it," he murmured.

Lorraine cringed, but the Babe decided it was funny. He let out a big guffaw and gave Marcus a pat on the back that almost knocked him out of his seat. "That's right, kid," he said. "You do the drawing and I'll do the hitting."

Just then somebody on the field called out, "Let's go, Babe! Game time!" The Babe turned and they could see the big "3" on the back of his uniform. He started to trot away from the stands.

"Wait!" Charley cried out. "My ball! You've got my ball!"

The Babe heard him. He stopped and looked back. "Right you are!" he yelled. "Here! Catch!"

With that, he threw the ball back toward Charley. Now, it wasn't a hard throw at all. Just a lazy lob up in the air. But Lorraine gripped the metal arms of her seat. It was going to be embarrassing if they had to lead Charley up the aisle with blood flowing from his nose. But she knew he'd never forgive her if she reached over to catch the ball for him.

Then Charley raised his hands. He was wearing a baseball glove on one of them. And as Lorraine closed her eyes, she heard a solid "thwack."

It didn't sound like the ball hitting Charley's nose. It sounded more like . . .

"I caught it!" Charley yelled, surprised himself. People in their section of the stands saw the catch. Even though they didn't realize how amazing it was, they applauded good-naturedly.

"Nice catch," the Babe called with a wave. "I'll hit a home run for you."

Actually, that day, he hit three. Charley said it must have been because he had been cheering the Babe from the front row. Lorraine figured that there must be such a thing as luck after all.

A Few Historical Notes

When people talked about "the Great War" in 1927, they meant the war that we now call World War I. It began in 1914 in Europe, but the United States did not enter the war until 1917. People thought the conflict was so terrible that there would never be another one like it, so they referred to it as "the Great War."

The year 1927 was filled with memorable events. As you've read, in May Charles Lindbergh became the first person to cross the Atlantic Ocean alone in an airplane. The feat made him one of the most famous people in the world. Babe Ruth, already the most idolized athlete in American sports, set a new home run record by hitting sixty in that year. The first "talking" motion picture, *The Jazz Singer*, starring Al Jolson, opened in October 1927.

The trial of Nicola Sacco and Bartolomeo Vanzetti, two Italian immigrants, is one of the most notorious in American history. They were accused of killing two people in the course of a payroll robbery in Massachusetts. Though there was little evidence against them, they were convicted and sentenced to death. Many people felt that the judge in the trial was biased against them because of their radical political beliefs. Despite worldwide protests, Sacco and Vanzetti were executed on August 23, 1927.

Dubbed "the Roaring Twenties," the decade between 1920 and 1930 was one of the liveliest of the century. The Eighteenth Amendment to the Constitution (ratified 1919) had made alcoholic beverages illegal. Ironically, alcohol consumption seemed to rise after the law's passage, and criminals such as Al Capone prospered by fulfilling the demand for illegal liquor. On the other hand, women took part in a new spirit of liberation after the Nineteenth Amendment gave them the right to vote in 1920. During the twenties, women's hemlines rose to the knees for the first time and many women imitated the "flapper" style—smoking, drinking, dancing, and driving their own automobiles. The stock market also rose to new heights, creating a sense of prosperity that ended abruptly on October 29, 1929, the day the market crashed.

Many African Americans moved from southern states to the North during this decade. They came in search of greater equality and economic opportunities. Tens of thousands of them settled in Chicago, encouraged by Robert S. Abbott, the publisher of the Chicago *Defender*, a newspaper that circulated among blacks throughout the South. Though the vast majority of blacks in Chicago lived on the South Side, several thousand found homes in a formerly Italian American neighborhood on the Near North Side.

The Dixon Family

John Henry (1892–)   *m*   Frances (1894–)

Nancy (1912–)   Lorraine (1915–)   Marcus (1917–)

The Vivanti Family

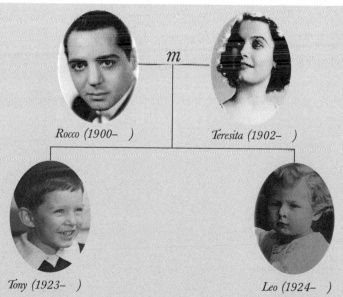

Rocco (1900–)   *m*   Teresita (1902–)

Tony (1923–)   Leo (1924–)

The Aldrich

Lionel
(1833–1902) ———————— *m*

Richard *m* Laura
(1866–1912) *(1867–1912)*

m

William (1867–)   Anna (1868–)

Harry (1887–)   Jack (1888–)   Peggy (1889–)   *m*   Charles Norman Sr.   Nell (1900–
(1888–1918)

Charley (1917–)

Family

Adele
(1838–1910)

Zena
(1840–1919)

m

Maud *(1872–   )*   Nick Woods *(1870   )*   George *(1870   )*

Molly *(1898–   )*   Polly *(1898–   )*   Freddy *(1899–   )*

Things That Really Happened

1920

KDKA, the first regularly scheduled radio station, begins broadcasting from Pittsburgh, Pennsylvania. There are an estimated 2,000 radio sets in American homes. By January 1, 1924, there will be 2.5 million.

Congress ratifies the Nineteenth Amendment, which gives women the right to vote.

Prohibition officially begins.

1921

First White Castle hamburger restaurant opens in Wichita, Kansas.

Nicola Sacco and Bartolomeo Vanzetti are convicted of murdering two men during a payroll robbery in South Braintree, Massachusetts. A campaign begins to gain a new trial for the two Italian immigrants.

1922

The tomb of Pharaoh Tutankhamen ("King Tut") is opened by British archaeologists in Egypt. The splendors of the tomb set off a fad for Egyptian styles.

1923

Russian immigrant Vladimir Zworykin invents a camera for broadcasting television pictures.

George Eastman, head of the Eastman Kodak Company, begins selling 16-mm movie cameras that can be used by amateurs. The first "home movies" are made.

1924

The first Popsicles are sold.

J. Edgar Hoover is named director of the Federal Bureau of Investigation (FBI). He will remain head of the FBI

During the Years 1920-1929

until his death in 1972, gaining enormous power and assembling files on millions of Americans including prominent politicians.

Congress passes the National Origins Act, which sharply restricts the number of immigrants from European countries and bars any new immigrants from Asia.

The first FM radio stations begin broadcasting.

1925

Nellie Tayloe Ross of Wyoming becomes the United States' first woman governor. Later in the same year, Miriam Ferguson of Texas is elected governor of her state as well.

John T. Scopes, a high school teacher in Dayton, Tennessee, is charged with violating a state law banning the teaching of evolution. In the trial that follows, Scopes is defended by famous attorney Clarence Darrow, while former presidential candidate William Jennings Bryan assists the prosecution team. The trial receives nationwide coverage. Scopes is convicted, but ordered only to pay a small fine.

1926

The National Broadcasting Company (NBC) links together 24 radio stations in the first broacasting network.

Gertrude Ederle becomes the first woman to swim the English Channel.

1927

Kool-Aid is first sold.

May 27, Charles Lindbergh completes a 33½-hour flight from New York to Paris. He is the first person to fly over the Atlantic Ocean alone.

After their defense team exhausts all appeals, Sacco and Vanzetti are executed.

The first automobile radios are introduced.

The Jazz Singer, starring Al Jolson, is the first full-length motion picture with a synchronized soundtrack.

Babe Ruth of the New York Yankees hits 60 home runs, a record that will stand until 1961.

1928

The Democratic party nominates New York governor Alfred E. Smith as the Democrats' candidate for president. Smith is the first Roman Catholic to receive the presidential nomination of a major party. However, he loses the election to Herbert Hoover.

Richard E. Byrd flies across Antarctica and the South Pole in an airplane.

Minnesota Mining and Manufacturing Company (3M) introduces clear cellophane tape: Scotch Tape.

Walt Disney makes his first animated cartoon movie with sound, featuring the character that would become known as Mickey Mouse.

1929

A group of gunmen thought to be working for Chicago gangster Al Capone shoot seven members of a rival gang in a garage. The event becomes known as the St. Valentine's Day Massacre.

October: Prices on the New York Stock Exchange, which have been rising steadily throughout the 1920s, suddenly collapse, triggering what was to be known as The Great Depression.

DATE DUE			
JAN 7			